"Mercy Me!
This *Is His Mother?* . . ."

At that moment, Elephant Man, returning anxiously along the lichen-covered ledge to get to his photograph, suddenly gasped and his legs shot out from under him. He hung suspended for an instant, his fireplug body thrust forward, his good arm reaching out to break his fall onto ground that was no longer quite under him, his broad hat askew and his cape streaming behind him. And then soundlessly he dropped from sight.

"Jesus Christ, Jesus Christ!" Leffingwell wailed, his words torn from him by the wind and dragged away into the absolute silence of the high and empty air beyond. "Only I could bring a million-dollar idea up two thousand feet and drop it off a cliff!"

Russell M. Griffin

THE BLIND MEN AND THE ELEPHANT

A TIMESCAPE BOOK
PUBLISHED BY POCKET BOOKS NEW YORK

Another *Original* publication of TIMESCAPE BOOKS

 A Timescape Book published by
POCKET BOOKS, a Simon & Schuster division of
GULF & WESTERN CORPORATION
1230 Avenue of the Americas, New York, N.Y. 10020

ISBN: 0-671-41101-2

First Timescape Books printing June, 1982

10 9 8 7 6 5 4 3 2 1

POCKET and colophon are trademarks of Simon & Schuster.

Use of the trademark TIMESCAPE is by exclusive license from Gregory Benford, the trademark owner.

Printed in the U.S.A.

ACKNOWLEDGMENTS

I should like to thank those who helped me through this book's elephantine gestation, especially George Blake and Stephen Spector, who read and encouraged me through the manuscript's many revisions, and Crocker Bennett, Peter Clark, Victor Miller and Curtis Suplee, who helped give the book its final shape.

RUSSELL M. GRIFFIN
1975–1979

For my father

Chapter 1

Feeding Time

Swaying, swaying, trying to remember, idly watching through the seine of veil the scalloped shore slide past.

"Hey, mister."

A boy of eight stood by the empty aisle seat in miniature adult's flared denims and wide belt.

Macduff, he thought. The boy's red hair and transparent eyebrows made him recall the name. But he didn't know whose name it was.

"Hey, mister, you all right? You sick or anything?"

He ignored the boy, thinking of other things. They wouldn't get to Butler in time for *The Young and the Restless.* Harry had said they'd just be passing Philadelphia by then.

"How come you got that tent thing on your head?"

Snapper doesn't know the girl he's engaged to is a former prostitute, he thought. His sister knows, though.

"How come you're wearing that thing on your head, I said. Can't you talk?"

"Of course I can talk," he answered.

The boy jumped back, slamming his head into Harry's stomach as Harry returned from the cafe car, Harry lifting the cardboard lunch tray out of the way just in time. "Watch it, kid." He was a round little man with a gray, sagging beagle face and caterpillars of fuzz in his ears. His suit, once a cacophony of bold blue and white checks, had been muted by stains and soil, and the cuffs were frayed white. He stepped around the boy and slid into the aisle seat. "Okay, U.B., got you a turkey sandwich."

"How come he can't talk?" the boy asked Harry, pressing his belt buckle against the seat arm.

"He can talk."

"No, he can't. I asked him if he could talk and he just made this kind of hooty noise."

Harry glanced back down the aisle nervously. Just before the kid had collided with him, he'd seen another of them! God damn it, still there! They were always the same—young and trim in light summer suits, wearing sunglasses and sometimes a hearing aid with a wire running down into the shirt collar. Harry had mistaken the first of them for a dapper blind mute, but the second had been pretending to read a newspaper through his dark glasses. They'd dogged him ever since his application for Elephant Man's exhibition license in Washington, and he'd grown used to them there. But he'd never expected them to follow him out of the city.

"Talks funny is all," Harry said, turning back to Elephant Man. "You get used to it. He's a good old boy." He pulled the tab from a can of Diet Pepsi and inserted a straw. "Why don't you go to the can or something, kid?"

The shape next to the window took the Pepsi with both hands, one normal, the other gloved and swollen, and slipped the can up inside the veil, feeling with the little finger of the ungloved hand to be sure the straw found its way into his mouth.

"What's the *matter* with him?" the boy asked, leaning over the arm rest.

Harry's eyes flicked impatiently, waiting for the Pepsi to reappear so he could get on with the sandwiches. Obedient even to Harry's expressions, the one next to the window produced the can.

"Stop humping my chair, kid," Harry said. "Beat it."

The boy didn't move.

"All right, there's *nothing* the matter with him. Now get lost."

"Then how come he's got that tent thing on his head?"

"It's a beekeeper's hat."

"How come?"

"BUZZ!" said Harry suddenly, poking a menacing finger-stinger. "He stings."

"No," insisted the boy, undaunted. "How come?"

"Because this here is the famous Elephant Man, kid, the world's ugliest mortal. He covers up with the veil so the folks on the train here don't throw up."

Swaying, swaying, Elephant Man slipped the can back inside the veil to sip while Harry was preoccupied. Snapper's sister came to dinner not knowing who Snapper's fiancée was, he thought, and then their eyes met at the door and Jill recognized she was a painted woman. Will Jill tell Snapper today? Because the girl really has reformed, and she really loves Snapper, and if she loses him it could drive her back to those telephone appointments with gray-haired men in dark suits. What does it matter who she is or was, so long as he loves her and she loves him? How beautiful love is.

"Can I look at him, mister? I won't throw up, honest."

"You got to pay."

"How much?"

"Forget it, kid. If you want to see him, you come to the parade tomorrow in Massachusetts. We're doing an exhibition right afterwards."

"We're getting off in Hartford."

"Too bad, kid, you just have to go look at something in Hartf—oh, for Christ's sake!" Harry twisted toward Elephant Man, dabbing at the front of his jacket with a paper napkin where the Pepsi had dripped from under the veil. Harry yanked the can away. "Can't you be careful?"

"Still thirsty," said Elephant Man deliberately.

"What?"

"Still thirsty."

Harry wiped the Pepsi from the sides of the can. "No wonder—you drooled most of it on yourself. I'll give you more in Philadelphia. Now eat the sandwich."

Elephant Man took the dry roll and sliced turkey loaf and slipped it inside the veil, finding his mouth with the little finger and then dropping it in. He chewed.

"Get lost, kid. U.B. wants to eat."

The boy was trying to look through the heavy veil to see whatever was going on inside. Harry feinted as though to grab him, and the boy fled back down the aisle toward his parents.

As he sat back, Harry caught another glimpse of the trim man in sunglasses. His scalp and back of his neck blossomed with cold prickles. "And don't slobber all over your coat," he snapped, tearing at the wrapper of his own sandwich.

But Elephant Man was thinking about Snapper and trying to remember who Macduff was but getting nothing more than a flash of hands and then gray light and a wall of stones dark with wetness where a bee clung paralyzed by the cold and a distant voice called to him out of the fog while another voice close by warned him that Froggie was coming. And swaying.

Chapter 2

Mr. Laffy

Claudine Leffingwell, still half asleep, heard the pounding on her bedroom wall, rolled over, and drove her knee into her husband's kidneys.

"Urmpf," he mumbled. "Chickens."

"*Dur*wood," she groaned, Bette Davis tortured by the Gestapo.

"Hey in there!" called a muffled voice through the wall from the next apartment. More pounding. "Telephone!"

Even as Gilbert Roland, the menacing but still terribly attractive oberleutnant, pressed with black-gloved hand his riding crop against the clinging silk of her dress and into the soft flesh of her abdomen, Claudine recognized the high gravelly whine, like the squeal of air from the neck of a balloon—Mrs. Adams, throwing all three hundred pounds into each thump. "*Dur*-wood!"

"Scratching," he muttered. "Pecking."

She rolled back, arms above her head and face in profile against the spray of auburn hair on the pillow. No matter what they did, they'd get nothing more out of her.

"Thousands all over me. Looking for corn." Durwood Leffingwell suddenly thrust himself upright, snapped his eyes open, twisted just enough to see his wife's pale face and matted hair. "Jesus, I dreamt I was a farmyard."

5

Claudine grimaced, eyes screwed shut. *"Listen!"* Even if they ripped her dress so her slip's shoulder strap showed, she'd reveal nothing, no matter how attractively menacing Gilbert Roland's riding crop was.

The pounding came again.

"All right, all right, Mrs. Adams," Leffingwell shouted. "I'm coming." A farmyard, he thought, shaking his head. All covered with chicken shit.

Gritty with sleep, he swung his feet to the floor and into the collapsed legs of his pants where he'd jettisoned them last night, grabbed his workshirt from the radiator, and padded barefoot down the stairs.

A low growl stopped him at the kitchen door.

As usual, Krishna Gandalf II had been standing with his front paws on the counter, staring out the window over the sink. He dropped to all fours and tensed, already salivating.

"Nice boy," Leffingwell gurgled.

Krishna Gandalf II was Claudine's second black Afghan hound and had cost four hundred dollars. "It's worth the extra money," she explained at the time. "You wouldn't want another one with epilepsy, would you? Anyway, we'll make it back in stud fees."

Claudine's Afghan mania had subsided two years before, after two supervised assignations had left one bitch still barren and another the mother of a litter of sad-eyed, un-Afghanish puppies bearing more than a casual resemblance to a free-running Saint Bernard down the road. But for Leffingwell, the difficulty with Claudine's Afghan phase, as opposed to her earlier flirtation with pottery, was that pottery's only legacy was easy to accommodate, a slab-method cigarette case with a lid that didn't fit and room for two cigarettes diagonally, whereas the Afghan period had left them with a monster that shed a miasma of fine hair over everything, ate more than a pound of meat a day, took up the whole couch when it napped and thirsted for Leffingwell's blood.

Leffingwell reached gingerly through the doorway to the garbage bag on the counter. Just as Krishna coiled to spring, Leffingwell flung the bag toward the far corner, coffee grounds pattering and chicken skins slapping against the wall. Krishna veered in midair and came down on the mess, and Leffingwell charged through the room and out the back door, hearing, as he slammed it behind him, the satisfyingly lethal crunch of chicken bones.

His smile faded in the daylight, and his eyes hurt. Sunday, his one free day, and he was up before eight o'clock, even before the fog of yesterday's heat, rising from the river into the night-chilled air, had begun boiling over the banks and rolling up the valley. He squinted and staggered across the scrubby grass to knock at the adjoining unit's screenless door.

"Just a minute, just a minute." A shadow appeared on the printed yellow flowers of the door's window curtain. "That you, Durwood? It's so early, don't have my face on yet." A hand swept the curtain aside for something white and bloated to stare out from a corona of red hair. Then the door opened.

She was wrapped in an old overcoat, a swatch of flame-colored terry cloth robe showing just below the hem, legs angling outward from the knees like two thirds of a tripod into a pair of her late husband's decaying slippers. On the stove behind were piled pots and pans filled with greasy water where shreds of egg and hamburg floated like harbor debris. The room was over ninety degrees.

"Telephone," she coughed, pulling the overcoat tighter. "Think it's your station again."

Leffingwell nodded, following her to the living room. "Your thermostat broken? I think your heat's on."

"Got a chill this morning," she whined. "You know, you really got to get a phone, Durwood. This is a real pain in the you-know-where."

"Had one once," he answered tersely. Amongst the pile of bills from Master Charge, Bank Americard and Gulf Oil every month was Bell Telephone's increasingly ominous reminder about six months of exotic calls for which Leffingwell still owed.

"But don't a newsman have to have his own phone?"

Sweat was collecting under his arms and between his shoulder blades. Hotter than an incubator—agh, chicken thoughts again. His eyes picked through the Dr. Pepper cans and magazines and overflowing ashtrays. "Where's the phone this morning, Mrs. Adams?"

"I'll call Fern," she said. "She loves seeing you." It was Mrs. Adams' firm belief that Durwood Leffingwell, the housing project's only college graduate, afforded a valuable role-model for her fatherless girl. "Fer-ern! That nice Durwood Leffingwell's here to see you!"

"She's probably busy, Mrs. Adams." Leffingwell blotted his forehead with his sleeve. "You remember where you left the phone?"

"Fern, you answer me, you hear? *Fer*-ern, you got that TV on up there? She wanted to show you her new kitty, see?" Mrs. Adams pointed to a bird cage by the sputtering radiator. Inside lay a gray kitten, eyes shut and tongue out.

"Is it sick?" Leffingwell asked.

"Course not—just sleeps a lot. Cute as a button, isn't it?" She swept a pile of clothing from the couch and toppled onto it full length. "FERN!"

Leffingwell spotted the red wire running from behind the couch across the floor and into a copy of the *National Tattler*. "Why do you keep it in a bird cage?" he asked, squatting to uncover the red princess phone.

"So it won't poopy on the floor. FERN! GET YOUR TAIL DOWN HERE!"

"Leffingwell here," he said into the receiver.

"You took your sweet time," said the thin telephone voice. "*What's* on the floor?" It was Mr. Trammel, Vice President for Programming, sounding more harried than usual.

"Poopy."

A long pause. "I don't have the time, Leffingwell."

"No, of course not."

"Because I'm trying to cope. Trying to cope with a little prob we've got down at this end."

Leffingwell took a deep breath and let go of his day off. "Shoot."

"It's about our live coverage of the parade today—"

"Just about to tune in and watch," Leffingwell lied.

"You know it's the biggest thing we've done. We've got thousands tied up in telephone line rental and the remote van and the pro switchers from Boston. . . . I mean, Leffingwell, this is a *live remote!* This is the *big time!* This is like ABC doing the Olympics!" Trammel paused, letting the grandeur of it sink in. "That's why I was just sick when I got the call from St. Joe's just now."

"The hospital? Oberon didn't slash her wrists again, did she?"

"No, it's Tanker Hackett. He's in traction."

"Traction?"

"They totaled Curt's VW Rabbit."

"Curt too? Is he all right?"

"Yeah, but his Private Cusp suit's just a lot of fiber-glass tooth crumbs all over Route 111-A. Leffingwell, Sergeant Smile and Private Cusp were supposed to attract kiddie viewers. We've got *no moppet interest*. WE'RE ABOUT TO SEE THREE THOUSAND DOLLARS GO DOWN THE TUBE!"

Leffingwell was silent, suspecting where Trammel was headed. Ever since Leffingwell's promotion to weatherman on the *Ten O'Clock News*, he'd been supplementing his $97.50 a week take-home by helping out on *Sergeant Smile and the Tooth Brigade*, usually as the mute end of the many-toothed Mr. Laffy the Horse.

"How about Hap?" Leffingwell asked at last. Hap Little, the previous news anchorman, was Mr. Laffy's better half.

"Wife says he's on another bender. But there's one last name on my list, Leffingwell. My niece Dawn's already on her way to the mobile broadcast booth with Hap's half of the costume. If you slur and mumble, I figure by the time it gets out of the horse-mouth nobody'll know it's not the regular Laffy."

Leffingwell's shoulders sagged. "All right, where do I go?"

"That's the spirit, Leffingwell. The booth's on the rear of a six-ton truck on Textile across from the library. You can't miss it."

"What's air time?" Leffingwell asked, knowing it was forty-five minutes from his New Hampshire apartment to the Channel 29 studio outside Butler, Massachusetts, and he'd have to allow an extra fifteen minutes to get downtown to the library.

"You've got thirty minutes."

"Hey, Durwood," said Mrs. Adams. "You're in news, right?" She had rolled onto her side to peer down at the *Tattler* that Leffingwell had removed from the phone and tossed by the couch. "What would a newsman think about this? Says here this woman had a normal husband and two healthy kids and then she had this frog for a baby."

"I only do the weather, Mrs. Adams," Leffingwell said.

"Is someone talking about frogs, Leffingwell?" asked Trammel.

"It *is* her house, Mr. Trammel. I'd better get going." He hung up.

"Must be real disappointing for a mother to go to the hospital and everything and then have a frog," Mrs. Adams mused. "Wonder if it was a boy frog or a little girl frog. Do you think she had insurance or maybe the newspaper paid her?"

"You mean a frog-*baby?*" Leffingwell began to edge back toward the kitchen.

"Nope, a goddamned *frog*. See?" She pointed to the newspaper photo, perfectly indecipherable from Leffingwell's vantage point by the kitchen door. "One mother, one father, two kids and a frog. I think it's pollution or radiation or chlorine or something. I'd sue if I was her. Think if I could have one of these I could sue?"

"It's a birth defect, that's all," Leffingwell said. "A human embryo goes through these stages, sort of like a TV instant replay of evolution. First it's got gills like a fish, then it looks amphibian, then reptilian, but—"

The kitten made a feeble effort to rise, toppled against the wire of the cage, and melted back into inactivity. "FERN!" screamed Mrs. Adams, standing up. "Kitty wants to do his duty!"

"—if anything happens to arrest its development, it gets born looking like the stage it stopped in—a fish, a pig, a frog or whatever. See?"

"My, my, what a smart thing for a person to know. FERN!"

"I'm doing something else, Ma," answered a small voice at last.

"She's watching that TV her father left her. Fern, if you don't come down this second, I'm letting your kitty out, and if it does its duty on the floor, you're going to be sorry."

"Don't let it out, Ma," pleaded the voice.

Mrs. Adams bent down, puffing, and unlatched the bird cage door. Uncertainly the tiny muff tumbled out, shook itself, squatted.

"It's piddling on the floor!" yelled Mrs. Adams. She waited until it had scratched rug lint onto the wet spot before she sent *Family Circle* after it, pages flailing, to splatter against the wall and cascade floorward in separated signatures.

Leffingwell, desperate to escape the heat but somehow unable to tear himself away, watched the kitten stagger past.

"FERN, I said your kitty did its duty on the rug, just like I warned you. Now get down here and clean it up!"

"I *told* you not to let it out, Ma," sulked a voice over the slow clumping of feet down the stairs, and then Fern herself slouched into the room in rhinestone glasses, sweat shirt and jeans, a jelly doughnut in one hand and a Dr. Pepper in the other, twelve going on thirteen and already approaching her mother's proportions. She watched woodenly as the cat squatted beside the kitchen sink. "What'd you have to frighten it for, Ma? It just makes it mess all the more."

"Maybe it needs more solid food," Leffingwell observed.

Fern blinked lizardlike, pushing the frames of her glasses back up the bridge of her nose with the back of her doughnut hand's bent wrist, then made a face and slumped toward the stairs.

"Fern, you stay here and clean up. Mr. Leffingwell wants to talk to you."

She stopped, her back to both of them. "I told you, I'm doing something else now."

"Where's your manners, Fern?"

"How's it going, Fern?" Leffingwell smiled.

Fern didn't turn. "Miss Nicky says I'll be premiere danseuse of the Nick-Nackettes this September."

"That's great," said Leffingwell. "Premiere danseuse. You've sure come a long way since that time on *Tooth Brigade*—" He stopped himself.

Mrs. Adams hadn't been listening. "She's premiere danseuse because everybody else in the class is eight years old. Jesus, the money I spend on those dancing lessons, and every time she turns around she knocks something over and gains five pounds." She collapsed onto the sofa again. "Money, money, money."

Fern glared, soundlessly mouthing something to her mother.

"Garbage-mouth," sneered Mrs. Adams.

"Really, *really* got to go, folks," said Leffingwell, backing through the kitchen.

"Screow," said the kitten as he stepped on it.

Leffingwell knelt down and picked up the small, limp

thing, his stomach knotted with horror. "Maybe it's not dead," he said hopefully as Fern clumped into the kitchen. It was the second time he'd done something horrible to her without meaning to, and the first still gave him nightmares. Why, why, why did it have to happen? "Maybe it's just asleep." He handed it to her.

"Asshole," said Fern.

Chapter 3

Sharp and Sided Hail

The sun was well up, but inside room 19 of the Down-towner Motor Hotel it was dark except for the far corner where Elephant Man, glowing moonlike in the television light, huddled in a blanket. As always, he'd spent the night in an armchair, knees drawn up to cradle his massive head, lullabied by ancient films, Roto-Rooter ads, driving tips, alcoholism spots.

He didn't mind that the ads and films and series reruns were the same here as in Mycenae, Texas, or Troy, Alabama, any more than he minded the sameness of motel rooms from one town to the next. Indeed, he liked the continuity they gave him, liked seeing people live on one screen and a month later seeing on another the same lives lived again in perfect duplicate, Lucy Ricardo scheming with Ethel Mertz to get herself on stage with Ricky's orchestra, Captain Kirk and Mr. Spock cleaning the Enterprise of Tribbles while Scotty tried to keep the dilithium crystals from breaking down again, Archie Bunker becoming a grandfather. It was the same reason he liked *The Young and the Restless,* because every day almost the same words were spoken in the same way about the same things. Just as he now paused at the steady rush and clacking of a train passing behind the motel to hear each wheel click predictably over the same splice in the rail at the same interval.

"—Channel 29 subscribes to the Television Code of Good Practices. Live today at eight-thirty on *Spotlight of Love* with Monsignor Francis Legume, Im*mac*ulate Conception—"

Harry had gone out to get breakfast, warning Elephant Man to keep his veil on in case the cleaning lady came by, but he had barely heard the warning, watching Herman Munster help Grandpa prepare a powerful concoction in his lab. Now as *Spotlight of Love*'s credits began to roll, he realized sadly that it wasn't one of his beloved and familiar reruns, but a live show.

Suddenly he tensed, looked away from the TV. It was going to happen again; he could feel the words coming.

aiyuvde zairdug owearspringznawt fayl. . . .

The chain of jumbled images and garbled sounds arced up from some ravine or fissure of his brain, tantalizingly exposed but impregnable. If he could just find some word or picture wedge amongst his shards of memories to isolate one fragment of meaning. Then the arbitrary divisions he'd made encoding what he didn't understand would ripple away on either side like falling dominoes, and one after another real words would emerge.

"—this Sunday morning, *Spotlight of Love* focuses its beam on Immaculate Conception Home for Boys, one of the many good works of the Sisters of the Seven Sorrows of the Blessed Virgin Mary. Hello, I'm Monsignor Francis Legume, and beside me here in the Channel 29 studio are Mother Margaret Rachel, who is the Provincial of Immaculate Conception—"

Elephant Man stared, but the screen showed only a glimpse of her smile and nod as it moved on. So familiar, like Lucy, Captain Kirk, Archie. . . .

aiyuvde zairdug, came the thought again, *owear springznawt fayl.*

"—Father Tim Fagan, a priest who wears two hats—or should I say 'stoles,' Father Tim?—as assistant pastor at St. Anthony's Parish *and* as chaplain to the boys at Conception."

Yes, Elephant Man thought. He remembered him, too. But it wasn't possible. How could he suddenly remember these people? He trembled with hope and fear. Close, so close.

"—and Mr. John Buridan, one of Holy Assumption Academy's lay teachers who coaches foot—"

"The *only* lay teacher," Buridan corrected.

"Yes, thank you. And I do want to discuss with you in a few minutes the recent strike by lay teachers so we can clarify for our viewers the pros and cons of destroying our parochial system, but right now—"

Elephant Man could not remember this one.

"—turning to you, Mother Margaret Rachel, that Holy Assumption is actually an outgrowth of Immaculate Conception?"

"Yes, Monsignor, that's right."

"Call me Father Frank."

"Yes, Father Frank, that's right."

"And I see in my notes here that the Academy's original purpose was to serve the orphans of Conception?"

Elephant Man watched Mother Margaret open her mouth to respond and then close it as Legume swept on.

"But, as I understand it, the Academy was opened to others when changing social and, ah, medical *conditions* more or less dried up, to coin a phrase, the orphan supply, so while there are still some orphans at Conception—now I want you to correct me on this if I'm wrong—many of the boys there are actually boarders from broken homes and so forth. So what I was really getting around to is the fact that you're probably a great believer in the old adage that there's no such thing as a bad boy."

"Frankly, I've never thought much of that adage."

Elephant Man looked longingly at her face. *aiyuvde zairdug owear springznawt fayl.* It was her voice speaking those syllables in his memory, he was sure. But where? When?

"You're thinking of Spencer Tracy in that movie about Boys' Town," Father Tim was saying. "What was it, *Going My Way?* Now *there* was a priest. Wasn't Mickey Rooney the bad kid in that one?"

Elephant Man knew if he closed his eyes he could see her again, bending over him. But he was afraid to miss an instant.

"I wouldn't know." Monsignor Legume adjusted his glasses.

"As a matter of fact, I've seen some *very* bad boys in my day," Mother Margaret said.

"I think it was *Bells of St. Mary's,*" said Buridan. "Mother used to say if Bing Crosby became a real priest, she'd have her heart's desire."

Desire, Elephant Man thought. *aiyuvde zairdug.* He rearranged the syllables. *aiyuv dezaird dug,* desire, desired, *aiyuv desired dugowear, aiyuv,* I, *I have desired dugowear.* So clearly her voice came to him. His tearless eyes burned, and he touched his little finger to the spittle collecting at the corners of his mouth to dab each aching eyeball. *I have desired to go wear springznawt fayl.*

"—philosophy at Holy Assumption's a little more like the parable of the Devil sowing tares amongst the clean corn, if you remember, where the farmer tells his workers to let the corn and tares grow together. Our job is to do the best with the boys we've got, good or bad. Of course, the parable goes on to the harvest time, when the farmer tells the reapers, 'Gather ye together first the tares, and bind them into bundles to burn them: but gather the wheat into my barn.' We don't get involved in that end."

Harvest, he thought. Summer, fall, winter, spring. *wear springznawt fayl, where springz, where springs nawt, not, where springs not fail.*

   I have desired to go
       Where springs not fail

He saw her clearly now, younger, towering over him, a huge black shape. *What on earth?* she seemed to be saying, as the thing in his hands suddenly seemed to burn his fingers and he dropped it. *I thought I heard a voice in here. What are you doing?*

He backed away, baring his teeth at her, and she came forward and bent down to pick up the thing he'd dropped. *This old book?* she said. *And this page, too. Well, no wonder —I guess it'll always open to it. But why were you talking out loud? You weren't . . . you weren't reading this, were you? The woman said you could, but I never believed a child so little. . . . Go ahead, take it. Read it to me.*

The memory flickered and went out like a lost station signal.

"Getting back to Spencer Tracy," Father Tim was saying, "it's not that a child's ever *really* that bad, but that we always expect them to be angelic, so they're always a bigger disappointment when they misbehave than they ought to be. As the poet says, 'Lilies that fester smell far worse than weeds.'"

Lilies, Elephant Man thought.

"In the Inquisition," Buridan began, "they——"

Lilies, *to feeldzwearflaiz no sharpinsaided hail lilies blow, to fieldz wear, to fields where flies no, lilies blow.*

> *I have desired to go*
>> *Where springs not fail*
> *To fields where flies no sharp and sided hail*
>> *And few lilies blow.*

She was towering over him again. *That's simply amazing,* she said. *But you're holding the book upside down. Just like that brilliant man—was it Ruskin?—who taught himself to read sitting opposite his father reading the newspaper at the table, so he learned to read upside down. Is that it? Did you learn by seeing things in people's laps at the center, Mac——*

The door swung open and Elephant Man felt the crash and sudden light sear through him.

"Breakfast," Harry said, coming in and putting a McDonald's bag on the blonde night table between the two beds. "Cleaning lady didn't pop in, did she?"

Elephant Man shook his head, trying to hear.

"——very interested in poetry, Mother Margaret? I'm sure a lot of our viewers would like to know why, because I know the first thing I think of when someone mentions poetry is, 'What a waste of time.' "

"Well, no doubt you're right, Father Frank," she said. "At one time I was very fond of Gerard Manley Hopkins, but I suppose every nun that can read goes through a Hopkins phase. My favorite used to be 'A Nun Takes the Veil,' because when I entered my novitiate, I was like the girl in the poem, planning to retire from worldly conflicts and be 'where no storms come.' But if I've learned anything over the last twenty-five years, it's that no member of a teaching order ever escapes the way the nun in the poem expects to."

"Can you recite a little of it for us?" Monsignor Legume yawned.

"Recite it from memory? It's been so long. . . ."

Elephant Man strained to hear over Harry's rattling inside the McDonald's bags.

"I think it goes something like this," she went on. " 'I have desired to go——' "

Casually, Harry walked over and tapped the off button. "Some religious show?"

"Spotlight of Love," Elephant Man whispered, staring helplessly at the blank screen.

"What say? *Sporelight of Lore?* That about plants, then?"

"No, Harry. Harry, I was watching that. I know that woman from somewhere."

"You're crazy," Harry said, returning to the bag. "You've never been around here before."

"How do you know? What was I doing before you found me? I was starting to remember something important, I know I was."

"Got to eat before it gets cold," Harry said. "Parade starts in forty-five minutes."

"But Harry, all I remember is you, trains, buses, fairs, motels, circuses——"

"Sausages? Nope, got us Egg McMuffins this time." He unwrapped one of the sandwiches and tossed it onto the other bed. "Truckload of stuff to do. Got to get to them TV folks. . . ." He sat on his unmade bed, his sandwich in his hand. "Make sure we're on the list of floats and stuff," he went on, chewing. "You know, got to get in that old plug when we go past the camera."

"Harry, when you found me——"

"Now, let's see. Got the signs from the printer yesterday," Harry went on, "and the keys to that storefront we're renting. Some dump, eh, U.B.?"

"Harry, that picture I had with me—you still have it?"

"Come on now, eat or you'll get sick in front of the crowd. Did you see the gypsies or whatever when we checked the place out? Some kind of fortune-telling massage parlor, read your fortune on your thing, I guess. And then that Greek guy on the other side with his hair dripping thirtyweight. What was that place, an accordion shop? Say, you don't play the accordion by any chance, do you, U.B.?"

Elephant Man shook his head, picking up his sandwich and poking between the cold poached egg and ham. "Harry——"

"Didn't think so. How about those little black flute thingies kids play in school? No, I guess you couldn't. Will you go ahead and eat, for Christ's sake? You got to eat to keep your strength up."

Elephant Man bowed his head, slipping the sandwich up inside the veil and dropping it inside his mouth. "Is today Sunday?"

"That's right. Boy, we'll knock the stuffing out of them.

You'll come by all mysterious—we're right after a Boy Scout troop—in your hat and cape, and all the gawks'll start wondering what's so disgusting we got to keep it hid. Then they'll see the sign on the side of our car about our exhibition this afternoon—"

"No *Young and the Restless*, then," said Elephant Man.

"And they'll be lining up outside the storefront like ants at a picnic, ready to pay for a look."

"No *Love of Life*," he said, bits of muffin and egg and ham dropping onto his chest.

"Come on, let's try out that new magician's cape I ordered. Stand up, will you?"

"No *Search for Tomorrow*."

"And hush up." Harry crumpled the McDonald's paper and boxes and tossed them at the wastebasket. Then as Elephant Man rose, Harry removed the long black cape with a red lining from the clothing box on the bed beside him and draped it over Elephant Man's shoulders, adjusting the veil over the cape like a knight's camail.

"It's a knock-out," he concluded after eyeing the ensemble critically for a moment. "Okay, U.B., let's get our tails outside. They'll be lining up down to the high school by now."

At the door, Harry paused and peered out between the slats of the window's Venetian blinds, afraid he might see another of the trim young men in summer suits. But the parking lot was empty. He opened the door and went out. Elephant Man followed him to the threshold and squinted, looking for the rented limousine. Even through the veil, the sunlit asphalt was blinding.

"Over here," Harry called from beside a green Ford Pinto hitched to an orange U-Haul trailer. On the trailer's side was one of the large, neat plastic signs with raised letters Harry had ordered from Washington in advance:

!! UNBELIEVABLE—HORRIBLE !!
BRING THE FAMILY
SEE THE ONE, THE ONLY
ELEPHANT MAN
THE FREE WORLD'S UGLIEST MORTAL
AND EIGHTH WONDER
NOT A FAKE, NOT A PHONEY
TODAY, 1–5 P.M., 689 CANAL ST.

"Where's the limousine, Harry?" Elephant Man asked.

"Well, see, they don't make convertibles any more," Harry said, patting the side of the U-Haul, "and I had to find some way folks could see you. I tried a couple of undertakers for one of them flower cars, of course, but no deal. One was busy all day, another one said it wasn't dignified for his flower car to be in a parade." He gestured for Elephant Man to get in.

Obediently, Elephant Man hobbled to the trailer and tried to lift himself over the side with his left arm.

"Jesus, clumsy as a June bug," Harry sighed, giving him a boost from the rear. Elephant Man got one leg over, then the other, but his foot caught in the ribbing of the hot metal floor and he sprawled face down into the pulverized leaves and dirt.

A scream from behind them. A woman standing in the door of her room, hand over her mouth, staring. Harry's eyes snapped back to Elephant Man: the beekeeper's hat had fallen off, uncovering the awful head.

"Sorry, Harry."

"Jesus Christ," Harry muttered, vaulting into the trailer. "Jesus H. Christ. It's okay, ma'am," he said, slapping the hat back on Elephant Man like a trash can lid and brushing off the rented cape. "Most people got to pay—stand up, can't you?—got to pay to see this."

But the woman had already fled back into her room and slammed the door.

"Shit," he said, easing himself back down to the pavement and then brushing his own suit clean. "That's the North for you, ain't it? Well, just keep the cape clean, you hear? And flip it back a little so that red lining shows."

Elephant Man reached to the side for support. "Got to sit down, Harry. Feel sick."

"Sit *down*? How can they see you if you're sitting down? I got the one with the lowest sides they had, but—"

"So hot," Elephant Man said.

"All right, all right, look. You can sit down for now—but mind, just till the parade starts. Otherwise we both starve. And don't sit on that cape."

"Thank you, Harry."

Harry turned and got behind the wheel. A moment later, the motor turned over and exhaust smoke began billowing over the trailer's front rim. Elephant Man coughed.

But Harry, intent on his side mirror, lurched backward and then forward, banging the gas tank on the incline from the parking lot to the street, the springless orange U-Haul bouncing behind in exaggerated imitation of the Pinto's every move, freighted with the free world's ugliest mortal and eighth wonder. Halfway down the block, a trimless gray sedan nosed from the curb just as the car and trailer rattled past, and slipped out into their wake, following with sharklike calm.

But Elephant Man didn't notice. Through his dark veil he watched, dry-eyed, the tops of buildings sliding past, each one as flat, squat and ugly as the last, like a monstrous hedgerow pruned back to thick and leafless stumps. He was chanting to himself.

> *"I have desired to go*
> *Where springs not fail,*
> *To fields where flies no sharp and sided hail*
> *And few lilies blow.*
> *And I have asked to be*
> *Where no storms come,*
> *Where the green swell is in the havens dumb,*
> *And out of the swing of the sea."*

Chapter 4

Live from Butler

Durwood Leffingwell arrived at the mobile broadcast flatbed-truck booth in downtown Butler in one of his fouler moods.

It wasn't the fact that his hairbrush had been missing—he'd found it on the way out, anyway, under the coffee table where Claudine had left it full of Afghan hair after Krishna's grooming—or that it had required a frantic search to turn up his car keys behind the bureau, or that Claudine had been free to drift back into sleep and had been lying, at the moment Leffingwell launched himself down the stairs, deep in some celluloid fantasy from her cinema class, mouth turned up in an enigmatic Carole Lombard smile.

It wasn't even that he'd been forced to walk two blocks to his car. He was used to it, after all: ever since he'd moved in, what remained of Mrs. Adams' black Packard had been parked diagonally across his space and hers. He'd never asked her to move it because he needed the use of her phone and because he'd soon discovered that it was somehow a memorial to the late Mr. Adams. Just as Queen Victoria, Empress of India and mother to a continent's royal spouses, had commanded that Albert's state papers and personal effects remain precisely as he'd left them, as though he were coming down in the morning, so the Packard stood exactly where it had lurched to a stop on Mr.

Adams' terminal evening, his last Blatz and Carling emp-
ties visible through the passenger's window, still strewn
across the floor.

First the tires had gone flat, then the axles had collapsed,
and this past spring the Packard's belly had settled onto
the asphalt where, like an atomic clock powered by the
decomposition of its elements, it measured the return of
Mr. Adams' primal parts by its own decay.

There was more to the Packard, too; Leffingwell didn't
understand it and had no wish to ask, but somehow the
car summed up everything that had gone wrong for Mr.
Adams, which is perhaps why Leffingwell couldn't help
wincing the morning he'd found vandals had smashed the
headlights and windows. "Kids," Mrs. Adams had said
that morning, looking at the empty headlight sockets above
the skeletal grin of the bumper and grill. "Nothing's sacred
to them."

Nor was it Leffingwell's own '69 Rambler that had so en-
raged him, though it too had betrayed him. When he'd
leapt in and slammed the door, the latch had crumpled
with a sickening *thunk* and the door had drifted open
again. He'd thrown his whole weight into the second slam:
the back of his seat had collapsed and sent him sprawling
into the rear even as the door had bounced harmlessly off
the latch's bent teeth a second time. He'd driven into Butler
hunched forward on the backless seat, holding the door
shut with his left hand except when he had to shift or
press the secret button in the directional-signal lever that
activated the twin fifty-caliber Brownings mounted behind
his grill to send two ribbons of tracer bullets streaking into
the gas tanks of cars and trucks that contemptuously
pulled ahead of him. "The price of discourtesy," he would
whisper to the flaming hulks of once-proud competitors
as he overtook them, still rolling in the breakdown lane,
"is death."

No, what finally made Durwood Leffingwell furious was
discovering that the six-ton truck from which he was
supposed to describe Butler's Annual P. T. Barnum Labor
Day Parade had been parked so he couldn't see the street.

"Three reasons," said Stackpole, sleeves rolled up and
one black-skinned arm draped over his camera. As head
switcher, he was floor director in the studio, but today he
was on camera one because the switching was being handled by the professionals hired with the rented white van

parked by the truck. "One, the scaffold for the street camera's on top of the cab, so Capella thinks the angle's better
if we park facing out."

Leffingwell looked up at Capella, sighting through his
camera five feet above the cab roof atop a pipe-frame
scaffold. "What's two?"

"Two is Capella forgot the lights, so we need the sun
on your face."

"And three?"

"Three is the head Van Man down there says it's the
professional way. Says nobody in the big leagues ever *sees*
the Tournament of Roses or Macy's Thanksgiving Day
Parade."

"Stackpole, how am I supposed to describe a parade I
can't see?"

"Well, Oberon's got a list of floats—"

Oberon Ricketts, a small woman with deepset, desperate
eyes that darted and glittered like a chipmunk's, held up
several trembling pages of typescript from her seat at the
commentators' card table. Behind her a backdrop curtain
had been draped over the rear of the cab, and the plywood "29" from the *Ten O'Clock News* set had been suspended in front of it from Capella's scaffold. A puff of
breeze riffled the curtain and the "2" twisted slowly
and lazily around until it dangled backward.

Leffingwell closed his eyes.

"Easy, my man," said Stackpole, who made it a policy
to be as serenely and unflappably black as possible. He
took a lumpy yellow home-rolled cigarette out of his pocket,
lit it, and offered it to Leffingwell. Leffingwell knew the
pungent smell; Stackpole grew it himself along with tomatoes, cabbages and turnips behind his silver Airstream
trailer, and with it he and Leffingwell had passed many
evenings in the studio. "We got a monitor hooked up for
you on the crate there beside Oberon. You're going to
do it just like Lorne Greene and Betty White."

"Great. I describe the parade to the folks watching it
on television by watching it on television." He dragged
on the cigarette.

"Hey, man, it's okay. Everybody knows art's got to
imitate CBS."

"Sorry I'm late," a voice called from the rear of the truck
bed. "I kept hitting all these one-way streets." Dawn Trammel tossed a shopping bag up onto the truck bed and then

clambered up after it. She was completing her first year as the news director's desk man and gofer after graduating from Cambria College with a B.S. in Communication Arts. The cathode ray tube and the written simple declarative sentence were equal mysteries to her, but she was Mr. Trammel's niece. And not unattractive, Leffingwell thought as she turned sideways to get past Stackpole's camera, despite an undeveloped, girlish figure and a self-effacing pragmatism of dress—flannel shirt, jeans, L. L. Bean hiking shoes. "And not a bad fuck," Stackpole had reported after her third day of work. "But man, that girl always look like she hitching to Chicago."

Stackpole suddenly held up one hand for attention and pressed the earphone against his ear with the other. "Van Man says two minutes," he reported.

Dawn flashed a shared-memories smile at Stackpole, who immediately ducked down and pretended he had to be checking his camera's built-in monitor. Leffingwell lifted his costume out of Dawn's shopping bag.

"Move it," Oberon hissed through clenched teeth, eyes wild but mouth already frozen in a video smile. Her fondness for diet pills had already proved nearly fatal once, and this had been another extra-pill morning.

Leffingwell unfolded the costume and stared blankly.

"Come *on*, come *on*, get *in*to the *cos*tume!" Oberon shrieked without moving her mouth, forming the words with the raising and lowering of her eyebrows.

"Dawn," Leffingwell said, "this is *my* half of the costume!"

Dawn was standing with her hand on Stackpole's rump while Stackpole continued to stare resolutely into his finder. "Sure—you're the one that's here, right?"

"Move your *ass*," Oberon choked.

"That's just it!" Leffingwell snapped. "She's brought me the *ass* end of the horse suit! You were supposed to bring *Hap's* half!"

"One minute," Stackpole relayed from the unseen pro in the van.

Dawn gave Leffingwell a *c'est égal* shrug. Like a condemned man on the scaffold, Leffingwell searched the faces of the living around him for some hint of help, found none, and pulled the top over his head like a grain sack, horse tail waving atop his hidden head like a Black Hawk scalp lock. "I can't breathe," came his muffled voice as he groped for his seat and stumbled into the card table. Oberon snatched the microphone away just as it toppled toward the floor, and Stackpole grabbed Leffingwell, took hold of both padded haunches and ripped them apart. From the darkness within the slit, Leffingwell's face appeared. "Thanks," he gasped, and sat down.

"Stand by," said Stackpole, back at his camera. "Ten seconds."

Leffingwell pushed the haunches back together with his hooves so his face wouldn't show as Stackpole held up his hand palm out and fingers extended. Four fingers. Three fingers. Two. One.

"Good morning on a beautiful sunny Sunday morning from downtown Butler, where the Big Parade is just about to start," cooed Oberon. "As I'm sure all of you out there in our Channel 29 viewing area know, I'm newsperson Oberon Ricketts, here to describe all the wonderful bands and floats for you on this beautiful sunny Sunday morning. And as a special treat for all you kids out there, guess who's sitting right here beside me! That's right, it's your special friend, Mr. Laffy the Horse!"

Stackpole panned from Oberon to Leffingwell. "Hi, kids," said the distant voice. "Yesiree bobtail, I guess you can see how excited I am, because I'm standing on my head!"

"And now let's cut away to our live remote camera high above Textile Avenue," monotoned Oberon, "to see what's happening."

Leffingwell peeked out between the haunches at the monitor screen, washed clean by reflected sunlight. "Yesiree bobtail, Oberon, looks like—"

The street was empty.

"—like Mr. Street's, uh, all ready for the first marchers." For the second time that morning, Leffingwell felt the sweat collecting in the creases and hollows of his body.

"It sure does, Mr. Laffy. And it's just, well, an absolutely perfectly sunny Sunday morning for us to be bringing you all this live remote coverage of the city of Butler's annual P. T. Barnum Labor Day Parade."

"It's just the kind of sunny day you'd want for a parade, isn't it, Oberon?"

"It certainly is. Perfect parade weather."

"Sunny," he said.

"You can say that again. Just absolutely perfectly, well, sunny," Oberon said, desperately scanning her typescript for background. "I believe our first marchers will be the Francis Gary Powers Regional High School Marching Band. 'First organized in 1962 to lend spirit to the athletic squads of the newly built regional high school,' " she read, " 'these musical wizards have cast a smell wherever they've gone.' "

In the monitor, Leffingwell saw movement far down the street. "Hold it, Oberon, I think I see something."

"Well, that's just *got* to be the band," she said, relieved. "Let's just sit back and listen."

Silence.

"They don't seem to be playing," she said at last.

"Actually," Leffingwell said, scrutinizing the screen, "it seems to be an animal of some kind."

"Yes, I think you're right, Mr. Laffy. It's not walking on its hind legs like a person, is it?"

"A dog, I think."

"I guess there's been a change in the order of march," Oberon said. "First it was supposed to be the musical wizards, then the Ancient Order of Nobles of the Mystic Shrine, which, of course, is open only to thirty-second degree Masons and Knight Templars."

"Could be a fire dog, Oberon. We'll be seeing a lot of fire companies and their engines from all over this morning, yesiree bobtail. Nope—dog's not officially in the parade."

"How can you tell, Mr. Laffy?" Oberon gritted. "Some special *horse sense?*"

"Because he's left the official route. He's gone up on the curb by that spectator there next to the fireplug."

"Do you think we could pan away for a shot of the library?" Oberon asked.

Stackpole leaned forward and stuck the joint through Mr. Laffy's haunches. Leffingwell toked again and felt better. "There she is, Oberon," he said, beginning to feel expansive, "Butler's municipal library. A really stunning architectural achievement. I'm not up on these things, being a horse and all, but I'd say it was nineteenth century harem style. See the minarets?"

"Actually, the windows remind me a little of Chartres," Oberon said, looking up from shuffling her papers. "I went to Europe before I got married, you know."

"The Winged Victory in front there is a nice Classical

touch," Leffingwell mused. "It's got a head and arms, too, which is more than you can say for the original."

"Just all over Europe," Oberon continued. "Paris, Rome, Monte Carlo, uh, Paris, Munich—did I mention Rome? First we stopped in Reykjavík to refuel. . . ."

Leffingwell had gotten Oberon's Grand Tour too many times before. "Wasn't the library donated by P. T. Barnum?" he prodded.

"What? Oh, yes, the great Butler benefactor this parade's in honor of." Again Oberon went through Dawn's typescript for something illuminating.

"Said it reminded him of his home town," Leffingwell said, ignoring Stackpole's arm-waving and dragging repeatedly and deeply on the joint. He watched little gray dots float upward from beneath his lower eyelids. "Bridgeport, Connecticut, another all-American industrial slum. Confidentially, the Russians and Americans have this top-secret 'Please Nuke' list. In the event of nuclear war, we promise to bomb Roumania, and they're pledged to hit Butler, Bridgeport, North Philadelphia, and Parma, Ohio." He stifled a giggle with another hit.

"Aha!" Oberon, who hadn't been listening, had found something. "While we're waiting, Mr. Laffy, we could take this opportunity to reflect on the man our city is named after."

"Shoot," said Leffingwell, trying to reposition the roach between his thumb and index finger so he wouldn't burn himself.

" 'Yes, Benjamin F. Butler, Civil War general, statesman, and native son of Lowell, Massachusetts, whose fame throughout the Merrimack Valley's sister cities made it inevitable that the last of the Sisters of Industry to be built should—' "

"He was cross-eyed, you know."

Oberon looked at him, her smile constricting. "No, I didn't."

"Yup, and fat as a tick. Blew every army command he had, so they made him military governor of New Orleans. Folks down there called him 'Beast Butler.' "

Oberon slapped her hand over the microphone. "Would you stop smoking those funny cigarettes?"

"No," Leffingwell said, and giggled out loud.

"Ta-ra-ra-BOOM-de-ay," rang the Francis Gary Powers High School Band from far down the street. Oberon slumped back in her chair with relief, and Leffingwell reluctantly returned the exhausted roach to Stackpole.

It seemed to Leffingwell the hour would never end. Fire truck after fire truck eased across his monitor, swarming with blue-caped volunteers with close-set eyes in broad, moronic faces. They rang the bells on the hoods of their trucks. Leffingwell bit the base of his nail to keep silent.

There were Cub Scout packs, Brownies, Girl Scouts, and Campfire Girls. There were Boy Scouts with knobby wrists and red pennants with black beavers and woodchucks rampant. There were gaggles of baton-school prepubescents in sequined skirtlets, scuffing their white vinyl boots and dropping their batons.

There was the Benevolent and Fraternal Order of Moose. The Knight of Columbus. The Holy Assumption Academy Chamber Orchestra and Marching Band. The Mayor in an open car. The Air National Guard. The Thomas Cromwell Technical High School Bugle Corps. The Polish-American Club. The Greek-American Club. The Fried Skulls Motorcycle Association. The St. Anthony Parish Ladies League. The Police Auxiliary Band. The Cambria College A.F.-R.O.T.C. The Gold Star Mothers. The Daughters of the Nile. Leffingwell nearly bit though his nail, switched to the other thumb, and finally stuffed the crusted flannel of one haunch into his mouth, shaken by uncontrollable giggles. Stackpole gave him another joint.

"What's next?" he managed at last, peering red-eyed from between the haunches.

"Post Five Eighty-Seven of the Foreign Legion, Mr. Laffy," Oberon snapped. "That's what's next." Her glare was a scalpel that bisected him from his head through his crotch, so he had to concentrate to keep the severed halves of himself from toppling over in opposite directions.

"Don't you mean the *American* Legion?"

"What I mean are the vets of Franklin Roosevelt's charge up San Juan Hill, Mr. Smartie-Horse, the men who marched to the Philadephia-Sheraton—"

"Hold it, Oberon, here comes another of those hilarious trick cars from the Shriners. Oh, great! Yesiree bobtail, kids, watch this! The car's going to go in a circle, tip on its rear, and then drive past. Just like all the last ones. Get ready now—don't miss it! Watch it . . . there it goes . . . tipped right up, down . . . and gone. Dynamite."

"Next we've got the Pawnee Council of the Indian

Guides, followed by the Bluebirds. Now the Indian Guides are a YMCA—"

"Looks like a Ford Pinto with a U-Haul trailer to me, Oberon. Seems to be a gray sedan right behind it."

Oberon squinted at the monitor. "Oh-oh, guess you're right, Mr. Laffy. Some little man named Gland or something stopped by with a note before—yes, here it is. 'The One and Only Elephant Man.' "

"What?"

" 'The ugliest mortal in the Free World,' " she read cheerfully. " 'A sensation throughout the southland—extended engagements in Georgia, Alabama, South Carolina, North—' "

Leffingwell watched the monitor as the Pinto slowed before the camera. The driver leaned out his window to peer back into the trailer. It seemed empty.

The Pinto slammed to a stop and the driver leaped out and ran back, reaching in the trailer to shake something violently. Then he saw the sedan and leaped back behind the wheel. There was a squeal of tires and the Pinto lurched off with the U-Haul bucking behind. Calmly the sedan followed.

"I think the sensational Elephant Man's passed out back there," Leffingwell observed. "Maybe he caught something from the American Legion."

"It's just because it's so sunny," Oberon said. "It says here he'll be available for public viewing at—I can't read this, Leff—Mr. Laffy. . . ."

Stackpole, as usual showing no effects from the joints, was holding up a piece of shirt cardboard with "10 sec. to 60 sec. spot" written on it in magic marker.

Leffingwell was stunned. The first commercial? Could there really be forty-five minutes of this left to go?

Somehow he sensed the first pulse of electricity entering the red "on" light of Stackpole's camera as the switcher in the van cut from Capella's street view to the commentators. Instantly he let the haunches flap shut, catching the joint between them. "Don't ask me," he coughed, the smoke thick inside his suit. "Horses can't read." He crumpled the note in his hoof.

"And we'll be right back," smiled Oberon, "with more of the parade right after these important announcements." She waited until Stackpole pantomimed slitting his throat with his index finger. "Durwood Lef-fing-well," she sang sweetly.

Leffingwell emerged hacking and choking, and folded the haunches back around his neck to air his steaming head.

"You shithead," Oberon purred. "You're going to regret this, I promise you."

Stackpole held up his hand, listening into his earphone. "Van Man's patching through a call from Trammel." He listened. "Leff, Little Man wants to know, and I quote, 'What the fuck is the story on this "Please Nuke" list?' "

Leffingwell groaned. Oberon smiled.

"Says he'll talk to you later about General Butler. Says— hold it—yeah, says he doesn't mind seeing a horse's rear doing commentary, says he's used to it on the news, but he says to tell the horse to take the cigarette out of its ass."

Behind Leffingwell's head the plywood "2" revolved, twisting slowly, slowly in the wind.

Chapter 5

The Darksom Hole
of Errour's Den

"Personal mass, my man," said Stackpole, his elbow out the window of the Rambler's passenger side. He yawned and stretched, pressing his back against the seat.

"I wouldn't do that if I were you," Leffingwell warned, hunched forward on his backless seat like a benched football player. He let go of the door to grab the wheel with his left hand while he shifted with his right, then tapped the accelerator to make the car lurch just enough so the door swung back toward him, a technique he'd mastered that morning.

The car coughed and died.

"I mean, look at you, man," Stackpole said. "Trammel gets a little P.O.'d, and off you go to find a way to make Little Man love you. Fuck him, that's what I say." He leaned out the window to give the finger to the driver tormenting her horn behind them.

Instantly, Leffingwell slumped down, hoping to hide from the car behind but forgetting about the missing back of his seat. He lost his balance and rolled into the rear, feet in the air like an overturned beetle. "I'm not doing this to make Trammel love me," he said, struggling to sit up. "I'm doing it for myself."

His head was still below the level of the window when the car behind squealed out and passed them. "Dipshit!" shouted a distant female voice.

"Get stuffed!" Stackpole bellowed out his window after her. "I'm moving into your neighborhood!"

Leffingwell regained his seat and turned the ignition. The Rambler yelped.

"You were saying?" Stackpole asked.

"I was saying that I'm doing this for myself. I mean, what kind of a future is there in weather?"

"There's always weather, Leff."

"Yeah, yeah, but the big-time jobs are going to guys with degrees in meteorology these days. Did Dr. Frank Field start out with a crow puppet?" The motor caught and the Rambler stuttered ahead.

"Light's red now," Stackpole said.

Leffingwell took his foot off the accelerator and the car died. "And that crow I've got to work with! Aren't you offended when Hap has it say, 'What's de wedder, boss?' "

"Why should I be? Has it got something to do with me?"

"The point is, with my background, the only way to get anywhere is to break into straight reporting. Then maybe Plattsburgh'll catch me and like my stuff. Or Worcester. Or Burlington. And I'm on the way up."

"You think a film of Durwood Leffingwell talking to this freak . . ."

"Elephant Man."

"You think Plattsburgh is going to lap that up and offer you a contract?"

"Look, somebody's already done My Lai. Woodward and Bernstein split Watergate and made a mint. I've got to take what I can get."

"Light's green, Leff."

Leffingwell held the clutch halfway in and raced the motor as they ground their way across the intersection.

"It still comes down to personal mass," Stackpole said.

"What the hell is personal mass?"

"Body bulk. Look at me." Stackpole sucked his beer belly up into his chest. "The more personal mass, the harder for people to hassle you. Every day I split wood before work, man, build up my chest and arms. Look, one semester in college I took my scholarship check, eased on out the door and bought this '59 Jag with real wood interior, red leather seats and holes in the floor."

"What's this got to do with personal mass?"

"I'm getting there, Leff. So by and by old Bursar calls me in. 'What did you do with the scholarship check for tuition, Stackpole?' says this dude with glasses so thick you just know he wipes his ass with graph paper, so I stick out my chest and fill his door with personal mass. 'Bought a Jag,' I tell him. 'Well, well,' he says, starting to sweat, 'what an innovative idea, Mr. Stackpole. How much would you like your new tuition check for?'"

Leffingwell's head still popped and buzzed with the morning's joints, and he had the nagging feeling he'd missed a crucial part of the narrative. "He was probably afraid you'd start a riot or liberate his office or something."

"Leff, don't be such a honky. I don't make out by being blacker, I make out by being cooler. Personal mass is cool."

Leffingwell didn't answer. Stackpole had been a friend for three years, but Leffingwell was still never sure when Stackpole would accept a racial comment and when he'd be offended by it. In fact, there was much about Stackpole that remained a mystery: he'd grown up in Texas, for instance, but he had a neutral collegiate accent except for saying "the-ayter" for "theater," which Leffingwell regarded as an affectation, like his occasional mimicking of ghetto talk. Leffingwell had no idea whether Stackpole's family were sharecroppers or landlords, or even what his first name was. "I knew a guy whose middle name turned out to be Apollo when they read it at graduation," Leffingwell had prompted once. "Nope," Stackpole had answered. "It's not Apollo."

"Well," Leffingwell said at last, "I don't see how personal mass would help me with Trammel. I've never even seen him—he's just a voice on the telephone."

"He's a little guy," Stackpole said.

"You can't stick your chest out at a telephone receiver."

"At least," Stackpole said, squinting reflectively at the car roof, "I *think* he's a little guy."

They were finally on Canal, a meandering secondary street that followed the tracks made by Butler's first drays picking their way between the textile mills and canals a hundred and fifty years before. The air grew thick with Greek seasonings and loud conversations.

At last Stackpole announced they'd just passed number 689. Leffingwell swung down the next side street and parked. "Don't forget your keys, my man," Stackpole reminded him as they clambered out.

"I'm leaving them here on purpose," Leffingwell answered. "I'm hoping somebody steals it. I don't like to think I'm parking this car; I like to think I'm abandoning it."

Stackpole paused to pull his Bolex H-16 out of the back. He'd started in television as a news cameraman, and even now as head switcher he liked to keep his hand in by going out on occasions like this afternoon's. The camera was over twenty years old, silent and had to be wound by hand, but Stackpole could pick the f-stop without thinking, and set the distance and shoot without looking in the viewfinder.

Down the block, Stackpole paused before a storefront window. "CHICAS DE TODAS NACIONALIDADES," read the cardboard sign inside with O's like hearts. "FORTUNES READ—MASSAGES. YOU'LL LOVE IT." Draped over the curtained window railing behind was a dark woman who seemed to be forming a word with her lips.

"What's she trying to say?" Leffingwell smiled nervously. "Is it 'lick'?" In back of her he caught a glimpse of someone in a suit and sunglasses. Her pimp, no doubt.

"It's a nice thought," Stackpole said, wiggling his fingers in goodbye. "Beats the kind of whoring you want to do."

"Lick, lick, lick," mouthed the woman after him.

They stopped again two doors down. The swirls and Roman columns of the cast-iron facade had grown dim and uncertain beneath the mottled layers of dark green paint and rain-streaked dirt. The corners of the empty display window were deep in the corpses of many seasons' flies.

On a sheet of butcher paper taped inside the window was a forest of crude, feather-duster palm trees, amid which stood a monstrous figure in a leopard-skin loincloth, club in one hand and feet wedged into two impossibly tiny brown oxfords meticulously traced from a catalogue. But what riveted Leffingwell's attention was the head—the head of an African elephant, trunk raised and tusks exposed threateningly. Like Babar dressed up as Tarzan.

The door was open a crack. Leffingwell knocked and, hearing no response, pushed the door open. Stackpole followed.

The room was unlighted, and Leffingwell had to blink to make anything out after the brightness outside. Toward the back of the room appeared to be a bedspread hung from a length of rope to mask the rear of the store, with "Downtowner Motor Hotel" embroidered in the center.

"Hello?" Leffingwell called.

Silence. From somewhere deep inside, the buzzing of a fly at a window. Then a strange slapping sound, like someone beating out a rhythm on his thigh with his hand.

"Hello?"

"I heard you the first time."

Leffingwell jumped back. The voice had come from the shadows right beside him. He peered into the darkness and found a small man sitting on a packing crate, his head lowered as though he held it in his hands.

"You the Elephant Man?" Leffingwell asked.

"Fuck you, Mac."

"Then you're *not* the Elephant Man?"

"Do I look like an elephant? Do I got a trunk?"

"I really can't see in here," Leffingwell said. "Is there a light?"

"Elephant Man likes the dark," came the voice. "You get used to it."

"Well, we're from Channel 29, where today's news is a real pleasure, as we like to say, and I'm here to do a kind of upbeat human interest story on the Elephant Man."

The man looked up, a small, pinched face, muscles at the edges of the mouth like taut cords. "You got to be kidding."

"Semi-human interest?"

"You're about five minutes too late," said the man.

There was a scraping sound from behind the makeshift curtain, like a foot dragged across the gritty floor.

"Too late?" Leffingwell asked. "Isn't the Elephant Man still here?"

"Of course, but there's no exhibition. See this?"

"Not very well," Leffingwell said.

"It's an injunction," the man said, holding up a crumpled piece of paper. "Damn those fuckers in sunglasses—they did it. Here, listen to this." He uncrumpled the paper and held it close to his face. " 'Aforesaid'—no. 'One Harry'—no. Here—'cruel and inhuman.' Can you beat that? What's cruel about U.B. earning a living? And inhuman? Ain't an Elephant Man *supposed* to be inhuman?"

"You've got me there."

"Wait, boy, there's more. Now get this: 'repugnant to the

moral and aesthetic sensibilities of the community.' Can you beat that? Why would anyone come if it *wasn't* repugnant? That's the whole secret of show business."

"I suppose so," Leffingwell said.

"Course it is. Confidentially, I don't see how *anything* could be repugnant to people in this town. Christ, around here if you want to see something disgusting, you just turn your lawn chair around and look at your house. If ugly's a crime, this is sin city."

Leffingwell shrugged. "All old mill towns look ugly after the mills close down."

"Tell me something, boy, you see a guy outside in sunglasses and a hearing aid?"

"Someone blind and deaf? Friend of yours?"

"Just tell me yes or no," said the man.

"I didn't notice," Leffingwell said. "You going to appeal the injunction?"

"Appeal it? Who's got the time for appeals? Who's got the money? As long as I don't pay the motel bill, I got exactly enough for one ticket back to Georgia."

The slapping sound from behind the curtain grew louder.

"Not that I'd just leave U.B. flat like that," the man added loudly. "Wouldn't think of it—not unless he had somebody else to take care of him. After all, we used to do pretty good together at the state fairs and all."

He stood up, brushing dirt and splinters from the seat of his pants. "U.B. was just dynamite in those days. His face could change overnight—well, almost. Cost me a fortune in new posters all the time." He began to pace, inspired by the happy recollection. "Monday it's the world-famous Guppy-Man, creature of your hidden fantasies. Tuesday it's Thoth, dread vulture-god of the ancient Pharaohs. He wasn't your average freak, he was a one-man menagerie—a freak's freak, la cream de la mint."

Leffingwell pinched the bridge of his nose; he was getting a headache. Stackpole examined his camera with great care.

"But then I had to hit the big time, just when U.B. was kind of settling into this elephant rut. Got turned down for a license in Washington, so I come up here when I hear about the parade. A *Barnum* parade, I says—how could I go wrong? Some parade. Where's the midgets? Where's the elephants? Where's the bearded ladies? It was all fire trucks and Cub Scouts."

"Yeah, I know. We did the TV coverage."

"Look," Stackpole said, "do you think we could see this Elephant Man of yours and get it over with?"

The little man studied Leffingwell and Stackpole for a moment. "Okay—I guess you're legit. What harm could it do one last time? Maybe even some good."

The man pushed the bedspread aside. The room beyond glowed with a cold gray light filtering through two grimy windows to the rear. Against the far wall was slumped a figure in a beekeeper's hat, form and features hidden by a black cloak and heavy veil, tapping out a rhythm on his thigh with the fingers of his left hand. The other arm was inside the cloak.

Stackpole looked briefly to Leffingwell to be sure he wanted to go through with it, scowled, racked the turret's medium lens wide open and raised the camera to his head with the graceful ease of long practice. The motor began to whir.

"Why is he tapping his leg?" Leffingwell whispered.

"Because he can't whistle," Harry answered. "On account of the tusks. Does it when he don't want to hear something, like me talking about money. Stand up, U.B."

Leffingwell saw the figure rise. It was surprisingly unimposing, below average height, perhaps five foot one.

"What's U.B. stand for?" Stackpole called from behind his camera.

Harry shot Elephant Man a quick glance. "It's for 'Ugly Bastard,'" he whispered, "but I don't say it out because it'd hurt his feelings. Doesn't have a real name, at least not one he can remember. Take off your cape, U.B."

Elephant Man let the cloak drop back to his folding chair. He was dressed in a boy's striped jersey that was much too small, dungarees rolled up at the cuff and basketball sneakers. Leffingwell assumed he was retarded.

"Go ahead," Harry said. "Hat and shirt, too. The whole show."

Elephant Man reached with his left hand and removed the hat, the veil rising and gliding away like the bunting from a statue at a dedication. Leffingwell turned away for a moment, swallowing hard. Then he forced himself to look again. Stackpole's camera never stopped.

Atop a slight, almost adolescent body was perched a head the size of a man's waist. The huge, bony forehead was distended in a breadloaf ridge above the eyes, small, deeply recessed, shadowed by the jutting brow. Where the nose should have been, hung an elongated, spongy bag of flesh like a rooster's wattle, while from the upper jaw above the teeth protruded two bony pink stumps that turned the upper lip inside out, the tusks shown so literally in the window sign. Spittle collected on the lower lip, pearling and beading and finally dropping from the mouth that could never quite close.

As the creature turned to remove the shirt, Leffingwell saw the back of the head, swollen into a second spongy bag that hung downward, trembling obscenely with Elephant Man's every movement. Along the right arm and back, now bare, were smaller bags and beginning swellings, the last dangling just above the belt. The right arm itself was twice the size of the left, ending in a hand broad and flat as a paddle, radish-like white bulbs of fingers just visible amongst the folds of flesh. The left hand and arm were normal, even delicate and feminine by comparison.

"What the fuck is wrong with him?" Leffingwell gasped.

"You got me," Harry said.

"But is it catching?"

"Him and me lived close as brothers over two years, and I don't look like that, do I?"

"Well, it *is* pretty dark in here," Leffingwell said, stepping away gingerly. "Where's he from?"

"Got me again. Carny I was with went bust down in Georgia and I was a little down on my luck and sleeping out in the woods, and one morning I wake up and there this guy is, leaning up against the next tree. Wasn't like this then, understand—head just a little swelled, see, and his hair all different colors like he spilled bleach on it. Mostly it's fallen out now, I guess. But the minute I laid eyes on him, I knew he had talent written all over his face."

"He's young, then?"

"Guess so, come to think of it. He's grown maybe six inches since I found him. Pretty fast grower."

Stackpole lowered his camera. "I don't know about you, Leff, but this is it for me. I'll grab an exterior shot for you, and then I'm going to see that dude with the shades and get his girl to tell my fortune."

"*Shades?*" said Harry suddenly. "You mean *sunglasses?* Did he have a hearing aid?"

"Never heard of a handicapped pimp before," Stackpole said.

"Say, look," Harry said to Leffingwell, with a nervous glance toward the door, "I got a confession to make. U.B.'s career is kind of bogged down at the moment, see, and it's really my fault. I don't got the contacts he needs—I know carnies and sideshows, but the only real future for a freak these days is television. I love him like a brother, understand, so it ain't fair for me to hold him back. But a real humanitarian like you with your TV connections—you could make an absolute killing. How about a TV campaign to find his mother, say? 'NOT EVEN HIS MOTHER COULD LOVE HIM!' Confidentially," Harry said, leaning closer to Leffingwell, "if I didn't have to run, I'd want to do it myself. But I've had my shot, right? Wait a minute—got a picture you could use for your promo." He dug into his rear pocket for his wallet and pulled out a smudged and dogeared picture torn from a magazine or perhaps a school yearbook.

Elephant Man said something indistinct and took a step forward. He seemed anxious or upset about the picture, even though his trunk and tusks rendered his face immobile and expressionless as granite.

"Take it easy, U.B.," Harry said sternly. "He'll be careful." He turned to Leffingwell. "Had this in his hand when I found him. I figure it's his mother."

Leffingwell looked. *"This* is his mother?"

"Sure—why else would he carry it around? He says he doesn't remember."

"But . . . this woman looks like a *nun.*"

"A nun? How can you tell? It's just her face. You mean that shawl thing on her head? I thought she was just Italian or something, but what do I know? I'm a Baptist." Harry edged slowly toward the door. "But hey! That's a great angle—NUN MOTHERS LOVE-CHILD, TURNS MONSTER. Love, sex, divine punishment—it's a million-dollar idea."

"A million-dollar idea?" Leffingwell asked dreamily, his eyes misting. He'd had so many—his cure for bad breath in older dogs, his letters to Revlon about a revolutionary line of cosmetics and deodorants for yet untouched parts of the body—Navel Base, Ear-Wick ("an aural hygiene formula to make you ear-resistible") and Nip-Stick.

Leffingwell was just recalling how Mary Quant's own

brand of breast makeup had deflated his balloon when a doorslam jarred him back to reality.

"He's split, man," Stackpole said. "Just bopped out the front door. Look, it's getting late. You want to drop me downtown at my car?"

"Yeah, okay," Leffingwell said, absently stuffing the picture into his shirt pocket. He took a step toward the door and stopped. From behind him came the smart slapping of a hand on a thigh. "But shouldn't we do something about . . . ah . . . you know. We can't just leave him here."

"Just what did you have in mind? Taking him to your house? Claudine doesn't even like it when *I* come over."

Leffingwell shifted uncomfortably, terribly aware of the eyes boring into him from behind, relentless as a TV camera. "What about your trailer, then?"

"Forget it," Stackpole said. "My advice is stay out of this and call the ASPCA when you get home. I'll be outside getting that exterior shot for you when you're ready."

"But the guy said a million-dollar ide—"

Stackpole was gone. Leffingwell hesitated, desperate and sweaty, and he never did know whether it was genuine compassion or his piles of bills at home that made him turn back.

"Excuse me, Elephant Man?"

Elephant Man raised his hideous head.

"You . . . you want to come with us?"

Elephant Man rose obediently and put on his hat and veil. Then he took the cape and swung it around him with the grace of an enchanted prince restored to his former shape.

After dropping Stackpole, Leffingwell drove the hour back to Quidnunck in silence, listening to Elephant Man tapping out his whistles in the back seat, unable to use the secret button in his directional-signal lever. By the time they reached the housing project, it was dark. Leffingwell parked his customary two blocks from the apartment and walked back, pausing every few paces for Elephant Man to catch up. As they passed the Packard, Leffingwell saw there weren't any lights on in his place. He hoped, sincerely hoped, that Claudine was out. Gingerly he unlocked the door and pushed it open.

"Claudine?" he called softly.

"GRRRRR," said Krishna Gandalf II, and lunged.

Chapter 6

Monday, Monday

Leffingwell awoke unconscionably early again, but before he could get back to sleep, he heard the television on downstairs. He glanced over, saw Claudine blissfully asleep beside him, and *remembered*. Moving as slowly as he could so as not to awaken her, he eased out of bed, slipped on some clothes and tiptoed down the stairs. He stopped halfway down, still out of sight.

Oh, Bunny Rabbit, Bunny Rabbit, I have a nice big bunch of carrots for you, Bunny Rabbit. Mr. Moose, is Bunny Rabbit in his hutch?

It was worse than he'd thought. Elephant Man was interfacing with *Captain Kangaroo*. Leffingwell eased himself down a few more steps until he could make out the squat, caped figure hunched in front of the TV.

I think he went out to the barn to help Mr. Greenjeans with the baby wallabies, shrilled Mr. Moose.

Really ought to go in and sit down with him, Leffingwell thought, embarrassed. Act friendly and all. And there's stuff I could learn from the Captain—that's a really slick production.

Instead, he came down the rest of the way, paused awkwardly at the foot of the stairs and waved hello. The moment Elephant Man turned to acknowledge him, Leffingwell grinned hugely and shot into the kitchen. What had he gotten himself into? What was he going to tell Claudine? This was the dumbest thing he'd ever done.

Morosely, he heated a pan of water, then dumped a spoonful of coffee crystals into his mug. "I'M A COFFEE-LOVER" it said in red letters on one side.

"EEEEEEK!"

Claudine rushed into the kitchen with Krishna whimpering at her heels. "Who's sitting on my *couch*, Durwood?"

"I was going to tell you when you got up," Leffingwell said. "I didn't want to wake you up when we got home."

"I was tired. I was at school all day yesterday for the Rondo Hatton film festival."

"I thought you finished that cinema course," Leffingwell said.

"I *did*. Now I'm taking Poetry and Film-Making. *Durwood*, who *is* it? *What* is it?"

"Well, ah, he's called Elephant Man."

Claudine sat down hard at the table. Leffingwell poured the boiling water and handed her his Coffee-Lover's mug. "But what's the matter with him? *Why* do they call him Elephant Man?"

"Because," Leffingwell whispered, "he looks like an elephant, sort of."

"AGH!" said Claudine.

"You don't have to shout."

"He's the reason Krishna's a nervous wreck this morning!"

"Well, Krishna jumped us at the door, and then he got a good look at Elephant Man." Leffingwell fought to hide his smile as Krishna, huddling behind Claudine's chair, glanced nervously in the direction of the living room. "I think it surprised him."

"You mean it's dangerous, too? I come down in the morning because the TV's so loud, I find some freak in a cape watching *Captain Kangaroo*, and if that isn't enough, I find out it's an elephant that attacks innocent dogs. You must be kidding. It's got to go!"

"No," Leffingwell said.

They both heard the click of the channel selector from the living room. *Aww, I don't wanna go to school*, Spanky said through the worn soundtrack across some fifty years.

"You are absolutely out of your mind, Durwood Leffingwell."

"Claudine, the poor guy's . . . well, his trainer, I guess . . . abandoned him in this empty store yesterday, and I happened to be there filming a story with Stackpole—"

"Stackpole again!"

"Anyway, I couldn't just leave him there."

"Oh, you couldn't? Have you ever seen *Freaks?*"

"Shh," Leffingwell whispered. "Watch your language." He nodded toward the living room.

"Well, it's by Todd Browning—Mr. Miasma showed it to us last semester. It's all about how these disgusting freaks in a circus disfigure this beautiful trapeze artist."

"Oh, yeah, isn't that the one where she marries a midget and then makes fun of him or something and has this affair with—"

"Durwood, I don't want him in this house."

Leffingwell regretted not being a more aggressive personality, because the kitchen was filled with things he could have hit her with.

"And another thing, Durwood. You were all over the bed again with one of your chicken dreams."

"Was not," he said, not sure. "I remember my dream perfectly well, and it had nothing to do with chickens."

"Oh, really? Then who were you saying 'cockadoodle-doo' to?"

"My dream was being in this huge garage with the door closed, and I tried to commit suicide in the Rambler. But I couldn't get it to start."

"Durwood, what is it with you and chickens?"

"The police broke in," Leffingwell went on, getting a mug for himself out of the cupboard and dumping a teaspoon of crystals in. "I was perfectly all right, but the battery was pronounced dead at the scene."

"Durwood, will you be serious? Why are you afraid of chickens?"

"I'm not," he answered, stirring his coffee. "It's dinosaurs I'm afraid of, but I have chicken dreams instead because they're only a couple of genes away from dinosaurs. Simple psychological mechanism, really."

"Why can't you ever make *sense?*" Claudine wailed. "The point is you're the one that brought this elephant-thing home, and now you can just find some jerk at the station who needs one of whatever it is."

"All right, all right," he said. "I'll try to figure something out. But we're going to miss out on a million-dollar idea."

"A million-dollar idea, Durwood? *How?*"

"Well, it's . . ." Somehow the magic of the little man's glowing descriptions yesterday had oozed away during the night. Now it all seemed so stupid.

"Never mind," Claudine said. "We'll discuss it while I drive you to work."

"What?"

"I need the car today. I've got to go to school."

"Jesus, you and your endless school. You're over thirty, Claudine—it's not going to make you twenty, you know." He didn't look at her because he knew she'd be mad. That was all right: he was mad, too. He hated being stranded at work without a car. It was like being fifteen and getting rides from his mother. "Isn't today a holiday?"

"This is a special conference with Mr. Miasma. He wants to go over my shooting script."

Leffingwell slammed his mug down. It hadn't seemed so bad when it started two years ago. He worked until eleven-thirty at night, so night courses made sense for her because she didn't like sitting home alone, and her computer communications course made sense to him because computer people were supposed to make big money. But she'd dropped the course two days after it was too late to get a refund, and now two years and fifteen hundred dollars later here she was learning how to make super-8 films of her poetry. Even pottery had been better. He turned and strode into the living room.

Elephant Man was hunched forward on the couch, intently watching the television set through his veil.

"Enjoying yourself?" Leffingwell asked very loudly and slowly. "Guess Captain Kangaroo's over, eh?" He could see it was *Our Gang,* and Alfalfa seemed to be in some kind of singing contest and had laryngitis.

"How soon would you like me to leave?" Elephant Man answered, slowly and steadily.

Leffingwell jumped back. He'd come to think of the creature as more elephant than man and hadn't expected a real response. "What?"

Elephant Man had great patience. "How soon do I have to leave?"

Leffingwell was astonished. They almost seemed to be real words. "Half a reave? What?"

"*Leave*." The voice was firm without being too loud. "Me. How soon?"

"Oh." Leffingwell wanted to sit down, but there was no place except next to the shrouded, alien figure on the sofa. He remained standing. "Leave? How soon do you have to leave?"

"Yes."

"Why, ah, *you* don't have to leave," he said. "You're my guest."

"Your wife is afraid of me."

"What?" Leffingwell settled gingerly on the arm of the sofa.

"*Wife*. Afraid. Me."

"Wipe your face?" The thing's syntax was primitive, of course, but it really did talk. "Just help yourself. I mean, you go bathroom any time, wash face." Leffingwell pantomimed washing his own face. "Or take bath. Up to you." He pointed to signify who 'you' was.

"WIFE."

"Oh, Claudine?"

"Your wife seems to be afraid of me."

Leffingwell listened intently to the slushy, indistinct sounds, and suddenly he understood. "My wife seems to be . . . afraid of you?"

Good God, Leffingwell thought, he wasn't retarded at all. It was just a matter of getting used to the way he pronounced things, like learning to interpret the speech of deaf people. "Oh, no," he laughed. "Claudine *loves* guests." It didn't occur to Leffingwell that Elephant Man had been fully competent the whole time and had heard everything he and Claudine had said; somehow Leffingwell imagined the creature had been retarded right up until Leffingwell's realization had conferred human intelligence on him, like God's finger investing Adam's clay with life.

Elephant Man sighed and sat back on the sofa. There was no point pursuing the matter further. He looked around the room. "I don't think I've ever been in anybody's apartment before," he said. "It's very nice."

"Say what? Apartment? Yeah, it's a real dump."

"I've seen plenty of motel rooms," Elephant Man said slowly. "Buses and trailers, circus tents, trains, even a baggage car." He went through the list slowly. "Even a hospital once . . . a long time ago, I think. But this is the first time anyone invited me to his home. I guess Harry didn't have one. It's really very good of you."

Leffingwell was embarrassed. He realized that if he'd expected gratitude, it had been something on the order of a puppy wagging its tail. Real compliments were, well, genuinely human responses. "It's nothing," he said. "I mean it. And I really do want you to make yourself at home."

"Do you think it's all right if I stay long enough to watch *Young and the Restless?*"

"Jung and who?"

"The Young and the Restless."

"You mean that soap opera? You watch those things?"

"Whenever I can. I like *Love of Life,* too."

"Of course," Leffingwell smiled paternally. Pathetic, he thought, a monster cut off from everything but the sick imitations of life on television, like a million housewives. Leffingwell began to swell with his own beneficence. "Look, I really mean it about making yourself at home. And if there's something special you want to do or anything, you just tell me, whatever it is."

Gee whiz, said Spanky from the TV, *what happened to your voice?*

"Anything?" Elephant Man bowed his head reflectively. "There is something—but it's not possible."

"Anything's possible," said Leffingwell.

"Not for someone like me."

Leffingwell shuddered, knowing he'd want sex. Well, there was that fortune-massage parlor. Wasn't that their business, doing it for money with people who couldn't get it any other way? Or he could ask Capella, though for all Capella's talk Leffingwell suspected Capella's experience was actually confined to the *Screw* magazines he brought to work and the occasional coverless copy of *Sex Sandwich Weekend* or *Prudence and Her Pets* he left on the dashboard of his Plymouth.

"But if I could," Elephant Man continued, the television screen glinting from his eyes through the veil, "I'd want to go to the opera."

Leffingwell watched the voiceless Alfalfa gulping with embarrassment. "The opera?"

"Yes, the way you see it in old movies with people

like Adolphe Menjou and Walter Pidgeon all dressed up in tie and tails, taking a taxi to the opera."

"Tie and tails. Sure."

"Movies are fine for most things," Elephant Man said. "Even Shakespeare. But for opera, you've really got to go in person. It's sitting right there in a box and watching through opera glasses."

Why couldn't he have been retarded, Leffingwell wondered. And this Alfalfa thing was kind of cute, in a way. If only he could watch it.

"No problem," Leffingwell said. "If it's the opera you want, that's what you get. There's a company in Boston, I think. I'll check and see if they're doing anything." Leffingwell had never actually seen an opera. He had vague recollections of record jackets on clearance-sale tables, middle-aged, jowly faces doll-like with eye liner and rouge. "I suppose you've seen *Phantom of the Opera?*"

"Which one?" asked Elephant Man.

"What do you mean 'which one'?" It was like talking to Claudine.

"Well, there's the 1925 silent with the first Lon Chaney on educational television sometimes. Then there was a remake in 1943 with Claude Rains, and then Hammer Studios did a version in 1962 with Herbert Lom—"

"I was thinking of the one where he wears a mask and falls in love with this soprano, but his face is all—um. . . ." Leffingwell rose, embarrassed. "That reminds me, I think you ought to see a doctor."

"What for?"

"Why, ah, to see if there's anything he could do for you. That guy who was with you—he never took you to a doctor, right?"

"No, but I'd been to doctors before."

"Oh? When was that?"

"I . . . I guess I don't remember," Elephant Man said, seeming to stiffen. "I just know I've been to them."

"Well, there's always the chance a new one could help you, even if the others couldn't. It's not an exact science, you know."

"I know."

"And it couldn't hurt to be sure you're good and healthy. No wasting diseases. Nothing, ah, catching." Leffingwell flushed at revealing himself and hastened to change the subject. "Say, this is kind of weird, you know, but you never told me your name."

"Name? Elephant Man."

"No, your *real* name. Before somebody thought up Elephant Man for you. That's just a stage name."

"The Dog-Faced Boy."

"Before that."

"I don't remember. Guppy-Man, I think."

"But you've got to have a real name—everybody does. They call me Mr. Laffy on *Tooth Brigade*, but in real life my name's Leffingwell. Come on, try to remember."

Elephant Man thought deeply. "I don't know—yet."

"*Durwood*," Claudine called from the kitchen. "Will you come in here? I've got to talk to you—*alone*."

"In a second," Leffingwell answered.

"Should I call you Durwood?" Elephant Man asked.

"I hate Durwood," Leffingwell said. "The name's Leff."

"*Durwood!*" Claudine shouted.

"It's really exciting to actually meet someone that works in television," Elephant Man said. "It must be a terrible strain, all that responsibility."

"Responsibility?"

"To the people who watch you. Living up to your image, worrying about how what you do on the air can affect people."

"Oh," Leffingwell said. "Yeah, of course." He paused, confused. "But that reminds me, you'll probably be on the tube yourself tonight."

"*Me?*" gasped Elephant Man.

"Yeah, all that film Stackpole shot of you yesterday. I won't be home, of course, cause I have to do the weather, but just flick on Channel 29 at ten and watch yourself." Leffingwell felt himself expanding again. "I imagine you'll get a real kick out of that, won't you?"

Elephant Man was silent for several minutes. "I guess so," he said at last. "By the way, there was a rock version, too."

"Rock version? Of what?"

"Of *Phantom of the Opera*. It was called *Phantom of the Paradise* and it had Paul Williams in it, but I haven't seen it because it hasn't been run on TV yet."

"Sooner or later it will. Everything winds up on TV."

"I'm sure the plot's the same, though," Elephant Man said. "They wouldn't change that."

"No," Leffingwell agreed. "They wouldn't change that." He stood awkwardly at the kitchen door until the great veiled head turned back to the television screen.

"DURWOOD!" screamed Claudine, and Leffingwell was gone.

"I don't like it when they change the plot," Elephant Man said to himself.

Chapter 7

Reruns

It was an hour later that the outside door slammed shut, and Claudine and Leffingwell's bickering had faded into nothingness. Elephant Man plucked his beekeeper's hat away, revelling in the sudden, unveiled brightness and coolness that swirled in upon his naked head. He shrugged off the cape and drew the glove from his right hand and felt cooler still.

Leffingwell and Claudine had left early, and Leffingwell had said *Young and the Restless* wouldn't be on for forty-five minutes. Idly, Elephant Man's eyes drifted from a quiz show to take in the room.

After the barrenness of motels, where the folding suitcase rack was as important as the bed and outranked the dresser, Leffingwell's living room seemed rich and cluttered. There was the sofa bed where he sat, a yellow butterfly chair in the corner with one pocket torn so the canvas seat flapped uselessly from its three remaining moorings, a floor lamp from the fifties whose shade was fuzzy with dust. Everything faced the GE nineteen-inch black and white portable atop the bookcase. Below, several large, encyclopedialike tomes with gilt lettering—*Prosser on Torts, Henn's Corporations* and several spiral-bound books published by Dilbert, followed by *Cinema as Art, Film as Film, The Screen Plays of Ingmar Bergman* and *Student*

Filmmaking. Beneath these were a number of tattered student paperbacks with sweat-stained backs: *Moby Dick, The Merchant of Venice, L'Étranger, A Farewell to Arms* and *Existentialism from Dostoevsky to Sartre,* culminating in *Knots, Zen and the Art of Motorcycle Maintenance* and *All Things Bright and Beautiful.*

Leffingwell was like Harry, Elephant Man thought. And things would probably work out the same way in the end—Leffingwell would help him for a while, and then Elephant Man would have to find someone else. It wouldn't be Leffingwell's fault any more than it had been Harry's. For while others might have raged against a fate that denied them independence, Elephant Man accepted it as an inevitable part of the destiny that had shaped him as he was.

His eyes found the quiz show again.

He didn't like quiz shows. They were unpredictable and made displays of unsuspecting people like the fat woman he saw now, flesh rolling up and down her body a half beat behind each of her frenzied, ponderous hops of greed. If people were put on display, he thought, they ought to know it, and they ought to get more than a chance at a quiz show prize.

The truth was that Elephant Man labored under two curses. The first was that he looked like a monster. The second was that he'd never managed to develop a monster's spirit. He had no defenses. Harry once explained by saying Elephant Man had watched so much television he thought life was a sitcom where people were essentially good and even the meanest was no worse than Mr. Honeywell on *My Little Margie.*

Elephant Man showed such lamblike patience and kindness with others and with every inconvenience of his life that at first his fellow carnies had thought he was stupid, until they found he could read books as fast as he could turn the pages. He could tell you that September 1 would fall on a Tuesday in 1981 without even pausing to think; he could figure twenty years of fractional interest compounded daily in the time it took him to repeat the problem; and he could remember verbatim months later conversations about the weather.

But while he was anything but stupid, it was also true that Elephant Man believed in the world of Romance which television brought him, a world where virtue always triumphed and vice could ultimately be defeated or at least contained in cycles based on multiples of thirty minutes. It was one of the patterns he occupied himself with as he probed each day's interlace of reruns and old movies for the threads which might lead him, like the endlessly interwoven ribbons and acanthus branches around the border of a Romanesque psalter, back to the missing beginnings of his life. All he knew for sure was that, like television itself, he was an entertainment and a child of technology.

Now, thoughts drifting from the woman on the screen, he felt again the hot blast from the asphalt of some forgotten shopping center parking lot, the air thundering with the whir of machinery, carousel music, the amplified shrieks of the Haunted House ride. He'd often taken his breaks from the sideshow hovering in the no-man's land between the parked trailers and the plywood false fronts that were bolted up panel by panel at every stop to disguise the fact that each of the attractions was the gaping hind end of a tractor-trailer.

There were small gaps between the panels, and Elephant Man could peer out from behind the fancifully painted images of himself, the Humungous Fat Lady and the Armless Marvel at the crowded midway. To the left was always the Haunted Hosue with Lester Fish lounging in one of the cars with an Orange Nehi as he waited for customers with three twenty-five-cent coupons to take the terrifying descent into all the hell that could be crammed into a semi, while above him a fiberglass witch blared taped cackles from her revolving broomstick.

The Haunted House was popular with teen-agers and couples. Teen-agers liked the sideshow, too, especially the boys, but couples rarely entered and families never did. As though they feared what they saw might compromise their own genetic legacies, paunchy men in work clothes and chunky women in bermudas and sleeveless blouses pointed at the representations painted on the panels behind which the real Elephant Man hid, and shrieked with delight that, by however narrow a margin, they were still outside and the freaks safely in.

As Imelda, the Amazing Filipino Pigmy Queen—the only other freak who ever talked to him—observed, you've got to be smarter than average to stop hiding what you never got or grew an extra of and make a profit on it.

The quiz show woman again, jiggling on the TV screen.

She reminded him of an earlier time—the nervous face and leaping eyebrows, the mouth taut and then stretched into a smile and then pursed in concentration. He remembered being in a big room filled with . . . children? . . . watching a show like this. He remembered concentrating to see if he could make the skin wrinkle on his forehead like hers or make his eyebrows rise. He tried it now, alone in Leffingwell's living room: he felt everything move forward and hover at the front of his head. A faint tingling, nerve impulses popping and dissipating ineffectually. But his forehead and eyebrows wouldn't move.

Suddenly the back of his neck prickled with some ancient, animal sense of another presence in the house. He was just reaching desperately for his beekeeper's hat when there was a sharp intake of breath behind him. He clapped the hat on his head and turned.

A large, puffy girl stood frozen in the kitchen doorway, her small eyes preternaturally wide with her glimpse of the back of the Elephant Man's head. "I wasn't doing nothing!" she protested suddenly, whipping her hands behind her back as though to conceal something.

"Good morning," Elephant Man said as slowly and distinctly as he could. "Are you a friend of Leff's?"

Her eyes narrowed. "Sure I am," she said. "He has me come over when he's away to make sure he hasn't been robbed or anything. You know how it is these days with the crime on the news and all. And see? I found this little transistor radio right out on the counter where *anybody* could steal it." From behind her back she produced a small black cube. "See, I'm going to put it right here on the chair where it'll be safe, okay?"

She did so nervously, then straightened. When he didn't challenge her, she seemed to relax. "Anyway, what're *you* doing here? He never told me about *you*."

"I'm visiting him for a little," said Elephant Man.

Fern squinted. "Visiting? I usually know about any guests. He tells me, you know."

"Well, he met me through his work," Elephant Man said. "In fact, he's going to have me on the news tonight."

"On TV? He put *me* on TV once."

"That must have been nice," said Elephant Man.

"After what it did to my dance career? One little word— I just forgot one little word and he absolutely *abandoned* me. Not only that, but he *kicked* me. Kicked me in front of millions of viewers."

"That doesn't sound like Leff."

"You'll find out," she sniffed. "Not only that, but he never invited me back on *Tooth Brigade,* just when I was *that close* to being a star. But I know what he had in mind—just like the rest of those TV biggies. They're all after one thing, like the guys in Ma's secret books—like *Network Sextortionist.* Killed my cat, too. Probably thought he could take advantage of me because I was an orphan."

Elephant Man was puzzled. A perfectly nice girl like her wouldn't hate Leffingwell without a reason. That was what made life so complicated—every time you talked to someone, you got a different view of the same facts. Like the way they tantalized you on *Perry Mason* by making you think it was the gardener, and then the nephew, and then the social secretary. "I'm sorry you're an orphan."

"Well, half an orphan. My mother's still alive, as if *that* made any difference. Might as well be a full orphan."

"I don't even *know* if I had a mother or father," Elephant Man said cautiously, hoping to cheer her up.

"That's stupid. Everybody's got to have a father and mother. It's biology."

"What happened to your father?"

"Ma says his life was so lousy his body needed a break. I was too little to remember. All I know is, he left me the TV in his will. If it wasn't for that, I think I'd go crazy."

Elephant Man saw the flicker of passion in her dull eyes. "I understand," he said.

"At least till I get my career going. *Then* the kids'll stop being so snotty about 'potato face' and 'Moby Fern' and all. *They'll* be sorry."

"I think you look very nice," Elephant Man said.

"What do *you* know? I saw the back of your head—you're—"

"I know," said Elephant Man.

"Anyway, I can get away up in my room from everything and just talk with Walter Cronkite or see what's happening on *Young and the Restless*—"

"Do you watch that?" Elephant Man asked excitedly. "It's my favorite show." He made as though to get up.

"EEK!" she shrieked, leaping back, eyes wide. "Oh, my God!"

"I wasn't going to—"

"No," she said, pointing at the TV. "It's the theme! I'll miss today's episode!" She flew from the room.

Elephant Man turned back to the set, shaking his head, and focused on the screen through his heavy veil. Before him was Dr. Ben Casey in a surgical gown, mask dangling around his neck, cap pushed back on his head. Elephant Man felt the torment of the flickerings of an unformed smile tugging at his immobile lips: an ad for an afternoon rerun.

—run a GI series, came Dr. Casey's voice reassuringly through the worn sound track's hiss and pop.

Yes, Elephant Man thought. He remembered this one. Then he felt it happening again. *Series, series.* Like a hook, the word dredged up first one bit, then another. *Ames mutagenic series.*

He felt himself dwindling into something very small and looking up to find mountainous monsters in green gowns towering over him. He looked at the vast legs going up to the bottom of the gowns and wondered whether the gowns were solid or they had more legs going up inside. Their heads seemed very far away, tops and bottoms green, separated by a band of flesh where the eyes lived.

—as part of the autopsy, one of them was saying.

You mean biopsy, don't you, doctor?

I mean what I mean, Dr. Sykes.

That's murder.

Hardly. Nobody calls the police when a lab puts a rhesus monkey out of the way, do they?

Later the one who was Doctorsykes came back in the dark time. *Don't be afraid,* she said, bending over him, her eyes glistening and wet. She scooped him up and carried him toward the door where time and again he'd seen the green ones disappear into nothingness, and even though they usually came back, he began to scream with fear.

I'm trying to save you. Hush, she said, and then suddenly he was through the door, and he hadn't wisped into nothing. He was in a long room with more doors. But then she reached up and pulled off the green bottom of her face.

What in the world is the matter with you?

Instead of the emptiness he'd feared, he saw a mouth-hole and chin like his working with the words. So the green was only some kind of covering, he thought. That meant the others probably also had faces like his.

That was why he was interested rather than surprised and didn't scream when she pulled off the green top of her head, and he laughed with delight to see hair like his cascading down.

There's a good boy, she cooed. *I know someplace you'll be safe.*

Now he was sitting in a very wide chair beside her inside a small place hurtling forward, the air rushing hard against his face. He began to scream again.

It's only a car, she said. *You don't have to be afraid. You'll probably be riding in them all the time after tonight. If the wind bothers you, I can roll up the windows.*

And the place they had gone. . . . Elephant Man concentrated very hard, trying to make himself remember. He glanced at the TV—Ben Casey still. Doctors, doctors, he thought. He felt himself swell and grow slightly from what he had been, but he was still very small, seated on a bench in a dim room with his feet swinging free of the floor. Beside him was a person in black. He could remember nothing about her except that her name was Froggie and they were both listening to what was being said on the other side of the door.

Hi, Wally, how's business? said a man's voice in the next room. For an instant Elephant Man's heart leaped at the thought that that was his name and someone was speaking to him, but then he realized the voice was talking to someone else. *Been taking wings off flies?* the voice went on.

Dr. Herzberg, please, said a motherly voice. *He's been through so much today already.*

Doctor Herzberg, Elephant Man thought. Was this the same doctor Skyes had talked to about murder? Was Sykes in that room, too? But this wasn't anything like the room Sykes had taken him from.

Okay, okay, take off your shirt, Wally. Let's see that manly chest.

He told *me he was having funny smells. If only I'd believed him, this wouldn't have happened. . . .*

Don't torture yourself, said the doctor. *His funny smells are just his body's way of telling him he needs a bath. Except when one of the sisters gives an exam. Anybody threaten you with a test today, Wally? Never mind—open your eyes and let's see into the depths of your soul.* Pause. *Just what I thought. No one home.*

You shouldn't joke with him like that, said the motherly voice.

Elephant Man remembered himself staring down past the white rubber tips of his sneakers at the floor and trying to imagine what the doctor was doing to Wally.

So this was the big enchilada, Wally? Never had a grand mal before? He been taking his anticonvulsants?

Sister Infirmarian administers them every day.

Whole thing, then, right? Tonic stage and cyanosis?

What?

He fall down and turn blue?

Yes, down the stairs. He was raving about the new boy.

Then the clonic stage—legs jerking, arms, the whole bit?

Yes. One of the sisters tore the hem off her habit and stuffed it in his mouth so he wouldn't swallow his tongue.

Well, cheer up, Wally—Caesar had it too. We'll get you a new prescription and in a few years you'll be supreme consul of the Western Hemisphere. But for tonight I think we'd better get him down to St. Joseph's for an EEG, a little of his spinal fluid and an x-ray of that thick head of his.

You heard the doctor, Walther. Go up to your room and get your things together.

Aw, shit, said a third voice.

Walther!

The door opened. Walther did not look at him. He ran his hand through his red hair to hide his eyes and walked as quickly as he could to the hall door. He glanced swiftly to be sure Froggie wasn't watching. *Freak,* he mouthed, and was gone.

Now what's the story on this new kid? came the doctor's voice through the still open door.

Well, I feel foolish, really. It's just what Walther said before his seizure. He seemed genuinely frightened . . .

Just what was it he said?

Elephant Man felt Froggie looking hard at him, but he didn't look back.

Nothing. Crazy things. There was a pause. *He claimed, well, he claimed the boy had said something about not having any parents.*

What's so unusual about that? asked the doctor's voice. *This is supposed to be an orphanage, isn't it?*

No parents ever. That he was some kind of test-tube baby . . .

All right, have the sister out there bring him in. But when I get Wally down to St. Joe's, I'm signing him up to see Lucy the kid-shrink right after we get his x-ray.

The truth is, we really don't know much about him, the woman's voice went on as Froggie rose and led him from the bench into the room. The doctor was on a stool beside a desk where an older woman in black sat. Elephant Man tried to remember her face, but somehow his memory veiled it. *And Sister Infirmarian noticed he'd been running a fever since he came, and if there's any truth. . . . Well, no matter. It's our policy to have a* doctor's *exam for every new boy.*

Elephant Man remembered thinking that he must never again reveal anything to Walther.

He looks fine to me, Herzberg said. He was putting tubes into his ears that joined into one tube at his chest, from which dangled a silver disc, but Elephant Man had seen such things many times before. *He got any other symptoms?*

We thought you could find—

Sister, doctors don't look for symptoms. We wait for the patient to notice them, and then we try to figure out what they mean. Try to remember I'm doing this for free, and I'm not even an RC. Take off your shirt, kid.

Don't rip it, snapped Froggie. *Unbutton it first.* Her black shape bent over him and cold white fingers began to pick at the buttons. He tried to look past the hands at the tips of his sneakers. Then the shirt was gone and his chest and shoulders were cold. Herzberg was whipping a glass tube.

Here, hold this under your tongue.

The glass tube went into his mouth and then the round flat thing was on his chest. It was very cold.

Stand still. Well, we're a big boy, aren't we? How old are we, four?

Not quite three, said the Mother. *That's what the woman who brought him said.*

Didn't think you took them that young, and he's pretty big for under three. You sure?

Well, we did notice the clothes we first gave him turned out to be a little small.

Take it from a pro, Sister, the kid's four. The doctor looked at his watch, listening through the tubes. Then he turned him around and the cold disc was on his back. *Now breathe in. Again. Again. Now turn sideways. I'm going to shine this light in your ear. It won't hurt. Say, Sister,* he said, squinting through the instrument, *you read about that kidnapping up the road?*

The Mother seemed suddenly upset. She went to the window and lowered the blinds. *Yes,* she said. *There was a picture of the poor woman's car in today's paper.*

Whole thing sounds fishy to me—now the other ear. No, turn the other way. Abducted by two men in a gray sedan with out-of-state plates. . . .

It's just terrible, said the Mother. Froggie listened.

Yeah, but they left her car, and the state police claim its plates were phoney—couldn't be traced. And her signing the motel register as Smith. That's got to be phoney. Who's named Smith, anyway?

Descendants of Captain John Smith, I suppose, said the Mother absently.

The doctor leaned forward and pulled the glass tube from under his tongue and looked at it. *Well, we'll give Wally the benefit of the doubt and say he was hallucinating instead of lying.*

Nothing abnormal?

Well, temperature is a shade under a hundred and one, but kids run fevers all the time. Could be a low-grade infection, or he could be one of those people with a high normal temperature. Have your sister infirmary keep checking him, but remember ninety-eight-point-six is an average, not a law.

Then he hasn't got anything . . . contagious or some laboratory—

He's just fine. But if you see the rats stagger out of their holes and fall over dead, take two aspirins and call somebody else in the morning.

Suddenly on the screen before him was a man's monstrously deformed face. He was wearing a stocking.

It was Peg remembering, of course. Elephant Man had seen the original rape on *Young and the Restless* and watched it repeated several times in later episodes whenever Peg remembered what had happened to her. The man in

the stocking mask: *I'm not going to hurt you. Don't scream.*
Coming at her, whispering, and she gurgling: *Please, no.*

It was terrible. Peg's sister hated Ron because she thought
he had raped her, too, and she was persuading Peg that
Ron had been the man in the stocking. And Peg was
probably going to finger Ron as the rapist in tomorrow's
lineup because of her sister's prodding. Poor innocent boy.

He closed his eyes and saw again Walther's red hair
and averted face, slinking across the room, *freak,* and he
wished he'd called out something to reassure him. What
was it, really, he'd told Walther about his parents? What
had he known in those days he no longer remembered? But
nothing came, and so he thought about Fern, about Alfalfa's voicelessness and humiliation, about Ron's desperation,
about Peg's eternal nightmare of the grotesquely swollen
face in the mask.

Chapter 8

The Halls of Ivy

On their way out that morning, Leffingwell had grabbed a coat hanger and a trash can. At the car, he'd flipped the driver's seat forward and wedged the trash can behind it; then he'd bent the coat hanger around the door's armrest and hooked it through one of the seat's exposed springs. Claudine had sighed and slid across from the side with the working door to take the wheel.

They did not speak for some time. As the highway flashed by, Leffingwell tried to remember exactly where yesterday he'd left the flaming hulks of the higher horse-powered and arrogant.

"You know, he's not retarded at all," he said at last.

"Durwood, you're getting that thing out of the house by tonight or I'm not coming home."

"All right, all right, I'll try to work something out at the station. You picking me up tonight?"

Claudine squeezed the rim of the wheel. "I don't know how long my conference will be. Can't somebody give you a ride?" She hated the long drive from Cambria College, north of their apartment, all the way down to Butler in the midnight dark when the road was deserted by all but occasional packs of trucks.

"Nobody lives near us. Watch that car—he's going to pull out in front of you."

"I *see* it, Durwood. What about Stackpole's trailer?"

"Will you stop riding the brake? Just because the guy ahead has his brakes on doesn't mean *you've* got to—cars with automatics tend to brake more. Just ease off the accelerator."

Claudine gripped the wheel tighter. "What about Stackpole?"

"I hate asking him again."

"Then isn't there some girl or something that went to C.C. and still has an apartment there?"

"Dawn? I guess so. You better slow down and let that truck in. It's dangerous to be beside—"

"Shut up, Durwood. Shut up or I'll drive into the next bridge abutment."

They were silent again until Claudine swung down the exit ramp onto 111-A, once a highway but now merely a divider between the vast parking lots of shopping centers on either side.

"Careful at the light," Leffingwell said at last. "It's tending to stall. I think the timer's off."

They didn't stall. "That's 'timing,' Durwood."

"You're riding the clutch. No wonder the clutch is always going."

Claudine cut diagonally through a Gas Paradise into the parking lot behind Stop and Shop, Medimart, and Bradlees toward the low pink cinder block home of Channel 29 and pulled to a stop by a red Sunbeam with a police bubble-gum flasher bolted on the trunk and a large cardboard sign taped inside the windshield that read "PRESS." Claudine knew it belonged to the attractive, curly-headed *Ten O'Clock News* anchorman, Lance Ricketts.

Leffingwell opened the door and swung his legs out. "Can you believe it?" he said. "He wants to go to the opera."

"No," said Claudine, looking straight ahead and tapping her index fingers on the rim of the wheel. "I can't."

"Well," Leffingwell said lamely, "you don't have to pick me up tonight. I'll get a ride home." He swung the door shut and she watched him walk with stooped shoulders across the last stretch of asphalt to the door. Then she sat for a moment, savoring the empty passenger seat and the quiet. But with no air moving, she began to smell the rich and fermenting world of new life in the thick ichor at the bottom of the trash can behind her head. She shifted into

first and rode the clutch back through the parking lot to
111-A, the right-hand door that Leffingwell hadn't quite
latched rattling steadily in a base line to the clank of the
trash can handles.

Ramblers, she thought. She always noticed them on the
highway because they were one of the few cars she could
ever pass, and that was because at the wheel was always
some stiff-necked, dim-sighted octogenarian with a pipe
and a dark, snap-brim 1947 hat who resolutely straddled
the line between the first and second lanes at thirty-five.

Durwood. They almost never made love any more, it
seemed. They'd gotten out of the habit when Durwood
had started at Channel 29: he got home too late for either
of them to be interested, and there was something unnatural about making love before breakfast coffee. Now
when they were together on Sundays, one or the other
would pick a fight so there would be no danger of affection.

The last time they'd made love was on the sofa in
the living room by the glow of the television set. She remembered being hot and wedged into the sofa's crotch,
looking over Durwood's shoulder to watch Mary Richards
give her reasons to Lou Grant for wanting to be executive
producer, while Durwood tried to lie beside her on the
cushions.

"Is your news room like Mary Tyler Moore's?" she had
asked.

"No, they're too professional. Jesus, Claudine, every
sex primer in the country says you shouldn't talk about
irrelevant things when you're going to have sex. It spoils
the mood."

They had made love and Mary Richards' first show as
executive producer was a success, but Claudine had known
it would be; she'd seen the episode before.

"Do you love me?" she had asked when Carol Burnett
came on.

"Why?"

"You used to say you loved me."

"Okay, I still do."

"Do what?" she'd asked.

"Look, Claudine, why say it? You know how I feel."

"I *don't* know. That's why I want to hear you *say* it."

Leffingwell rose and pulled up his pants. "If I didn't, I
wouldn't be here."

"Will you just say it? Will you just come back here and put your arm—"

"I've got to go to the bathroom, all right?"

She'd listened to him go up the stairs and heard the bathroom door close. "I HATE CAROL BURNETT!" she had screamed.

EXIT 14-B QUIDNUNCK N.H. ½ MI.

She would go home and take a shower and freshen up. Maybe she'd sit down and watch *General Hospital*.

EXIT 14-B QUIDNUNCK N.H. 1000 FEET

Suddenly she remembered. Durwood's miserable creature was sitting like a fireplug in the middle of her living room sofa. At the last second she veered back out of the exit's mouth, closing her eyes at the sudden blast of an air horn inches behind her bumper. With a roar the huge tractor-trailer pulled beside her; she rolled her window up. Then she smelled the trash can. She rolled the window down.

She knew perfectly well why she'd hated the thing in jeans and sneakers the moment she'd seen it, despite its covered head and shoulders. It had reminded her of her retarded uncle.

Uncle Samuel. The reedy treble voice, the flat white face, the patches of stubble on his cheeks and chin he invariably missed when he shaved, only to have Claudine's grandmother send him back to the bathroom three and four times. "People who are *different*," her grandmother once explained, "have to be very careful about the ways God left them to be the same." An Irish immigrant still unsure of her respectability, Claudine's grandmother had been adamant about superficial details like always wearing your best underwear downtown, in case you were run over by a truck. It was the same reason she made him practice printing his name, despite Claudine's father's objection that if no one could read Sam's signature, they'd think he was a bank president.

He'd been everywhere, like smoke. Unable to amuse himself, he'd tagged after her, and until she turned sixteen and could escape in the family Dodge, she would look up and find him grinning vacantly at her from around the garage or through the lilac, or following down the sidewalk a block behind. He had even found his way into her locked diary. At the bottom of an exclamation-studded entry ("Diary, I'll just *die* if anybody ever sees this!!") about Dicky Ianello ("this really *neat* guy in 9th grade!!") she'd found, in those inimitable block letters, "SAMUEL GRADY." That he couldn't read had been no consolation.

Gradually, Samuel had dwindled into a contemporary, until at last she had simply grown past him and he, caught by time, had accepted her as another superior. Even now, fiftyish and white-haired, he still shuffled through her parents' house in perpetual childhood, watching Saturday morning TV and being sent to bed early.

She almost envied his freedom, except she knew how he yearned to be grown up, how he secretly tore bra and girdle ads from Sunday magazines and kept them at the bottom of his sock drawer, poised forever on the threshold of sexual awareness and not knowing what to do with them. How he'd taken up pipe smoking in imitation of Claudine's father but never learned to puff in instead of out, sending showers of burning cinders sifting down on everyone's heads until the night he forgetfully stuffed his lighted pipe in his jacket and hung it in the closet. After the fire, the pipe had been taken away.

She'd outgrown her embarrassment and resentment. She knew now, living with something long enough, no matter how repulsive, made it familiar as the furniture. But she wasn't going to let herself become like her mother, slave to some in-house grotesque. She'd waited twenty years to escape from it.

Funny, though, she thought, driving slowly along the shaded street toward the entrance of Cambria College. Years before, Uncle Samuel had become convinced—after watching a *Twilight Zone* show—that everyone had a perfect double, and his was in China. She'd laughed at the idea of anyone so weird having a duplicate, especially a perfect, white-faced, second Samuel Grady among the almond-eyed millions of China, laughed with the same cruelty that made her at six or seven walk behind him to mock his penguin's rolling gait until she'd looked up to find her grandmother watching from the porch, mouth taut with anguish.

And now, through some bizarre conjunction of the stars and planets, her husband had brought Samuel's spiritual twin to sit in her living room and watch her television set.

Claudine eased the Rambler into one of the student spaces near the tennis courts, determined to think no more about Durwood, his monster or Uncle Samuel, and hoping to find a partnerless student on the courts for a set or two before her conference. She liked using student parking. Her registration didn't say "older" or "returning," it just said "student"; it was like being able to erase these last years.

She took her tennis racket and can of dead balls out of the trunk. Durwood had played tennis; they'd even met the first time on the courts. He had been in a sweat shirt, jeans and loafers, his serves had been wild, but he'd been amusing in those days. He'd been planning to go to cinema school and get rich, so she'd escaped Uncle Samuel by getting married and going along to the University of Southern California. There they'd eaten beans and lived on New Hampshire Avenue in a Mexican neighborhood where the men spent all day sitting in their Chevy convertibles in their driveways playing their car radios. For his animation course, Durwood filmed a pair of pliers eating an aspirin tablet in super-8, and a week later Claudine had gotten cramps and found the pliers had eaten their last Bayer. At the end of the year he'd filmed her running up stairways and through doors in a condemned building for his final project. At the end she burst into a room where an actor-friend was supposed to pull a rented boa constrictor out of his fly, but at the climactic moment, the actor had reached inside his fly with a bewildered expression while the snake dropped down his pants leg and slithered through a hole in the floor. Durwood substituted a sparkplug from their Volvo, but his professor, a former pro who'd met Franchot Tone, found the symbolism muddy. Two D's in a row and thirty dollars to the pet store for losing the snake. Durwood said you had to know somebody big to make it in Hollywood, and they'd packed everything into their red '62 Volvo and come back east.

Durwood had worked intermittently for Manpower and enrolled at Boston College law school the next September, but in October she'd come home from an employment agency and found Durwood jumping up and down on *Prosser on Torts*. In November he'd heard about an opening for a film editor at Channel 29 for fifty-two hundred dollars a year, and they'd moved to New Hampshire and traded the Volvo "for a commuting car."

Six years ago, Claudine thought, toiling up the rise to the courts. Eight years altogether, from start . . . to finish.

The courts were empty. With a sigh she crossed the asphalt to the green wooden backboard at the far side, took out a ball, tossed it into the air, rose to the balls of her feet and rifled the thing to New Jersey. Back it came. Returned it once (Delaware), twice (Virginia), lost it.

Durwood refused to play after they returned east. She had kept her tan by sitting in their scruffy back yard through the summers and under a sunlamp in the winters, while Durwood had turned whiter and puffier. Once he'd driven her to Butler's municipal courts, but they'd been full; later she'd found the metal racket she'd given him their first Christmas under the couch, strings blurry with accumulated dust. She had put it back and never mentioned it again.

Angrily Claudine threw a second fuzzy sphere into the air and caught it flat with the racket. It bounced crazily off the backboard to the side, rattled the chain-link fence and dropped into the tall grass. She walked over to look for it, but it eluded her because the night was beginning to collect in the nooks and crannies around the edges of the court.

They'd tried children, of course, but Durwood had been no better than Krishna. She'd suggested a fertility clinic. "Just what I need," Durwood had said. "Some doctor sticking his finger up my ass. Forget it. I'll take the blame—I'm sterile, okay? Satisfied? Go see if you can find a sperm bank that takes Master Charge."

She returned to the line for a final serve, lofted the ball like a pigeon she was setting free and smashed it. She caught it too high. The white speck flashed up and to the left, beyond the backboard, and winked out in the gloom.

Oh, well, almost time for her conference anyway. She walked back to the car, threw her racket and empty ball can past the trash can and pulled out her papers for the walk to the Humanities Department. On the way, she paused at the plate glass at the field house entrance to assess herself. Not good, she thought, but not bad. No one would guess thirty, anyway. Maybe eight years ago there hadn't been that gentle roundness to the breasts and tummy, but then eight years ago she wouldn't have dreamed of going on the courts in jeans and a cardigan.

Humanities 112: Poetry and Film-Making was Claudine's fifth course at Cambria College. When she had discovered in Computer Communication that she couldn't communicate with the computer, probably because the keyboard terminal was in a janitor's closet that smelled of ammonia, she'd taken up pottery; but even though the cigarette case had made a stunning earring box, she'd gone on to an English course with a strange, bearded man who laughed quietly to himself while he showed slides of Blake engravings. Then C.C. had begun its Women's Continuing Education Weekend College, and she'd signed up for the Raised Feminine Consciousness in Cinema with Professor Jack Miasma. The first two classes had been devoted to clarifying the fact Jack Miasma was not only a cinematographer himself ("The Urinal," b & w, 16mm silent, 2 min., Second Runner-Up in the Northern New England Experimental Film Festival; "Windpoem," color, super-8 silent, thus far denied the critical acclaim it deserved), but a heavily published and widely read younger poet (two major pieces in *Mineshaft,* a journal appearing irregularly in parts of Colorado). After that they'd seen *Freaks, King Kong* and *Road to Morocco,* and then the budget had been depleted and Professor Miasma had assigned whatever was playing at the Capitol in town.

She knew perfectly well he was a fool, of course. He hadn't accomplished a bit more than Durwood, but he was oblivious to his own pointlessness, and that made him more interesting. And so the next semester she'd signed on for Poetry and Film-Making.

The walls on either side of Miasma's door were papered with *Mademoiselle* contest fliers, graduate writing programs and summer workshops in cinema. The door was open; inside, pounding at the typewriter, was Jack Miasma in a cowboy shirt and baggy Einstein sweater, oily skin gleaming in the sheen of his oily hair.

"Mrs. Leffingwell!" he said, looking up. "Come in, come in. I hope this wasn't a bad time for you, but I'm just *so* busy during the day—students wanting to see me, phone calls from editors . . ."

"It's fine, really," she said, sitting in the oak chair beside his desk. "I'm just grateful you could find the time to see me at all. It was so, I don't know, embarrassing when that girl laughed at my poem. I mean, I can't film a poem people are going to laugh at." She had a flash of the still classroom, the ten or twelve undergraduate faces that seemed ever younger, her own voice quavering and higher than normal. And then the laughter from the girl Claudine had all along so generously thought had real talent. Her eyes had been hidden behind the reflections on her round glasses, blank as two plates, but her mouth had been drawn up in a mocking smile.

It seemed so much warmer and more comfortable here in Miasma's office.

"Here," he said, leaning forward to take the sheet from her hand. "Let's see, it's called 'Feet That Yearn to Run and See No More.' "

"That was where the girl laughed," Claudine said.

"Well, maybe it was the way you read it. Poetry has to be *performed*," he said, voice growing more resonant. "It's what I call the 'orality' of art."

Claudine looked at his sincere eyes, his full lips, his skin shining in the blue-green of the fluorescent tubes, and wondered whether her backboard tennis had made her cardigan too sweaty. She flipped her hair back over her shoulders.

"But this certainly has strong visual possibilities," he went on. "I see maybe thirty seconds of . . . feet, see . . . maybe, ah, *running*."

She nodded. It was more or less the way she'd seen it herself.

"But confidentially, Mrs. Leffingwell—actually, do you mind if I call you Carol?"

"It's Claudine. Please do."

"Good. I think art works best on a first-name basis. Confidentially, I can't put my finger on it, but there *is* something wrong somewhere. Hmmm. Maybe it's the whatsis, the, um, you know, da-*dum,* da-*dum,* da-*dum*—"

"The rhythm, Professor Miasma?"

"Call me Jack. Yeah, something like that. Or how about if you put in a bunch of 'feet' and some 'oh's,' like 'Oh feet, oh feet, oh feet'—see?"

"I guess so."

"But I wouldn't worry about that girl laughing. Oh, she's got a slick, superficial talent, fine for *New Yorker* or Hollywood, but she's got no *depth,* Claudine. This poem *has.* When I look at you"—he looked at her—"I can see you've got something you can't get out of a book or a class. The Poet's Scar."

"I do?"

"You *have* suffered, haven't you?"

She didn't have to think much about it. "Yes."

"I *knew* it. So have I. You might not guess it to look at me," he said, leaning back and pushing back his glistening hair with the palms of his hands so hard that the corners of his eyes were pulled back in mock oriental. "But in high school no one liked me."

"I'd never have guessed."

He leaned forward again, intensely, his face gleaming directly in front of her. "What's really wrong with this poem is you're not getting in touch with your Scar."

"But honestly, most of the time I *do* want to run away."

"Yes, yes, but running away is just a whaddayacallit, a *symbol* for something else. The thing that's under the Scar, under all that suffering, is your sexual beingness."

"What can I do?"

"Use four-letter words. That's what I do in my own work to make sure I'm really in touch with myself. Here, let me read you something."

He turned to his desk and rummaged amongst his papers, finally extracting two single-spaced typewritten sheets. "This is from the book of sonnets I'm working on, *Unlisted Numbers*. Looking Glass Press is very, *very* anxious to get it, and they're even promising I'll start making back my investment after four hundred copies. This one is '866-5463.' "

He cleared his throat.

> "*At the NASA exhibit i see*
> *a glass case containing*
> *a reflection of me*
> *redder than sunrise &*
> *a cruel piece of moonrock.*
> *O moonrock O moonrock*
> *you don't understand*
> *except moonrock-talk*
> *not even butterflies & sunshine.*
>
> *what do you care if yesterday*
> *i read in the new york times which I have a*
> *   subscription to*
> *some woman gave birth to a frog?*
> *?*
> *what do you care if Tomorrow's*
> *Iron Fist smiling cruel as adolph hitler*
> *the german politician*
> *to kick me in the gut*
> *?*"

Her thoughts drifted away to Jack Miasma pulling back his hair and scalp until his eyes slanted, to Uncle Samuel's double somewhere in China ...

"Well?" Jack asked.

"Pardon?"

"What did you think?"

"Oh," she fumbled. "Well, I guess you were really in touch with, um, your hostility to the rock there."

"No, no," he said. "The last part, about 'erection' and 'hardasnails with deepseated yearning, thrusting, churning, rotating,' and then where I talk about, ahem, 'getting my rocks off,' and, um, the really primal stuff about seeing me 'cream.' "

"Very good," she said. "Very, ah, vivid."

He raised his eyebrows. "Like the film I was going to make of my wife giving birth to our little girl, Bloodstone. I shot hundreds of feet of really rock-bottom primal visuals. God," he said, suddenly thoughtful. "That would have been really prize-winning footage. Goddamn lens cap." He paused. "You know something, my wife and I conceived Bloodstone right where you're sitting. In that very chair. One evening, in fact, just about this time."

"Really?" Claudine said. Part of her was angry and resentful at his talk of the child he'd created when she and Durwood couldn't. But the rest of her remembered the Rambler somewhere in the darkness outside with its door held shut by a coat hanger and its seat propped up by a trash can, and she looked at his eyes. Deep, intense, almost beautiful.

"Did you know," she said, leaning forward so only a few inches remained between their faces, "for a poet, you have very, very hazel eyes. Just the purest hazel."

"Tonight," he answered, "I'm absolutely sure we're going to be able to put my finger on what's wrong with your poetry."

Chapter 9

The Walls of Cinder Block

The Channel 29 studio occupied a low, cinder block building which had been the warehouse terminal for B&B Trucking Co. until the conviction of B&B's managerial cadre for extortion, grand theft, receipt of stolen goods and tax evasion, which had not only cost the principal stockholders, the Bagliarini family, the loss of considerable capital investment, but had lopped off the three remaining twigs of the late, lamented Anthony ("Fat Tony") branch of the Bagliarini tree—Tony, Jr. (a k a "Sonny," president), Ernesto (vice president), and Kitty (secretary-treasurer)—for a period of not less than ten nor more than twenty years.

Channel 29's corporate structure was considerably less certain because the only executive whose name was known was Vice President Trammel. One year, in fact, a citizens' group petitioned the FCC, claiming that the Bagliarinis were more than Channel 29's landlord, but the complaint lost its momentum after the group's leader, as Lance Ricketts dutifully reported on the air, accidentally beat himself to death after hanging himself on a meat hook in the processing room at B&B Packing Co. nearby.

Channel 29's News Department was located in what had

been a hallway, a line of desks against one wall and their chair backs against the other. Originally the *News* had consisted of two fifteen-minute broadcasts where Hap Little, a disc jockey who also did magic acts and puppet shows at P.T.A. Christmas parties and Scout camporees, read stories snipped from the newsaper with occasional file photos and UPI actuaries or audio tapes of presidential addresses.

Ratings were so abysmal and ad dollars so scarce that Trammel had considered dropping the news altogether until someone reminded him it might jeopardize the station's license. In desperation he'd hired a team of New York media consultants. They had come north in Nehru jackets and medallions, cursing the B&M and the snow and blowing their noses, watched a day's programming, and then rated the station ("Minus three on a scale of one to ten, darling. Do they have Bufferin up here?") and made suggestions ("Action film beats a talking head every time, dear.") and taken a bus home.

First, the two news broadcasts were combined into a single thirty-minute show at ten o'clock where it might attract news buffs among nursing mothers, the infirm, the elderly, and others unable to make it until eleven. Second, Hap Little and his bottle of Southern Comfort were bundled off to *Farm Fantasies*, and Lance and Oberon Ricketts, the state's first husband-wife anchor team, were brought in on the next train from Norman, Oklahoma, and three reporters (an unemployed sports writer from a local weekly and two college seniors) were hired, along with Durwood Leffingwell, who was supposed to edit their film and do stick-on-alphabet graphics in his spare time.

Like any piece of fine machinery, the *Ten O'Clock News* required constant adjustments. When Lance and Oberon kept interrupting each other in their joint conference calls to the weather bureau, Leffingwell, who seemed free of visible tics or noticeable abnormalities, was promoted to weatherman. Thus had the bitch goddess Fame found Durwood Leffingwell.

Today in the newsroom Leffingwell found the reporters off on stories, and only Lance and Oberon at their desks.

"All right, Lance," Oberon was saying, "do I get the three full minutes for my piece on the plastic surgeon or not?" Since the beginning of their tenure at Channel 29, she had been galled by the fact that while they had been hired as co-anchorpersons, Lance had actually been named news director: it was he who decided what stories would be covered, who would cover them and how much air time they would get.

Lance ignored her. He was smiling at something Fred MacMurray had said on Channel 29's rerun of *My Three Sons* blasting from the monitor bolted to the wall over his desk.

"Hi, all," Leffingwell said.

Lance held up a hand so he wouldn't miss Bill Frawley's rejoinder.

"Durwood," said Oberon, "I want to thank you for what was certainly the very worst morning of my entire life."

Leffingwell smiled modestly. The thing uppermost in his mind was how serious Claudine was about his finding another home for Elephant Man and whom he might ask. Obviously not the Ricketts.

"Rollo," purred Oberon. Lance, of course, was a *nom de tube,* and Oberon used his real name only when she had to. "I'll put Ex-Lax in your prebroadcast coffee, sweetums."

Lance glared at her. "All right, all right, two minutes, but I've got this feeling there's going to be a very heavy late-breaking story. Got to keep a slot open."

"Two and a *half* minutes?"

Leffingwell wandered on to the unbearable clatter of the teletype closet, where Dawn was ripping the wires and waiting to monitor the three o'clock TN feed for Lance.

Leffingwell sorted through the coiled ribbons of teletype on the floor, looking for the UPI national temperatures and weather as the beeps of the ten-second countdown came from the monitor over the machines. He found a TN printout with the in-cue, out-cue, slug line and description: "China Quake—Earthquake Rocks Peking and parts of People's Republic."

"I tell you, something really big's about to break," Lance was shouting at the other end of the room. "I can feel it in my bones. Call it my newsman's sense."

"Rollo, you haven't even got common sense."

"I do so. I've got that sixth sense of the great reporter."

"That's why you're news director, I suppose."

The screen showed a pinched, shabby man in a trench coat hunched in front of a wall. He was talking about what had happened in Peking. But he wasn't in Peking. He was in Tokyo.

"They got no real visuals, Lance," Dawn called. "Just a talking head."

"Then we'll get our own. Go down to the film library and see if they've sent yesterday's afternoon movie back to the rental agency."

"You mean *Sodom and Gomorrah?*" Dawn asked.

"You're *kidding,*" said Oberon. "That's unethical."

"Ethical shmethical, we'll be the only station in the country with footage of Peking coming down around Chairman Mao's ears. We'll scoop the world."

"Here's a hot flash for that sixth sense of yours, Rollo. Chairman Mao's as dead as a coat hook."

"Come off it, Oberon. You and your stupid jokes."

Dawn waited for the next story and Leffingwell headed on toward the processing room, where he felt more at home. It was a water world, purged of human babble, floors perpetually wet, walls vibrating with the rush of water through the pipes to the film washer, air acrid with stop bath and fixer. Somehow it seemed more real.

Waldron, the darkroom technician, had his door closed and the red light on, while Hollis Burrows, Leffingwell's successor as film editor, was at the island in the center of the room beside the two editing consoles, doing graphics for tonight's show.

Burrows was a morose young man from Idaho who held Leffingwell personally responsible for the large number of leftover K's, V's, X's and Q's he'd inherited from Leffingwell's old stick-on alphabets. "Whatever happened to the KKK?" he would say wistfully sometimes. "Why aren't more people named Quinlan and Quarry?"

Today he looked up and said, "You know, I've been thinking. Why the hell didn't George VI have a son? Then I'd be doing George VII instead of Elizabeth II, and I'd have every fucking V used up by Christmas—I mean, X-mas."

"You'd run out of I's. What's on the viewer?"

"Sarazin's footage. Came up on the twelve o'clock bus today." Obligingly, Burrows flicked the editor on as Leffingwell watched.

Trammel had hired Sarazin as a Boston stringer because so many things kept happening in Boston, though whether or not this had anything to do with Boston's being the state capital was too metaphysical a question for Trammel to speculate on. Sarazin had been issued a 16mm sound camera and told to bring in the goods every day in time to ship it up by Greyhound.

Leffingwell had never met Sarazin personally, but he liked his work: it was abominable. Leffingwell sensed a kindred spirit.

Knowing nothing about cameras, Sarazin had started out preferring the dramatic tight framing of a moderate telephoto lens. He'd managed well enough filming the subjects of his interviews, asking questions as he peered through his viewfinder. But he'd had trouble when it came to the cutaways—reshooting the questions after the interview with the camera on the reporter, so pictures of the interviewee and interviewer could be spliced together to give visual variety to otherwise boring stretches of qualified people discussing things they understood.

Sarazin had to guess where his head would be, set the camera on automatic and then stand in front of it. In the first month, his chest asked two probing questions, his right ear expressed skepticism and a disembodied voice exchanged quips with the House Minority Leader from the ornate ceiling of the State House. After seeing himself thus dismembered, Sarazin had switched to the widest angle on his camera's lens turret for the cut-aways. Thereafter, tight shots of interviewees were interspersed with wide-angle shots of huge rooms, often with the subject's chair now visibly empty, while Sarazin, a tiny spot in the center, would re-ask his questions like an asteroid hailing our solar system from the vastness of interstellar space.

Even when Sarazin stopped decapitating or omitting himelf entirely, he still couldn't remember his questions. "Are you promising the new sewage-treatment plant will be operational in three weeks?" he might ask, and the official would answer, "Absolutely, Todd." In the cut-away he would ask, "Exactly when will the treatment plant be operational?" "Absolutely, Todd," the official would beam witlessly after final editing.

Leffingwell liked to watch the out-takes and try to reconstruct the technical disaster. Today it was a loose tripod mounting.

"This is Todd Sarazin reporting from the Federal Court Building," said a distant speck against the panorama of Boston, Revere, Chelsea, Cambridge, Back Bay, Roxbury and Jamaica Plain. Slowly the world in the frame began to tilt as the tripod mounting gave way. "—where today

reputed Godfather and alleged Mafioso chieftain Giovanni
Bagliarini, known as Johnny Bag to the mob, arrived to
plead—"

The world spun wildly and then there was only empty
sky; the weight of the camera had tipped the rig over. Suddenly Sarazin's huge face appeared close up and a hand
came forward to flip off the switch. "Shit," said Todd
Sarazin, and the frame went dark.

An upright world burst back onto the screen, then
Todd Sarazin's diminishing back as he walked the endless
distance from the auto-start button to his place as reporter. "This is Todd Sarazin reporting off the Feder Bort
Kilding—"

Tilt. Even as far away as Sarazin was, Leffingwell could
see him gamely leaning to one side to keep himself vertical
in the frame.

"—where today reputed Godfather and—"

Tilt-tilt.

"—alleged Mafioso—"

Tilt-tilt-tilt.

"—chieftaingiovannibagliariniknownasjohnnyb—"

Crash. Sky again.

"—AG TO THE MOB—OH, THE HELL WITH IT!"

Sarazin's face appeared again, and the frame went dark.

The processing room door opened and Jerome Gompers,
General Manager for News and Public Affairs, appeared.
"Say, has Waldron processed that Sarazin film yet?"

"It's on the fucking viewer right now."

"Mr. Trammel says if it's about Mr. Bagliarini again,
deep-six it. He doesn't want any part in crucifying an innocent man."

"Crucifying? Bagliarini's a mobster. You know, Al
Capone, like that. This isn't the first fucking time Trammel's killed a Mafia story."

"Burrows, Mr. Trammel is the V.P., and as far as I'm
concerned he's got a license to kill whatever he wants."

Burrows shrugged. "God knows *I* don't give a shit
whether there's *any* fucking thing on the news tonight." He
flipped the retainers down, yanked both reels, and dropped
them into the trash. Gompers closed the door behind himself.

Poor Sarazin, Leffingwell thought. "Say, Burrows, you
married?"

Burrows had his hands on his thighs and was looking at the empty screen. "Why?"

"I was just wondering if you lived alone."

"Yeah, what about it?"

"You ever thought about a roommate?"

"You having trouble with your fucking wife, Leffingwell?"

"Well, yes and no. The thing is, I know this guy—"

"Forget it," Burrows said. "Last guy I let stay in my apartment got drunk on Boon's Farm apple wine every night and threw up in my bathtub."

"This guy doesn't drink."

"Worse. Nondrinkers are very fucking gloomy people."

Leffingwell nodded and accepted defeat. "Did Stackpole drop off the film he shot yesterday?"

"Yeah, I think Waldron just got around to it."

"I want to see it when he's done," Leffingwell said.

Dawn appeared at the door. "Lance says to remind you he wants that cost of living chart for tonight's inflation story."

Burrows nodded and looked unhappy.

"What's the problem?" Leffingwell asked. "You'll get to use one of your V's in 'living.'"

"Yeah, but you were right about the I's just now. I'm out of them. And there's one in 'high' and two in 'living.' God, life is fucking brutal."

Leffingwell smiled guiltily, squeezed through the door past Dawn, and headed for the bridge.

The bridge, once the loading dock for the B&B truck bay, had been glassed in to contain all the complicated electronics required to operate a television station. In the center was an island containing a large bookstand like the lectern for the Bible in a medieval cathedral; it was the log, the second-by-second account of what was to be shown every day, from *My Three Sons* at two-thirty to whether the eight o'clock station break would be the logo slide (a rooster crowing on a fence) or the chaste "29" superimposed over the Butler skyline, made out five days in advance by the Continuity Department, two elderly women with a pathological love of order and details. The rest of the island was given over to the film-chain, two 16mm projectors and a carousel slide projector for transferring movies, commercials, station ID's and static ads onto broadcast tape.

On one side of the room were the three VTR's, two audio tape decks and a small soundproof booth for announcers to prerecord the next day's sign-in's, spots, breaks and sign-off's. Leffingwell had the duty today.

The bridge's busiest time was from three in the afternoon to eleven at night, when there were five switchers on duty to see that the right segment of *Bewitched* included the right spots, and that the reels of the Homemaker's Movie appeared in their proper order (unlike their much heralded evening screening of *Citizen Kane,* which had opened with a long dolly across the acres of Kane's possessions to a tight shot of the sled "Rosebud" burning in the furnace). At the same time, the switchers were expected to pretape the difficult switches for the one-man night and morning shifts.

In addition, the switchers handled the news broadcast live at ten and whatever studio taping there was from three to six in the afternoon. On Mondays they taped in-house ads and editorial replies, offering aid and encouragement to neither. On Tuesdays they taped the following week's five fifteen-minute segments of Oberon Rickett's *Koffee Klatch,* a show rich in macramé wizards, self-help and cookbook authors and transcendental meditators—whomever publishers had sent on the road. On Wednesdays they taped Hap Little's early-morning *Farm Fantasies* by wheeling him into the parking lot with a section of split-rail fence and a steel drum painted to simulate a wooden barrel, where he would do fertilizer spots, pull at his flask of Southern Comfort and, on at least two occasions, try to plant things in the tarmac. On Thursdays they taped sermonettes on a rotation basis that each week shifted the burden of humiliation and embarrassment to a different major faith. Also on Thursdays they taped Monsignor Legume's *Spotlight of Love* and—until recently, when an intracongregational dispute had brought it to an end—the Unitarians' *No One's Stopping You.* And on Friday afternoons when Tanker Hackett wasn't in traction, a busload of children from a local grade school received dog tags and serial numbers, formed a column of twos and double-timed into the studio for *Sergeant Smile and the Tooth Brigade.*

All in all, the switchers were the mainstay of Channel 29. Not being unionized, they not only rode the bridge boards and manned the cameras, but built sets, moved props, set up lights and, in slow moments, worked on their cars.

This afternoon, Leffingwell found the bridge the usual eighteenth century madhouse. Stackpole stood by the island, eyes flicking from the line monitors to the broadcast monitor—the countdown for an upcoming spot, a Borax commercial for next morning, the taping from the studio floor, and on the broadcast monitor, Fred MacMurray presiding over the conclusion of yet another wild and funny family misunderstanding. Stackpole prided himself on seeing every switch executed flawlessly, without pauses, dead spots or fumbles. He had nothing but contempt for management and viewers alike; he drove himself only to fulfill some strange inner yearning for perfection.

Leffingwell walked between the island and the VTR's to the glass overlooking the studio. Below was a huge puddle of water and a Buick hub cap; a figure in glistening black was just flapping flipper-footed toward the side door, like the Creature from the Black Lagoon returning to his primordial ooze. Crazy Stan of Melchizedek Chevrolet had just completed another commercial.

Crazy Stan was one of a unique breed, the businessman who continued to do his own ads. While Channel 29 plugged the usual nostalgia records, amazing health insurance offers, Florida geriatric condos and combo fishing-pole-fish-gutters from Grand Central Station addresses, the bulk of WHCK's revenues came from the station's two roundheeled time salesmen, who passed among local advertisers like broad-beamed Phoenician trading ships. Their principal gimmick was the offer of free commercial production to any local merchant buying air time. What they didn't specify was that the station provided one camera, one cameraman and fifteen minutes to get a usable tape—no director, no camera movement, no editing and no help.

Before the camera's uncritical but unblinking eye passed a succession of the frantic and terrified to expose the poverty of their imagination and the limit of their wit. Plumbing contractors, sewer routers and reamers, furnace cleaners, roofing and siding specialists, restaurateurs and exterminators shouted or mumbled their way through sixty seconds and went home to be tormented, at regular intervals and in time slots they were actually paying for, by their flattened faces, shortened bodies, magnified tics and nasalized voices. Thereafter, most paid the modest fee for

Hap Little, Leffingwell or Dirk Pataud—who weren't "newsmen" in the strict sense—to read their copy.

But Crazy Stan was not troubled by visions of all Greater Butler doubled up with laughter when he appeared on screen. Whether he was oblivious to what others thought or a closet masochist, he had become hooked, and over the months he had transformed himself into a low-grade local celebrity on the order of a medieval village's demented hunchback.

He'd started in front of a studio curtain and spoken in an aggressive monotone of his many wonderful formerly owned Chevrolets and other type cars. He had looked like a first-term project from embalming school. He had loved it.

In the following months, he had returned with various members of his family—his big-eared son, his beehive-coiffed wife, his drooling, dotard sire—until the day he had touted his formerly owned cars as real cream puffs and then had his brother-in-law throw a cream pie in his face. Crazy Stan had invented symbolism.

The next time, he had one of his used cars brought into the studio (no problem—the rear wall was still a garage door from the building's truck terminal days) and then put a sledge hammer through the windshield to demonstrate how he was smashing prices. It was such a success that the following month he slashed prices by taking a butcher knife to the upholstery, and over the next half year he hacked his way down to the frame and rims in a frenzy of metaphor.

The frogman outfit obviously marked a new phase in the artist's creative life. Leffingwell watched the auto industry's Jacques Cousteau disappear.

"Lock up, motherfucker!" shouted Stackpole's voice, followed by a terrific pounding. Leffingwell turned to find him kicking one of the VTR's, his usual method for making the machines lock in on a frame on the tape. The monitor showed only crazy streaks and flashes, and then suddenly the image jumped and a computer-style 5 appeared. 4, 3. Stackpole froze it to give himself the usual two-second segue, then cued it at the precise moment the console switcher punched in "broadcast." As the countdown 1 faded from the line monitor, a litle girl appeared on the broadcast monitor tenderly stuffing a vinyl nipple into a vinyl face. "Baby Alive, soft and sweet," sang a distant female voice. "She can drink, she can eat."

Stackpole, earphone around his neck and disconnected audio plug dangling at his waist, went to the end of the island to consult the log. "How's that freak of yours, Leff?"

"Claudine wants me to get rid of him." Leffingwell tried to find a section of wall where he wouldn't be in the way. "Any chance you'd put him up for a while in your trailer?"

Stackpole laughed as his eyes swept the monitor.

"Claudine says she'll move out if I don't get rid of him."

"So?"

Leffingwell shrugged. "I'm addicted to our level of hostility." He paused. "He's really kind of interesting, you know?"

Stackpole signaled a switcher to punch in the second spot. "Weebles wobble but they don't fall down," sang a male voice.

"You got *Batman* on the film-chain?" Stackpole demanded.

"No, really. You know what he told me this morning? He'd never been in an apartment. Can you believe that? Just motels and stuff. I mean, I could see this really in-depth analysis—monster discovers amenities of middle-class life. Like the reverse of taking a Zulu to New York, see?"

"Leff, the Zulu know all about cities."

"Well, you know what I mean."

Stackpole was at the log again. "Go get a philosopher to script it, that's what I'd do. Course, I'm no critic, but who knows? Maybe you could sell a minute or two to TN or UPI or some network news outfit. Okay on *Batman*—five, four, three, two, one, and IN."

Suddenly it all fell into place. Of course! Each moment of the monster's discovering new facets of modern life and the natural world he'd been denied lovingly recorded on film. First shower. First buttercup. First fuck. Elephant Man, freed from exploitation and oppression by D. Leffingwell, the Great Emancipator. A documentary film-maker's dream. Leffingwell could be an artist, humanitarian and a lot richer at the same time.

"Know any philosophers?" he asked.

"My father. Used to whip me and say, 'Hard head makes a soft ass.' You got Barbie's Malibu Beach House locked in for the first spot?"

"No, we want someone with more formal credentials."
Leffingwell paused. There was probably a philosophy department at Cambria College, but he didn't want anything
to do with Claudine's school. "Hey, I've got it! Remember
that little guy Buridan that was in for *Spotlight* last Thursday and got into an argument with Legume over the teachers' strike?"

"You got me, but I recall that strike of theirs lasted
about fifteen minutes. Okay, slap Baby Says-So on projector
two. After we run Barbie and Says-So, I want to get back
to tomorrow. Let's see, we got the Borax on tape, so next
the log says we want Mop n' Glo at ten-thirty-thirty——"

"What do you say, Stackpole? You with me?"

"What?" Stackpole's attention was divided between today's Commissioner Gordon picking up the Bat-phone on
one monitor and tomorrow's Mop n' Glo on another.

"Help me film it. Fifty percent of the profits."

"What about your star, Elephant Man?"

Leffingwell blushed. "Yeah, I forgot. All right, how
about a three-way split?"

Bruce Wayne and Dick Grayson were talking to Aunt
Harriet. Alfred answered the phone. A mop mopped clean.

"The whole idea's stupid, my man. But seeing you're a
friend . . ."

"Beautiful," Leffingwell said. "I'll go line up our philosopher. And we can kind of test the water tonight when we
run that footage you shot yesterday of Elephant Man."

"I can't get Baby Says-So to lock up," interrupted one
of the switchers. Leffingwell headed out the door. "Come
on, Baby Says-So!" echoed Stackpole's voice down the hall
after him. Bam-bam-bam went his foot against the VTR.
"LOCK UP, MOTHERFUCK!"

"TO THE BAT-POLES, ROBIN, OLD CHUM!"

Chapter 10

The Journey

The only light in Immaculate Conception's chapel was from votive candles guttering in their red glasses on the rack at the front. Sister Ann's, probably, and Sister Agnes's. Mother Margaret Rachel genuflected and went forward, down the aisle and through the railing, and took her regular seat in the choir to the side of the altar.

Comforter, where, where is your comforting?
Mary, mother of us, where is your relief?

It had been the woman's letter today that had made her so agitated. It had made her remember what she'd struggled—how many years was it?—to forget.

But at last she began to feel the peacefulness of the room. The boys' footsteps in the hall upstairs pounded across the ceiling, yet they seemed very far away.

She slipped forward onto her knees and began to recite the rosary, emptying her mind of everything but the mysteries of the Blessed Virgin, joyful, sorrowful, and glorious.

The sixth decade of the rosary began the sorrowful mysteries. The first small bead, Christ's agony in the garden, contrition. *Hail Mary, full of grace; the Lord is with thee: blessed art thou among women, and blessed is the fruit of thy womb, Jesus.* The second, Christ scourged at the pillar, purity. *Hail Mary, full of grace.*

She did not look up until she had finished the full fifteen

decades of the rosary. Purged, calm, she lifted herself back onto her seat and looked around the room's oak paneling, dark with age. Seventy years since workmen had refinished it as a chapel. What purpose had it served in the life of the family that had lived here before the neighborhood had become unfashionable? A study?

Then the room hadn't changed so much, really. But what would those Butler aristocrats say if they came back in their turn-of-the-century frocks and cutaways and found some weak-willed nun had let a tribe of bees burrow deep in their mansion's timber? And what would her own stern-faced predecessors have said, those grim photographs pasted neatly in the office scrapbook?

She remembered seeing Mother Immaculata come here often, and she imagined the others had come in their times, too, each with her own moments of doubt and self-loathing. But they had known better what their priorities were and where their loyalties lay. Her own spirit leapt and wavered like the votive flames, and from the brightness of this morning's resolve to venture into the world it had dwindled into uncertainty.

She ought to have been worrying about Immaculate Conception. Monsignor Luce from the Bishop's Chancery, cold hands, puffy grub-white face, exceptional idle grace a few heavy men develop. Whenever she saw him, she couldn't help imagining him gliding from one subterranean counting house to another beneath the Renaissance Vatican.

This was an old building, he'd told her, uneconomical to operate. He'd sucked his tea like a fat white spider emptying the liquid from a fly's fragile shell. She'd argued that their support came not from the Diocese, but from their boys' families, and the Sisters could always have fund-raising drives. Sell blown Easter eggs, he'd snorted. Anyway, however infinite *caritas* might be, earthly charity was based on the supply of dollar bills, which was finite, so any money she raised meant that much less in the local parishes. And since Chapter 766 of the state law meant public schools must now provide the special services that Immaculate Conception's least fortunate charges required, the academy and orphanage could be closed with a clear conscience and the money freed for needier Diocesan projects.

She'd threatened to go to the welfare people, which by law paid a stipend for any otherwise unsupported child; a secular orphanage had done just that, she'd heard. But even then she'd secretly doubted she had the strength to defy the hierarchy. And now this letter.

She would have to go. There is no way to ignore the desperation in the letter. And she herself wanted to know what had happened to the woman after that night. And, of course, Mother Margaret owed it to her to tell her the boy was gone.

She thought back to that first night five years before. She tried to remember the face, but all she could recall was the fear in the eyes of the woman she'd mistaken for a stranger, clutching the child against her. It might have been in the woman's voice when she'd made the appointment by phone, too, but Mother Margaret had dismissed the quavering hesitations as another of distance's distortions, like rising pavement heat rippling a far-off mountain.

The children had been coming toward the woman, filling the hall with squeals and shrieks, and instinctively the woman had backed away from the foot of the stairs toward the outer doors, hiking the sleeping child higher on her shoulder. Mother Margaret had stood firm as her charges swirled past on either side of her and tried to wave the woman toward her office door halfway down the hall, but the woman hadn't responded. She was too frightened or didn't understand.

The boys were just boisterous after Vespers and anxious to get to the TV room upstairs, but Mother Margaret knew how menacing they looked to outsiders. Pitiful victims, too broken or twisted in body or spirit even to be adopted; but strangers always shuddered, seeing rather gargoyle caricatures of boys.

Two of the gentler ones had stopped beside the woman, stretching their necks to see.

"A little baby, Kevin," shrilled Luis over the pounding of the rest up the stairs. "Lookit." He balanced on his good leg, the other with its brace and corrective sole drawn up beneath him like a heron's.

"Is it coming to stay, lady?" Kevin had asked.

The woman had raised the child higher.

"Sister Agnes," Mother Margaret had called as the old nun emerged from the chapel door. "We have a visitor."

"Very busy, yes, Reverend Mother."

"I say, *we have a visitor.*" She gestured down the hall. "Can you hurry the boys upstairs?"

Smiling and nodding, Sister Agnes had swept down the

hall, arms extended to wave on the stragglers, and waded into the crowd at the foot of the stairs to start the lift for the three in wheelchairs as the other Sisters came from the chapel.

Mother Margaret had brought the woman and child into her office, wondering about the nurse-white shoes, the expensive overcoat (odd in the August heat), the snatch of green beneath the hem like a surgical gown. It wasn't until she'd gathered her skirts and seated herself at her desk that she realized she knew the woman.

"Yes," the woman had answered. "It's Sykes. I used to do volunteer counseling for unwed mothers. I came here with some other volunteers for a seminar one day, before you were elected Superior."

Mother Margaret nodded. She remembered the woman had been a child pathologist in some hospital. Maybe she'd done the volunteer work to expiate the guilt of a grisly lifetime devoted to scrutinizing dead children's tissue. But she thought she remembered an exchange during the seminar when the woman compared the seeds of sin and the seeds of disease, saying studying dead children wasn't morbid because it was the only way to prevent disease in living ones. But why would a woman with such a medical specialty have been disturbed tonight by her boys? No matter how misshapen, they were at least living.

But before Mother Margaret had a chance to speak, the child stirred, stretched its arms, and raised its head from Sykes's breast. Mother Margaret noticed the hair was coarse and multicolored—brown streaked with black, blond, red, even gray, as though it had been splattered with bleach. Suddenly it snapped its body over, so it was lying on its stomach and staring at Mother Margaret over the woman's lap.

The eyes. They darted back and forth warily, like an animal's. But something more, something about the whites —a dead dryness, like the inside of a clam shell.

Then it spoke.

"New guy." It was looking at Mother Margaret, and for a shocked instant she was sure the low, husky voice belonged to some pitiful dwarf and the whole affair was an elaborate hoax. "New place."

"He's getting a cold," Sykes explained. "It's the air. He's been in a sealed environment—dust-free, humidity-free— for . . . well, for a long time. Because he's got no tear ducts or sweat glands." She pulled out a bottle and dropper from her purse. "He needs these regularly to keep his eyes moist. And without sweat glands his body temperature tends to run high. He shouldn't overexert himself, especially in this heat, but it helps if you put his feet in a pan of water."

Mother Margaret watched Sykes administering the eye-drops as she talked. The child submitted resentfully, and the moment she was finished, it slipped off her lap and scuttled sideways facing Mother Margaret, its arms held heavily over its head. It stopped in the center of the room, making sure it could see in all directions. An animal instinct.

It was like a huge crab, Mother Margaret had thought.

The child pivoted slowly, peering everywhere. Then it scuttled suddenly toward Mother Margaret, stopped, slipped backward effortlessly and wheeled to face Sykes. Mother Margaret found herself gripping the edges of her desk, her knuckles white.

"Don't be alarmed," Sykes said. "He's testing you. Macduff, stop that!"

Now the thing darted for Sykes and backed off. The teeth bared, arms held rigidly over the head. Only the legs moved. Not a crab, Mother Margaret had thought, but a scorpion.

"There's a certain jerkiness in motor skills," Sykes had said, unperturbed. "His growth rate at this point's very rapid. I think the nerve connections haven't kept up with the rest of the body, but it should normalize before long."

The child pivoted to face Mother Margaret once more. Again it scuttled forward, arms up scorpionlike, then back. A third time it came at her. But this time it was no feint. It kept coming.

Mother Margaret jumped sideways out of her chair, instinctively trying to keep the desk between herself and it. She felt an ancient, animal terror of its touch.

"Food, Macduff," Sykes called. "Over here, food!"

It stopped, glided sideways toward Sykes. She was crinkling a cellophane bag of cheese-flavored corn puffs to attract its attention. It snatched them from her, tore open the bag and extracted one of the elongated puffs to sniff it. A moment later it began cramming the rest of them into its mouth, some slipping from its fingers, two dangling from its wetted lips like wind-bloated yellow caterpillars. When it had finished the last of them from the floor, it broke into a crooked smile rimmed with crumbs and yellow grease. "Good guy," it had barked to Sykes.

"You mustn't be afraid of that game of his," the woman said, patting his head. "He senses it unnerves people. Aggressiveness is a fear mechanism, you see. Animals don't bare their teeth when they're attacking, only when they feel threatened."

Mother Margaret righted her chair, embarrassed, watching the child. It squatted next to Sykes's legs, sated, and didn't move again. The two women began to talk, and gradually, as now and then Mother Margaret glanced toward the child, she found it less and less terrifying.

Still, Mother Margaret was never sure, even afterward, why she'd agreed to keep the boy, even temporarily. Immaculate Conception accepted only older referrals from the State Welfare Commissioner or Catholic Charities; a child that young should have been sent to a foundling home for adoption. Not only that, but the record of birth, the only document Sykes had brought, had been hopelessly botched. The date of birth had been recorded as the previous December, though the child had to be close to three years old. No mother had been listed, and the father had been given only as "comatose male."

Perhaps the woman's enthusiasm had persuaded her. Though he was to all intents a feral child, Sykes said, who'd come to the Bay State team when they had taken in his terminally ill father, the boy had made tremendous strides. He was phenomenally intelligent. He had even taught himself to read.

Or perhaps it had been Sykes's own ill-concealed fear, as though someone were pursuing her. "I didn't want to burden you with this," she had said. "I drove around for hours trying to think of something else. But there's no choice."

Mother Margaret had tried to calm her by sticking to details. "The child's got no surname here," she said, "and the first name is listed as 'Macduff.' Funny choice. Like the one in *Macbeth,* 'not of woman born'?"

"We named him. We, ah, didn't have any information on the mother. Almost like he didn't have one, in a way."

"And you're listed here as attending physician. I thought you were a pathologist."

"I've been working at Bay State in cancer pathology and DNA research."

"A pathologist in obstetrics?"

"Will you take him?" Sykes demanded suddenly. "He's not . . . well, not *safe* at Bay State any more. They're experimenting on him . . . as though he weren't human. You know, a feral child. . . ."

So Mother Margaret had agreed. The child hadn't cried when the woman left. She'd given it a sad smile and handed the eyedrops to Mother Margaret. "In a very real way," she had said, "I'm his mother."

"This can only be temporary," Mother Margaret had reminded her, walking with her as far as the front steps. The air had been damp and sticky and still hot that night, like night in a primeval jungle. She had watched the woman dissolve into the darkness and heard the sudden and distinct slam of her door, but she had seen just enough of the light-colored sedan as it pulled away beneath a street lamp to recognize it later as the abandoned car at the motel in the newspaper picture.

The sudden slam and booming echo of the chapel door. Mother Margaret looked up, startled, and peered across the red glow of the votive candles as they dimmed and brightened in the sudden draft. Her chaplain, Sister Ursula, was standing respectfully in the shadows at the rear of the chapel. Mother Margaret rose, genuflected, made her way through the railing and down the aisle.

"You asked me to let you know in time to catch the bus," Sister Ursula apologized in a whisper. "Are you sure you don't want Father Tim to give you a lift—?"

"No," Mother Margaret said, shaking her head. "I have to do this alone."

She paused halfway down the outside steps to check her change purse one last time for the bus and taxi fares, then cut across the lawn alongside the building to avoid notice from the classroom windows across the street. Today wasn't the day she wanted to be caught and harangued by John Buridan, who more and more seemed always to be lying in wait for her on some bizarre pretext or another. At the corner of the building something flew at her. Instinctively she blinked and ducked her head. One of her bees. She watched it swoop upward to the top of the house.

August and September were the months of the angry creatures of the air. Early summer was soft and green, new lacewings, delicate mayflies. By the end of summer the sun seemed to have burned everything away but the hard and buzzing things, cicadas, dragonflies and hornets.

But her bees were different. They had terrified her that day four years ago, swarming out of nowhere, somehow knowing about the hole in the unused side door where a doorbell had once been. The Sisters had shut the windows and watched the bee cloud darken and condense into a pumping mass of insects patiently crawling over each other as one by one those at the center clambered in the hole. "I thought they lived in hollow trees," little Kevin had said, and everyone had laughed at the idea of mistaking Immaculate Conception for a tree stump. But Mother Margaret had not laughed; the bees had an unerring instinct for rotting wood.

They weren't really dangerous. Often of an evening she would come out to watch the workers returning from their flowers, legs thick with pollen, to form again a living knot around the hole, pulsing like a heart. Sometimes, of course, a stray would slip around the screen into the television room, and Mother Margaret would herd the boys out as the creature buzzed hopelessly at the ceiling light, knowing eventually it would scorch its wings away and fall on its back, tail arched and stinger out, beating stubs of browned cellophane against the floor. She would wait outside the door until the metallic sound of tortured insect parts had stopped, and then she would go in and sweep up the remains.

So many had wanted to kill them. Stanley, their maintenance man in the days they could afford one, had wanted to use gasoline. "I give dem de big bellyache wid it, knock dem right on their stingers." But she had told them all no. There was something warm in knowing that beneath the rotting clapboards the wall was thick with wax and honey.

Then there had been the time those boys plugged up the doorbell-hole with a stick. Which was it, now? Macduff, of course, with Kevin, though later she'd learned Walther had put them up to it.

She'd taken it out herself, her breathing rapid and shallow, stomach knotted around a hard lightness, back of her neck cold with sweat as she'd reached for the stick poking mockingly from the doorbell. She'd imagined them gnawing away inside and suddenly spewing out some crack in the baseboard and filling the chapel, thousands of black spots dancing and buzzing above the altar like notes from treble organ pipes materialized, demanding an eye for an eye. That was when she'd realized she had let them stay as an act of mortification, to exorcise her fleshly fear, an ancient terror of an alien, primitive society that challenged her own.

And then with a final, dry-throated swallow, she had grasped the stick with both hands and yanked. She stepped back, poised to run. But no column of angry insects had gushed out at her. The hole was empty. Had they suffocated? Had they given up?

And then at last a single bee had appeared in the hole, surprised, perhaps, to see the light, as though it had calmly resigned itself to extinction and didn't know what to make of this change in the divine plan. A moment later it left the hole, dipping slightly until it had gained power and then soaring away. Another had appeared and launched itself, and then another. Gentle creatures, accepting whatever happened with equanimity, not celebrating their resurrection but simply resuming the business of foraging for pollen.

She hurried on across the vacant lot, past the end of the house with the bees' doorbell, and then, when she was far enough to be hidden from view, she stepped from the curb and clicked across the street, her heart beating louder and faster. It was a formless dread she felt, perhaps awe at being out alone in the world after so many years, perhaps a fear that a gray sedan would suddenly nose into view; yet the further up the side street she went, the safer she felt.

There was no bus service on Canal Street near Immaculate Conception. As those Sisters who accompanied boys to the hospital or took night classes had explained, she had to cut through the Puerto Rican neighborhood to reach Sachem Street, where the downtown bus stopped.

She walked slowly past the irregular facades of the three-family houses, each with its three-tiered porch. She remembered vague impressions of the neighborhood from when she'd first ridden to Immaculate Conception in a station wagon with a Sister from the Mother Chapter. Then it had seemed desolate, solitary French-Canadian men on their front stoops with their elbows on their knees, women in shabby coats moving with bowed heads and string bags toward neighborhood groceries. There had been no children; fewer and fewer had been born since the mills

had begun closing, and those born before were already
coming of age and moving away.

Now the spirit was different. The houses were shabbier,
paint on doorjambs and steps and porch railings worn
through to bare wood. But Latin music pealed in explosive
celebrations from radios in windowsills, and laundered
sheets and shirts, no longer banished to the modesty of
back yards, flapped from lines strung between porches and
neighboring shade trees. And the children. They were
everywhere, clambering over fences and railings, playing
ball in the street, climbing through the windows of cars
gutted and stripped of chrome that rested at strange angles
by the curb.

It was no wonder her boys, fostered in the right angles
and scrubbed walls of Immaculate Conception, couldn't
relate to these people who brought their tropical sun with
them into the cold north. That, and the fact that her boys
were generally at the age where parents were half the
world and possessions the rest, and her boys had neither.
On the other hand, to the neighborhood her orphans were
shabby outsiders, treated with the primitive fear of Nean-
derthals driving away strays from rival tribes. She thought
of her bees.

Mothers and children and clusters of teen-aged boys in
club jackets warily watched the strange figure in black pass
by, head bent and eyes down. Custody of the eyes, it was
called, never looking to the left or right but walking demurely and purposefully with the eyes lowered. It was one
of the many subtleties taught her in her first days by the
Mistress of Novices, like remembering always to choose
the least comfortable chair in a room. Mortification of the
flesh.

It took her nearly an hour to reach the bus terminal. The
fumes on the local bus had been unbearable, and the terminal itself proved a bewildering procession of soldiers,
sailors and young people, wandering the filthy concrete
floor in a confusion of purposes while vending machines
and pinball games clanked and rang, lockers slammed and
loudspeakers barked garbled announcements into the din.
At last, however, she heard the call for her bus and
boarded, taking the right-hand front seat before she realized she'd done it for the luxury of looking through the
windshield, and then it was too embarrassing to force her
way back into the column of people shuffling down the

aisle. She sat back in the soft seat, rather liking the hot, close air after the drafty local. When at last the doors closed and the bus began to move, she felt like something of a veteran, and contentedly she watched the storefronts slide past.

Once they pulled onto the highway, however, the ride was a horror: for ten years Mother Margaret hadn't moved faster than her own legs could take her, and now she watched the roadway rush toward her, disappear at the bottom edge of the windshield and race unseen beneath her. Instinctively, she pulled her feet up for protection. Trucks that were specks ahead suddenly loomed hugely and then swept by only an arm's length from her window as her driver passed them. Passenger cars were hopelessly small and vulnerable as she peered down into them for glimpses of families or solitary salesmen.

But Mother Margaret said nothing. Speed was one of the conditions of the outside world, and the more it pained her, the better. She had ventured out, after all, as an act of mortification, the same way she had endured the fear of the bees. Immaculate Conception, she realized, had become too warm and familiar, not a discipline but a refuge which she no longer deserved.

She closed her eyes, trying to think of other things—of Monsignor Luce's thin lips drawing in tea, of the doom hanging over Immaculate Conception, but instead, again and again against the darkness of her eyelids she saw the strange adult face of the child Macduff.

The early days had been hardest. There had been that first night when she had returned after a cup of tea with Sister Agnes and found him prowling her office, holding a book upside down. He had read it aloud to her when she asked him, though clearly the words had meant nothing to him. Poetry. Hopkins. She had left the book on her desk ever since as a reminder; whenever she'd doubted him after that, it had made her remember how at least one of Dr. Sykes's impossible claims had proved true.

In the days that followed she had dropped by occasionally to check on the strange child, though it was her custom as administrator of both the school and the orphanage not to become directly involved with either: to be effective, a mother superior had to maintain a certain distance. She remembered the TV room on the second or third night, the boys ranged around the set watching some quiz show. It was criminal, she had thought. A prime hour for children and they showed nothing but quiz shows.

—and each of you open your boxes when I give the word, and the winner will get to choose which of the twenty-five packages she—

"It's going to be the fat one," Norman said. "They always give it to the fat one so she'll flop up and down when she gets it like—"

He'd meant to say Sister Theresa, but he'd seen Mother Margaret in time.

"They don't fix it," Luis said. "It's luck."

"They're all fixed."

EEEEEEEEEEE, I got it, I got it! screamed the fat woman.

Retarded Kermit pounded his fists on the arms of his chair in delight. "She get! She get!" he bellowed.

Mother Margaret's eyes had traveled the rest of the room to find Macduff. He was sitting in the corner with Kevin, who seemed to have adopted him as his special friend. Macduff was watching intently. His eyes were blank and empty, but his mouth was drawn up in a huge grin.

—there are some prizes there, and there are some real clunks, so you've got to be careful—

Mother Margaret glanced back at the set. The woman's demonic gaping smile was a perfect mirror of Macduff's face. Then a commercial began, a woman looking serious and holding up a soiled shirt. Mother Margaret looked back at Macduff. Slowly he was drawing his brows together and straightening the line of his mouth. Then he stopped and his face was expressionless. Then he began to knit his brows and straighten his mouth again.

As if, Mother Margaret thought, as if he'd never seen human facial expressions before, and were practicing how to make them.

Later, just before lights out, she had come to his room to ask about it.

"The shows are very interesting," he'd answered. "I like to watch the people get excited." His eyes were huge, as if the irises themselves had expanded; the pupils were tiny slits like a cat's in bright light. "No one ever got excited where I used to live."

And then later that week he had fallen near her and his head had hit the playground's asphalt with a terrifying thud. She'd tried to cradle him, but he'd made no sound, and when she'd pulled his head back to look into the eyes and see the tears of pain come welling up, it had been all she could do to keep her arms around the warm little body. There had been no tears. The irises had contracted and the whites were blank and dry as china.

Part of her had loathed him, and part of her had found something remarkable if terrifying in him. Still, she had not been altogether unhappy when the boy's uncle had come to claim him, despite her misgivings about the man. He'd shown no family resemblance. He'd had the pallid face of an office worker, but his shoulders had been broad and strong and his shoes had been scuffed with much walking. He'd shown her a snapshot of Macduff, shockingly small, eyes half-closed and skin washed white by the flashbulb. Behind him was a jumble of shadows and steel cases through which snaked hoses or electrical cords, and from the absolute blackness beyond had gleamed the starburst reflection of the flashbulb in what seemed to have been a large mirror. But the uncle had not only been able to provide identification for himself, he'd had a birth certificate and documents for a John Macduff Stewart, aged four years, eight months, which had made Mother Margaret smile at the memory of the botched forgery Sykes had shown her. Yes, he had said, the boy had been hospitalized periodically for a variety of glandular disorders. No, he wasn't feral, far from it; in fact, the parents had been so distraught over the last months that the uncle had begun to worry over the health of his sister-in-law and brother. That was just one of the reasons they hadn't called in the authorities. No, they weren't going to press charges; they would be satisfied with getting the boy back, especially since Dr. Sykes was clearly a sick woman and needed compassion more than anything else except, perhaps, proper treatment.

The boy hadn't cried when he had gone with his uncle, but later Mother Margaret had found an old yearbook from downstairs behind his bed with her own picture as the new English teacher snipped out of it.

Mother Margaret opened her eyes and realized that this time, as the bus slowed and pulled off the highway exit, they were finally approaching Tyler, the nearest town to Bay State Medical Center. The bus stopped in front of a small cigar store. The town taxi was parked next to it; the man's business was almost entirely the run from town to the Center with the diseased and dying the bus brought. He didn't help Mother Margaret into the cab, and he said nothing as he drove her along the wooded road.

"Do they do a lot of research here?" she asked.

"Wouldn't know," he answered.

As they drew nearer, Mother Margaret caught occasional glimpses of four identical gleaming white towers through the trees, and when at last they came to the parking lot, she leaned forward to look up through the windshield, across the roofs of row upon row of cars like the rounded backs of Muslim worshippers, to peer at the dizzying, almost blinding mass of concrete, as clean and functional and powerful as the ancient citadel of the Assassins.

Inside it was much like the lobby of a busy hotel, and four women in pale blue dresses worked frenziedly behind the main desk of imitation mahogany, answering calls, looking up names in long card files, giving directions to visitors and incoming patients.

"That's a restricted floor, of course," said the one who found Dr. Sykes's card for her. "You'll have to sign in and out."

Mother Margaret followed the woman's directions to the right elevator, painfully conscious of her habit's swishing and convinced everyone was watching her. Silly, she thought. She was just letting the paranoia of Sykes's letter rub off on her.

But when she stepped out on the fifteenth floor, she found herself inside a wire cage. Through the grill she could see the usual wall and reception desk, but for a moment she felt the sour taste of fear at the back of her mouth, and when the nurse let her in, she couldn't help thinking she had just been let out of one prison into a larger one. As she signed "Margaret Rachel, OSSBVM" in the register, she tried to peer down the hall. There was none of the nervous bustle of the other floors. Everything was silent, a kind of malevolent, midnight stillness except for the barely audible whine of distant air conditioners or dehumidifiers.

"Please respect all signs and do not touch exposed equipment," the nurse was saying as she led her down the darkened hall. The doors they passed opened not into hospital rooms but offices and small laboratories filled with the kind of equipment she'd seen jumbled behind Macduff in the photograph his uncle had shown her.

"Are you taking me to Dr. Sykes?" she asked, suddenly more frightened.

The nurse stopped and turned. "Why, of course. What did you think?"

Mother Margaret shook her head self-deprecatingly. At the end of the hall the nurse stopped and unlocked a door. Mother Margaret stepped in, convinced she would find another office, but instead it was a conventional hospital room, the center curtain partially drawn to separate the two beds. She heard the door shut and lock behind her.

Propped up on pillows inside the brown shadow of the curtain was a yellow sibyl's face fringed with wisps of colorless hair. With one eye the woman—could it really be Dr. Sykes?—looked absently at Mother Margaret. The other was a thin white slit with a darkened pupil; below swelled a reddish brown mass from the eyeball that stretched the lower rim downward, as though the brain itself were forcing its way out through the eye socket. Mother Margaret put her hand to her mouth and turned away.

"Mother Margaret?"

Gratefully Mother Margaret pushed past the curtain into the other half of the room. A second woman—thinner, but unmistakably Dr. Sykes—lay on the other bed beneath the barred shadows cast by the Venetian blinds. The skin of her face was taut and semi-transparent, and through it showed the shadowlike clusters of blue-gray veins.

"Thank you for coming." The voice rang strangely loud and clear, like china. "But it was stupid of me. I should have known they'd only let you in so they can follow you when you leave. They'll find Macduff."

"Let me sit down," Mother Margaret said. She had to gather herself together; she couldn't just blurt out where the boy had gone or how she'd learned the truth about Dr. Sykes.

A groan came from the other side of the curtain. Mother Margaret stiffened and looked questioningly.

"Nothing. Former colleague."

Mother Margaret gestured toward her eye.

"Choroid melanoma," said Dr. Sykes. "Don't worry about what you say. It's already spread from her liver to her brain—speech center's gone, can't talk. I think she's still rational, though."

Mother Margaret winced at the easy way the woman

could discuss the progress of someone's cancer as though she were still a pathologist instead of a patient. "How are *you?*" she managed at last, wondering what a mental patient was doing in the same room with a terminal cancer patient.

Sykes laughed sharply, a rasping against the back of her palate. "I'll be at the autopsy, of course, but I won't mind not seeing it. I can tell you right now what the histological profile's going to be—I've seen it so many times."

Mother Margaret looked at the fragile face, as though all the years in this dehumidified air had dried her to a brittleness that was, in fact, madness. "Do you mean some kind of physical illness?" she asked.

The laugh rasped again, and she suddenly pulled her hospital gown up. Mother Margaret caught a glimpse of two pitifully thin legs, then the hospital underwear and then a large, brownish bulge on the abdomen the shape and almost the size of a loaf of bread. Again she wanted to turn away, but she forced herself to look at Sykes's eyes.

"Shouldn't have been malignant, you know," Sykes said. "I knew all about it when I brought you Macduff. I left him with you because I thought I could have it surgically removed."

"You mean someone stopped you?" Mother Margaret asked, humoring her.

"Don't be silly. You mean here? If it weren't for them, I'd already be dead. No, they're very interested in controlling these things. We all were."

"Is it some kind of tumor?"

"Just the largest of the metastatic sites. It started out as a dermoid cyst." Sykes was pulling her gown back in place. "Only three out of a hundred are ever malignant."

"What's a dermoid cyst?"

"A form of ovarian cyst, usually benign, but it contains undifferentiated tissue, usually skin and hair. Sometimes they can even have teeth or a partially formed gland inside. Used to run across them a lot in the lab. A little like a diseased embryo—an unfertilized one, of course. It's a cancer of the germ cell—the cell of life. Kind of a perverse parthenogenesis—virgin birth where you come from."

Mother Margaret bit her lip.

Sykes shugged. "Men can have it, too, you know. It's rare, something like one in two hundred thousand, but it happens. The germ cell becomes cancerous and forms a tumor in the testicles. Often fatal—by the time they're big enough for a doctor to palpate, they've usually metastasized."

"You mean spread through the body?"

"Nice irony, don't you think? A cancer embryo is killing me. You know, some people think cancer's really just the cell's growth mechanism—that's how the embryo and infant grow so fast at the beginning. Then the cancer virus becomes dormant till age or some carcinogen activates it, or the antigens that controlled it break down. So the seeds of life and death could prove the same, if we ever figure it out."

Mother Margaret tried not to listen. Was this why the woman had begged her to come—to rave about the grisliest things she had discovered in a lifetime devoted to death?

"But what's really interesting about these cysts—actually, they're called teratomas, you know. Do you know what teratoma means? It's 'monster' in Greek. Anyway, what's fascinating is they're a jumble of body parts, so the metastases can be in the form of regular tissue cells. Rudimentary hair or teeth grow in the kidney, or an eye sprouts in the brain—"

"Please," said Mother Margaret, watching the woman's thin hands smooth the sheet over her abdomen and thighs with jerky, disconnected motions. "You still haven't explained—"

"Explained what?"

"Why you asked me to come."

Delicately Sykes pushed one last wrinkle in the sheet ahead of her index finger. "Macduff," she said at last.

"He's fine," Mother Margaret answered. She paused, summoning her courage. "But why was he so . . . different? Why did he grow so fast? Who was his mother?"

"Why do you say 'did' and 'was'?" Sykes's eyes narrowed. "What's happened to him?"

Mother Margaret bowed her head. The insane could be so cunning and perceptive sometimes. There was no point in lying, even to soothe her. "His uncle came for him, almost four years ago. He brought him back to his parents, but he said they've forgiven you—"

"Then he's dead."

"What are you talking about? He was perfectly—"

"Don't you understand? That wasn't his *uncle*. He never had one, any more than he had parents. He was—"

Mother Margaret shook her head.

"Listen to me," Sykes said. "For ten years I was here—
here—working on recombinant DNA technology for—
well, it doesn't matter. It was a little like bacteriological
warfare."

"What's DNA re—?"

"Genetic engineering. DNA is what makes the offspring
exactly like the parent cell. We learned to break down the
DNA chains in certain bacteria and viruses—we used *E.
coli* bacteria because they're common in the human intestinal tract, and we used Epstein-Barr virus because, well,
it's associated with certain nasal cancers and we had it
on hand. We created all kinds of hybrids by breaking down
the DNA chains with restriction enzymes and then combining parts of the bacterial DNA with parts of the viral
DNA. Eventually, we learned how to code the genes to
predetermine exactly the kinds of hybrids we'd get, hybrids capable of reproducing exact duplicates—"

"Changing genes? That's—"

"I know, you wouldn't approve. But Macduff came from
our research, indirectly, at least."

"Are you saying he was some kind of test-tube baby?"

Sykes held a finger to her lips and nodded toward the
door.

"That's against every teaching of the Church," Mother
Margaret went on in an angry whisper.

"I'm not asking for your blessing," Sykes said, "but
it had nothing to do with artificial fertilization of an ovum
ex utero, so you can forget about telling me how it's
adulterous to unite a sperm and egg in a test tube because
it's outside marriage—"

"That has nothing to do with it. It's unnatural—"

Sykes hushed her again. "I don't want to argue about it.
I want to give you something." She rolled over and reached
up under the night table by her bed, extracting a wad of
what seemed like toilet paper and the surgical tape that
had held it there. "I wrote it for the boy, to explain, so
he'd understand. Everything's there, the whole story. Now
that he's dead, there's no point. . . . But I, I just don't
want them finding it here, after I'm gone. You can think
of it as a kind of confession, if you want."

Mother Margaret accepted the wad; it was covered with
small, cramped writing. "Why do you believe he's dead?"
she asked.

"Because that's how afraid they were—of things like what's happened to my roommate over there. And to me. They thought there might have been imperfections . . ."

"Really, Dr. Sykes, even if the rest of this were true, why, God Himself spared His creations, though they chose imperfection and ate the apple."

Sykes began pulling at the cotton of her gown. "The project leader—you'll read about him in there—said he wasn't human, said it wouldn't matter any more than if they unzippered the atomic chain of some molecule they'd created. I tried to tell them he was unique—a kind of miracle. But in the end I had to sneak him out because . . ."

Mother Margaret found herself reaching for the rosary that hung from her waist to finger the beads. There was something in the woman's voice, a kind of conviction. . . . "But why wouldn't he have been human? You said he wasn't a test tube—"

"Exactly! Why wouldn't he? He was a living thing with rational faculties, wasn't he? He grew from a human cell, didn't he?" Suddenly she stopped, turning her head to watch the wisps of cloud racing in the horizontal slots between the blades of the Venetian blind. Her eyes glistened with tears. "I don't want to talk about it any more. He's dead. It's over."

Mother Margaret wanted to speak, but she held back. The loaf-sized swelling on the woman's abdomen was only the part of the cancer that showed; but cancer was insidious, burrowing wormlike beneath the skin. Instead, she put her hand on Sykes's arm, studying the shattered woman, the tear-streaks on her face like sharp and jagged cracks.

Mother Margaret had chosen too different a path to understand her fully, but at least she could sympathize with what must have been Sykes's desperate need to give meaning to her childless body's corruption by fabricating such a story of a corrupt thing she'd helped create. Psychiatrists would no doubt talk about externalizing guilt or something. Silently, she tucked the wad into her cuff.

She didn't think of it again until she was back on the bus. It was sunset, and she watched the low hills slip by, still green in the September evening but already flecked with occasional autumn reds and yellows where trees had turned early from too little water. She felt the lump in her cuff, retrieved the wad, thought briefly and then unfolded it and began to read.

She had to force herself to keep going at first. At every turn the woman's madness seemed to betray itself. Yet by the time she was done, her hands trembled with the realization that no one, mad or sane, could have made up such a thing. It had to be true. She felt sick to her stomach.

She refolded the paper and slipped it back inside her sleeve. Outside her window, the world rushing by had grown black, and in the glass she saw only the stars and her own reflection, startlingly old and coarse, flitting across the shadow trees, sad and substanceless as the ghost of some damned soul.

Chapter 11

The Live Side

The only Buridan among the news room's phone directories was a Mrs. Mary E. in Butler's Riverview section, but since Holy Assumption Academy was also in Riverview, it was worth a try. Leffingwell dialed the number; at one end of the room the demonic chatter of the teletypes began again, while at the other, a few desks away, Lance and Oberon were having a high-level discussion.

"Get you a pastrami to go? *Lance,* am I an anchorperson or what? I'm busy with the Valhalla power plant piece. Get Dawn."

"She's on the bridge with a preliminary script for Stackpole."

"Then get someone else."

Lance thought a moment. "Hey, Leffingwell?"

"I'm on the phone," Leffingwell said. It was the fifth ring.

Lance finally pushed himself away from his desk and wandered off. "Hey, anybody?"

Leffingwell heard the receiver picked up at the other end. "Hello?" he said.

Silence.

"Hello? Hello? Is this John Buridan's residence?" Obviously a breather or a child. Why did people let their children answer phones? "Can I talk to your mommy or daddy?"

"They're dead," said a voice at last. It was the voice of a middle-aged man.

"I'm trying to reach John Buridan," Leffingwell said.

"Why?"

"It's . . . well, it's hard to explain. Kind of a professional problem, you might say."

"Are you from the Board of Trustees?"

"Trustees? No, I'm Durwood Leffingwell from Channel 29, where today's news is a real pleasure."

"You're sure?"

"Of course I'm sure. Why would I lie?"

"You could just be *saying* you're you."

"Well, I'm me, and that's all there is to it, Mr. Buridan."

"Who said I was me?"

Already the conversation struck Leffingwell as hopelessly Cartesian. "Reporter's intuition. You in some kind of trouble?"

"Trouble? I'm the only lay teacher that hasn't been axed yet," he said. "They're replacing us—they're trucking in teaching nuns from retirement homes, nuns with rare tropical diseases, nuns with parts of their bodies missing in China. The teachers' lounge looks like a leprosarium."

"I'm sorry to hear that."

"Well, they can't get rid of me unless they drop football. I'm the coach. But I get phone calls. Someone's stealing my *Time* out of the mail. I haven't seen *People* for four weeks—that's got to mean something."

"Well, look, Mr. Buridan, maybe we could do a big exposé on all this later, but right now I'd like to ask you something in your professional capacity."

"I don't know the first thing about football."

"No, about philosophy."

"Philosophy? Mercy me, did you know after all those years I spent getting my master's, the nuns still won't let me teach ethics?"

"Anyway, I wanted to ask you about this, well, he's a freak is what he is, kind of. And the thing is, this guy, being a freak, has all these gaps in his experience. Now we're planning this documentary, and we thought it would be a good idea to have, you know, a technical advisor."

"I think you want someone in psychology or sociology."

"No, we want something very deep and profound."

"Let me see if I understand. You have some kind of Noble Savage you want to expose to the twentieth century? First Big Mac, that kind of thing?"

"No, he knows all about the modern world—he's a TV addict. But he's missing weird little things, like a walk in the woods."

"Very interesting—a Noble Savage innocent of nature. A kind of urban barbarian. Was this caused by any kind of sensory deprivation?"

"I—"

"Of course the eighteenth century would've been much better at this kind of thing. Take Diderot after they discovered a cure for cataracts, waiting for the bandages to be taken off a blind man to see if he'd recognize a triangle. Ideally we'd want to restore one sense at a time, like Condillac's statue. I can tell you, the eighteenth century would love to've gotten its hands on Helen Keller. Oh, and they were fascinated by feral children—wild boys—"

"About the film, Mr. Buridan."

"Yes, well, I'll want to be there myself."

"Naturally, but the thing is, where do you think we should start? Escalators? Ice cream cones?"

There was a long pause. "I just wish I had time to think through all the permutations and ramifications. My brain's just *buzzing!* This is a very rich lode. Has to be mined thoroughly and carefully. Mined . . . a *mountain!* That's it! What's grander among the works of nature than a mountain?"

Leffingwell was pleased. He understood a mountain. And Stackpole owned the back of Mount Shadrach for his trailer.

"Yes, we'll just trot him right up a mountain and see what he has to say about the view. Tell me, is he ugly or deformed in any way?"

Leffingwell was trying to think of phrases that meant goodbye. "They call him Elephant Man."

A long pause. "Oh, good, good. I'm looking forward to seeing him. I'm very interested in grotesques, you know, birth defects, accidents—eep! Hear that?"

"Hear what?"

"That click. They've tapped my phone to catch me saying something they can use to fire me. I KNOW YOU'RE LISTENING! Excuse me—have to run. Something's in my window."

"Look, if you want to see what Elephant Man looks like, I'm going to run some footage tonight on—"

But the phone had already gone dead. Leffingwell shook his head and hung up. No point trying to get a replacement; his own college philosophy prof had gone around campus with a dachshund he addressed as Schopenhauer, so they were probably all crazy. He went down the row of desks to clear the Elephant Man side story with Lance.

Lance was not impressed. "This isn't a sideshow."

"Look, it's human interest. Anyway, I was downstairs when Gompers killed Sarazin's piece on Bagliarini. What about that slot?"

"We've got loads of stuff—the China earthquake, a shopping center rape, local basketball coach murdered and the last TN feed was about this old lady that failed her driver's test nineteen times."

"And you're telling me you can't fit in something on a guy that looks like an elephant? Lance, give me a break. It's not fair I should be a weatherman all my life. This could be my big chance. Give me three minutes—two minutes. Introduce me as your *science reporter.* That's the way they do it in the big time, like Frank Field in New York."

"You're no reporter. What do you know about journalism?"

"What do I know about *meteorology?* Lance, this is Channel 29! This is Butler, Massachusetts! It's not for real! It doesn't matter what we do!"

"You've got to have *some* standards," Lance said.

"Since when?" Oberon said, looking up from her typewriter. "Around here, you're anything you claim to be."

Lance glanced briefly at the monitor. The Dynamic Duo were reeling in the knockout gas from Penguin's umbrella. "All right, all right, but I'll have to clear it with Gompers and Trammel. This is a pretty major change."

Leffingwell went back to his desk and dialed the US Weather Bureau. It was busy. It was always busy. Someday he'd get the number VIP's used so he could talk to a real forecaster instead of dialing the recording like some clown wondering whether it was going to be too rainy to take his outboard down to the boat ramp.

He took his B&B Trucking memo pad and drew a right triangle. Lance was talking on the phone while he watched Penguin put Batman and Robin in a vacuum chamber. Leffingwell drew a rectangle from one side of the triangle, and another triangle at the opposite end. It made a parallelogram, like half the feathers on an arrow. He drew another parallelogram that mirrored it. He drew the shaft. He drew the triangular arrow head. He drew a human body around the arrow head. He erased the tip of the head so it looked like the arrow was sticking into the body. His phone rang.

"Leffingwell? I've been calling all over the buillding for you since three o'clock."

"Sorry, Mr. Trammel. Had to check on some film, then see when the bridge wanted me to do Wednesday's sign-off's—"

"About the parade, yesterday, Leffingwell."

"Lost my head, sir."

"I could *see* that. What about that 'Please Nuke' business?"

"Yeah, I'm really sorry about that. Had no right to let it out. It's classified."

"Oh?" There was a long silence at Trammel's end. "Then that must be why—"

"Pardon?"

"There was a guy here this morning asking about you, Leffingwell."

"Who was it?"

"He never said, but I know the type. Used to see them all the time when I was assigned to the quartermaster's office. Washington snoop. Probably checking up on you letting this thing slip."

Leffingwell blinked and swallowed. There couldn't *really* be a "Please Nuke" List, could there?

"But frankly," Trammel continued, "I think his brains had gone soft. Spent most of the time talking about elephants. I told him to go see that neighbor of yours with the frogs."

"Well, Mr. Trammel, next time one comes by, I'd appreciate your sending him down to me. But I'd better get on those tapes now, right?"

"Right, Leffingwell. Say, though, one last thing. Do you by any chance live up there in New Hampshire because it just happens to be *far enough away?*"

"Far enough for what?"

"Well, if for *some reason* a crater should happen to be formed in this general area, would the rim of that crater just happen to miss your house?"

"No, the liquor's cheaper. State stores, you know?"

"Oh," said Trammel, obviously not believing him. "All right, talk to you later."

Leffingwell put the receiver back in its cradle and looked up to find Lance waiting for him. "Jerry thinks your idea about a science reporter is worth trying," he said. "As long as you don't want extra pay or anything."

Leffingwell held up his hands as though he were already hard pressed to spend what he made and departed with the sign-off script, stopping by the studio for the only directional microphone from Lance's plywood news-set desk. The others were omnidirectionals, the audio equivalents of Sarazin's wide-angle shots; they missed nothing, but while the face on the screen moved its lips, they made the voice sound as though it were coming from a barrel somewhere out in the parking lot. Back on the bridge, Leffingwell closed himself inside the audio booth.

Next to the processing room, it was his favorite place. It was close and stuffy, but it was tranquil—no phone for Trammel, not even a knock on the door as long as the red light was on. Leffingwell held one of the headset's phones against his ear until the switcher's cue. "Good morning," he said into Lance's microphone. "This is WHCK, Channel 29, beginning another broadcasting day for your viewing pleasure. Coming your way this A.M. will be your favorite and mine, *New Zoo Review,* and then big and brawny at seven-thirty, that champion of the oppressed, *Mighty Mouse,* followed by those wacky *Banana Splits* and *Crusader Rabbit.* Then for a change of pace at eight-forty-five, it's *Koffee Klatch.* Today newswoman Oberon Ricketts will be serving up this week's guest, Apocrypha G'Zyz, High Priestess of the East Islip Coven of Witches and Amalgamated Earth Mothers, Incorporated, and author of *Hexes for a Slimmer You.*"

After the day's attractions, Leffingwell worked his way through the breaks and spots. He rather enjoyed the way he could race through an entire day and then crumple it in the wastebasket, something he'd like to do with too many of the days he had lived.

"This is Channel 29, WHCK. Time now is twelve noon —do you know where your children are? Coming up at six o'clock, Mr. Spock finds out it's Vulcan rutting season, and Captain Kirk has a tough decision . . ."

Occasionally, to break the monotony, there were audio

tags for commercials—regional address dub-in's and daily specials for Crazy Stan—and finally it was over.

"WHCK is a public corporation owned and operated by Media Masters Corporation of Roxbury, Massachusetts, and broadcasts from a tower atop Alden Hill by microwavelength at an allowable power of—"

Already he was formulating the lead-in for his Elephant Man side story. He'd almost forgotten Elephant Man himself even existed as a separate entity that was, in fact, sitting at that very moment in his living room.

"And now, the 'Star Spangled Banner.' "

Leffingwell looked up at the clock above him. Six-fifteen on Monday evening, and already Wednesday was over without having to live through it. He pushed the door open, felt the shock of fresh air and noise and ran for the peace of the processing room.

Waldron had finished Stackpole's footage, and Leffingwell slapped the reel on the viewer. Not much. A few seconds of Elephant Man without his veil, fuzzy and obscure in the low light—no depth of field, degraded image. Degraded subject, too, Leffingwell thought. Then the bright exterior of the storefront.

By eight o'clock he'd spliced the exterior shot at the beginning and removed the darkest, blurriest sections, then ordered a key slide of Elephant Man's face from a frame of the film and cursed himself for forgetting the picture Harry had given him yesterday. By eight-thirty he was on the bridge with a draft of a profoundly moving script to have it timed and included in the news log. There wasn't time to pretape, so he'd have to do his side story live, which, counting the weather, meant two live spots. Leffingwell didn't mind; visions of Master Charge cards danced through his head.

Leffingwell was back at his desk by quarter of nine to get the weather report ready. Lance was watching Doris Day in *Pillow Talk* on the *Eight O'Clock Movie* and Dirk Pataud, bull-necked and bug-eyed, was at his desk with a transistor radio on full blast, listening for the Red Sox game while he wrote up the day's sports. Pataud, fired from a local weekly paper for being obtuse and abrasive, was currently being trumpeted in thirty-second spots as the area's only brutally candid sportscaster.

Leffingwell's phone rang.

"Hello, Mr. Trammel," he said, without having to ask.

"Gompers tells me you're doing some animal story?"

"Well, it's more like human interest with an animal ambience."

"Just keep it clean, Leffingwell. No mating animals. And nothing about dog poo on sidewalks or any of that shit, because people see enough of it in real life. Remember, this is Channel 29, where today's news is a real pleasure."

A moment later the phone rang again. "What kind?"

"What kind of what, Mr. Trammel?"

"Of animal?"

"It's about a guy with a head like an elephant."

Pause. "I hate political satire. Politics got no place in the news."

"It's for real. It's got nothing to do with politics."

Leffingwell left the phone off the hook and went to Mellor's desk to call the Weather Bureau, got through like the Bruce's spider on the third try, went to the closet to tear the latest UPI highs and lows and headed down to the studio with his trusty magic marker. The taping light was on over the double doors, and Leffingwell waited outside, watching through the little round windows as Toby Mellor, seated at Lance's news desk, taped his VTR side.

"Who's that knocking at my door? Who's that knocking—"

A moment later Hap Little hit the doors with his shoulder, turned slightly to give Leffingwell a broad, vacant smile and a cheery "Good morning," and rolled into the studio. Leffingwell stepped back from the cloud of White Owl cigar and Southern Comfort fumes, catching a glimpse of the crow puppet dangling from Hap's right rear pocket.

Hap crashed into Toby's desk, apologized to the fire extinguisher on the wall, and plowed across the set to disappear behind the weather board.

" 'Sony me fr'mover the sea,' says Barnacle Bill the say-lor."

There was a crash and silence.

"Okay, Mellor," boomed Stackpole's voice from the ceiling speaker. "Take it from 'crazed suburbanite.' "

At nine-forty-five the set was clear. Leffingwell went to the weather board to copy his UPI temperatures on the acetate sheet over the national map. He paid no attention to the gurgling snores from behind the board.

A few minutes later, Oberon took her seat at the anchor desk, Dirk Pataud waddled in and unfolded a metal chair behind the sports desk and finally Lance and Dawn appeared.

"Don't torture yourself," Dawn was telling him. "Maybe Mao died on your day off. You know how those Chinese are." She halted in the shadows by the cameras as Lance walked on into the light, squinted and sat down by Oberon.

"Where's my mike?"

"What's wrong now?" Oberon asked.

"Somebody stole my mike!"

"You and Oberon share the omni down there," Stackpole boomed from the bridge.

"Dawn!" Lance called. "Go find my directional. Quick, quick!" Dawn went out. "Jesus, what a headache I've got from no supper."

"One more word," Oberon said, reading through her script, "and I'll file for divorce."

"You'd break up Butler's first husband-wife reporting team?"

"*Reporting* team? You just sit there looking like Ryan O'Neal and read a script. You think a press sticker on your Sunbeam makes you a reporter? The biggest thing you ever went into the field for was a bridge dedication."

"Who was up all night with hurricane updates last fall?"

"You mean the one that veered out to sea by six P.M.?"

"It *could've* doubled back and hit us. They're tricky."

"Stand by," said Stackpole.

Capella had just rolled his camera into position for the first half of the opening two-shot—his camera showing the happy anchor couple, then camera two with Lance's head and shoulders. At five seconds Capella held up the count on his fingers.

"Bastard."

"Bitch."

A hush fell and Lance broke into a huge smile. "Good evening, everyone," he said. "This is Lance and Oberon Ricketts here to bring you the *Ten O'Clock News,* where today's news is a real pleasure." Red light out in camera one, on in camera two. "Tonight's big news—rocking and rolling in Communist China."

Lance read the TN story while on the monitor the columned arches of Sodom shivered and fell, and Gomorrah's shoebox temples toppled. As the dust settled on the Hollywood special effects table, Leffingwell imagined that in every Butler living room the TV's glow illuminated so many pillars of salt clutching beers.

"Coming up after this announcement," Lance said, "Nuclear fission could mean no fishin'."

The red lights were out. Capella wheeled his camera around for a side shot of Oberon as Findelmann Furniture's spot ran on the monitor.

"Well," Lance said, "if it's a divorce you want, then you can have it."

"Fine."

"Just remember, you're the one that said the word first."

"Stand by."

Oberon assumed her video smile. "The first word was 'pastrami sandwich,' Rollo. One anchorperson does not expect a fellow anchorperson to get him pastrami sandwiches."

"Only you would wreck two careers and a marriage over one sandwich to go."

"The simple fact, Rollo," she answered through tight lips, "is—"

Stackpole punched from line to broadcast; the red light in camera one glowed.

"—I'M SICK OF BEING MARRIED TO A HAMBURG," she continued to several thousand people. Her eyes snapped to Capella's lens. "Well, it's fish fry or no juice say the biggies at Mass. Edison to environmentalists complaining about thermal pollution at the new multibillion-dollar Valhalla Atomic Power Plant in nearby Bumberry, New Hampshire, where last year twelve local residents died of bladder cancer."

Leffingwell fingered his script nervously and waited.

"—said a lot of stuff about roentgens and neutrons, and claimed the local bladder cancer upsurge would be balanced by the lower national rates, so no cause for alarm—"

His first news story. His big break. Job offers flew to him. He waved goodbye to Bank Americard and Master Charge. Now he'd be getting American Express because he wouldn't have to worry about being able to pay the full balance every month.

He looked idly at the monitor. Camera two was on chromakey, its cobalt blue turned off so the blue wall behind Lance would register as an empty blank onto which could be superimposed slides or film. As Lance gave the lead-in to Donaldson's taped side about the murder of a local basketball coach, behind him flashed Burrows' chart of a shopping cart whose wire basket was a graph of consumer prices since 1970 labeled "HiGH COST OF LiV-iNG."

The slides were out of phase, Leffingwell thought, adjusting the lapels of his blazer. But something else was wrong, too, something about his own key slide. "—the J. C. Penney parking lot," Mellor's tape was saying, "where a man described by police as a crazed suburbanite in a red alligator shirt wielding a mulch-covered lawnmower blade—"

Leffingwell tried to flatten his shirt collar. It was the standard blue uniform twill worn by the cretins that worked the pumps at the weather spot's sponsor, Gas Paradise, and was forever curling up.

Another commercial, then Oberon began her live lead-in to a plastic surgeon story. Leffingwell was next. He re-read his opening lines, fingers icy and numb.

"—able to rebuild most of the face using grafts from the buttocks," said the doctor, "but the really big problem was the missing upper lip, which, of course, must produce mucus in order to—"

If he blew it, he could be a weatherman the rest of his life.

"—dawned on me that a graft from the inner vaginal wall, where secretions—"

The rest of his natural life.

On the monitor was a waxwork dummy. No, the mouth was moving. It was the plastic surgeon's creation. "No real problems," she was explaining. "Course there's always jokers saying, 'How's tricks, BLEEP-face—' "

Leffingwell pushed his hair back with his hands.

"—and now, a special report from our weather—our *science* reporter, Durwood Leffingwell."

Red light—Capella's camera. Leffingwell looked directly into the lens. "Good evening." Why was it so much worse than the weather? "Yesterday, thousands watched the grand spectacle of Butler's annual Barnum Labor Day Parade, little realizing that they were not about to witness a display of horrible yet pathetic deformity. For who among them could have known that the seemingly innocent U-Haul trailer, which might easily have been mistaken for just another float in the parade, actually carried a great load of prostrate and unconscious human misery?"

Leffingwell read the words without listening to them, letting them echo hollowly through his head. His chromakey slide was coming up and he glanced at the monitor. He had no chest.

"—the haunting question, 'who was this man's mother?' "

No *chest?* He looked again. A gaping hole, black as the farthest corner of the universe, an infinity of nothing in the triangle between his neck and lapels.

"—woman could nurture within herself with her own heart's blood a child for nine long months and then, when she had brought it into the world, be so heartless to abandon it?"

He slapped at his chest as though somehow he could bring it back, but still the monitor showed the hole. *That* was what he couldn't remember about his key slide—with the blue off in Capella's camera for the slide, Leffingwell's blue uniform shirt simply ceased to exist.

"—truly a child not even a mother could love?"

At that instant inside the Daliesque window of Leffingwell's heartless chest appeared the taut, expressionless face of the plastic surgeon's Pygmalion.

At last Stackpole switched to the film.

"—presently residing with this reporter, who is attempting, at his own expense, to provide a suitable home environment for the poor creature to spare it the humiliation of further public display—"

In the film, Elephant Man turned modestly away from Stackpole's camera, reaching for his shirt to cover himself.

"—which has in any event turned out to be illegal in Butler—"

He finished his script in a daze, rose, moved zombielike toward the safe familiarity of his weather board. Dirk Pataud was beginning the sports.

"—especially tragic for such a promising coach," fearlessly editorialized the brutally candid sportscaster. "And I want to say right here and now—and I don't care *who* hears me—murder has no place in high school athletics."

Leffingwell did not hear. His mind was a blank until the second time Hap's trembling hand, inside the cigarchewing crow wearing a jaunty boater, nudged him and Barnacle Bill's voice demanded, "What's de wedder, boss?"

He stumbled through a forecast for torrential rains, barely remembered to ask Stackpole for a ride and rode home in silence. And when he had slammed Stackpole's door shut, he did not see the tall, muscular figure in sunglasses slip into the shadows behind the late Mr. Adams' rusting Packard.

And inside Leffingwell's apartment, Elephant Man still sat as he had an hour before, paralyzed by the moment when the television screen, always a window on the world's fond past dreams and fantasies, had been transformed into a mirror of yesterday's awful reality, and instead of finding the old, familiar faces of his reruns, he had seen his own head—hatless, uncovered, loathsome in its nakedness.

Unable to get up and turn it off, he had sat, eyes closed, trying to blot it out by replaying old series and movies in his head. In *Bride of Frankenstein,* he remembered, was the haunting, agonised look Karloff had given the German peasants at the instant they raised up the pole to which he'd been tied. He had hung there for an eternity, suffering their jeers, and then they had tipped the pole over and let him topple into the hay wagon they had brought.

Chapter 12

A Little Lettuce for the Big Taco

"Yuck."

The tendons of Claudine's neck stood out to pull the corners of her mouth down. She was looking at the living room door as though she expected the TV strains of the violin theme from *The Young and the Restless* to materialize into wisps of pale, noxious smoke. Before her was a cup of coffee Leffingwell had just made.

"It's the same stuff we always have," Leffingwell snarled, returning the saucepan of boiling water to the stove.

"Not the coffee," she said. "I saw your news last night." Even saying it reminded her how the wonderful, nervous lightness after Miasma's conference had fretted her too much to go home, how she had drifted through the student lounge and glimpsed her husband on TV . . .

"Yeah?" Leffingwell was surprised because Claudine always refused to watch him on TV. "Well, anyone could have made the same mistake about wearing blue. The sponsor *makes* me wear that shirt, and we normally don't do weather-spot chromakeys. Where would *we* get a satellite photo?"

"No, I mean the pictures of . . . you know."

Leffingwell sat down with his Coffee-Lover mug.

"Durwood, if I'd had any idea what it really *looked* like under that netting. Could it—where's my spoon?—could it rub off on the sofa or anything?"

"What are you talking about?"

"Those *things* hanging off it. I mean, that's all I need, sitting down and finding . . . You *promised* you'd get it someplace else to go, and then I get home last night and . . . Didn't you give me a spoon?"

"No, I forgot. It's not enough I made you coffee?"

"Durwood, when I make *you* coffee, I *always* remember to give you a spoon." She pushed her chair back and reached into the silverware drawer. "It's not I don't feel sorry for him, but he *can't* stay. He reminds me—never mind. Krishna's so terrorized I had to push him down the stairs this morning."

"Like hell he was terrorized. He was too comfortable on my pillow with his nose tucked up his ass."

Claudine shrugged and tipped a spoonful of sugar into her mug. "Well, you weren't using it. I heard you fall off the bed at four this morning."

"I don't remember."

"You remember waking up on the floor just now?"

"Krishna pushed me."

"Durwood, I was awake. I saw the whole thing. Nobody pushed you—you went over the side locked in mortal combat with another giant chicken. Now you find someplace else for the Beast from Twenty Thousand Fathoms or else."

Leffingwell tried to merge his nod of assent with lowering his head to sip his coffee. He had no intention of doing anything of the sort. The Elephant Man documentary was going to be the Big Taco, and he didn't want anyone else getting close to Elephant Man and doing a rival film. He'd think of some excuse for Claudine by tonight; he'd make her relent one day at a time.

"I suppose you didn't read the mail this morning," Claudine said.

Leffingwell always checked the mail when he got up, but he only opened envelopes with handwritten return addresses. Letters with corporate logos, glassine windows for his address and, worst of all, anonymous P.O. box returns —these he wouldn't touch.

"This month's letter from Master Charge was pink. They want to know if there's any way they can be of help."

"That's nice."

"Durwood, they don't want to be of help. It's just their way of asking why we haven't sent the minimum payment for three months when we're already over our credit limit."

"Who cares? It was a really insulting limit. Four hundred dollars! I was talking to Capella last week, and *his* credit limit is a thousand. Look, when this documentary gets rolling, they'll beg us to take a million-dollar limit, believe me."

"Durwood, Gulf Oil didn't even bill us. Their credit card company asked us to cut our cards into two or more pieces and send them by return mail."

"Claudine, I've got to keep my head clear. I've got to *think*. Who needs Gulf Oil?"

"The car seems to, Durwood. You remember, the Rambler with the optional trash can? I thought you were going to fix it."

"I did."

"Your idea of fixing something is leaning one wreck against another and hoping they don't both fall over."

Leffingwell hated talking to anyone before he'd finished his coffee. And he hated especially to talk to Claudine when she was just-out-of-bed bitchy. "It's *your* fault, anyway. If *I'd* had the car I'd have stopped at a gas station and gotten the whole thing taken care of—you've got to have the right *tools* to fix these things, you know."

"Where, at a Gulf station?"

"All right, all right, so in a little while we'll get a Mercedes."

Claudine sighed, lowering her eyes to her mug. She sat in silence for some time.

What he does isn't important, Mother, said a voice from the television. *As long as you* cared *for him. So what if he was the plumber?*

We were both so lonely, said another voice. *Something in common, something to* build *on. Just two old dogs—*

"Say," Claudine said, looking up. "Where *is* Krishna?"

"I tricked him into going outside with some old liver."

"From the *refrigerator?* That was *dinner*."

"I hate liver."

"But you're not home for dinner. That was for me. I *love* liver."

Leffingwell rose, put his mug in the sink, and ran water into it. "I never knew anyone that liked liver, except somebody's parents. People's *mothers* always like liver. *People* never do."

Mrs. Adams began pounding on the wall. "Durwood! Telephone! Your station!"

"Coming, Mrs. Adams!" Leffingwell left the water running, peeked out the back door to be sure Krishna wasn't within lunging distance and made good his escape.

It was Fern who opened the back door at the Adams' apartment, head tipped back, mouth pulling at a Dr. Pepper. She turned away as soon as he stepped in.

Leffingwell wanted to ask her about the kitten, but he didn't dare. She'd hated him ever since the time he'd sidestepped her request for her own variety show by getting her a guest shot on *Tooth Brigade*. Sergeant Smile was donating two minutes per show to the Jimmy Fund as his public service, and every week he'd introduce kids who'd held fairs and mowed lawns to raise money for research in children's cancer. The fifth and sixth grades at Quidnunck Regional Grammar had pooled their efforts selling cookies, and Fern was designated to hand over her classmates' two dollars and twenty cents in person.

She'd arrived at the studio that Friday afternoon fully rehearsed and decked out by her dance teacher, Miss Nicky Nackalis of the Tap 'n' Toe Studio. For the occasion, Miss Nicky had created a rooster suit of terry cloth dyed a bright flame red and flecked with scurfy patches of similarly dyed pillow feathers; in addition, Miss Nicky had choreographed an interpretive tap étude entitled, "L'Après-midi d'un Poussin." First, however, was to be the presentation, for which Fern had penned her own lines:

> *Cockadoodle-doo, cockadoodle-doo,*
> *Rooms three and five gave*
> *Twenty cents plus dollars two*
> *For* CANCER—*WOO!*

When the big moment came, someone had to push her center stage.

"Well, Miss Rooster," Sergeant Smile had said, untroubled by the sex angle. "What's the good word?"

Miss Rooster had stared speechlessly into camera two.

"Isn't it something about 'cockadoodle-doo,' Miss Rooster?" Sergeant Smile had urged hopefully.

Miss Rooster had remained mute.

"I think it's about rooms three and five giving two dollars and twenty cents for cancer-woo, sir," Private Cusp had lisped.

Still no word. Leffingwell had been behind her in the sightless rear end of Mr. Laffy the horse. He felt personally responsible for the fiasco, and guessing at her location by the sound of Sergeant Smile's voice, he'd landed his hoof squarely on Miss Rooster's terry cloth tail.

"Cockadoodle-DOO!" Miss Rooster had yelped.

But after the temporary return to lucidity, Sergeant Smile had had to pry the envelope of nickels and pennies from Miss Rooster's paralyzed wing, after which Private Cusp had led her in disgrace to the oblivion of shadows beyond the lighted set. It had been about twenty minutes later that they had gotten to the list of names for that week's "Birthday Root-a-Toot Salute."

"And a special big Birthday Smile to you, Todd Gillette, Michele Gompers and Johnny Hale," Sergeant Smile had said, brandishing his forty-five automatic. "Michele's daddy works here at Channel 29, too."

"Oh, Sergeant, sir," Private Cusp had said, pooting through a raspy toy trumpet. "Let's not forget a grin for Natalie James, Roddy Meechum or Barbie Morris!"

"Bless my chompers, that would never do," said Hap, Mr. Laffy's head. "Not to mention Rip Panella, Jodie Pappilard or the Stockton twins, Sandy and Rocky—"

Suddenly a very powerful little voice had come out of nowhere:

> *"Cockadoodle-doo, cockadoodle-doo,*
> *Rooms three and five gave*
> *Twenty cents plus dollars two*
> *For CANCER—WOO!*
> *Let me go, fucker!"*

And so it was now that Leffingwell hesitated before addressing her. Though he'd never told Claudine, he knew what caused his chicken nightmares. "Morning, Fern."

She didn't answer.

"Beautiful morning."

"That's not what you promised me last night. You said it'd be pouring."

"I never—oh, you mean on TV? It's not like I lied to you personally. That was a weather bureau forecast—we were all duped."

"FER-ERN!" Mrs. Adams called from the living room. "Is that Durwood?"

"Got to go," Fern said. "I never miss *Young and the Restless*. I *adore* Snapper." She ducked through the door with her Dr. Pepper, and Leffingwell heard her clumping up the stairs. He went on into the living room, glancing anxiously at the corner. The kitten's bird cage was empty.

"Durwood, how long is this going to go on?" Mrs. Adams was wrapped in her overcoat on the couch, leafing through *Better Homes and Gardens*. "I mean it, when are you getting a phone?"

"As soon as I'm rich," he said. Today the phone was out in the open, on the floor by the far wall. He picked up the receiver. "Hello?"

"Woody?"

He looked at the receiver to see what was wrong with it. *"Woody?"*

"Woody, this is *Dawn*."

"Dawn? Oh, sure, Dawn. What can I do for you?"

"Nothing. I just thought you'd want to know right away that Western Union just called. There's a moneygram for you and you've got to go down to their office and pick it up."

"A moneygram?"

"Yeah, they said it was for a hundred dollars. Wait, I wrote it down—it's made out to 'The Weather Guy at Channel Twenty-nine for the Elephant Man.' "

"Jesus Christ." Leffingwell had believed everything Harry had said about Elephant Man's potential, but to have it happen—to actually feel a million-dollar idea taking root and see the first tender treasury-green tendrils breaking through the moist spring earth. "You say it's made out to *me?*"

"Yeah, but that's not all. The TN stringer in Billerica called. He caught your side last night and wanted permission to do his own story."

"Oh?"

"I told him no—you had exclusive rights."

Leffingwell was very impressed. He would have said

yes and not realized till next morning that the profit would go to the stringer.

"Then I called TN headquarters in New York for you—I figured you wouldn't mind. Paid for it myself. They'd already talked to their stringer, so when I laid it out for them, they said okay."

"Okay what?"

"Three hundred and fifty dollars for national first-run rights to use your footage on the feed. They want it air freight some time today."

"Jesus, three hundred and fifty dollars. No wonder those guys all have ties that match their socks."

"I already called for times and rates. There's a three o'clock Emery flight out of Logan—I can make it if I leave in fifteen minutes."

There were unsuspected levels of efficiency in Dawn. And just out of Communication Arts, too.

"And I've kept everyone else here out of it. Lance was positively drooling over the film. Of course CBS called, too."

"CBS!"

"Yeah, but they said they'd only pay for footage from someone that wasn't directly involved, like Zapruder, say, or from a convicted felon, like Haldeman. They said you were a news source so they couldn't give you money, and they wanted to send their man up from Boston. I told them to sit on it. They can just switch to their local independent station in New York and watch it on the TN feed."

"You told CBS to sit on it? Look, Dawn, just drive the film down to Emery for me and I'll reimburse you or something."

"Don't worry about it, Woody. By the way, you also got calls from *National Tattler* and *Meteor*. I told them you'd get back to them—there's no rush, and I figure if you keep them waiting maybe they'll up the ante for exclusive print rights, okay?"

"Fantastic."

"So what're you going to do with all this money, Woody?"

"I, ah, hadn't thought much about it. I've got a lot of bills, but I need a new car. I guess it depends on whether there'll be more. This could be just the beginning, you know?"

"I *know*," she gushed, and the diaphragm in Leffingwell's earpiece buzzed with the overload. "Bye, Woody."

He realized as he hung up that Mrs. Adams had been listening intently.

"You come into some money, Durwood?"

"Not really. The guy that's staying with us did."

"You mean the monster with that sombrero thing on his head that's been hobbling around? Fern's scared to death of him. Thinks he's some kind of sex maniac."

"Sex maniac? He's perfectly harmless—pathetic, even."

Mrs. Adams shook her head. "She still thinks he's a sex maniac."

"YOU LYING BASTARD, RON BECKER!" a voice from upstairs shouted. "YOU KNOW YOU RAPED PEG! YOU DIDN'T HAVE ME FOOLED ONE MINUTE!"

Leffingwell raised his eyebrows questioningly.

"Just Fern," Mrs. Adams explained. "Yelling at the TV. Sometimes I swear she talks to it. She's up there watching it all day."

"Well, it's too bad she's afraid of Elephant Man. They've got a lot in common."

Mrs. Adams looked hard at him. She brooked criticism of her daughter from no one but herself.

"No, no," Leffingwell said hastily. "I mean she likes *Young and the Restless* so much. That's one of his favorites."

"Yeah, well, I don't think it's healthy. It's all she ever thinks about. I should move the thing down here before her brain rots."

"Why don't you? Then you could both watch it."

"Because her father left it to her. To me he left the Packards."

"Packards were nice cars."

"You're telling me. We used to have eighteen of them."

"Eighteen *Packards?*"

"The livery business Bradley inherited. Mainly rented to undertakers when they needed extras for a big job or a busy day. We had three flower cars and two hearses for the heavy season."

"WHY CAN'T YOU SEE THROUGH HIM, NAN-CY?" shouted the voice upstairs. "FORGET HE'S YOUR HUSBAND. HE'S A RAPER!"

"But you got to keep up with the latest styles," Mrs. Adams went on. "So we bought all new Packards in fifty-four, and then Studebaker merged with them and dropped the Packard. So there was the competition with garages full of slick Cadillac hearses and us with eighteen discontinued Packards. I could of cried. Our undertaker friends were sorry, but they had to think of their deceased's feelings, see, taking their last ride in a fifty-four Packard. By fifty-six, we couldn't of hired out to a Polish wedding. We were screwed."

"That's too bad."

"Oh, well, when Bradley died nine years later, at least he had one bang-up funeral—two hearses, three flower cars, everything my brother-in-law could get running again."

She sighed. "Nowadays there's all these car buffs paying top dollar for Packards, and kids fixing up hearses for rec vehicles, but in nineteen sixty-five I had to sell them for next to nothing to Crazy Stan. You remember that car he kept smashing up in those ads? One of Bradley's Packards. Guess even Crazy Stan couldn't sell them."

"Very sad," Leffingwell agreed.

"Yeah, Bradley was a real jerk."

"Well, I've got to go."

"Anyway, must be pretty nice getting extra money," she said, tossing *Better Homes and Gardens* onto the floor and picking up the newspaper folded beside her. "Comes in handy. Look at me here, food stamps, Aid to Dependent Children, going through the classifieds for work. Know what I come up with? A big nothing. 'Computer programmer with two years' experience,' 'Salad chef, references required.' Sure could use some extra cash."

Leffingwell shifted uneasily. "Claudine's had the same problem finding something right for her. Well, say goodbye to Fern for me."

"Oh, by the way, there was some guy here asking about you."

"Really?"

"Yeah. Wanted to know all about how you lived and what you did, stuff like that. And all about that sex maniac of yours."

"What did he look like?"

"Oh, he was dressed real nice, suit and tie. He was wearing sunglasses so I didn't see much of his face."

"Probably a tax assessor." But Leffingwell was beginning to think about what Trammel had said yesterday, and about the cryptic comments of Harry just before he'd left for the New York train.

Outside, he spotted Krishna at the kitchen door and circled around to let himself in the front way, only to find himself face to face with Elephant Man. "Uh, hi."

"I didn't get a chance to talk to you last night—you just rushed in and went right upstairs."

Leffingwell put his hands in his pockets and looked at the tips of his shoes. "Well, it was a hard day. I was figuring on catching you this morning."

"I just wanted to tell you how . . . nice it was of you to put me on television. It was quite an experience. Will it be repeated?"

"What say? Oh, *repeated?* No, they don't rerun news stories. But there *is* something along those lines I wanted to tell you about. We were, ah, thinking of maybe doing a movie all about you. That is, um, if it's all right."

"A movie about me." The unseen head shook the veil and hat back and forth in what Leffingwell took for disbelief.

"Yeah," Leffingwell said, warming slightly. "We were thinking Saturday we could go to this mountain and film you going up for the view."

"A mountain? Did you ever see that movie with Spencer Tracy about how the old mountain climber goes up to see if there are any survivors of the plane crash, but his corrupt son Robert Wagner takes the watches and jewelry from the bodies, only on the way down the snow gives way—"

"That, uh, kind of reminds me. If the movie makes any money, we were thinking of splitting it three ways."

"Money? I don't need any money while I'm staying with you. I probably *owe* you money."

"Right. That's right. Your share could be like room and board. By the way, somebody did send a moneygram for us."

"Really?"

"Yeah, just a few dollars, but maybe we could buy you, I don't know, maybe a new hat or something."

"I like this hat."

"Well, it's a quality hat, you can see that. You want me to open a bank account in your name, then?"

"Whatever you think is best."

"Right," said Leffingwell, glancing at the television. Suddenly it seemed important to change the subject. "Say, how's *Young and the Restless?*"

"Terrible, just terrible. Peg identified Ron as the man who raped her because her sister persuaded her he's the one. He tried to talk to her and reassure her and that just convinced her all the more, so an innocent man's going to go to trial for a rape he didn't commit."

"Happens all the time, but Fern next door seems to think he did it."

"Oh, no, he's *innocent.*"

"Yeah, well, you know these are all just *stories.* They're *actors.* None of it's *real.*"

Elephant Man tapped on his thigh. "Of course they're not real. That's why I like them. I wouldn't want *real* people that miserable."

"Of course not. But there's one thing about those soap opera characters—at least they're all doctors and lawyers with big incomes."

"Durwood," Claudine called from the kitchen. "You back?"

"I'll be right there. Say, E.M., there's one thing I wanted to ask you about. That agent of yours, Harry—he said something about guys in sunglasses he was afraid of. You know anything about that?"

"Harry never talked to me most of the time. Do you still have that photo he gave you? I'd like it back."

"Sure, it's upstairs somewhere. I'll get it for you in a minute."

"Durwood! Will you come *out* here?"

Leffingwell went into the kitchen. Claudine was standing at the counter where she'd arranged a row of boxes and jars like the state's exhibits in a trial.

"You see these?"

"Yeah, what about them?"

"Durwood, you used to drive me crazy taking the last thing and leaving the empty package in the cabinet. But I got used to it, because I learned which ones to check— Oreo cookies, Ritz crackers, Spanish peanuts and anything with chocolate in it. But this! I can't take it!"

"What are you talking about, Claudine?"

"An *entire* jar of mayonnaise—yesterday it wasn't even

open, this morning it's scraped clean. The cardboard bottom from a pound and a half of hamburg, the wrapper from a fresh pound of bacon, and an empty box that had two pounds of spaghetti yesterday."

"*I* didn't do it."

"I *know* that. I just got through saying you were an Oreo specialist. Your little *friend* in there did it."

"Okay, so he was hungry. Did you make him anything to eat yesterday?"

"I certainly did not. But there's something else—I didn't wash any pots or pans yesterday, and those *same* pots and pans are soaking in the *same* water I put them in."

"So?"

"So this, Durwood. Aside from the cost of the food, try to reconstruct the *meal*. Yesterday your friend ate two pounds of uncooked spaghetti, a pound of raw bacon, a pound and a half of raw hamburg, and covered it with *a pound of Ann Page mayonnaise!*"

Leffingwell put his finger to his lips. "Shh," he said. "There's something you ought to know."

"Unless it's that he actually has his own hotplate and didn't eat that stuff raw, I don't want to hear it."

"The phone call," Leffingwell whispered. "Somebody sent us, um, *fifty dollars* for keeping him. A kind of contribution."

"Oh?" Claudine said.

"That's not all. The wire service's buying my film."

"How much?"

"A hundred dollars."

"A hundred dollars?"

"You can buy a lot of liver with a hundred dollars, Claudine. A lot of raw hamburg. Didn't I tell you this time it was a million-dollar idea for real? This is just the beginning!"

"Just the beginning," Claudine mused.

Leffingwell had been hunched forward to keep his voice down; now he leaned back and smiled.

"By the way," Claudine said, "I'll need the car again today. Mr. Miasma cancelled class, but he's having a poetry reading or something instead, and I promised I'd come."

Leffingwell's smile faded. "For God's sake, Claudine, a

hundred-fifty dollars and I still can't drive myself to work? What's the point?"

"Durwood, you've still got nine hundred ninety-nine thousand eight hundred and fifty to go."

Leffingwell crammed his hands into his pockets and turned to go upstairs.

"By the way, Mr. Weather Hotshot," she said to his back. "You won't need your raincoat today."

Chapter 13

Onan in Drag

After dropping Durwood off at Channel 29, Claudine had gone directly to Jack Miasma's office. Now she lay face down with her chin on her forearms, staring gloomily from one end of a seat cushion to the floor three inches below, while from the other end the rest of her drooped to the floor, skirt hiked up around her waist, a draft from beneath the locked door traveling coldly and disinterestedly across her naked buttocks.

Behind her she heard the whispered padding of Jack Miasma's stocking feet as he paced back and forth in short, oriental steps, belt buckle dragging from the trousers coiled about his ankles.

A repeat, she was thinking. Maybe she'd pushed things. Maybe she should have given Jack a few days to get over yesterday's failure.

"You shouldn't worry about it," she sighed. "It can happen to any man, God knows." Durwood's doleful face flashed through her thoughts like a face on a station platform glimpsed from a rushing subway. "Even twice in a row. I've seen it happen a thousand times."

She dug a little of the accumulated grime out of a crack between the floorboards and examined it balled on the tip of her nail. If she couldn't have a career, why couldn't she at least have a sleazy affair? It was a basic human right, wasn't it?

She rolled onto her side. "Jack?"

Jack Miasma had stopped pacing and was staring at the drawn shade. The bare backs of his legs glowed a luminous white in the dim light.

"Jack, wasn't there anything, well, *special* I could have done to make you, uh, excited long enough? I mean, I'm no teen-age innocent." She paused, fighting back the fear that there was something wrong with her instead.

"No," Jack said, peering down at his limpness dangling between his open shirttails. He shuffled over to the chair by his desk, pants still crumpled around his ankles like a hobble, sat down, and brought the heels of his hands up to press his hair back and squeeze his eyes into slits.

"It just shows how I'm in touch with my bodily needs. Sort of like listening to millions of teeny little voices. It makes me very responsive to my own touch. Usually I can stimulate myself when no one else can, like tonight." The light filtering through the shades glinted from his forehead. "It's the artist's self-discipline—otherwise my creative juices would just drain away. So don't feel bad—I don't want you to think it's *your* fault."

Claudine bit her lip.

"It's the price I pay for art," he said.

Claudine waited a moment. "Why did you, uh, want me to stay? You didn't even *look* at me." Claudine had imagined herself a living *Playboy* centerfold that inspired his private passion, but when she'd looked through lustfully heavy-lidded eyes, she'd found him watching himself. She reached for the blue scrap of her bikini underpants. "At least now I understand where they get the term 'jacking off.' "

Miasma didn't follow. "No—I needed you. To watch." He thought for a moment. "You got a Kleenex?"

"No," she said glumly. "But there's some poems on your desk." She tucked her feet through the leg-holes of her underpants.

"Bond paper's got no absorption. And it scratches." He thought again, then pulled up his pants. "What the hell, you've got to be flexible in this business."

"I can see that," she said. "Well, I guess I'll be going."

"Don't forget the poetry reading tonight. Encino's virtually a neighbor, and her first book was published by

Doubleday or somebody really big. I want to impress her with a big turnout. Maybe she could put in a good word for me."

"I'm not sure I'll be there," she said.

His eyebrows butted together. For the first time he noticed she wasn't entirely pleased. "It's not always like this. Sometimes it just takes, well, a couple dry runs." His eyes were two fathomless pools of sincerity. "We could come back here after."

She took a deep breath and nodded. Outside, her legs felt weak, and she left the asphalt path to sit on a large boulder. Affixed to it was a weathered bronze plaque:

> **HERE LIES**
> **H. MENDIP PARSONS**
> **FOUNDER OF CAMBRIA COLLEGE**
> **BUSINESSMAN EDUCATOR PHILANTHROPIST**
> **WHOSE DREAM WAS MIDWIFE OF TOMORROW**
> **1887–1956**
> **WELL DONE, GOOD AND FAITHFUL PRESIDENT**
> **GIFT OF THE CLASS OF 1957**

Funny she'd never noticed this. She'd always heard the old geek was buried on the fifty-yard line.

Well, it was obviously time to look for a real lover. She wasn't going to be reduced to employing Jack Miasma's methods for fulfillment—she could do that without leaving the house. She sorted through the faces of the men she knew, but all the husbands in the housing project were slack-lipped morons who clustered on front stoops drinking beer from cans, their foghorn hoots of laughter fading into silence whenever one of their wives came within hearing distance, though everybody knew they were only discussing football, cars and the cup sizes of filing clerks at their factories.

So she'd meet somebody new. Maybe a faculty member or one of those Vietnam veterans she occasionally saw walking alone from class bundled into thick army parkas. Weren't men always supposed to be preoccupied with sex and salivating for an opportunity?

Poor Jack Miasma—his technique reminded her of those make-out sessions with Dicky Ianello's successors in high school. French-kissing until the only thing she could taste next day was salt, and even her teeth had hurt. The night

Buzzy Kaplan's hand had crept up her back until, as though by accident, it had lost its grip and plunged from the summit of her shoulder. Heart beating, she'd made no objection when it worked its way under her sweater to brush a sweaty palm across the raised embroidery of her brassiere cups, boldly squeezed her breast like Clarabelle the Clown working the rubber bulb of his horn and finally gouged her trying to dig its fingers between her flesh and the bra.

And then she'd heard a shuffling sound and pushed herself up from the couch just as Uncle Samuel had come grinning into the room. "Okay I watch a TV? Lone Ranger on," he had said.

She had been nervous when she'd decided to go all the way, parked among the dark pines just off Kirk Pond Road, but after the pain had come only the relief she'd felt after making it across the tracks in the face of the onrushing commuter train to prove herself to the sixth-grade boys. Glumly she had found her cotton underpants crumpled against the firewall on the car's passenger side where Buzzy's gritty foot had pressed them as he'd squirmed on top of her, banging his head on the bottom of the steering wheel rim in each of the three heaves it had taken to satisfy his lust.

The earthy cold of the boulder began to seep through her skirt to chill her buttocks, as though H. Mendip Parsons were reaching from his vault below to pinch one last ass. She shivered and went on to wait at the library, where, pipes creaking and clanking with the gush of the season's first steam, she suffocated in a tropical nightmare and browsed among the periodicals for the ones she'd subscribe to if she ever got money.

At last eight o'clock came, and she departed for the recital hall at the Center for Fine Arts and Applied Sciences. She saw Jack on the stage, deep in conversation with a large, heavy woman in black. Scattered through the three hundred seats were some ten students from class and two adults: another teacher dragooned into swelling the ranks —handsome but tired in a suit either British or from the last decade, a self-deprecatory smile licking at his lips like a shipwrecked Bostonian at a New Guinea wedding hoping a New Bedford whaler might still happen by—and a strange young man in sunglasses and a smart tan suit.

Claudine made her way to the front row where she

found taped to the back of every seat a scrap of paper with the warning "Reserved for Friends of Professor Miasma." She dropped into the aisle seat feeling terribly conspicuous and alone, and glanced back just in time to see the mocking Pierce girl whisper to the boy beside her, her glasses two blank and gleaming discs.

From the stage, Jack kept looking up to see if anyone else was coming, his forehead and lank hair glinting in the houselights. Next to him was Encino, seated on a metal folding chair in front of the American flag, a large, brass fire extinguisher and a six-foot gray wooden box housing the PA speakers. At her feet were the crushed paper cups and cans from Saturday's campus movie. She was perhaps forty, with thick, straight, close-cropped hair and the massive, earthy beauty of a Russian peasant or a government center. Claudine immediately disliked the startling contrast of her greasy black leather pants, vest and heavy boots with her plump arms—easily twice the girth of Claudine's—bare to the shoulder.

At last Jack seemed to recognize Claudine in the vast crowd. With a smile he stepped self-importantly from the stage, trailing wisps of glory down to her.

"Hi there," he said.

She nodded.

"Were you, ah, still planning to drop by after the reading?" He raised his eyebrows slightly.

"If you want me to, I guess."

"Of course. I'll have to say good night to Encino first and give her the check. Hope it doesn't bounce. But then . . ." He winked and made a clicking sound, then clambered back onto the stage.

As clumsy as Durwood, she thought. And that same vulnerability that made her want to comfort and protect, the vulnerability Durwood had lost when he elected to protect his Uncle Samuel clone.

Suddenly there was a terrible squeal. She glanced up to see Jack center stage, adjusting the microphone. It squealed again.

"Testing, testing, one, two, squeee-uck-óur. Okay, I guess we're bleee-ack-peep."

A small, acned student with glasses, close-cropped hair and a sense of mission bounced down the aisle on ripple-soled shoes and up onto the stage.

"Squawk," said Jack Miasma. "Pee-op poot fwack."

The young man began doing things to the microphone while Jack grinned sheepishly at Encino but finally despaired after several long minutes. He tipped the stand over and dragged it toward the side like a stricken grenadier, catching the heavy metal base of the claw-shaped flag stand. The man in sunglasses leaped to his feet as the American flag teetered threateningly, but Encino slapped her fist around it and it stood Plymouth-Rock still. Somebody clapped.

Jack Miasma held up his hands. "Mumble mumble mumble," he said.

"LOUDER!" came a cry from the back.

"HEY, ANGLO, HEY, HEY!"

"CAN'T HEAR YOU!"

"THIS BETTER?" Jack called.

"NOT MUCH!"

"FUCK IT, JUST GET ON WITH IT!"

Jack waited for the audience to quiet down. At last he began in a small, thin voice.

"It gives me great pleasure as Director of Cambria College's widely respected Creative Writing and Cinematography Program to introduce this year's widely read Visiting Artist, who calls herself simply 'Encino,' after the famed metropolis. Her first collection of poems, *Motorcycle Twixt My Thighs,* which electrified America's literary beachheads, sang of the simple joys and sorrows of her two years with the Fried Skulls Motorcycle Association in nearby Butler, Massachusetts."

"I'll have copies for sale as you go out the door!" Encino shouted.

"Thank you, Miss Encino." Jack cleared his throat. "Following the temporary disbanding of the Fried Skulls—"

"Seven bucks apiece," Encino said. "Forget the sales tax!"

"Thank you. As I said, following their sentencing, tonight's poet journeyed to New York, where she came under the influence of our greatest living concrete poet—and my personal friend and admirer—Jeremiah Swagg, creator of the justly famous 'Fireplug Poem' and 'Stand Pipe Rondeau.' However, while executing her poetic manifestoes, she was arrested by the Transit Police in a graffiti crackdown—"

"I'll have some eight-by-ten glossies at the back, too," Encino said. "Two bucks a shot."

"Thank you. Her two months in the Women's—"

"But that's genuine Kodak paper, and every one's signed individually. No rubber stamps."

"—REFORMATORY FOR DEFACING AN IRT TRAIN only served to strengthen her resolve, and once again she walks amongst you and I. I give you . . . Encino."

Jack retired to his folding chair, and Encino rose, a sheaf of papers and photos under one arm, and walked heavily to the center of the stage to scattered applause.

"I've had my head turned around a whole bunch of times, I can tell you," she began in a booming voice. "But this time I'm here to say I've really got it all together, and tonight I'm going to read you some things from my new book, *Secretions*. This is like, you know, a spiritual journey like Homer trying to find his house in the *Iliad* for ten years, about how I got my consciousness jacked up. I call the first one 'Pulsar'—kind of gives it a science fiction feel, right, Jack?"

Jack nodded.

> *"thrustingthrusting*
> *rammingramming*
> *im a millionmile vagina im*
> *a bigblack empty hole*
> *so*
> *fuckme fuckme*
> *fill my interstellar cunt*
> *cause*
> *god hates*
> *a*
> *vacuum"*
> *."*

There was an awful silence.

"Now that kind of shows you where Sherwood Anderson was at when he said, 'Everyone in the world is Christ, and they are all crucified.' Right, Jack?"

"Close enough," Jack smirked, but his eyes were suddenly empty and desperate. Was Sherwood Anderson the one that wrote plays?

"But back then, I just thought I was a *receptor*, a wet tube with a need, and I even went down to Washington after the pigs busted the Skulls, looking for the ultimate cosmic orgasm—for my poetry, see—thinking that meant finding the world's biggest cock. So I did up a little smack and then the answer hit me—go fuck an elephant!"

The hall was very, very still.

"So I like whip over to the Zoological Park, you know, and I tell the first guard I see what's on my mind. Like, what could be the problem, right? It was early, hardly anybody there, elephant wasn't busy, and you could hardly even tell I was stoned. Well, you wouldn't believe the hassles and the runarounds. First guy sends me to the Special Events Office, and *they* send me to the Bicentennial Office, and Bicentennial laterals me to Animal Husbandry. I mean, these chauvinist zookeepers couldn't *comprehend* my headspace. Look, we all know if some *guy* had come in wearing an overcoat and rubber boots and told them he wanted to be alone with the camels, would they have batted an eye? But let a woman come in and be honest about her sexuality, and they're all *threatened*. Why, can you believe it—they've had guys trailing me and bugging my phone ever since?"

Encino glanced meaningfully toward the back of the hall.

"So leaving the zoo, I'm all depressed and losing my buzz, when like it started to *dawn* on me. I looked at the elephants. Like really *looked* at them. And you know what? They're really heavy, man—a girl could get crushed. And all dry and dusty with straw and shit, and their *skin*, man, all *baggy*. So I says to myself, who needs it?

"So that's how when the matron brings me in and locks the cell on that graffiti rap, and I hear this chick in the next block singing 'You Only Hurt the One You Love,' I start thinking. Who do I *really* love?

"Like, who is the *only* person who never gets a headache at the wrong time? Who's *always* sympatico?"

Even all the way across the stage, Claudine could see Jack's eyes widening with longing.

"So in the next poem, 'Master Stroke,' I—"

Claudine stopped listening and looked away toward the huge and silent speaker box, then past it to the bare brick at the back of the stage, then to the oil painting to one side of some forgotten simp in a black cap and gown, maybe H. Mendip Parsons himself. Whatever odes to masturbation Encino read, Claudine didn't hear them. She was trying to tell herself that what Jack did made no difference to her. Master stroke indeed. He and Encino were two of a kind—them and their poetry. And what kind of a first name was "Encino" anyway? Why was she keeping her last name a secret? Probably something awful, like "Goatbreath."

Vaguely Claudine became aware of random, isolated claps.

"Don't forget, I'll be up at the back. Seven bucks for the book, two for the photos."

All at once Claudine found someone standing over her.

"Uh, look," Jack said, leaning forward confidentially. "It may take a little longer than I thought to get Encino on the road. Maybe we'd better make it tomorrow night instead."

"I won't be here tomorrow."

"Thursday after class, then?"

"We'll see."

She got up and walked slowly toward one of the side exits, pausing once to look back across the empty seats to the rear where Jack and Encino were already in intimate conversation beside a pile of slim volumes.

Claudine waited in the dark just outside the Center for some time, unsure whether she was hoping to see Jack and Encino or the tall, handsome teacher. When at last no one appeared, she headed reluctantly for the parking lot. But when she reached the Rambler and opened the door, the light from the street lamp behind glinted off the metal rim of the trash can.

"NO!" she sobbed, slamming the door. Her eyes burned with tears and a hot lump grew at the back of her throat. Jack was still better than nothing, better than Durwood and his monster.

She ran back toward the Center for Fine Arts and Applied Sciences, yanking the doors open and pounding almost blinded across the lobby to burst through the double doors of the recital hall.

The curtains had been drawn across the stage, leaving only the American flag and the fire extinguisher exposed, but from behind the curtains she could hear the high, thin whine of an electric motor.

"I know you're in here, damn it!" she shrieked at the curtains.

There was no answer, but suddenly Claudine guessed what the throbbing motor signified.

"So!" she shouted, her voice echoing through the recital hall. "It doesn't matter to you *who's* watching, you fickle bastard!"

Encino's face appeared at the juncture of the two curtains. "You want to just hang on, lady?" she said. "It's hell on the batteries to keep stopping and starting."

Chapter 14

God's Hinder Parts

It was Saturday, and Durwood Leffingwell had the accelerator all the way to the floor as the Rambler shuddered in first gear up the gentle incline toward Stackpole's. Today was the day they were to film the first footage of *Elephant Man Story*. Stackpole had rented the equipment and Buridan had at least hinted he would be there with a written version of the philosophical game plan he'd outlined on the phone. "Who knows?" he'd said as Leffingwell had scribbled notes. "Perhaps up there we'll all discover something about ourselves, as well."

It was the kind of New Hampshire morning that let Leffingwell forget Channel 29. In the early gray, the tree trunks were black with wetness, leaves glistening, and a ground fog hung at treetop level in the low spots, rising occasionally to wrap itself about the shoulders of the low, wooded hills on either side. "The old lady has her shawl on," his grandmother would have said.

As they moved farther up the base of Mount Shadrach, Leffingwell listened to the laboring of the motor and the faint clanking of the handle of the trash can, then shot a quick glance at Elephant Man. Leffingwell hadn't seen him without his veil since those few moments in the rented store last Sunday when all this had begun, except for reviewing and editing Stackpole's footage of the same moment for Monday's broadcast; yet he knew well enough that even if Elephant Man were bareheaded, there was nothing in the immobile face that could so much as twitch in response to whatever went on behind the glittering eyes.

But Leffingwell had some notion, at least, of the creature's thoughts. On Wednesday, the last time Leffingwell had blundered forgetfully into the living room and been forced to talk to him, Elephant Man had said something about trying to remember things, and Leffingwell noticed that several times during the conversation Elephant Man had grown quiet and thoughtful. So apparently Elephant Man liked to run repeats of his own life. It was definitely not healthy.

"You have breakfast this morning?" he asked now to break the monotony of the drive.

"I had a box of Rice Krispies before you got up," answered the voice from inside the veil.

"Aha!" Leffingwell joked. "So *you're* the one that finished all the milk before I had coffee."

"No, Leff. Claudine made herself some hot chocolate when she got in last night."

"Did she make some for you?" Leffingwell asked.

"No."

Leffingwell sighed. "Look, I'm sorry she hasn't cooked you a meal or anything since you came. We're, you know, kind of in the habit of eating separately—we just grab whatever we can from the refrigerator when we get the chance. Claudine's just not used to the idea of having someone around she could eat with. I mean, I'd make you something myself, but, well, you know. . . ."

"Leff, I don't think she'll ever get used to me. Every time I try to talk to her, she runs out of the room."

"She hasn't learned to make out what you're saying."

"It's all right, really. It doesn't bother me. I'm used to it."

"Well, it bothers *me*," Leffingwell said.

Elephant Man tapped a tune on his thigh.

"Say, how *did* you eat those Rice Krispies?" Leffingwell asked at last.

"Dry."

"Gack!"

"They're not bad—kind of like rice popcorn." Tap-tappity-tap-tap.

Leffingwell listened to the tapping as long as he could

stand it. "By the way, E.M., how come you always wear that cape? I mean, isn't it going to get all ratty and everything? I've got some old sweaters. . . ."

Elephant Man pulled the cloak tighter. "I like it."

Leffingwell considered buying him a spare and then thought better of it. He had aready unconsciously transferred Elephant Man's share to his own slush fund, and if Elephant Man preferred the old cape, so be it. Far be it from Leffingwell to impose himself. He cleared his throat. "Enjoying yourself?"

Tap-ti-tap-ti-tappity-thwack. "Sure."

"That little guy . . ."

"Harry?"

"Yeah, Harry. He never took you to the woods for a picnic or anything? You know, nature and all?"

"I remember something about a river, but I think that was before he found me."

"Well, we're changing all that, right?"

"We certainly are. You're a thoughtful person, Leff."

Leffingwell felt suddenly much, much worse, but a moment later he had found Stackpole's hidden mailbox and was winding his way up the three miles of driveway which, in the damper spots, melted into a corduroy road that rotted so quickly in the acid soil Stackpole couldn't keep up with repairs.

It had always mystified Leffingwell that Stackpole, who had nothing of the pioneer in his manner or background, should choose such a life.

"It's in the genes," Stackpole had told him one evening. "It's the instinct to cut down palm trees and build a hut. We're jungle warriors."

"No, but I mean—you're an engineer," Leffingwell had protested, tongue thick with Stackpole's weed. "Shouldn't you be doing technological stuff like bringing electricity or running water into your trailer?"

"My man, you'll never learn. You got to leave what you do at the office." Stackpole had lowered his voice as though he were the old innkeeper about to relate the fearful legend beneath the very shadow of Castle Dracula. "Think of the alternative. As soon as the juice was in, I'd get a TV set, and every weekend I'd be watching the spots and switches I pretaped on Friday."

A moment later Leffingwell caught the glint of the silver Airstream trailer beyond a stand of pines, just as his motor died and he coasted to a stop amidst the crackling of his tires over the fallen branches and dead leaves.

They found Stackpole with two men, one small and slight, the other tall and robust and ruddy, waiting by Stackpole's Land Rover and a white Ford station wagon with a black metal clerical cross over the license plate. The short one turned out to be John Buridan in an uncommunicative mood; the taller was Holy Assumption's part-time chaplain, Father Tim Fagan, who had given the licenseless Buridan a ride in his parish's station wagon.

"Glad you could come," Leffingwell said to Father Tim, but he wasn't. Priests made him nervous.

"Yes, well, it was this or going to the Golden Agers' dress rehearsal of *Arsenic and Old Lace,*" the priest laughed. "But I've already promised to go to the performance, so this way I can nurture my fond memories of the film a little longer. The man taking Cary Grant's role is seventy-nine, if you know what I mean." He shook his head and smiled. "And you must be the Elephant Man."

Elephant Man tipped his head, but he seemed preoccupied, as though he were staring through his veil at the priest's face.

"It's a proper name," Leffingwell corrected. "No 'the' in front of it. And just call me Leff."

"Still haven't figured out a name for yourself?" Stackpole asked, flashing a smile at Elephant Man. "Well, it beats 'U.B.,' anyway. Leff, the sound camera's in the Rover. I rented thirty-five millimeter—if you want to try for theatrical distribution, you got to go thirty-five, even though the film's twice as much."

Leffingwell shrugged. "We're all right. We're starting to get a little money."

"I heard," Stackpole said. "Dawn mentioned some mail donations."

"Enough to cover film, anyway," Leffingwell scowled, wondering exactly how many people the altogether too efficient Dawn had confided in, even if Stackpole were the third partner.

"Anyway," Stackpole went on, "we better head on up. Mr. Buridan here tells me he's got to be back by noon."

"I've got to coach this afternoon's game with Powers Regional High," Buridan said. "They're going to cut us to ribbons."

"I keep telling you, John," said Father Tim, "you can't take these things so seriously."

"Do you know what I think?" Buridan said confidentially to Leffingwell. "I think those kids are losing games on purpose, to get rid of me. I think they're pawns of the trustees. They haven't let me win a game for ten years. Do you know what I am?"

"The coach?" Leffingwell asked.

"The butt of the Northeast Central Regional Athletic Conference."

Stackpole swung his door open to put an end to the talk, and all five clambered into the Land Rover: priest, philosopher, weatherman, cameraman and monster. Stackpole had Elephant Man sit in the front because of his bad leg, and the other three squeezed into the back, as they jounced from stone to stone along a road apparent only to Stackpole. Buridan announced he expected to be killed.

The fog grew thicker as they drove further and further up the mountain's shoulder; Leffingwell could no longer see anything of the peak, but he was sure it was entirely obscured by clouds, despite Stackpole's promise that it would burn off by the time they'd walked the last part of the trail to the summit.

The trees amongst which they passed were generally small and close together. "This was logged for hardwood back in the twenties," Stackpole called over the motor's whine. "Strongest trees haven't squeezed out the weak ones yet. Would you believe this whole mountain was stripped naked in twenty-six? Ran in a railroad and an old Filer and Stowel logging engine."

"Where do you learn all this stuff?" Leffingwell asked.

"No television."

At last the forest began to thin and the trees were more twisted and gnarled. Stackpole let the Land Rover bump to a stop and set the emergency brake.

"We got to walk the rest of the way," he announced. "Too steep for the Jeep."

His voice's echoes came back muffled by the fog and trees below, and Leffingwell was suddenly aware of the chorused hollow drips and patters of the beaded rain dropping from higher to lower leaves. Occasionally there came the distant snap of a twig as an animal, frozen at the sound of the intruders' approach, decided at last to risk dashing away.

There was a sharp slap. Buridan struck his own face again.

"You all right?" Leffingwell asked anxiously. All he needed was to have his philosophical advisor go off the deep end.

"No-sees," Stackpole explained.

Silently they formed a single column behind Stackpole to follow a path ribbed with roots exposed by the rain's finding its way back down the mountain. It wound upward into the fog between boulders clustered like maggots where the retreating glacier had abandoned them ages ago. The only sounds were the steady tramp of their feet and an occasional slap when another small stinging thing struck.

"I've really got to rest," Elephant Man said at last. He had been protected from the flies by his heavy veil and hat, but his bad leg was obviously bothering him, and he had been falling farther and farther behind. He dropped onto a fallen tree where barnacles and fungus, flowers of decay, glowed with livid whites, yellows and scarlets in the gray light.

A needle of pain drove into Leffingwell's cheek and he slapped. He was damp with fog and sweat, hair limp and clinging, and he was annoyed at stopping where it was too dark to film.

"See that trunk down there, E.M.?" Stackpole asked as Elephant Man limped up and sat down. "See how the bark is all chewed off at the bottom?"

"Yes," said Elephant Man.

"Porcupines. They have meetings, I think. They all get together around these meeting trees and eat the bark and figure out how to run the forest."

"Porcupines. They have those stickers on them," Elephant Man mused. "I'd always imagined them alone."

"What'd he say?" Stackpole asked.

Leffingwell translated.

"Shit," said Stackpole, "even a porcupine's got to make little porcupines. Nothing's so ugly it don't mate." He stopped himself short, but Elephant Man either didn't mind or didn't make the obvious connection. The huge bee-keeper's hat nodded in agreement.

"Reminds me of Moses," Father Tim said hurriedly to change the subject, gesturing toward the veil. "When he came back down from Mount Sinai, you recall, he wore a veil to hide the glorious shining of his face from other mortals."

"I don't recall," Leffingwell humphed.

"Moses!" Buridan said. "There's something that's interested me since I was a child. When Moses asked to see God's face, God said it would kill him, but he told him to stand on a rock and he'd let him see his 'hinder parts.' Now I'm an atheist, Tim, but I've always wondered what it was God showed him. Does the Church feel God has a . . ."

"You're a caution, John," laughed Father Tim, but it was obvious he either couldn't or wouldn't answer.

Buridan turned to Leffingwell. "That brings to mind your promise," he whispered, "that I could, ah, see . . ." He nodded toward Elephant Man.

"Later," Leffingwell said, and stood up to go on.

A little further on they broke through the last scrubby pines. By now Stackpole had dropped back to film Elephant Man picking his way carefully along the rock slippery with fog-wet lichen. He limped even more, now, and Father Tim often had to help him across the more treacherous parts.

"Take your time," Stackpole cautioned. "It's your show, E.M."

Buridan was again beside Leffingwell. "My interest in seeing him isn't morbid . . . understand," he panted. "Had a life-long interest in the grotesque . . . kind of hobby. Comes from the Italian word *grotto* . . . used to put fancifully—oof—distorted sculpture in grottoes to amuse the nobles. Later the meaning was extended to . . . include earlier whimsy like gargoyles."

Leffingwell looked ahead at the small, squat figure in the flowing cape and oversized hat as it stumbled upward, clinging to Father Tim's right hand. The flies were gone, now, but the air was still cold and damp, and what little Leffingwell could see of the mountain above, until the fog closed it off, was empty, windswept, desolate.

"In the Middle Ages they thought deformity—umph— was the devil's work . . . physical manifestation of a cancer in the body of humankind. But they accepted grotesquery. Had to—more deformed people in those days, plague, birth defects, no medical cures to speak of. Why, even when I was little—huff-huff—at least you saw an occasional club-foot or amputee, but nowadays any oddities are shut away by government agencies. You never see—"

"Shit," Leffingwell said, stubbing his toe.

"So they were even whimsical about ugliness," Buridan continued. "For one thing—huff-huff—sin was only dangerous when it was hidden, like a disease. Out in the open, sin and ugliness were harmless folly, something to laugh at. Like Bosch's paintings of hell with all those sinners with feathers up their, you know, rear ends. Lots and lots of rear ends. Silly."

They had passed beyond even the suggestion of soil, and the ancient gray granite was deeply grooved where the glacier had dragged boulders across it to deposit them far below.

Suddenly Leffingwell looked up. Instead of the blank wall of fog, he could make out distinct, ragged wisps moving slowly across their path, and a moment later he began to see patches of blue sky beyond. And then all at once, as though an unseen hand had ripped a cloak from the mountain's face, the morning opened up and the quartz and mica in the granite began to glitter and the browns and grays about them glowed sienna and umber in the golden light. Off to the right and below appeared the valley, still gray-white with fog where the sun hadn't penetrated, but beyond, brilliant with light, rose the green-purple mantles of Mounts Meshach and Abednego, two mighty monarchs surveying kingdoms just redeemed from darkness. Stackpole started filming.

"Beautiful, isn't it?" Leffingwell prompted, hitting the Record/Play key of the cassette machine that hung from his shoulder and mentally editing and scoring the answer print with Handel's *Messiah*. He cleared his throat. "I *said*, E.M., it's beautiful, isn't it?"

"I don't know."

Leffingwell held the microphone forward while trying to stay outside the frame of Stackpole's camera. "What say?"

"I DON'T KNOW."

"Jesus Chr—you don't *know*? If that isn't goddamn *beautiful,* I'll goddamn *eat it!*"

"I'm sorry, Leff. It's just . . . well, there's so *much* of it. A television picture always has a top and bottom and sides. This . . . goes on *forever*. It doesn't seem real."

Leffingwell looked up to the heavens and shut off the machine. "All right, we'll just go with the *Messiah* and do a voice-over later or something."

"I think he's just a little overwhelmed, Mr. Leffingwell,"

said Father Tim with a nervous glance toward the camera to see if he could edge closer unseen to offer comfort.

"Have you ever heard of a 'Claude glass'?" asked Buridan.

"Jesus *Christ!*" bellowed Leffingwell. "I'm losing my mind!"

"They used to carry them in the eighteenth century," Buridan went on. "They were mirrors with picture frames, so instead of looking directly at nature, you could turn around and see it like a framed painting. Some of them were even tinted to look like the varnish glaze of the Old Masters."

"It makes me very lonely," Elephant Man said as Leffingwell motioned the others back to clear the view for Stackpole's camera. Elephant Man stood apart, hunched before the glorious panorama in his cloak, his weight on his good left leg. "It makes me think about, well, a higher power. Don't you think so, Leff?"

"Never got the knack for higher powers," Leffingwell snorted, relieved that he alone could understand Elephant Man's indistinct and slushy speech. "Nothing over two cubed."

"Three cubed," mused Elephant Man. "That would be a kind of perfection because it's the Trinity raised to its own power."

"What's he saying?" called Stackpole.

"Where'd you get that?" snapped Leffingwell.

The hat and veil turned toward him. "I don't know. It just came and went all of a sudden. I don't remember anything else about it."

"Perhaps you were raised in the Church," Father Tim said.

Leffingwell stuffed his hands in his pockets angrily. So the priest could figure out what Elephant Man said through his slobbering without Leffingwell's help. The last thing he wanted was the religion angle—he hadn't considered it for a long time. Suddenly he became aware of the whirring of Stackpole's camera. "Why're you filming *this?*"

Stackpole kept his eye at the finder. "Whose picture is this, my man? Do you just want what Buridan makes up, or do you want what really happens?"

"What really happens, of course. I never said we should fake anything. But why bother with this? It's not like going to his first opera or anything."

"This could be what we call a religious experience," Father Tim said gently, "if you can have one in the middle of a crowd."

"Yeah, right," muttered Leffingwell.

"What's the matter, you never have a religious experience?" asked Stackpole.

"Of course I have," Leffingwell blurted. "Even had a vision once. My mother let me stay in the car while it went through the carwash once. Water's drumming on the roof and cascading over the windshield and everything, and then through the streams of water I see something. It's the Sacred Heart of Jesus. Knitting. The Sacred Heart is knitting this afghan. Then it says, 'I'm checking out, kid. Take any messages and tell them I'll call next time I'm in the neighborhood.' "

Leffingwell was suddenly conscious of how the echoes of his anxious, high-pitched chatter filled the mountaintop, but at least they were no longer pressing Elephant Man on the religion thing.

"God sometimes works in strange ways," Father Tim managed at last, his face perfectly blank.

"I guess so," Leffingwell said. "My mother died about a month after that." For some reason he suddenly remembered Mount Golgotha School for Boys where his desperate grandparents had sent him afterward, despite its reputation for fire-breathing Protestantism. He had been one of five Catholics allowed to drive to mass in town wtih a reedy little math teacher named Mr. Tendril, the only confessed RC on the faculty. The whole thing had been so shabby, Leffingwell had converted just to stop being an outcast and go to chapel with everyone else.

"I'm cold," said Elephant Man.

"Just hang on a few more minutes and let me get around for more of the south face," Stackpole said. "I can get a good side light on you, and there's a dairy farm partway up the mountain, so the background's more photogenic."

Leffingwell watched Stackpole angle off to the side. The mountain hadn't been a good idea. In fact, none of it had been a good idea. After all, if he hadn't been able to get that boa constrictor to stay in the actor's pants when he was working from a script, how in the world could he expect to get anything to work when he was dealing directly with life, which was always unpredictable, perverse and pointless? How did great artists elevate human passion, thought and action above the banal when all they had to draw on was mere shabby human experience? How could you get the idea for a Hamlet from people?

"What else were you planning for the film, Mr. Leffingwell?" Buridan was asking. "Will you show his face?"

"I think I'll do something with his boyhood."

"Oh, very good. You mean about his religious upbringing?"

"No, about his mother," Leffingwell answered with a malevolent gleam in his eye. Already he was filling the silver screen with the sad and solemn face of the adulterous young nun. He'd send a complimentary ticket to the meddlesome Father Timothy Fagan and watch him squirm.

"Mother!" Buridan breathed. "Of course—I'd never thought about that. And if he'd been born during the Spanish Inquisition, she'd have been burned at the stake for fornicating with the devil. You know, when the Suprema turned someone over to the secular authorities for incineration, it was called 'relaxation'—nice turn of phrase, and my doctor's always telling me I need more of it. Where does she live? Will you interview her?"

"No idea," Leffingwell said. "E.M. doesn't remember anything, and all we have is a picture."

"A picture! Can I see it? Does she look like him?"

Leffingwell glanced at Elephant Man alone on the ledge, framed against the rolling dairy pastures far below.

"He ought to be a little more careful," Buridan observed. "One time a man using a Claude glass was contemplating a romantically wild vista behind him in his mirror, but when he stepped back to frame it better, he went right off a precipice. Wasn't found until the next thaw."

Leffingwell was digging in his wallet for the picture. "I've been meaning to give it to him, but I don't think he'd let me have it back. I mean, he's normally passive, but this is something special in some way." He looked up. "Look like you're enjoying the view, for Christ's sake!" he called. "Look thrilled, will you? Fake it!"

Elephant Man turned slowly and stood with his arms dangling at his sides, gazing forlornly out at New Hampshire and Massachusetts receding dim and blue into the distance. "It's making me nervous," he said. "I don't like it."

"Nobody cares," Leffingwell said.

"Mercy me!" Buridan exclaimed. *"This* is his mother?" Everyone but Stackpole turned at the sudden shout.

"Is that my picture?" Elephant Man called plaintively. *"Please,* Leff, let me have it."

"You *know* her?" Leffingwell asked, ignoring his star.

"Know her!" said Buridan. "It must have been cut out of a yearbook from *ages* ago, but there's no mistaking—"

At that moment, Elephant Man, returning anxiously along the lichen-covered ledge to get to his photograph, suddenly gasped and his legs shot out from under him. He hung suspended for an instant, his fireplug body thrust forward, his good arm reaching out to break his fall onto ground that was no longer quite under him, his broad hat askew and his cape streaming behind him. And then soundlessly he dropped from sight.

"Jesus Christ, Jesus Christ!" Leffingwell wailed, his words torn from him by the wind and dragged away into the absolute silence of the high and empty air beyond. "Only I could bring a million-dollar idea up two thousand feet and drop it off a cliff! What an asshole I am! Stackpole, how much of that did you get?"

But Stackpole had already dropped his camera and was scrambling over the rock ledge in the direction Elephant Man was probably still falling, while Father Tim ran to the left to find a less precipitous way down.

"Mercy me," Buridan chirped.

"Would you kindly get stuffed?" said Leffingwell, scrambling after the others.

Chapter 15

Macduff

Elephant Man saw only flashes of light and dark through his endless spinning, heard more than felt the crackling branches break as he plummeted through them. Then something exploded beneath his back, tremors flashed to every extremity, air was driven from his lungs. He lay gasping and empty as before his eyes the air of breaths he couldn't take danced with shimmering, waterlike globules that rose dizzyingly upward.

There was a moment of profoundest calm and quiet, the sky above him white as a vast stone tablet where he might, given the chance, have read the secrets of the universe. Something appeared above him, a monstrous head transfigured into a golden splendor by the sun.

"Moo," it said.

And then darkness crept inward from the corners of his vision, constricting the brightness into a smaller and smaller circle until it was only a point of light, and then it was gone.

Again and again he strove to climb up from the darkness, occasionally as he neared the top catching glimpses and fragments. Someone—Stackpole?—shouting, "I've found him! Over here!" Feet crashing through the brush behind. "Shoo, Bossy! Get on out!" More footsteps thundering up around him.

"Dear God in heaven, is he alive?"

Of course I'm alive, he thought, drifting back into the dark. And I'll be right back after this important message.

"—to the Land Rover—"

"—mercy me, the nearest doctor—"

Doctor. Litter. *Littultaim. Ahlittultaimayjor weenedalittultaim.*

The snatch of light turned gray, like the mountain's morning fog. Fog at Durwood's house. Fog piling above the river in great puffy mounds and then spreading outward, rolling up the banks and rising faster than the new sun.

It would stay storm-dark until eleven, when the pale disc would begin to burn through. Then the oak tree would emerge from the far end of the playground, and finally the slope down to the river would appear behind it.

With another boy he was leaning against the stone wall near the oak. The stones were wet-black, and the cold came through their sleeves like electric current where their elbows rested on the wall. They watched the wisps of fog moving through the diamonds of chain-link fence above them.

Walther's around today, you know, the boy said.

He watched the fog merging endlessly with the fence.

He told Sister Elizabeth he was smelling funny things. That always gets them because once he actually did smell something funny and he had this fit. Now he says it when he don't feel like school. Like my stomach aches.

Most of them went across the street in the morning and then the ones that moved on chairs or had things strapped on them went outside and a yellow bus came and took them away till afternoon. Then he would have to sit with the littlest ones, or Kevin when he was sick, and Sister Catherine would make them sing or handle pieces of wood with little wheels and squeeze the things with flapping eyes saying *waa* until recess when he could go into the fog and be away as long as he answered whenever a sister called his name.

I saw him when Sister Elizabeth was taking my temperature. He rubbed his sleeve under his nose. *I don't get Walther. Who'd want to stay here? Up in sixth grade you change rooms and everything. But I guess he's always getting in fights and stuff.* He rubbed his nose again. *Hey, how come you're not talking? I mean, I'm your new friend and all so you're supposed to talk to me.*

There you are. A shape appearing out of the fog, something in one hand. A stick. *I was looking for you. They let me get up because I said I wasn't smelling stuff any more. It was close, though—thought they were going to send me to class late.*

Hi, Walther.

You got the creep with you again? Does it talk yet?

He talks better all the time, don't you, Macduff?

Well, who cares? said Walther. *Hey, look at that.*

The stick rose and pointed at a small black and yellow striped thing clinging to the wet rock of the wall.

They can't move when it's cold and wet like this. Walther reached until the stick touched the bottom of the thing. *And it's old, too, like all summer old, which is like a hundred years old. You ever touch a bee?*

They got germs and everything, Kevin said, and the sleeve went across the nose with a snuffling sound. *They walk on dogshit all the time. I think they eat it.*

Those are flies, Walther said. *God, are you gross, Mooney. Anyway, flies don't eat it, they just like climbing on it. Frogs spend all their time in water, but that doesn't mean they eat it.*

Yeah, well, frogs eat flies, Walther, so there.

He thought about Froggie bending down to lick the bee off the stone. He walked beyond the stick to touch the bee where the stick had. He could barely feel it at the end of his finger.

Don't do that, Kevin said. *You want to get sick and die?*

Old? he mused. *Like Sister Agnes?*

Yeah, Walther said. *Say that bee is Old Pit. Watch this.* He put the end of the stick on the bee and pressed and there was a crackling sound like the yellow puffs when you ate them, and then the stick came away and there was a black splotch of wetness on the stone with a hair-thin leg dangling from it.

Why did you kill it? he asked.

Then the stick was in his face and Walther was holding it there. At the end of the stick hung a yellowish glob, a bit of wing, another leg. *Cause bees are bad. They sting people. Buzz, buzz, BUZZ.*

The stick came closer to his face and he looked from it to Walther's face and Walther's eyes looked away and then Walther went toward Kevin.

No! Kevin yelped. *Don't touch me with it! Help me, Macduff!*

It's dead, he answered calmly. *It doesn't work now.*

Help! No!

Keep it down, Walther hissed. *If Froggie comes over here, I'll really fix you. I'll put something in your supper and you'll wake up dead tomorrow morning.*

What's the matter over there? A black shape was coming out of the fog toward them.

Nothing, Sister Catherine, Walther said.

I might have known Macduff would be involved. What were you doing to Kevin, Macduff?

The sounds of the other children were very far away.

Nothing.

That's no way to address me. Use my name. Use it. Nothing what?

Froggie, he said.

You beast! she snarled, and her hand came from nowhere and pain splashed through his cheek. *I'll speak to Reverend Mother about this. Walther, put that stick down. Sticks are dangerous.*

Yes, Sister Catherine.

Thanks, Mooney, you bastard, Walther said when she was gone.

I couldn't help it, Kevin whimpered.

Yeah, well you just wait till supper, squealer. You just eat up, and about ten o'clock you'll start puking and puking till your heart falls out. I got this special stuff from a kid I know.

Please, Walther, no.

Walther was silent a moment. *Hey, want to see something?*

No.

Look, I won't put the stuff in your supper, so long as you keep quiet next time. Come on.

He led them along the fence to a place where the chain links were loose at the bottom. He pushed them up and crawled under, and then waited for the other two. Kevin held the fence for Macduff. Then they walked along the fence until they could see the building's dim shape emerge from the fog.

Isn't this where the bees live? He thought about how Kevin had acted, and he began to feel afraid.

So? Walther's voice was strange and distant.

The Sisters all said keep away, Kevin said. Froggie said they could swarm on you and sting you to death.

There were so many, he thought. All alike.

They won't do anything now, Walther said. It's too cold. What are you going to do?

Get rid of them, Walther answered.

You better not. Kevin's voice was frightened. Reverend Mother said—

God, what a moaner you are, Mooney. Just watch. Here, kid, what's-your-name, stick this in the hole there.

Walther forced the stick into his hands, but he did nothing.

Do it or I'll break Mooney's arm. Walther twisted Kevin's arm behind his back.

He hesitated, even more frightened, then went up to the sealed door and put the stick into the hole. When he took his hand away, the stick stuck straight out.

Now who's afraid of bees? Walther gloated. Look at it, will you? It looks like a boner. Hey, want to see something else? Something really good?

What, that Mercury Montego model you bought with the money your old man sent you?

Naw, I stuck matches in it and crashed it yesterday.

Are you going to show us a squashed fly? he asked.

No, this, he said, unzipping his fly. His face was flushed. I was trying it this morning and it finally happened. I been doing it all day. I just make it hard by squeezing it—

Kevin looked anxious. *That happens to me all the time in the morning. It just means you got to pee. My stomach's starting to hurt.*

Yeah, well, when I start pulling, this white cream stuff comes out. Come on, you take yours out and let me see. We can do it together.

No. I feel sick.

But I'll be doing it in front of you.

Nobody asked you to, Kevin said.

It's how you make a girl have a baby. You just grab her and pull down her panties and stick your thing up her ass and then jack off.

I knew you were making it up, Kevin said. Nobody's going to let you do that.

You make her, that's all. Walther laughed deep in his throat. There were flecks of spittle at the corners of his mouth. *Once you start doing it they like it. Girls are different.*

Kevin turned away. *I think it was dumb burning up that Montego. I wish my mother sent me money. She just sends me these retarded presents. Last Christmas I told her I wanted Evel Knievel and his stunt cycle, and you know what she sent? Steve Scout with a Boy Scout uniform and a Steve Scout weather station and two signal flags. God, it was dumb.* Your mother ever send you money, Macduff?

I never had one.

You mean she's dead?

He thought very carefully. *No, she just never was.*

That's crazy. Everybody's got a mother.

Maybe Mother Margaret, then, he said.

Walther stared at him a moment, then turned toward Kevin. *All right, if you don't want to see mine, let's see yours.*

No, Walther. I said no.

Come on, let's see it.

I feel sick, I told you. No.

Walther pushed Kevin down and climbed on top of him, digging at Kevin's crotch as Kevin tried to draw his knees up and roll to one side. The bigger boy straddled Kevin's legs, forcing them down with his buttocks like an attacking bee lowering its abdomen to strike, his erection spearing from his open fly like a stinger, still digging with his hands. They were both giggling hysterically.

He grabbed Walther's wrist. *Let go of him!*

Suddenly a dark figure loomed over them. Walther, still straddling Kevin's thighs, doubled over and tried to turn away to hide himself, but his posture held his fly open. Mother Margaret saw. *Stand up,* she said.

Walther dismounted and struggled up with his back toward her, zipping his fly. Then he faced her, wiping his knuckles on his pants leg.

Well, this is a fine scene, she said. *Sister Catherine has been everywhere looking for you three. What have you done to the bees?*

I feel sick, Kevin said.

Then go to bed, she snapped. *And keep your hands on top of the sheets. I'll send Sister Infirmarian.*

I've got to talk to you, Walther said, shifting nervously.

About what, Walther?

Walther's glance caught Macduff's. *About, oh, uh, nothing, really. Forget it.*

"What's the difference whether it's his real name or not?" Leffingwell's voice was saying from high above. "It's the only one he's got."

There was a sigh. "Is that 'Man, Elephant,' or 'Elephant, Man'?"

No, he thought, trying to make his voice give the right answer.

"Jesus!"

"Now we're getting somewhere. 'Mann, Jesus.' That's at least a name I can work with. Puerto Rican?"

"Can we get him to a doctor?"

"Not without the forms. You're just holding everything up. Was it a family fight or are you going to try to tell me it was a household accident?"

The name, he thought, the name. . . . And then he was falling again, upward, up stairs . . . marching up the stairs with Kevin. Behind came Walther and Mother Margaret.

But I'm starting to smell funny things all over again, Walther was saying. *He made me do it, the little one. He's some kind of freak, he never had a mother, he even said so, and he's got these weird mental powers or something and he made me go with him and watch while he—*

Nonsense, Walther. Why did you stop up the bees' nest?

He did it, I tell you—ask Kevin. He's like some Frankenstein monster, I know it.

Then I'll attend to him. Go to your room, Macduff, and wait for me. As for you, Walther, I think you'd better go to class and we'll discuss this later.

Walther stopped, his body stiffening. He began to sway. Mother Margaret gasped and reached out to him, but he gave a shrill scream and toppled backward away from her, landing flat on his back, arms above his back and legs pointing rigidly up the stairs.

A seizure, a seizure! she called. *If only I'd believed him—*

Sister Catherine was coming up the stairs, tearing a strip from the hem of her habit. She pried his mouth open and wadded it inside. Suddenly the arms and legs began to jerk and Sister Catherine clung to him to keep him from rolling further down the stairs. Other boys were coming down the hall and crowding in behind Macduff and Kevin to see, while below, the sisters were running from their quarters.

It was over in a few minutes. Sister Catherine and Mother Margaret helped Walther to his feet. He looked around sleepily and didn't recognize Macduff when he was led past him and down the hall to his room.

Again now Elephant Man heard the voice of Dr. Herzberg *open your eyes and let's see into the depths of your soul* droning through the rerun of Walther's examination later that *just what I thought no one home* morning. Again he saw Walther come out *big enchilada* deliberately looking away and go to the hall door *like a stinging bee lowering its abdomen to strike* to pack and be taken to the hospital for observation. Again Sister Catherine rose and brought him into Reverend Mother's office for his own *he's just fine but if you see the rats stagger out of their holes and fall over dead take two aspirin and call somebody else in the morning* examination.

And then afterward, shirt buttoned again, he stood alone in the outer office and heard the voices through the door.

No need to apologize, Dr. Herzberg was saying. *I was planning on coming by anyway. Kevin Mooney's tests came in last night. Guess I should have called right away, but I thought it would be better in person.*

What is it? said Reverend Mother.

It's a mistake they warn you against in med school. Nausea, dizziness, ringing in the ears—they could mean a lot of things, but I spotted the enlarged spleen and lymph glands two months ago, and the reticulocyte count was normal and a sternal bone marrow puncture turned up negative. Everything pointed to anemia. The tests yesterday were just routine precautions after you told me about the joint pains and stomach aches. But this time the puncture was positive and the white cell count was sky high.

You mean—?

Acute lymphocytic leukemia.

But he'll live, of course. They're treating leukemia now, aren't they? There's all the work by the Jimmy Fund—

There's always hope, ma'am. Chemotherapy. The chance of a spontaneous remission.

But not much in Kevin's case—that's what you're saying, isn't it? Should we . . . should we tell him?

What good would that do? Herzberg said. *Nowadays everybody runs around being so honest with kids, the kids are unbearable. You know what I think? I think honesty is a lot of bullshit.*

Doctor, said Reverend Mother's voice at last. *I remember reading somewhere leukemia was connected with a virus in some way.*

You're worried about an epidemic?

Well, yes.

It doesn't work that way in humans, as far as we know. It's not Asian flu.

But there are viruses?

Some Herpes viruses are associated with some cancers. And they've transferred cancers from sick to healthy rabbits and rats, but that's with laboratoy serums. No, it's only the boy himself you've got to worry about.

Poor Kevin, she murmured. *So little time.*

Littultaim. Ahlittultaimayjor.

She stood in the doorway to his room at lights out that night, her face gray. *I spoke with Kevin, Macduff,* she said. *He told me Walther was the one who made you put that stick in the doorbell hole.*

He sat silently, imagining bees in the dark crawling over one another, stingers out, dripping trails of venom.

I suppose you have a right to be angry, she said. *But I have to be Reverend Mother to every boy here and sometimes I have to act before I'm able to find out the whole truth. I'm sorry about giving you the detention before I knew the facts.*

He nodded. *Like a real mother,* he said, looking anxiously to her.

She didn't seem to hear. *I was just upset because it would have been so wrong to let the bees die. God filled the world with as many different creations as he could— that's what makes them all beautiful. You can't be like Walther, afraid of things just because they're different. Thank goodness we saved them in time.*

So little time for Kevin, he thought.

Littultaim. Ahlittultaimayjor. Weenedalittultaim. Time. Little time. A little time, Major. We need a little time.

Time? What for? I can see the scientific interest of this thing, Carpenter, but where's the practical application?

Far away was the constant hum of some machine.

What Dr. Carpenter means, Major, is we can't give you practical applications till we've worked out the theoretical problems. We've only just got him back, remember.

Soares, Washington has already wasted a lot of money on this, and it's my job to see the agency doesn't wind up with egg on its face. We brought you all the way down here, and all you've come up with so far is something that grows fast. It's like having ten pounds of shit from a Martian. Interesting, maybe, but not exactly useful. The decision is to cut ourselves loose and save what we can—dispose of the—

Now wait. We've already told you it's got high levels of EA's, antigens indicating Epstein-Barr. And we've shown you EB's got very attractive possible links with Burkitt's Lymphoma and nasopharyngeal carcinoma. Now we know the contagion factor of our hybrid EB's is very good through ingestion because we're using the modified plasmids in the E. coli *bacteria as a delivery package. But if the indications from the follow-up data from Butler test out—I mean, if he's actually capable of transmitting the stuff himself, we'd have a lot more than a medical textbook freak.*

What would we have?

A complete delivery system. The possibility—if we can isolate the original generative mechanism—of endless disposable humanoids like that one who can carry the stuff undetected inside wherever we want it—

> *How contagious is it? I mean, how long does the exposure have to be?*

Don't worry, Major, you're all right. And as long as we keep him drugged, no matter how big he grows, he—

The memory swung away and was lost. For a moment there was only darkness, and then he realized the black was becoming gray.

"You're *sure* these injuries were sustained this morning?" a familiar voice was asking.

"Of course I'm sure," Leffingwell answered.

"But they're almost *healed*." He *knew* the voice, he was sure.

"Gee, I'm sorry."

"Wouldn't be surprised if the broken bones were almost healed, too. The whole thing's crazy. But we'll keep him in traction a little longer and then take him back to x-ray. And tomorrow we'll start testing and find out exactly what your friend here is made of."

"What do you think?" asked Leffingwell.

"What do *I* think? Nothing. I'll have to check medical

texts, case histories—I've never seen anything like him before. Do those pouches on the right arm and back cause him pain?"

"No," he answered for himself, opening his eyes.

"Hey, E.M.," Leffingwell said, leaning over. "Good to see you. I can tell you, I thought you were a goner when I saw you fall."

But Elephant Man was preoccupied, trying to make out the doctor in the white coat.

"Any pain?" the doctor asked.

Elephant Man stared. It wasn't possible! He must have slipped back into his delirious memories. But no—the man he saw was real flesh and blood! Dr. Herzberg!

"We're going to be running some tests, Mr. Mann," Herzberg said.

Bits of dream exploded in his brain, arced in streamers of fire, fell and congealed. Elephant Man looked up, his body trembling. "Macduff," he said. "I am Macduff."

"Hey, E.M.!" Leffingwell cheered. "Is that your name? Did you remember? Hey, Doc, can you have a kind of reverse amnesia, you know, hit your head and—"

But Dr. Herzberg was staring silently at Macduff. Then he shook his head, dismissing the possibility as too outrageous. Macduff opened his mouth to call to him but something stopped him. His memories were too new. He needed time to sift them, to understand.

"Would you call the nurse and ask if they've found my beekeeper's hat?" he said, raising the sheet to spare her the sight of his naked head. "I think I need to sleep."

Hours later, when he was alone, the burning lump at the back of his throat became unbearable, and he wished that he could cry. Silently he wet the little finger of his left hand and dabbed moisture onto each eyeball. He had been wrong: the search was over, he had found his past, knew who and what he was, and it had brought him no relief. Still he wished he might someday feel real tears trickling down his cheeks. But as he lowered his head to cradle it on his knees, his eye caught something in the doorway. Dr. Herzberg was standing there, watching.

Chapter 16

Blunt Instruments

Because Macduff was miraculously recovered by the second day, he spent the better part of November in St. Joseph's Hospital. Dr. Herzberg refused to release him; he hovered at the doorway, staring, and every day he thought of a new battery of tests that kept Macduff sitting cold and forlorn in hallways far from his TV. The only concession he won was the right to wear his beekeeper's hat. For the staff, watching the strange creature shuffle past in his paper slippers and impossibly large hat and veil became a spectator sport second only to the most grisly accident cases.

But the longer Herzberg kept him and the harder he pried, the more determined Macduff became to tell him nothing of their former association, though in fact it made little difference: after three weeks, Herzberg had filled a dozen folders with test results, but he still couldn't understand a word his patient said.

In the meantime, Leffingwell visited more or less regularly. The first day he showed up with Stackpole and the camera rolling to get footage of the patient recuperating, part for another *Ten O'Clock News* science report, and part for *Elephant Man Story* on the grounds that medical sequences had big box-office appeal as long as the ailment was exotic enough for the audience to titillate itself with the thought of having the same thing without really believing it did.

"Say, you look tremendous," Leffingwell called cheerily. "You feeling better, E.M.?"

"Macduff," he said softly.

"Eh? Oh—Macduff, then."

"Please, I need to talk to you."

Leffingwell looked annoyed as Stackpole lowered his camera. "All right, what is it, E.M.?"

Macduff sighed heavily.

"Do you remember Father Tim, the priest who was with us when I fell?"

Leffingwell grimaced. "What about him?"

"I want to go to the orphanage where he works."

Leffingwell looked puzzled. "What in the world for?"

Macduff looked from Leffingwell to Stackpole and then back again. "Because," he said at last.

"I can't think of anywhere worse to go," Leffingwell said. "How about if—"

"I want to go. I have to."

Leffingwell paused. "Has this got anything to do with your past? I mean, we could take the camera and—"

"No cameras, please. I just want to visit. Will you take me?"

There was an even longer pause. "Yeah, sure," Leffingwell said.

"Thank you."

Later, in the hall, Herzberg stopped Leffingwell. "He's got no tear ducts," he said. "He wets his eyes with saliva from his finger. You know if he has relatives around here?"

Leffingwell's eyes narrowed. E.M. wanting to go to Immaculate Conception, now this. "No, why?"

"Oh, it's just I ran into a similar case a few years ago— a kid though, perfectly normal looking. Except the name— no, never mind. Couldn't be. But it gave me the idea to run a routine check on the sputum. Did you know this guy of yours is a double-Y?"

"Beg pardon?"

"YY chromosome structure. Men are usually XY, and women are XX, so the ovum is always X and the sperm can be X or Y. If an X sperm penetrates the ovum, the kid's XX, a girl. If a Y sperm gets in there instead, you've got the old XY combination, a boy. But if you get incomplete mitosis and two Y halves that should have gone their separate ways get stuck together—"

This kind of talk had never interested Leffingwell even when he was going to be quizzed on it the following Monday. "So what do I have in Elephant Man?"

"Double-Y is supermasculine macho aggressive. They did a study a while back and found it was really rare except in males in prisons and institutions for the criminally insane."

"E.M. is about as aggressive as a sofa," Leffingwell said and left.

The next several visits, Macduff kept bringing up the orphanage and Leffingwell kept trying to find out what it was all about, but the more he pressed, the more morose the creature became, answering only in monosyllables. Leffingwell also had the distinct impression that Macduff was beginning to resent the film, though what had changed his attitude Leffingwell couldn't guess. Leffingwell even apologized for the accident, though it was perfectly obvious it hadn't been his fault at all. He left in a huff, only to be stopped in the hall again by the ubiquitous Herzberg.

"There was another Elephant Man, you know," he told Leffingwell.

"No, I didn't."

"Neither did I till a friend told me about the memoirs of a surgeon named Sir Frederick Treves, *The Elephant Man and Other Reminiscences.* Back in the 1880s he found this guy named John Merrick touring Europe as the Elephant Man. I don't have the time for movies and stuff myself, but they tell me there's been a play and a film, a bunch of books—"

"You're telling me the one and only Elephant Man is a rerun?"

"Yes and no. Their physical appearances are really surprisingly similar. But of course Merrick had neurofibromatosis."

"Pardon?"

"Von Recklinghausen's disease."

"Oh."

"The connective tissue around the nerves grows, but usually only in the skin. Merrick's case was the worst on record because even the nerves in the bones were affected. His skull got so huge he broke his neck one night trying to lay his head back."

"So Elephant Man has von Richtofen's—"

"I didn't say that."

"What *did* you say?"

"I said John Merrick had it. I ordered several biopsies. It turns out the fleshy sacs on his chest and back and arm —well, they seem to be modified tissue cells with aplastic tendencies. They're definitely descended from skin and bone cells, but they're more generalized—they're no longer skin or bone, strictly speaking."

Leffingwell had discovered he didn't need to say anything, because Herzberg always went on anyway. He waited.

"Now, if some experienced pathologist were looking at the samples in a lab, he'd probably assume he was working with autopsy material from a terminal cancer patient."

"Jesus Christ!" Leffingwell said. "Are you telling me he's got cancer?"

"Not exactly," Herzberg answered. "The aplastic cells seem to be coexisting with the specialized tissue cells. And the specialized cells are coarser than you'd expect, as if they came from the undifferentiated cells rather than vice versa. But there's no metastasis per se."

"What does it mean?"

"It means he's defying every law of nature except gravity. He's up there in his room eating junk food and watching TV, healthy as a bull. I'm stumped."

After that, Leffingwell's visits became less frequent, but in fairness it must be said that Leffingwell was getting very busy. His Elephant Man update on the *News,* combining some of the mountain footage with the hospital shots and Handel's *Messiah,* produced an overwhelming response. The very next morning more contributions started pouring in, and it was all he and Dawn could do to count them.

At first, Leffingwell showed restraint. He reimbursed Stackpole for camera rental fees, and he took forty-five dollars in cash to a costume rental agency and bought Elephant Man a cape to replace the first one, now a cloth boa of black and scarlet tatters folded neatly in the closet of Elephant Man's room at St. Joe's.

But his restraint failed him at the crest of Malvern Hill when the Rambler's motor died. He sat ferociously twisting the key in the ignition for several minutes while the car answered him in anguished whines of steadily diminishing volume. He tried it in first, in second, in third. He tried it with the emergency on, and with the emergency off.

Finally, he put both hands around the steering column and tried to strangle it.

When a last turn of the key yielded only an empty click, he got out, opened the hood, turned the fan by hand, methodically wiggled every wire he could find and checked the oil dipstick. Nothing worked. His feet were getting cold and he was going to be late for work.

Smiling, he reached inside, put the shift in neutral and slammed the door. It drifted back toward him. He kicked it and it swung in and out again instantly, catching him on the knuckles and shins before he could get out of the way. Grimly he went to the rear of the car and began to push.

At first it wouldn't yield, but then slowly the trunk and bumper began to pull away from him and he heard the satisfying, gritty crackle of the tires moving over the gravel road. He gave one last heave and watched it lumber down the hill, faster and faster, the treacherous door on the driver's side flapping like the wing of a stricken bird. At the foot of the hill it left the road at forty miles an hour and plowed into a stately oak by a stone wall. In slow motion, the door snapped forward and fell away, the fenders crumpled into an embrace of the tree trunk, the hood popped up, the trunk flopped open, the driver's seat back went through the windshield and the trash can flew out the door, bounced twice on the far side of the tree and rumbled hollowly to a stop.

Leffingwell stood smiling at the top of the hill for some time, until even the hood had stopped wagging and the Rambler lay still at last. "Here's looking at you, kid," he said, and went to find a telephone.

Later he gave Stackpole full credit for the inspiration.

"You mean pushing the old one down the hill?"

"No, no, I mean your story about using your scholarship money to buy a Jaguar."

"Oh, *that*. Well, Leff, I've got to say you've gone me one better on this one."

"But it's something I really needed," Leffingwell said.

"I agree, my man," Stackpole answered. "Everybody needs a new Mercedes."

Leffingwell's acquisition of the Pride of Wilhelm Maybach coincided roughly with an acquisition made by Channel 29. Shortly after Elephant Man's fall, the local ratings service had delivered the figures for the Sunday of the

Butler Barnum Parade: they'd knocked the pants off *Davy and Goliath,* an animated children's show with a Christian moral that had taken the lion's share of 9 A.M. Sunday viewers for three years, they'd devastated a female evangelist who demonstrated the rewards of Christian living by preaching in gowns from name designers and they'd wiped the floor with *Insight, Christopher Closeup, Worship for Shut-Ins, Oral Roberts* and *Library Lions.* For the first time, WHCK had the lead in a time slot.

For two days Trammel called everybody in the station hourly, and a glow seeped through the very wood of his closed door. He had seen the future, and the future was the live remote biz. At the end of the week, two self-contained minicams and a completely equipped mobile TV van arrived. "Go for the gold," he said.

"It'll take two years for the switchers to figure out which buttons to push," Stackpole observed sourly.

"What are we going to do with it?" Leffingwell asked Lance Ricketts.

"Cover fast-breaking stories, of course," Lance answered. "On-the-spot reportage."

"Of what?"

"Whatever happens in Butler."

"What *has* happened in Butler, Lance?"

"There was a parade this year," Oberon smiled. "I imagine there'll be another one next year."

"Don't forget sports," Dick Pataud said. "Live football! Cromwell Tech's undefeated this year."

"Great," said Leffingwell. "All this for our combined raises for the next thirty years."

But the van and the possibility of live remotes gladdened at least one heart, and it was a heart that—though normally stout and true—needed gladdening, a heart plunged into the Slough of Despond. The heart of Tanker Hackett. Like the rest of him, it was finally out of traction.

"It was terrible, wasn't it?" Tanker asked Leffingwell on the first Friday in November, just after taping his first episode of *Sergeant Smile and the Tooth Brigade* since his accident in Private Cusp's Rabbit. The mocking hoots of departing third graders filtered back down the hall as they were led to their bus.

"God," squealed a distant, tiny voice. "What an asshole."

"The whole thing was retarded," trilled a second.

Leffingwell cleared his throat, still in his Mr. Laffy pants held up by suspenders. "Actually, I thought your story about being laid up by a wound from the eternal war against tooth decay was a stroke of genius."

"Don't lie to an old trooper, boy." He had removed his steel helmet to run his fingers through the bristles of his crew cut. "My audience just drifted away while I was laid up. You can't hold kids with reruns—they're fickle. And you can't fight decay from a wheelchair." He thought for a moment. "What I need is a gimmick that'll knock 'em deader than this old forty-five of mine."

Tanker Hackett was not primarily a show business personality. He was Director of Physical Education at Henry Adams Elementary School and he ran a summer institute for overweight boys, Camp Savage (whose chief counselor, Curt Stropp, was the animating spirit and substance of Private Cusp), but, up in the attic one day to see if his old WWII tank corps uniform still fit, he had conceived the Tooth Brigade in one of those visionary moments granted only the rarest of men.

He'd started out with his uniform, an even older Felix the Cat cartoon and a backdrop painted to look like the inside of a mouth. "Strong teeth makes strong minds," he'd advised his first listeners, "and if those choppers aren't polished so I can see my face in them through these here magic binoculars, I'm coming over to your house and beat the living you-know-what out of you."

Usually the script, merely a guide for the ad-libbed performance, called for Sergeant Smile to prevent Peregrine Plaque, Commie Cavity or Fatty Food Particle (all played by Leffingwell) from abducting Private Cusp, whose principal function was to be menaced in the great tradition of Andromeda and other naked virgins chained to rocks. Since Private Cusp's fiberglass suit reached (if you included the roots) past his knees, occupied nine cubic feet of space and had no eye holes, it was not safe to let him do anything but jump up and down and squeal. Usually there was a battlefield lull for the "Birthday Root-a-Toot Salute" before Sergeant Smile flossed the villain of the week into oblivion with a tire chain. That was why Leffingwell preferred Fatty Food Particle's yellow parka with the fat-globule accent pillows sewn on it to Commie Cavity's protectionless black Viet Cong pajamas and conical hat.

"Mr. Leffingwell?"

Leffingwell turned to find the priest that Elephant Man wanted to see.

"They told me you were probably still here," Father Tim went on. "I've been meaning to visit your poor friend at the hospital for I don't know how long, but I wanted to check with you first to see if there's anything he'd like to cheer him up."

"Can't think of anything offhand," Leffingwell said. What was it, he wondered, between Macduff and this man? "Say, is there any chance there was someone at your orphanage a few years back named—"

"Halt!" said Tanker Hackett. "To the rear march, there!"

"Pardon?"

"Didn't I hear you say orphan asylum?" Tanker Hackett's eyes burned like those of a second St. Francis discovering poverty.

"Many of the boys are orphans, yes."

"What do you think of that, Leffingwell?"

"It's too bad," Leffingwell said.

"No, no—don't you get it? *Orphans!*"

"Orphans?"

"Orphans! Just think of that new van outside—our gimmick, soldier! A live remote of Sergeant Smile's First Annual Orphans' Christmas Extravaganza!" His huge hands closed around the arms of his wheelchair as though around the necks of two malingerers. "What would you say, Father, to a knock-em-dead professional TV show right at your orphanage?"

Father Tim laughed. "It would certainly beat Bill Podorsky from the Waterworks doing his magic show again. In all my life I've never seen anyone drop so many things in twenty minutes. But who did you have in mind, Captain Kangaroo?"

Tanker Hackett threw out his chest. "Me."

"And you are—?"

"*Sergeant Smile.* You'd get Sergeant Smile and the *entire* Tooth Brigade."

"Is that a children's show?"

There was a long pause as Tanker Hackett slowly collapsed in on himself like an inflatable duck suddenly exposed to cold air. Then he shoved violently at his wheels and shot out through the double doors.

"Did I say the wrong thing?" asked Father Tim.

"He was already pretty depressed," Leffingwell said, and tried to explain what a Tooth Brigade was.

"Oh yes," said Father Tim, "the strange man in the goggles and Eisenhower jacket. I guess I didn't recognize him without his helmet."

"He *does* tell kids to brush their teeth," Leffingwell went on. Already a plan was forming in his mind—a way to get an entire TV crew on location free to record whatever it was Elephant Man expected to find. "But why don't you consider it? It could get you a lot of exposure, and TV's a great way to bring in donations, believe me."

"Well, the money situation *is* pretty grim. Let me check with Mother Superior. I have a feeling she'd be delighted."

Father Tim left bubbling with optimism, and Leffingwell, feeling guilty, went to his news room desk to call Tanker. He found Dawn in a lumberjack shirt and army fatigue trousers seated cross-legged on his desk, opening envelopes. "Afternoon mail," she smiled.

Mrs. Hackett answered the phone. "Oh, God," she wailed, "he went straight to his den when he got home and he's been there ever since in his sergeant jacket, just staring at the wall. I'm afraid he's lost the will to live."

"Just give him the message," Leffingwell said.

"This makes close to five thousand dollars for the week," Dawn said when he hung up. "It's starting to slow down, but I bet if you zapped them with another update report you could probably shake another ten thou out of the trees."

"What's the grand total?"

"Forty-seven thousand, less the cape, projected hospitalization costs, and the down payment on your Mercedes."

"I *needed* the Mercedes, Dawn. He's got to get around town somehow, and the Rambler wasn't *safe.*"

"Of *course,* Woody," she soothed, ever so slowly unfolding herself and sliding her legs and then her hips to the edge of the desk, pausing at the point where her body weight was carried on her arms through the arch of her back to her pelvis, thrust out, as it were, unavoidably by the desk's edge, her fatigues pulled taut by the forward slide to follow precisely the contours of her flat stomach, firm thighs, and—

Leffingwell looked away to the monitor over Lance's desk. A man in shoulder-length hair and a waist-length beard, naked except for a short, furry skirt, was squatting over a pile of sticks within which a red lightbulb simulated fire.

Ugh, said the man. *Me invent wheel!*

After all, Leffingwell thought feverishly, hadn't Claudine taken *his* new Mercedes this morning and dropped him off *again?* And she'd been so distant, even though Elephant Man's hospitalization had given her back her living room.

"Woody, I've been wondering, . . ." Dawn said. Leffingwell could sense without looking that her toes still dangled a few inches from the ground and her body was still arched like the Tappan Zee bridge across his desk.

Now me glad! said the furry man. *Now me can go straight to Crazy Stan. Him so crazy, give me great trade-in on old wheel for brand new Vega hatchback at ridiculous—*

Of course, Leffingwell thought. How could he have failed to recognize Stan Melchizedek even under all that hair? Last time he'd been a frogman. Now it was up from the ooze to caveman. Well, that was evolution for you.

"Have you ever thought about *incorporating?*"

"Beg pardon?" Leffingwell said.

"Well, I want you to see if you can follow my thinking on this one, Woody. Elephant Man is a kind of natural resource you're exploiting, right? Now, considering all the options, especially in the taxation area, and assuming that the corporation had a competent executive officer who could devote herself entirely to the business end and leave you and Stackpole free to concentrate on the *creative* part—"

The telephone rang.

"Leffingwell?" said the voice in the receiver.

Leffingwell put his hand over the mouthpiece. "It's your *uncle,*" he whispered. "Yes, Mr. Trammel," he added aloud. Dawn made a face at the telephone.

"Leffingwell, I hear you've collected quite a substantial sum for that whatsis of yours." As usual, the voice seemed farther away than upstairs.

"Elephant, sir," Leffingwell corrected. "Well, money doesn't go very far these days, you know, and then there's his hospital bills and custom-made clothes—"

"Yes, yes, of course, but the thing is, your reports went out on *our* signal, and the money was sent care of *this* station, so if any improprieties developed—say a contributor raised a question about your new Cadillac—"

"Mercedes, Mr. Trammel."

"Whatever. The point is, WHCK as a corporate entity has a legal responsibility to protect itself. Now I was just talking with our attorney, Louie Rinaldi—"

"Isn't he the one who's appealing that Bagliarini perjury conviction?"

"He's a prominent attorney, handles a lot of big cases," said Trammel. "Anyway, he thought the way to go was set up some kind of trust fund with an impartial third party as trustee—me, for instance."

Leffingwell's mind raced. "Gee, we've already set up a trust fund," he lied. "I'm the sole trustee."

"I see." There was a pause. "Well, Louie said in the eventuality of such an eventuality, you should tender us a copy of the instrument."

"The what?"

"The document making you a trustee, so Louie can go over it and . . . see where everyone stands. Said he'd send an associate over Monday morning to pick it up, somebody named 'Crusher' or something. But I'll have to get back to you on this, cause I've got a lot of correspondence—you know, applications from eager beavers wanting to be weather persons, people like that."

"Monday morning it is," Leffingwell gurgled, hanging up. He had to set up something ironclad over the weekend. If Leffingwell alone controlled the Elephant Man money, they couldn't afford to kill him. Hurt him terribly, yes, but not kill him.

He needed a lawyer. But he didn't know any. Wait— something in the *Golgothite* alumni magazine about that bastard who'd always gotten A's—what was his name? Greenbaum!—joining a law firm in Bumberry. Just enough time to make it before five o'clock and get back in time to do the weather.

"Dawn, how'd you like to take me for a ride?"

"Love to," she said. "Providing we discuss what we were discussing before."

"Anything you say," he promised, picking up the phone to get New Hampshire information.

Greenbaum's secretary had been with the firm longer than Greenbaum and apparently outranked him. She made no secret of the fact he was free for the rest of the afternoon. Indeed, she hinted, his appointment book was a virgin-white wasteland.

Outside, Dawn had Leffingwell drive her Honda because he knew the way. "Well, Woody?" she asked after a time.

"Well, what?"

"What I was running over with you before. About making Elephant Man a corporation. I don't care about titles—you could be president or something. But let me handle the business side—investments, mergers, tax shelters—"

"I don't think so, Dawn."

"But, Woody, I don't think you understand. I'm not just talking low risk and high yield. I'm talking, well, a lot of fringe benefits over the long term."

"I don't follow."

"I could, well, be useful in other areas. With my uncle, for instance."

"Frankly," Leffingwell said, "I've been thinking of moving back to L.A. I mean, doing the weather out there would be a really easy berth—it's always the same except for the earthquakes, and the news reporters handle those."

"And I'd fuck for it."

There was a long pause. Hondas were very responsive on corners, Leffingwell thought. Front-wheel drive.

"Didn't you hear me?" she asked.

"Yeah, well, the thing is, I don't know how interested the partners would be. I mean, Stackpole's already . . ."

"So what? It's *you* I'm making the offer to."

"Yeah, right, and you're very attractive, no doubt about that. But I've been married awhile, and straight sex doesn't interest me much anymore. Right now I'm into, uh, black stockings and corsets."

"I could get into those."

"And enemas," Leffingwell said desperately.

"I *love* enemas," Dawn gushed.

"But, see, for me sex isn't the noblest expression of love. Sex is . . . it's a way of humiliating another human being. I mean, take high school—you're humiliated when she slaps your hand away, or she doesn't and then you're humiliated when she cries because she was saving it. And when you finally score, it's all weird noises and funny postures. It's like toilets, proctologists, and Y locker rooms—anything you've got to take your pants off for has got to be humiliating."

But Dawn had already leaned over so her left shoulder pressed against his right arm. She ran her right hand from his chest to his stomach, and then, flattening it like a spatula, she slid it between his abdomen and the elastic waistband of his underpants.

"Why don't you pull in at the next roadside rest area?" she asked.

They arrived at Bumberry Center rather later than Leffingwell had intended, and more precious time was lost locating the offices of Roach, Shrike and Greenbaum over a luncheonette. The secretary was putting her Kleenex in her pocketbook and getting ready to go home. "In there," she said with a jerk of her head. "He's watching the read-out on his digital wristwatch."

Greenbaum was in his early thirties, medium height but slight, with curly red hair and a sparse and scraggly Vandyke, six moles and horn-rimmed glasses. He listened to Leffingwell explain the situation and picked his nose reflectively. "What school did you say we went to together?" he asked when Leffingwell had finished.

"Mount Golgotha. See, the Alumni Office finally found out where I live, and they've been sending me the *Golgothite*. Usually I just check the obituaries, but I happened to spot your—"

"Ah, *prep* school." Greenbaum looked at what was on the tip of his fingernail; Leffingwell remembered watching him do it during chapel, because Greenbaum had been in the choir and had sat at the front between the two pulpits. "I knew from the way you handled yourself it wasn't Northeastern Law. But this is going to cost, you know. I didn't get here handling out freebies."

"Oh, sure," Leffingwell said. "I just figured what the hell, if I'm going to pay for a lawyer, why not an old friend?"

"We were in the same dorm?"

"I lived next door to you."

"Funny, I thought I had a corner room."

"You did. I was on the *other* side."

"Oh. Oh, yeah, now I remember—there *was* some guy living there. Absolutely covered with zits. Was that *you?*"

"My roommate, Herbie Hinkle."

"So Herbie had a roommate? What do you know. He was absolutely disgusting—never washed his hands after he took a crap and he had so many zits on his earlobes they looked like bladders. I didn't think anybody could stand to live with him."

"He had a nice hi-fi," Leffingwell shrugged.

"Look," Dawn said coldly, "do you want to draft the document or not?"

"Pardon?"

"The trust agreement that gives us power to disburse funds as necessary for the needs of the corporation, and makes damned sure we're the only ones that can get at it."

"No problem," Greenbaum said. "You'll need a witnessed signature from this elephant person, of course."

"That's easy," Leffingwell said.

"Now, how do you want it set up? You're married?"

"Business associates," Dawn said.

Leffingwell looked at his shoes.

"And we'll also need you to draw up some articles of incorporation," Dawn continued. "I think you can use a set of standard forms."

"Say," Leffingwell said, "your father still in the junk business?"

"My late father," replied Greenbaum, "was a speculator in previously owned metal goods."

After Dawn had typed up the forms for Greenbaum, who didn't know how, he saw them to the door. Suddenly he brightened. "Durwood *Lester!*"

"Leffingwell."

"Right. Jesus, *now* I remember. You and Herbie Hinkle." He put a fraternal hand on Leffingwell's shoulder. "Jesus Christ, Durwood Lester. After all these years." He shook his head. "Say, Durwood, sometime when you've got a minute, you've really got to tell me something."

"What's that?"

"Whatever became of you?"

Dawn drove back to Channel 29, but even at her ferocious pace Leffingwell had to go on and ad-lib the weather —he gave a thirty percent chance of precipitation, since there were more clear days than rainy ones.

Dawn gave him a ride home, and she made another detour through a rest area, as a pledge of good faith. Leffingwell felt utterly drained as they neared his apartment.

"Are you sure that friend of yours passed the bar?" Dawn asked. "He doesn't act like he can handle the assignment."

"Well, he's not much in the memory department, but he got all A's. I don't know—maybe he cheated. Still, he's with an established firm—"

"Woody, they're over a luncheonette," she said, pulling to a stop in front of Leffingwell's unit.

"Hey, wait a minute," he said. "Something's wrong. I can't put my finger on it, but . . . Of *course!* That's our *Mercedes* parked there!"

"What's so strange about that? Hasn't Claudine been coming home from school every night?"

"It's not that, Dawn. Where's the Packard? Somebody's towed the Packard away! Do you think it was the police?"

Leffingwell got out and stared in puzzlement at the asphalt as the buzz of Dawn's Honda dwindled into the night. Even in the darkness he could see the pattern of the Packard's underbelly traced like a Jurassic fish in the accumulated rust and dirt deposits.

"—that overlooks the av-ah-noo—" puffed a voice. Leffingwell glanced up to see a bloated figure jerking toward him out of the darkness. Elephant Man singing?

No—it was Fern! She bore down on him, shrieking and waving her arms and shaking first one leg and then the other. A seizure of some kind.

"Hold on!" he called. "Just take it easy! I'm coming!"

He grabbed her by the shoulders to keep her from falling at the edge of the parking lot. "Get hold of yourself, Fern! You're going to be okay!"

"Course, it's better with music," Fern gasped, huffing and blowing. "You got to kind of imagine the orchestra playing 'in some seek-looded rendayvoo.'"

"What?"

"You know, 'Cocktails for Two.' You like it?"

"Like what?"

"My audition! Don't you think it'll be *super?* Ma told me all about the film you're making, and I figured—"

Oh, my God, Leffingwell thought. Under no conditions would he ever get involved with Fern again.

"What's going on out there?" It was Mrs. Adams, standing in her doorway. "You let go of my baby, whoever you are!"

"It's just me, Mrs. Adams," Leffingwell said. "Really, Fern, it's not that kind of movie."

Mrs. Adams heaved herself down the steps and lumbered toward them in her slippers and overcoat. "Durwood Leffingwell? I'm surprised at you! Fern, you get in the house this instant!"

"But, Ma, you told me to show him—"

"GET IN THE HOUSE!"

Fern slunk away.

"Really, Durwood, *you* of all people."

"Mrs. Adams, I was just trying to save her from falling. I thought she was having a fit or something."

"YOU'VE RUINED MY CAREER!" Fern screamed from the doorway.

"Honey, there's a million girls in Hollywood that got sweet-talked into thinking this was the way to stardom," Mrs. Adams shot back. "You know what they're doing today? They got ten kids and they're waiting table. Read the *Tattler*."

"I HATE YOU, MA!"

The door slammed.

"There's nothing wrong with fooling around, of course," Mrs. Adams went on calmly. "But grown men ought to stick to grown women, if you know what I mean."

Fool around with Mrs. Adams? There was something terribly wrong here, but Leffingwell was too tired to fathom it.

"By the way," Mrs. Adams went on, producing a copy of the *Tattler* from under one armpit, "'you see about this doctor?"

"Which doctor?" Leffingwell asked, turning toward his own door.

"The one that poor woman's family's suing for a cool million," she said. "He gives her some anes—, aneth—, knock-out gas so he could diddle her on the sly, and her head swole up like a beach ball and afterwards she grew a beard and died."

"Sounds like it's worth at least a million."

"Says here jury settlements are getting bigger all the time," Mrs. Adams said.

"So I hear. You thinking of suing your doctor?"

"Not exactly," she said with a strange edge to her voice. "Not unless Fern starts to swell up like a beach ball."

Leffingwell took a step toward his door, imagining Fern swelling up like a beach ball. Suddenly he stopped. Was that it? Was Mrs. Adams setting him up for some kind of paternity suit? No—couldn't be. It was too preposterous, and he was too exhausted to think about it anyway.

"Course, Durwood, I *could* use the money," she said, returning to her familiar whine. "I hear *you're* doing all right, though."

"Well, it's not mine," he said, stopping. "It's Elephant Man's."

"That's right," she said. "Nice new car you got there, by the way. But *I'll* never say anything. After all, you got to take what you can get. If you got it, spend it."

"By the way," Leffingwell asked, "what happened to your Packard?"

"I had a tow truck take it away."

"Why?" he said, unlocking his door.

"Oh, I don't know—guess I wanted some kind of change. I've been getting this funny feeling lately, like my luck is finally going to turn, you know?"

"Maybe it's just some kind of change in the weather," Leffingwell said and stepped inside.

Chapter 17

Hark, the Conquering Hero Comes

Earlier that evening, Claudine had been waiting nervously in the Cambria student union, staring at the pattern of intersecting coffee rings on the formica table top and idly snapping bits of her styrofoam cup rim inward until she reached her starting point, when she would carefully detach the shattered circlet, stuff it inside, and start again. It had been her second cup.

"Oh, shit!" a girl shrieked two tables away, leaping up to brush spilled coffee from her overalls.

When Claudine had been in college, she thought, girls didn't jump up and say shit in mixed company. It was all part of being in touch with yourself, she guessed. Jack liked seeing shit in poems, too—the more shit the better, as far as she could tell. It was like finding your roots or something.

Gloomily she began snapping away another ring. Jack—that was what had brought her here. She'd barely seen him since Encino had arrived, and those few times he'd begged off on the grounds of Muse-induced impotence. "I'm really cooking tonight. A poem's coming over me—like electricity in my fingernails. 'Um, among . . . among the greenest green of, um, grass . . . I smell the dandelion's rich perfume and—"

"Dandelions don't have any smell, Jack," she'd told him. The problem was that Encino lived just up the road in an organic vegetable commune that Jack described as "the last of the flowery sixties." Jack fancied himself a keen observer of imponderables like the differences between the sixties and seventies decade-wise, though there was always a startling similarity between his insights and items in the previous Sunday's *Parade* magazine. Jack claimed he read nothing but the *New York Times*. "Now level with me," she went on, "is this Encino really famous or is she just handy?"

"There's no law a famous person can't live within driving distance. Look, Robert Frost had neighbors, I think. Maybe even Allen Ginsberg, too."

No doubt somebody lived next to Paul Newman, for that matter, she thought. She left defeated.

. Oh, she'd tried other things, of course. A job, for instance. But the woman at the employment agency had told her she was overqualified. "There *is* an electronics firm with Affirmative Action problems that needs a woman vice president of personnel so they can keep their government contracts."

"I guess I wouldn't have the experience," Claudine had said.

"It's not that, dear," the woman had answered. "They're looking specifically for a vice president who can type sixty words a minute. I'm afraid you don't have the skills for that kind of top management slot."

She'd even tried Durwood, really *tried*, but even with the Uncle Sam beast safely in the hospital, they were more estranged than ever. Part of it was money: she'd believed his stories about getting small contributions and investing every cent in the documentary, but then one day he'd shown up in that Mercedes. He hadn't been lying for any consciously nefarious purpose—Durwood wasn't the type to run off to Brazil—but because long ago they'd stopped trusting each other.

So she was back to Jack. But this time she had a plan. Where it had come from she couldn't say, perhaps the old resentment of Sam, but perhaps also pity for the way he, and Elephant Man, had been excluded from the adult world. At least she tried to tell herself that her plan wasn't entirely without altruistic motives, but at that moment, as she hoped, she saw Encino in her greasy leathers emerging from the cashier's line with a package of brownies and a large Coke. Fighting back the surge of anxious lightness in her stomach, Claudine waved frantically.

"You flagging me?"

"Hi, Ms. Encino. Just wondered if you had a minute."

Encino sat down with an exhausted sigh and a frown at the shattered cup. "Do I know you?"

"We met after the poetry reading," Claudine said.

"Oh yeah, right. You had some beef with Jack. You a student?"

"I take courses now and then to keep busy."

"Putting off menopause, eh?" Encino unwrapped her brownie.

Claudine blushed. "I think you've got to keep on learning. Otherwise you stop growing. Do you remember what you said at the poetry reading?"

Encino chewed reflectively. "You mean about who never has a headache?" she said, mouth full of wet black brownie lumps. She wiped her lips with the back of her forearm.

"No, before that," Claudine said, looking down at her own pile of styrofoam scraps. "About that phase in your spiritual growth when you were thinking about, you know, relations with an elephant as the ultimate cosmic experience. Do you still kind of, ah, contemplate the possibility?"

"Nope. I got radicalized and mechanized."

"But if an opportunity happened by, wouldn't you, just for the sake of the experience, wouldn't you be just a *little* interested?"

Encino's eyes narrowed. "You got a horny elephant or something, honey?"

"Not quite. But I know someone who . . . *is* an elephant, kind of."

Encino leaned back, crumpling the brownie's cellophane in her fist. "What do you mean, kind of?"

"Well, an elephant *man*." The moment she said it, Claudine felt that pang of guilt again, but she forced herself to go on. "Even if he's not a *real* elephant, wouldn't doing it with him be *pretty* cosmic?"

Encino looked thoughtfully at the ceiling where a bread knife, embedded in the nicotine-yellowed soundproofing by some student long ago, hung handle downward.

"I guess we all got weak spots for old dreams," she said at last.

"Somehow I thought you'd say that," Claudine said. "I think deep inside you're really a very soft and sentimental person."

Encino wasn't listening. "It ought to be some kind of artistic statement, of course, maybe another concrete poem. You need pictures for that—otherwise, it's just a *happening*—but I think Jack's got an Instamatic . . ."

At first Claudine's heart sank. The whole point had been to separate the two of them by giving Encino a new interest. And then she realized it was perfect—photographing that great fat thing coupled with the elephant creature covered with sacs of flesh would absolutely *have* to turn Jack's stomach.

"We'll use my barn," Encino was saying.

"Oh, he's not that big," Claudine began, but Encino was staring off into space.

"Shit," she said at last, slapping her thigh. "And Catherine the Great thought *she* made history."

When Claudine got home, her stomach was fluttery and her fingers numb with elation and with nervousness over how she would broach the subject to Durwood. She went straight to the cabinet over the refrigerator where they kept their bottle of liquor whenever they had one. One of the things Claudine hated about her life was that she and Durwood could only get the money together for a bottle when they were having company, but she thought there might be some scotch left from when they'd had that dreadful Tony Capella and his wife over last spring: Durwood didn't like scotch because he couldn't mix it with Coke or Kool-Aid.

Claudine found the 100 Pipers far back in the cabinet and poured three fingers into a Bugs Bunny glass. They had been giving them away if you bought a large Coke at Burger King in Gordons Notch a couple of years ago, and she and Durwood had had dinner out there twice. She left the bottle on the counter and slid along the wall into the living room as though Elephant Man still sat there—it was for his own good, really—and slipped up the stairs. Even with him gone, the room made her wonder what it must have been like for the poor woman who'd given birth to the creature. It made her feel better about the fact that she and Durwood hadn't had children.

In the bedroom she flipped through the tattered covers of their record albums—she'd set her Lafayette stereo among the dust balls of the bedroom floor when Elephant Man had taken over the living room—and found *Sergeant Pepper's Lonely Hearts Club Band*. She put it on and lay back on the bed while the blaring voices swirled around her like the tingles from lying in a bath that was a little too hot. College, freedom . . .

Suddenly a sharp, real voice broke through the fruity, boxed sound of the recording. "Maybe it's just some kind of change in the weather," she heard Durwood saying.

She tensed, still waiting for some inspiration for how to broach her Elephant Man plan to Durwood, as she heard the thunk of the latch and shuffling feet. Krishna growled from the foot of the bed.

"Well, you're having a tall cool one, I see."

She jumped even though she'd been expecting his voice for what seemed an eternity. Nerves. She looked up and forced a smile. Durwood filled the doorway, leaning with one arm on the doorjamb, looking tired and old.

"Who gave you a ride?" she asked.

"Uh, Dawn, uh, dropped me off."

"You look worn out," she said. Somehow saying it almost made her feel sorry for how exhausted he seemed. "Why don't you make yourself a drink?"

He thought a moment. "I guess that's a good idea."

She sighed with relief when he disappeared to clump back downstairs. Another few moments of the music's peace, another few moments alone to think.

"God, this scotch really *is* terrible." Durwood was back in the doorway, making a face at his matching Tweetie glass. "Capella was right."

"What are you having?"

"*What?* I can't hear you with that fucking music so loud." He squatted and turned the volume down until the voices singing that things were getting better, a little better, were distant squeakings. "Scotch and Seven-Up," he said.

She allowed herself no expression. "Maybe the Seven-Up was flat."

"Nope, see the bubbles? It's the scotch."

She studied Durwood's lank and matted hair. When she'd first met him, he'd worn his hair close-cropped, a relic of his prep school days, like the fuzz of a fledgling bird. Or, she realized now, a large tennis ball.

She took another swallow of her drink and motioned him to the bed. He sat obediently, dandling the glass between his legs.

"Tired?" she asked, and waited. When nothing happened, she moved her hips once as though settling down, and waited again. At last she felt his hand on her haunch and she manufactured a satisfied sound.

"No headache tonight?" he asked.

"Let's not talk about it," she said.

There was silence. Then the hand began to move, kneading the flesh of her thigh. She felt a strange reluctance in the movement, as though he acted out of duty rather than desire. Maybe it was just lack of practice.

"You know that Elephant Man of yours?" she began.

The hand stopped.

"No, keep going."

"What about him?" His hand kept kneading without beginning in any new directions.

"Have you ever thought about the fact he's never made love to a woman?"

He didn't answer.

"But don't you think he ought to? You've been doing all this talk about exposing him to the normal experiences of life and all."

"What did you have in mind?"

"Goodness, Durwood, I didn't mean *me!*" She put her empty glass on the night stand and undid her snap and zipper to slip off her pants. He had never understood the luxuriousness she felt when he undressed her, and he never bothered. His sexual aesthetic was somewhere out of *Hustler* or worse. He liked her naked and prelubricated, like a set of ball bearings. And he never used his elbows to relieve her of the weight.

She closed her eyes, heard the clink of his buckle and the downward burr of his zipper, then felt his weight move onto the mattress. He lowered himself onto her.

"Durwood?" said a voice.

"Groof!" barked Krishna.

"Jesus Christ!" shrieked Claudine, rolling to one side in a fetal crouch to cover herself.

In the doorway was the unmistakable outline of the beekeeper's hat and veil. "I didn't mean to, I'm sorry," he was saying.

"Ele—I mean, Macduff!" Durwood said, backing madly off the bed and fumbling with his shirttails to hide himself as he rose. "How'd you get here?"

"Father Tim," he answered. "He came by today and we, ah, had a talk. He agreed to help me get away from Herzberg. I'm . . . I'm sorry if I . . ." His voice trailed off, low and strangled.

"It wasn't anything, really," Leffingwell said.

"Absolutely nothing at all," Claudine agreed.

"Well, I'll . . . I'll just get some blankets out of the linen closest and . . . go right downstairs."

"Make yourself at home," Claudine said gloomily.

"It's . . . um . . . really good to see you," Leffingwell said. "I'm really happy you're back."

But Elephant Man was already gone. They waited, frozen in the same postures, until Macduff's footsteps had gone down the stairs. They both sighed together.

"That's something, though," Durwood said, sitting on the edge of the bed with his pants draped over his crotch. "Just leaving the hospital like that—completely out of character."

Claudine said nothing.

"And did you notice how upset he was when he saw that we were, uh . . . you know, like the little kid finding out his parents really do it? Do you think no one ever told him about the birds and bees?"

Claudine drew closer to him. "That's what I was talking about." She reached under his pants. "Love is probably the most important single sensation. Do you want to deny him that?"

Leffingwell didn't answer.

She began stroking him. "I've found a woman that wants to, ah, introduce him to the mysteries of love."

Still he didn't answer.

"If you filmed it, you know, you could get an X rating for the movie." She pulled the pants away slowly and, lowering her head, closed her lips over him.

Leffingwell couldn't answer because he was concentrating on enduring the relentless prodding of hand and tongue despite the dull, painful throb of having already exhausted himself twice with Dawn. With all his will he concentrated on seeming excited lest he hurt her self-esteem. If this was really what she wanted, he thought, he didn't have the heart to tell her he wasn't interested. How did the characters ever manage in Harold Robbins novels? "All right," he said. "I guess you're right."

And Claudine read in his squirming and in his yes the inevitable response to her lips and tongue, even as she realized that the pungent musk she smelled and the metallic taste that almost made her gag had to be the secreted essences of her own body. With idle detachment she watched across her husband's knees the rhythmic jerkings of the stero's tone arm as it traveled endlessly along the record's final groove. The changer was broken.

Chapter 18

The Threshing Floor
of Love

Within two days, Macduff had agreed to let himself be led to the trough of love behind a procession of cameras and tape recorders. He had been so reluctant in his passive way that Leffingwell had been forced to play his trump card: he promised to bring Macduff to Immaculate Conception to meet Mother Margaret when they taped the Sergeant Smile Christmas show.

Stackpole had been almost as hard to convince, but Leffingwell had managed by being deliberately vague on the grounds that reducing the project to a mere naked outline would rob it of its subtleties and richness. Cheapen it, as it were. He elected not to mention it to Buridan or Father Tim at all.

On the day itself, the beginning of December, Krishna Gandalf II neither knew nor cared; it was nothing he could gnaw. Curled up on Leffingwell's pillow, he sullenly watched people bustling in and out of his bedroom.

"For God's sake, Durwood," said What's-Her-Name, "you can't wear that tie with that jacket! You want everyone in the restaurant to laugh?"

"Claudine, we're going with Macduff in his beekeeper's hat and magician's cape," said the Bad One. "I could wear an Exxon sign with this jacket and no one would notice."

Krishna stood up, stretching his front legs and lowering his head and shoulders. "Unnh," went his throat. Then he leaned forward, elevating his head and shoulders and squeezing out his hindquarters while an undulating tightness swept from his stomach along his lower half to a point just beneath his tail.

"Claudine!" shouted the Bad One. "Your goddamn dog's farting again."

"Grrr," went the sound in Krishna's throat. He jumped easily from the bed and walked into the water room, sniffing. Lap lap lap.

"Krishna!"

He looked up, chops dripping. What's-Her-Name stood in the doorway.

"Krishna!" she said again. She was forever using the word as though it had some mysterious significance. "What a *bad* doggie, drinking from a toilet. It's all *germs*. Now you go downstairs. Your dish is in the kitchen. Go on, now."

He paused a moment, glancing at her throat, but then padded past her and out the door because when she screamed it hurt his ears.

He stopped short on the last stair, hairs on his neck and shoulders bristling while a gurgling "Rrrr" came from his throat. But the dark shape on the sofa didn't move, and at last Krishna slunk past and on to the food place.

Sniff sniff. What was it? Sniff sniff. Not a dog. Not a cat. Sniff sniff. Not a squirrel, not a rabbit, not a mouse. Sniff. Not a child. Sniff. Not excrement. He opened his mouth and bit it. It didn't wiggle. He was disappointed. He thought if he could sink his teeth into something that moved and made noises and could shake it from side to side until the noises stopped and it hung limply from his jaws, then the uneasy feeling would go away.

Chomp. Swallow. He felt unpleasant, out of sorts, restless. Urp. He went to the counter and heaved his forepaws up and looked out the window. Something scampered past and tremors ran up his sides and a convulsion swept over him and *groof* came out of his mouth.

Something dark moved to one side of him. He lunged, raking his claws down his own shadow on the door.

"Does sweetums want to go out?" What's-Her-Name

again. "See how he's scratching to go out? And he's eaten *all* his Gaines-burger."

The wall opened, cold air against him. He lunged out to clamp his jaws around it and shake it, but instead it was all around him, blowing in his face. He narrowed his eyes and snorted and swiped his head sideways and licked his chops. His nose tingled with the faintest trace of musk. The uneasiness coalesced into a burning and a need that hunched his hindquarters. He wanted to get on top of something and hunch his hindquarters more, but then the scent was gone. He walked in a circle until he faced where the wall had opened. Then a different feeling swept up from his stomach to his throat and mouth and *groof* came out.

"He wants to come in," Claudine said inside.

"He just got out," Leffingwell answered, pouring hot water from a pan into his Coffee-Lover mug.

"He knows what he wants, Durwood. Why are you drinking coffee? We're just about to go out to eat."

"We only go around once, Claudine. You've got to grab all the gusto."

"Honestly," Claudine said, looking out the door's window at Krishna, "he's almost human."

"He probably *is* human," Leffingwell said. "The requirements get lower every year." As he picked up his steaming mug, the body dropped away from its handle, and Leffingwell watched the ceramic cylinder fall earthward like the spent first stage of a Saturn rocket. It hit the floor, spewed a tongue of coffee upward and fell to its side. Leffingwell carefully placed the uncoupled handle on the counter.

Outside, Krishna barked again.

"Are you planning to let it seep down and nourish the roots?" asked Claudine.

"No time to mop up if we're going to make it to dinner before the, uh, commune," Leffingwell said.

"Oh, all right," snapped Claudine, ripping a paper towel from the roll. "Let the dog in and see if your Elephant Man's ready to go."

"I really loved that mug," muttered Leffingwell, going directly into the living room. He found Elephant Man in front of the television set.

If we meet any crooks out there, sang the TV, *We'll even up the score.* . . . Two men were singing as they rode on a camel.

"What's on?" Leffingwell asked.

"Afternoon movie," Macduff answered distantly.

I'll lay you eight to five that we

Meet Dorothy Lamour.

"No, I mean what *is* the movie?" said Leffingwell.

"*Road to Morocco,*" Macduff said. "I'll be ready to go as soon as they finish this song. These are interesting. Hope is the fast talker, but Crosby always tricks him."

It had occurred to Leffingwell as he'd come in the door that he might, in some small way, be using Macduff. But here was this lump on the sofa telling him to wait so it could hear some thirty-year-old song—as though Leffingwell weren't about to provide this inhuman thing with a taste of what it could never have without him. Well, that was gratitude for you.

Leffingwell snapped the set off. "Let's move it."

Little was said in the car. Leffingwell was still enchanted by the sensations of sitting in the Mercedes' container of still air and yet rushing forward, the only sounds the eerie hum of the tires and the inevitable slapping of Macduff's hand on his thigh.

Oh-I-don't-want-to-set-the-world-slap-on-slap-fi-re-I-just-want-to-start-slap-slap-a-flame-in-your-heart.

"Does he *have* to do that?" Claudine asked. Only the outline of her face was visible in the glow of the instrument lights.

"It makes him feel better," Leffingwell answered, curling and uncurling his fingers over the rim of the wheel. "You go ahead, Macduff—whistle as much as you want to."

In fact, Leffingwell had found the slapping incredibly annoying, but now Claudine had said how much she hated it, the slapping provided Leffingwell with the exhilarating release bloody vengeance invariably affords.

I-don't-want-to-set-the-world-slap-on-slap-fi-re—

"You know," Leffingwell broke in for the sake of his sanity, "I never understood what people meant by 'hugging the road' till now. Those four big radials just dig their fingers under each edge of the pavement and—"

"You've got the soul of a poet," Claudine said.

I-don't-want-to-set-the-world—

"I mean, you couldn't shake it loose if you turned the road upside down."

Slap-on-slap-fi-re—

"Oh, shut up."

"Do you mean me or Macduff?"

"I mean *both* of you."

I-just-want-to-start-slap-slap-a-flame-in-your-heart-slappy-slap, slappy-slap, slappy-slap.

Leffingwell had arranged to meet Dawn and Stackpole at a Howard Johnson's near Cambria College and go on to the commune safari style. The idea of having dinner there had been a providential afterthought that would answer Claudine's eternal complaining that they never went out to dinner. For her part, Claudine had assumed that the Ho-Jo invitation was a cruel parody of her perfectly reasonable need to get out once in a while.

They waited at the laminated sign asking them to please wait for the hostess to seat them until Claudine recognized Dawn and Stackpole at one of the booths. Leffingwell kept several paces behind Claudine and Macduff as though he were with some other party, but he couldn't keep his ears from burning as heads snapped up from hamburgs and all-the-chicken-you-can-eat platters to stare at the wonderful procession. He prayed no one would mistake Macduff for a child out with its parents.

At the table, Dawn flashed Leffingwell a covert smile and then glanced aside, only to find the unseen presence behind the veil apparently staring at her. She pretended to read the little stand-up advertisement for the Friday night Clam Special.

Silence settled in like the summer river fog.

"We got an inquiry about Elephant Man from the San Diego Zoo," said Dawn brightly, trying to break the ice.

A longer silence.

"I've always liked the blue in Ho-Jo rugs," Stackpole observed carelessly.

"I think Durwood must, too," said Claudine.

But Leffingwell was preoccupied with the children's menu he had accidentally been given. He ordered the Jack-in-the-Beanstalk Special. "And a good stout ax," he added.

"Rare, medium or well done?" asked the waitress—whose laminated name tag read "Belle"—without flinching.

"Rare."

"You know, Durwood's never happy unless his meat leaves a puddle of fresh blood on his plate," Claudine confided to Dawn. "He's got the tastes of a Hun." She forced a laugh as though it were good-natured banter, but it grated like chalk on a blackboard and betrayed her. "Broiled scrod," she said to recover. "And extra tartar."

Another uncomfortable silence fell as the waitress departed.

"Well," said Stackpole, "here we all are."

"Yeah," Leffingwell agreed, "here we are."

Suddenly Stackpole slapped his hand around Leffingwell's wrist. "You see that?"

"What?"

"That dude over there staring at us."

Leffingwell sighed. *"Everyone's* staring at us."

"No, the one in sunglasses. I could swear I saw him before somewhere."

Leffingwell started at the mention of sunglasses.

"Sure!" Stackpole went on. "It's that pimp from the massage parlor!"

"What massage parlor, Durwood?" asked Claudine.

"The one where they told fortunes," Leffingwell said.

The man in the other booth had sensed their interest in him. Casually he put an elbow over the back of his seat and faced the wall.

"Just leave him alone," Dawn said. "He's obviously sensitive about too much attention, that's all. He's in a very touchy business. Really, you wouldn't believe the problems facing the small independent businessman."

There was little conversation during the meal, and Macduff seemed interested only in removing the paper-thin layers of turkey and rearranging them to expose the gray lump of stuffing underneath.

"Come on," Leffingwell urged. "Eat up. You're not *really* nervous, are you?"

"Would *you* have liked it this way?" The veil and hat seemed to be looking somewhere beyond Dawn.

"That's a silly question," Leffingwell said, startled, glad no one else at the table understood. Why in the world would it have to have been this way for *him?* He wasn't . . . well, *he* didn't look like Macduff.

"Say, E.M.," Stackpole was saying. "You sure you want to go through with this thing with the lady?"

"Woman," said Claudine.

"I think it's a trip," Dawn said.

"Of course he does," Leffingwell said.

"I'd rather hear *him* say it," Stackpole said.

"It doesn't matter," Macduff said after a pause. "I owe

Durwood a lot, and he's promised to take me to Immaculate Conception to see Mother Margaret. I'd do anything for that."

"What's he say?" Stackpole asked.

"He says he's really looking forward to it," Leffingwell translated, leaning back as Belle reached in front of his face to lift away the remains of the Jack-in-the-Beanstalk Special. "You got a dessert coming, ice cream or jello with whipped topping and chocolate jimmies."

"I'm too stuffed for dessert," Claudine said. "I'll just have a bite of Durwood's."

"You will not," Leffingwell said. "I'm looking forward to every bite that's coming to me. Otherwise I'll leave here dissatisfied, incomplete and unfulfilled. Pecan pie, please."

"Pecan pie's extra," said the waitress.

"I don't *care!*"

"Is he as much a bastard at the station?" Claudine asked, looking over toward Dawn.

Dawn smiled weakly and glanced away as though she'd just recognized someone on the far side of the room. There was something too sudden about the movement, something almost guilty. Claudine turned to Leffingwell and found he wouldn't look back. Stackpole was tracing his index finger along the intersecting lines of his paper place mat's map of every Howard Johnson's in the continental United States.

"Well," she said quietly. "Well, well. I guess . . . I guess I'll have the apple pie, then."

The ride to Encino's commune—Mercedes, Honda and Land Rover in a neat procession—was equally quiet, and when they finally found it, they discovered Jack Miasma had been right. It was a last relic of the sixties' sunlight and flowers bravely facing the present like a monastery of furiously copying monks defying the encroaching Dark Ages.

"Maybe," Claudine sighed as they bounced along the rutted driveway, "things would have been different if we'd gotten into communal living out in California."

"I hate sharing," Leffingwell said.

I-don't-want-to-set-the-world-slap-on-slap-fi-re—

"Is that how little *Dawn* feels about communes, *Durwood?* She seems to *like* sharing."

A-flame-in-your-heart-slappy-slap, slappy-slap, slappy-slap.

The house was utterly charmless, the kind put up in haste to answer basic needs and grown shabby over the years without becoming quaint, roofed in tin and covered in brown, brick-patterned asbestos shingles. Strewn across the lawn were lumpy wooden things with irregular wheels. Toys, Leffingwell supposed: they stimulated the imagination by avoiding not only the explicit representation of a truck or steamroller, but the abstract idea of either, as well. It was the kind of handcraft done by lost, uneasy, mindless people with no affinity for wood and no understanding of machinery.

Leffingwell remembered the white metal trucks of his boyhood. They'd been honest, commercial products, designed by someone who knew what trucks looked like and perhaps even admired what they did. He wondered now whether he had brought those trucks with him when he'd gone to live with his grandparents. He couldn't remember ever actually having the chance to outgrow them.

There was no need to knock on the door or even open it; it stood ajar, welcoming friends and December alike. Leffingwell stood aside and let Claudine lead the way— they were her friends, after all.

They found themselves in what appeared to be the kitchen, grease streaked and fly spotted. In the eye of the chaos, eight hairy and flannelly people still slouched at the communal supper table before unmatched plates, the routes of their forks and fingers preserved in the congealing streaks of some kind of greenish sauce. They were looking into each other's mouths, occasionally probing with a finger or fork tine like grooming monkeys.

"Oh, hi, man," said a woman, brushing back a cloud of frizzy hair. "We're checking for plaque." Her teeth were flaming pink.

"Pardon?" said Leffingwell.

"Disclosure tablets," the woman said, pushing a small bottle toward him. "Take some. Just chew one up and it'll turn all the bad-news plaque red so your woman there can scrape it off your teeth. Biodegradable, of course. Why get ripped off by some pig dentist? You want a fork or something?"

"I'll have to pass this one on to Sergeant Smile," Leffingwell said. "You were right, Claudine," he added in a whisper. "We missed the boat in the sixties. We could have been in Colorado by now, scraping each other's teeth and having nightly full disclosures."

"You, like, looking for someone?" said the woman.

"We're looking for an Encino somebody, I think it is," said Leffingwell, "and . . ."

"Jack Miasma," prompted Claudine.

"Oh, yeah," said the woman very slowly. "You're those TV people. Wow, and we don't even have a *set*. It's all garbage, you know, rots your mind away. Anyway, go through that door there. They're out in the barn. Hey, somebody die?" She was pointing at Macduff's veil.

"It's the Princess Anastasia," Leffingwell said. "Traveling incognito."

"Wild," said the woman.

At that moment a girl of perhaps six, naked except for a tattered woolen shirt, bounded into the room. "You should've seen the *sunset!*" she squealed. "It was like the *whole sky* was *tie-dyed!*"

"Dynamite, Sea-Shell," said one of the men.

"Oh, this is *freaky!*" said Sea-Shell, counting first the newcomers and then the people at the supper table. "There's *thirteen* grownups in this room!"

The table became a frozen tableau of horror, and the five intruders hurried through the door and down a narrow passageway, past a can that seemed less a receptacle for garbage than a target at which garbage was occasionally thrown, and into the barn itself.

It was even colder than outside, and their breaths smoked. On the back wall were nailed several decades of tractor license plates, and farther down were the dark, cavernous openings of the unused stalls, cluttered with hoes and shovels, about which strutted in awkward, staccato bursts several chickens. At the far end a starlike light bulb dangled by a frayed cord from a huge rafter, and directly beneath it, like an altar, a thin, lumpy mattress had been laid on a door supported by two sawhorses.

"Jesus," Leffingwell muttered to no one in particular, "how could anybody screw in this cold?"

At that moment he became aware of the thin, mosquito-like whine of a battery-powered motor, like an electric shaver. Suddenly a man of medium height emerged from the darkness of one of the stalls and came toward them, face and hair glinting with the reflections of the hanging bulb.

"Hi," the man said, pausing to push his hair and skin back with the palms of his hands. "I'm Jack Miasma, the widely known poet-cinematographer."

"I'm Mr. Laffy, the world-famous weatherman," said Leffingwell. "And this is—"

"Oh," said Jack, blinking dully in the light. "Hi, Cl— Mrs. Leffingwell."

"Hello, Jack," said Claudine, head erect. If Durwood wanted to play with teen queens, then he might as well find out other people could play the same kind of games.

"—our cameraman, Stackpole," Leffingwell continued absently, looking from Jack's face to Claudine's. So *this* was the inspiration for the enduring passion for poetry, experimental films and staying after school?

"Hello," said Jack, extending his hand. "It's always a pleasure to meet a Negro of the Black Race."

"Likewise," Stackpole said, clutching the camera with both hands to show he couldn't shake.

"I just want you to know I had no part in the millenniums of suffering you people have suffered," Jack said nervously. "I'm an Equal Opportunity Poet."

"And that's our star over there," said Leffingwell.

Macduff stood with his weight on his good leg, waiting.

"Oh?" said Jack. "Encino said he was some kind of elephant, I thought."

"Figure of speech," said Leffingwell.

Jack's eyebrows butted together in painful thought.

"Where's the, uh, woman?" Leffingwell asked.

Again the mosquito motor whine drifted through the barn's empty cold.

"Doing warm-ups," Jack said. "She'll be out in a minute."

The entire company stood awkwardly in the intense silence, glancing away from each other at the least hint of eye contact until the motor finally stopped. Leffingwell looked to see if Macduff were whistling again, but he wasn't. A moment later Encino emerged from her stall.

She was stark naked, a mass of white flesh creased and rolled but curiously featureless and amorphous except for the triangular thatch of hair at the juncture of the thighs and torso and another thatch on top of the head, tallow thighs swishing and something tied behind her by a length of clothesline slapping at her buttocks with each step.

"Howdy," Encino said, stopping directly under the light. "Hope I didn't keep you waiting. What do you think?" She turned around to display a green license plate:

```
┌─────────────────────────────────────┐
│  ○   NEW HAMPSHIRE TRACTOR   ○       │
│                                      │
│        LP1533A                       │
│                                      │
│  ○      LIVE FREE OR DIE      ○       │
└─────────────────────────────────────┘
```

"Didn't have time to do up a concrete poem," she added, "But this has a message, right? It relates."

"Leff, my man," said Stackpole, "I just cut myself out." He handed Leffingwell the massive camera. "You do anything you want to from here on, but you just do it without me."

"No, Stackpole," said Leffingwell. "Please."

"Forget it," Dawn whispered. "A three-way split beats a four-way every time."

"But *why*, Stackpole?" Leffingwell said feverishly, waving Dawn away as he followed him back through the door into the passageway.

"*Why?* It's inhuman," Stackpole said, pausing amongst the tin cans by the garbage pail. "I might have expected this from Dawn, but *you* . . ."

"We've got to think box office," Leffingwell said. "An X rating could make a big difference in our gross potential."

"This manger scene's got as much gross potential as I care to see," Stackpole said. "Look, Leff, the road back to the human race is through this door. Just turn left at the Biodegradables' Last Supper."

Leffingwell was suddenly alone next to the fetid pail, the heavy camera tugging at his arm. His faced burned. He hated himself.

"Shit," Encino was saying. "He doesn't look like he'll be all that cosmic. Let's see how elephanty his equipment is."

"Just let me get a flash cube in the Instamatic," said Miasma's voice.

"Maybe . . . maybe this shouldn't actually be filmed," Claudine quavered. "Maybe they want a little privacy . . ."

Leffingwell spun around and charged back down the barn just in time to see Encino yank Macduff's hat from his head, exposing the pink protuberances of trunk and tusks and bulging forehead wisped with multicolored hair, beneath which two glittering, anguished eyes looked directly at Leffingwell. At that instant, Jack Miasma inadvertently stepped into his path to frame an Instamatic shot. Leffingwell swung his camera to clear the way and caught Jack in the stomach: Jack doubled forward, then dropped backward onto his buttocks. He sat there paralyzed for almost a full second, as though deep in thought, Instamatic pressed to one eye, and then ever so slowly he unfolded backward. As his unconscious head came to rest on the dirt, his finger hit the shutter and the barn roof above was suddenly flooded with the flashcube's blue light.

In the meantime, Leffingwell hit Encino full force with his right shoulder, toppling her backward onto her mattress, then grabbed Macduff away as the door supporting her gave out a great creak and collapsed, spilling her onto the floor with a great *whoosh* of expelled breath. Numbly, Claudine bent down and picked up the beekeeper's hat. She held it out to Macduff.

"I didn't think . . ." she murmured. "I'm so sorry—"

"Oh, cut it!" Leffingwell raged. "You're not fooling anybody. It was all on account of this character with the Instamatic. Can't you even play teeny-bopper screwing her teacher without dragging everyone else in?"

"Well, you're no prize!" Claudine shouted back. "What do you think *you're* doing with your little fountain of youth over there?" She stifled a sob. "You're *welcome* to him!" she screamed at Dawn. "You're just going to love his chicken nightmares!"

"Please," Macduff whispered. "Please just get me out of here." His shoulders shuddered with a tearless sob.

Suddenly the door burst open and one of the crimson-toothed biodegradables tumbled in. "Cool it!" he stage-whispered. "There's a gray sedan parked out back and Sea-Shell says she heard someone on the roof. We think it's narks!"

Leffingwell thought of the man in sunglasses at Howard Johnson's, and his brain reeled with visions of Oberon Ricketts reading his arrest story on the air.

"My car," Dawn said. "If it is the cops, we can't afford this kind of publicity." She led the way to the barn's front door and out to the Honda. Leffingwell helped Macduff into the rear seat as Dawn slipped behind the wheel. Even before Leffingwell could shut his own door, Dawn was squealing down the driveway. Leffingwell looked out the rear window for any sign of pursuit. He saw Claudine getting into the Mercedes; he deliberately didn't try to see whether Jack Miasma was there, too. For better or worse, Leffingwell's choice had been made.

Later, in Dawn's apartment, Leffingwell stood guiltily before Macduff, who was drawn up on the couch, still trembling.

"If I'd realized—" Leffingwell began.

"I'd rather not talk about it," Macduff said.

"But I just didn't know what I was thinking about when I said yes to Claudine," Leffingwell said. "I even talked you into it. But I'll make it up to you, I swear."

"I wasn't made for love, that's all."

"No, really," said Leffingwell. "I want to do something special for you. The opera! Remember you said you wanted to see a live opera? Tomorrow I'll get on the phone—"

"Please, Leff. Enough is enough. All I want is for you to take me the way you promised to see Mother—"

"Yeah, yeah."

"You *promised.*"

"I *said* I would, didn't I? Didn't I tell you we're taping that Christmas special there next week?"

"All right. And no cameras when I see her?"

"No cameras."

"Come on, Woody," Dawn yawned. "I'm going to bed."

As soon as they were gone, Macduff turned on Dawn's little portable and sat wrapped in the single blanket Dawn had given him after he'd reminded Leffingwell he'd need some place to sleep. For a long time he watched the flickering faces, Richard Basehart, Gregory Peck in a Lincolnesque beard.

Blasphemy? Ahab demanded. *Speak not to me of blasphemy, man. I'd strike the sun, if it insulted me.*

And then he rose and, even before he knew what he was doing, flicked off the old movie. He sat down again, staring at the screen. In its blankness he saw Encino towering over him, flesh trembling obscenely, gradually dissolving into Walther struggling on the ground with helpless Kevin. And then behind them rose a great black shape, arms spread, calm, good, beckoning him forward to fold him in her blackness and mother him forever.

Durwood had promised.

In the darkness on the other side of the bedroom door, Leffingwell stared at the ceiling, uncomfortable in Dawn's unfamiliar bed. "Jesus," he muttered, "I should have known the minute I stepped in the door and saw the biodegradables sitting around picking each other's teeth. And that Encino —what a monster."

"Don't worry about it," Dawn said, lying down beside him. "It wasn't your fault."

"No, I guess you're right," Leffingwell said. *Halfway between the Last Supper and the Manger, tie-dyed sunset, Encino in the stall.*

"It's too bad, though," Dawn mused. "We could have used the footage."

White metal trucks with chipped paint and decaying rubber wheels, one lost or broken or something, he couldn't remember, only the crying, and his mother folded him against her to comfort him. Gone, like Claudine.

He shook his head to clear it. "Jesus," he said suddenly, "what an asshole I am."

"I told you, it wasn't your fault," Dawn said, slipping an arm under his neck.

"No, it's not that. I left the camera in the barn."

"Forget it, Woody," she soothed, drawing him to her. Gratefully he lowered his head and pressed his lips between her small, almost adolescent breasts.

"Business losses are deductible," she murmured.

Chapter 19

Pretaping Christmas

Father Tim Fagan sat in the drafty makeshift confessional at the back of Immaculate Conception's chapel, still aching with the December cold through which he'd walked this Saturday. He could hear at the altar the drone of the last boys at their penances, and he sighed with relief.

Of all his duties at his parish and at Immaculate Conception, Father Tim dreaded confession the most. It wasn't the sameness, though he sometimes joked the boys committed the same sins year after year and the Sisters never committed any. It was what the confessional reminded him of.

If it hadn't been for that, he might still have been in his own pulpit. Whatever he knew about his own weaknesses, he could at least pretend to wisdom and virtue before the anonymous strangers of a full congregation. But he couldn't bear to be closed into that tiny space and feel the weight of others' guilt mounting above his shoulders. It was like those desperate moments he'd known as a child, struggling half asleep in the hot, choking dark under nightmare-twisted bedcovers. But the child had always been able to wrench his head free, gulp fresh air, see his room's familiar wallpaper; and the priest was sworn to bury himself beneath his vestments without protest, however much the child within him might still be struggling to escape.

He'd always lowered his eyes as part of the confessional's etiquette, but now it was a compulsion, so he would not see that woman's eyes glittering through the lattice like shards of broken mirror, or remember when he had again seen her, olive skin drained a blotchy gray, sides of her blouse soaked deep and glistening red, the jagged scrap of mirror by her hand reflecting the washroom's single light bulb. Or hear the mocking litany of his advice—reassuring, resonant, fatal—replayed beneath the soaring treble descant of the cleaning woman's wail of horror.

But it was more than his usual fear of confession that troubled him this morning. Confession had gone so quickly because all of Immaculate Conception vibrated with anticipation at the arrival of the crew from *Sergeant Smile and the Tooth Brigade* at noon. That meant Leffingwell would be coming. And that meant—possibly—Elephant Man.

No matter how much he tried to avoid it, the same impossible question kept haunting him. Could the strange child he had known five years ago have become the pitiable monstrosity he had spoken with in the hospital? Were the two Macduffs the same?

Father Tim could not say what had made the thought occur to him. There was the obvious congruence of the names, of course, but that was hardly enough to justify a conclusion that so defied every atom of common sense. And there had been the odd hints that John Buridan had been dropping recently, insisting that Father Tim bring Leffingwell to his house this evening after the taping to hear what John claimed was a startling discovery.

But John had been stranger than ever this autumn— paranoid was a better word—and Father Tim knew perfectly well he himself hadn't even considered the possibility till that day in the hospital. There, when the awful reality of the sad monster ought by rights to have abolished any doubts, Father Tim had been seized by the certainty that the two *were* the same. It was nothing that was said, though Elephant Man had asked more questions about Immaculate Conception than one might have expected from a total stranger, more knowledgeable questions. It was the phrasing, the cadence, the alien quality of the thought behind the words—something indefinable that made Father Tim believe in his heart what his head knew could not possibly be.

He heard one of the boys get up and leave the altar, and

he distracted himself momentarily by recalling the joking rivalry among the Irish toughs of his boyhood over who spent the longest confessing or reciting penances. Many had found the only escapes from the nether world between the shanty and the lace-curtained house—the police and fire departments, prizefighting, the priesthood. The toll of the War and the years themselves hadn't left many of them, except Tim himself and Justus O'Toole, the little gamecock who'd been a fight manager before becoming foreman at the City Yard. Since his retirement he'd kept himself busy with custodial work at St. Anthony's, where Father Tim was an assistant pastor. Hardly the one Father Tim would have guessed years ago would become so devoted to the Church. But time had a way of changing everything.

Father Tim let himself out by the confessional's curtain and paused to watch Walther, the last, slogging his way through the rosary. Walther's confessions never matched his accomplishments, and today he'd admitted only to a desire—successfully repressed, he'd claimed—to touch himself in an impure manner. A veritable Saint Anthony in resisting the demons of temptation.

It wasn't easy for him, Father Tim thought. Now he was a gangling teen-ager caught between childhood and adulthood, but he had always been an uneasy, homeless spirit. The boys his own age had always rejected him, and he had asserted himself by bullying the younger ones. It wasn't cruelty, reality; it was the need to define the self by the reactions of others, even when they had to be extracted forcibly.

Father Tim thought of Kevin—before his death Walther's chief victim. He was ideal for someone like Walther—sickly and weak, but without an obvious disability like a brace or wheelchair that might have forced Walther to recognize any meanness in himself.

And Kevin brought Father Tim back to the strange newcomer Kevin had undertaken to befriend. The first Macduff.

Father Tim kept going over everything he could remember, trying to find the answer. Those confessions, for instance. Initially Father Tim hadn't known what was wrong with them, and then he'd realized it was their flawless perfection. The child simply aped what the other boys said without any substance. He supposed that was how all children learned, by imitation, but one day he'd tried to explain that the confessional was where you told the truth

about your real faults. "The boys don't just mouth empty
words, they're sorry and they want to make amends with
God."

"Walther wasn't sorry just now," he'd answered. "He
wasn't even telling the truth."

"Walther's not a good example of what I mean," Father
Tim had said. "Anyway, you're not supposed to listen to
the others' confessions."

Thereafter, Macduff's confessions had shown more in-
ventiveness, but Father Tim had still felt a kind of void on
the other side of the screen whenever Macduff was there.
It had made his flesh crawl because it somehow seemed to
expose the vacuum in his own soul. Well, it wasn't sur-
prising. From the little Mother Margaret had told him,
Macduff had been abandoned at the age children most
need cuddling and loving, and so he'd been robbed of most
emotions, and, feeling nothing, he'd been able only to imitate the emotions of the boys around him, from contrition
to simple love and hatred.

He looked at his watch as Walther rose to leave. Not
quite twelve, and before him lay the perfunctory Saturday
mass he'd agreed to expand for taping, the meeting with
Buridan, and . . . and seeing Elephant Man-Macduff again.
His throat was tight and dry with anxiety. Perhaps . . .
perhaps he'd take a run back to his rooms at St. Anthony's
rectory. A little early, he admitted, but there wouldn't be
any other opportunity to . . . fortify himself against the
cold.

He let himself out of the chapel and walked softly down
the hall, past Mother Margaret's office, to the outside doors.

Meanwhile, Mother Margaret sat glumly at her desk.
She had come to hate Christmas. Not because it made her
feel more powerfully the deprivation of her boys, but because it seemed to bring out the worst in other people, the
showiest and most substanceless generosities.

Wooly matrons with powdered faces and fresh corsages
would brave the wintry drive from the suburbs to represent
the K. of C. Women's Auxiliary or the St. Anthony's Ladies'
Guild and hand over a solitary canned ham, a twelve-
pound turkey, or a bag of canned goods. Or the firemen
with their good intentions and torn shopping bags of trucks
they'd fixed to run on three wheels and a thread spool, or
hydrocephalic restuffed teddy bears with mismatched button eyes. Whatever it was, she had to accept it graciously

and swallow her anger that for crippled children no one wanted, there were only castoff and mangled toys.

This year was worse than usual because her battle with Monsignor Luce and the Bishop had already brought several newspaper and television reporters. But any help was welcome, even when it meant pretending Christmas had come ten days early so that their ersatz celebration could be pretaped, edited and packaged in time to be shown for everyone else's Christmas. And what would be left for *her* boys the real Christmas morning?

Mother Margaret heard the dull boom of the front doors being flung open and the rumble of adult male voices. Dutifully she rose and walked through Sister Ursula's outer office to the hall, where she found four men carrying in heavy light stands and thick black electrical cords. Another man rushed up to her.

"Now here's the picture, Sister," he said. "What WHCK was looking to get by pretaping instead of going the live-remote route—aside from saving double-time for working the crew on Christmas—was two packages, you follow? One would be your basic *Sergeant Smile Christmas Day Extravaganza*, see, and the other would be your basic up-beat human interest story with a couple of the kids on your *Ten O'Clock* for a little Christmas hype on a slow news day. So what've you got, say, is some kind of handicap that's maybe not too noticeable for Oberon Ricketts to interview? I got an eyeful of some colored kid with his head kind of squashed over, and that's definitely what we don't want."

"That was Kermit, one of our retarded boys. You'll just have to pick whomever you want when the children come. They'll all be down shortly."

"Yeah, well, that's another thing—there's not enough room in your parlor, so I was thinking we'd get some shots of the kids in there and then get them out so we can do the show."

"You mean they're not even going to get to see it? I thought the whole point was to entertain the children."

"That's right," said Gompers. "Couldn't have said it better. Entertain the children. So we'll keep maybe five or six for audience reaction and then the rest can go play till the show's aired Christmas Day. What could be fairer?"

If she had the courage, she thought, she'd have ordered the whole pack of them out the door that instant. But the publicity, the potential for contributions . . . a million reasons for compromising instead of taking a stand.

A massive man in an Eisenhower jacket swung through the door on crutches. Behind him came a younger man in a Coors T-shirt and white leotards, carrying a huge fiberglass tooth under one arm.

"Tanker," said Gompers. "I want you to meet the head nun here, Sister Margaret. Sister, this is Tanker Hackett, better known to thousands of kiddies as Sergeant Smile."

"Who knows," said Hackett, grimacing a hello, "maybe even millions."

"My pleasure," smiled Mother Margaret.

"Curt," Gompers said to the unintroduced Private Cusp, "you go on in there so they can get a reading. It's that white tooth, you know, Sister. Drives the cameras wild. Now all we need are Hap and Leffingwell, and we're in business."

Curt hefted the great tooth above his head and slowly lowered it, extinguishing himself like the Ghost of Christmas Past. Then the tooth walked unsteadily toward the parlor.

"A little to your left, Curt," warned Gompers. "Now another thing is Oberon wants shots of the kids at the chapel service. We'll need—"

"Father Fagan will offer the mass," Mother Margaret said quickly, transferring responsibility so she could escape the confusion and animal heat by getting out the door. She squeezed past Gompers and made it into the welcome cold.

A sad-looking man was coming up the steps. His body ballooned out at the waist and his elephantine legs terminated in large black discs. A tail flapped behind him in the December wind. "Hi," he said. "I've got a message for you."

"You're a horse, I presume?"

"I'm the business end. My head's getting suited up in the van." He stopped and stared at her.

"You seem familiar somehow," Mother Margaret said.

"That's funny, so do y—uh, I mean, you've probably seen me do the weather on WHCK. Say, I hope you're not being taken in by all this schtick. I mean, the station wants to make itself look like Santa Claus. They could care less about you and your kids. Not to mention the fact we've never gotten official approval from the American Dental Association."

"It's kind of you to warn me." She looked past him to watch a small sports car with a flashing police light screech to a stop at the curb.

"Almost ready to go," Leffingwell said. "There's Oberon."

"You said you had a message, Mr. . . . ?"

"Uh, Leffingwell. Yeah, there's someone waiting in my car who's very anxious to meet you, but he wanted to wait till things quiet down after the taping. He's shy. But, uh, maybe you could come out and meet him here later on and we could, uh, film it." He looked around uncomfortably as though he were afraid of being overheard.

"I'll be in my office," Mother Margaret said. "Just tell him to let himself in."

Leffingwell hesitated thoughtfully at the door. "*Do* you think we've met before? I seem to remember your face from—"

"Let's GO!" came Gompers' voice from inside.

The decision was made to tape the chapel first, and then the audience shots of the parlor so that Oberon could leave, Saturday being her day off, while the crew went on with the *Sergeant Smile* show. Dawn was dispatched to find Father Tim. Some forty-five minutes later the boys were waiting impatiently in the chapel when Dawn reappeared with Father Tim in tow.

"Hello, Mother Margaret old friend!" Father Tim shouted, his face flushed. The idea of being taped must have been too much for him, Mother Margaret thought. He'd overfortified himself.

"We're gonna broadcast this Christmas Day, Father," Gompers said at the chapel door, "so if you do a sermon or anything, try to fake something appropriate theme-wise."

"This is the seventh day of the Octave of the Immaculate Conception," said Father Tim. "I'm not changing *that* to suit a television schedule."

"Fine," said Gompers, "just so long as it's Christmassy."

Father Tim went unsteadily into the chapel as Mother Margaret, lingering reluctantly outside to be sure everything ran smoothly, watched Capella hoist his minicam to his shoulder and flip the switch on the light mounted above it, flooding the chapel with more light than it had seen since the roof had closed over it seventy years before. Off and on it went through the progress of the mass as strategic moments were recorded.

And then, inexplicably, Father Tim chose to include a

sermon in the Saturday mass. "Christmas," he said, "is a time of great joy, but we mustn't forget, little brothers, that it is a joy bounded on every side by sorrows. On the one hand, the travail of Mary bringing forth new life, Mary whose own immaculate conception without original sin we celebrate today." He glared at the camera. "And let us not forget, on the other, the blessed Holy Innocents, those poor children slain by Herod in his vain hope to destroy the Christ he feared would become King of the Jews. Mere boys like you, ignorant of even the Lord Jesus' existence, yet they died for His sake and were His first martyrs, while Joseph, warned by the angel, fled with Mary and Jesus into Egypt. And of those first victims Matthew quotes Isaiah: 'A voice was heard in Rama, weeping and loud lamentation, Rachel weeping for her children, and she would not be comforted, because they are no more.' "

"What the hell *is* this?" muttered Gompers to himself, peering through the partly open door.

"And beyond their tragedy," Father Tim continued, "the Christmas birth is bounded by the pain and suffering of the Passion, the Babe born in December now hanging from the nails of the cross in His last human agony. But this intertwining of each Christian joy with its matching sorrows reminds us, my sons, that we must always be ready, for He is the Bridegroom whose coming is without warning."

"Bridegroom?" said Gompers. "Coming?"

"We must keep ourselves without stain to be ready for Him. We must not be like those who will at the end of time, as John the Evangelist tells us in Revelations, worship the seven-headed Leviathan, which will rise from the sea and be given dominion over men for forty-two months. We must not receive the beast's mark on our hands or heads, we must not be misled into false faith when the beast's wound is miraculously healed, we must not be betrayed into worshipping the Antichrist, for he and his followers and the great Whore of Babylon will, as John assures us, be cast down into perdition when the angels shall at last pour down those seven vials of wrath that shall turn sea and land to blood, and darken the beast's throne, dry the rivers, cause the earth to quake and cast down the sun itself at the end of time."

"Kill the lights!" Gompers stage-whispered into the chapel. "Who needs *this* on Christmas?"

And the little world of the chapel was plunged into sudden darkness.

Mother Margaret stood waiting in the hall, her ears burning for Father Tim until at last he announced, "Go, the mass is ended," and the boys responded with a heartfelt "Thanks be to God." She met him at the door and hurried him to the daybed in her office, reemerging just in time to see all but the six most docile boys dismissed after the audience shots and sent upstairs. A moment later a horse's head on a pair of human legs appeared in the hall and paused, swaying. "What's that running down my—?" it began to sing in a gruff voice when someone shrieked "Hush!" and pulled it ("Said the fair young maay-den!") into the parlor to be coupled to Leffingwell. The lights came on again.

"Front and center, Private Cusp!" barked the man in the Eisenhower jacket, now decked out in helmet and goggles. "What's the day to*day?*"

"A snip-snap tip-tap *hap*py day, Sergeant Smile, sir!" came a muffled voice from deep within the pith of the bouncing tooth, as it rolled like a tanker in heavy seas. "And what's our first car*toon* for Christmas after*noon*, sir?"

Mother Margaret quietly closed the door and sealed herself back inside her office. With a glance at the sleeping form of Father Tim on the daybed, she settled herself at her desk.

The four o'clock December dusk had begun to gather before he stirred.

"Holy Mother of God," he said, sitting up and rubbing his eyes. "I really did it, didn't I?"

"Oh, I wouldn't worry," she said kindly. "I've read all about editing. They can turn whatever really happened into anything they want. That's why they call it the miracle of television. I imagine they'll edit your sermon."

Father Tim shook his head woefully. "We're driven creatures, Reverend Mother. Some of us are very weak."

"Don't be hard on yourself, Tim. I'm sure they all thought you were a fine speaker."

"That's why they turned out the lights?" he said. "And what I said—the Massacre of the Holy Innocents, the beast with seven heads, the Antichrist . . . I should have been a Baptist."

He rose and walked to the window. Already the sky

beyond the river was black, but a row of tenements on the far side gleamed like red stars with reflected sunset.

"It was the pressure, I suppose," he sighed. "The fact you've never seen me this way before just proves how many burdens I can normally slough off onto others."

"Nonsense, Tim. I don't know anybody busier than you. Masses and confession here, masses and confession at St. Anthony's—"

"Reverend Mother, there's nothing safer than being chaplain to a bunch of boys. They're rowdy sometimes, but essentially they're too innocent to test anyone's spiritual resources. I'm the man who takes the weight of the occasional impure thought and act of disobedience. I'm the man the parish sends to see octogenarians do *Arsenic and Old Lace*. It's the way I've wanted it. Nothing there to wrench even a soul of cobwebs."

He was silent for several moments, as though wrestling with some anguish deep within. "There was a girl once," he began at last, "when I was pastor at St. Ambrose's. Lovely Puerto Rican girl. She was raped."

"How awful," said Mother Margaret.

"She came to the confessional," Father Tim went on, grinding one fist into the palm of his other hand. "She was pregnant. She wanted forgiveness in advance for an abortion. I told her how wrong that would be. I told her there was no such thing as absolution before the sin itself—how could you repent a thing and still do it? I told her to see someone at Catholic Charities and give the baby up for adoption after it was born. I said the child's conception wasn't on her conscience because it had been done to her against her will. I told her about all the martyrs who'd suffered as much and more." He looked at his hands. "Her family had disowned her—pride. And she was a passionate girl. She believed she'd been defiled. Even said it was the devil's own seed growing in her."

"It must have been one of those movies on television," Mother Margaret said. "About demonic possession and—"

"It doesn't much matter where she got the idea. She was determined not to bear the child."

"She killed the unborn child, then?" Mother Margaret asked. "An abortion?"

"She killed herself," he answered, pressing his forehead against the cool glass of the windowpane. The last touch of sunset had faded from the houses across the river, and they had melted into darkness. "In a public washroom, with a broken piece of mirror across the crook of her arm."

"Do you want to talk about it?"

He was silent a long time. "No, Reverend Mother. It's only what makes me weak, not what troubles me tonight. I can't talk about that yet, not till I've seen John Buridan tonight."

"Oh, dear," she said, trying to cheer him up. "Now you've come to one of *my* burdens. He's in to see me about some outlandish suspicion or other almost every day. And twice this week I've come into my office and found him standing at my desk. He'd just let himself in. I think he'd been going through my things. Not that he meant any harm. I just don't think he's quite himself any more."

"Christmas vacation is the end of next week. Maybe we can get him to take a good rest."

"I hope so," she said.

"Well, I'll be going along, then." He forced a smile. "Don't be so gloomy, dear soul. Here's one to cheer you up—remember, I was suckled on ethnic slurs. What's a mile long and has an IQ of eighty-five?"

Mother Margaret smiled patiently.

"The Saint Patrick's Day Parade!"

"Good night, dear Father Tim," she said.

He left, laughing hugely to himself, and she was glad at least for that. She sat alone at her desk in the darkness for several minutes.

Poor Father Tim. Now she understood something of why so good a man had ended as an assistant pastor. Perhaps he hadn't been intended for the Vocation. He'd always been a little too affable and lacked the concentrated force of intellect to rise to preeminence. As she had in her way come to the veil through the poetry of Hopkins, Father Tim had come to the collar, she sometimes suspected, by way of *The Bells of St. Mary's*.

Still, he was a good, kind, compassionate man, the last of a vanishing breed, the Irish priest. He still moved easily among the Rotarians and the Knights of Columbus, trading ethnic jokes and delivering drinker's prayers—he understood them because he'd lived as an adult in the secular world longer than most priests. The youngest of many brothers, he'd stayed to bring his weekly paycheck home from the factory and turn it over to the widowed, ailing mother he had privately sainted. He hadn't entered the seminary until after his mother's death, when he was nearly thirty.

She pushed herself away from her desk and got up. She would have to go down to the parlor and see if the TV people were finished. The hall was empty, the parlor a deserted jumble of dark furniture shapes except for a single table lamp left burning by one wall. She walked forward to snap it out.

"Hello, Reverend Mother."

"Oh," she gasped, looking up. On the shadowed sofa beyond the circle of lamplight something short but broad and massive sat. It seemed to be wearing some kind of broad-brimmed hat, its face covered by a veil.

"Hello," she said uneasily. "Do I know you?"

"I hope so," said the voice.

Chapter 20

The Wrath of the Lamb

While Leffingwell was not certain that Macduff was Mother Margaret's illegitimate child, he was convinced that she was the key to his past, and he was equally convinced that film of their meeting would be crucial to the documentary. On the other hand, after all his promises to Macduff, he had been reluctant even to admit to himself that he planned to break his word. Thus he went to Immaculate Conception without any real plan, looking instead for some fortuitous set of circumstances that would somehow justify his lingering and recording the event by accident, as it were. And thus he couldn't think of any way to put Buridan off when the strange little man accosted him right after the taping and demanded Leffingwell come home with him. He tried to plead other commitments.

"I have the real story for you," Buridan said mysteriously.

"The real story of what?"

"Macduff."

So Leffingwell abandoned his first plan and went with Buridan to his living room of outdated overstuffed chairs and low bookcases mounded with old class notes and un-returned student papers. There he sat, still in his Mr. Laffy pants, next to an ancient Motorola atop which, in the center of a yellowed doily, stood a framed, oil-tinted photograph of a white-haired woman whom Buridan nodded toward every time he mentioned his late mother. And there he endured—because, Buridan explained, they couldn't start without Father Tim—a litany of paranoid delusions.

Father Tim finally arrived, rubbing his hands up and down his arms and blowing with the cold. He came stiffly into the room and begged for something hot. The warm house, he explained, was making his head throb again.

"I was hired," Buridan was saying, "because Mother was Bishop Feeney's second cousin, but now he's gone, the trustees will do away with me. And I went to night school for *six years* to get a Master's in Philosophy."

"I think you mentioned that a minute ago," Leffingwell said.

"Six years. Mercy me, and when I was done, do you think the Sisters ever once let me teach Ethics, or Sixth-Form Moral Philosophy? Or even European History—even when that old bat Sister Agnes was so senile she kept forgetting to teach the Renaissance and ended the course every year with Pope Innocent III? *They did not!* No, I got things no one else wanted—Citizenship and Geography. Do you know what our team mascot is?"

"Pardon?" said Leffingwell, taken by surprise.

"Really, John," said Father Tim, "a little coffee—"

"Agnes the Paschal Lamb!" He snatched a tabloid-sized student newspaper from the rubble atop one of the bookcases. TECH TOPPLES HOLY ASSUMPTION, screamed the 72-point type. BATTLING PASCHALS BUTCHERED! "A winning team needs something like a tiger—even a duck! But every year they borrow a yearling lamb from some pious pig farmer. It's too late this year," he went on, eyes narrowing, "but next season is *tabula rasa.* If I could just inspire the team. Maybe something from the Inquisition, something lingering but not irreversible." He wandered out into the kitchen. "Hot coals or molten lead . . ."

Father Tim frowned. He'd never seen Buridan quite this bad before. Could it be the great secret he claimed to have? He glanced over at Leffingwell, but Leffingwell looked merely perplexed.

"Frankly," Buridan shouted in over the roar of the faucet, "I'd sell my soul for a victory, if I weren't an atheist. I wonder if *that's* it—the trustees know I'm an atheist? Regular? Black with sugar? Milk with no sugar?

No milk or sugar? That's what I like about coffee—only our permutations. Now with tea—well, you've got to uggle the lemon, too. Why, there are eight possibilities you count lemon and milk."

Buridan returned with a tray, three cups, a jar of Pream, nd a box of Domino sugar cubes. "The tap water'll be hot a minute," he said graciously.

"Of course, with coffee there's decaffeinated," Leffingell offered. "And Espresso, café au lait, Postum . . ."

Buridan gave him a mournful look and sat down.

"Look here, John," Father Tim said quickly, hoping to et it over with, "I've got a splitting headache and my aouth tastes like a Bedouin encampment. You said you ad something important to tell us."

"Oh, yes," said Buridan, rising again. "Of course, of ourse." He went to a bookcase and began rummaging mongst the papers, then moved on to the next and did ne same. "It's been so hard to keep things tidy since Mother passed on last year," he muttered after the fifth ookcase. "Oh, of course!" He reached into his jacket's aner pocket and pulled out a wad of tissue.

"What in heaven's name is *that?*" said Father Tim.

"Exactly what it looks like," said Buridan. "Toilet aper!"

In the silence that followed, Leffingwell and Father Tim voided looking at each other.

"But not just *any* toilet paper. I found *this* toilet paper *Reverend Mother's office!*"

"Is it a special kind for nuns?" Leffingwell asked.

Father Tim closed his eyes. "John, Mother Margaret nows you've been breaking into her office, and you're oing to get into real trouble if—"

"Yes, I imagine she was afraid I'd find this," Buridan aid. "Tell me, Tim, have you ever wondered about the aechanisms of the mysteries of your faith?" He waved ne wad tantalizingly. "If science could explain the Bible's aysteries?"

"Mysteries don't have scientific answers—not those kinds f mysteries, anyway," Father Tim said.

"But take the Parting of the Red Sea. It turns out when ne wind and tide are right, the bed of the Red Sea is emporarily exposed. No miraculous Cecil B. DeMille valls of water—Moses and the Israelites just walked across the wetlands, but the Egyptian chariots got bogged down in the mud."

Father Tim sighed. "I've read about that."

"Then haven't you ever wondered about the Virgin Birth?" He began to unfold the wad of tissue. It was covered with dense writing, like a medieval manuscript. " 'In the event of my death,' " Buridan began to read.

"What is this you've stolen?" Father Tim said. "Is it something Mother Margaret wrote?"

"I took it for a greater good," Buridan answered. "And it's not by Mother Superior, but whoever it was wanted this made public, not locked away. It's all about—where was that?—aha! 'The search for carcinogens amenable to covert introduction, producing rapid, irreversible results nominally attributable to natural causes.' You have to get used to the style—she writes in a kind of verbal shorthand, typical doctor. But what she's talking about here is she was part of some project looking for, well, secret ways of killing people."

"What people?"

"It doesn't say. Here she says, um, 'testicular tumors called teratomas investigated for low-profile neutralization because often overlooked until too late, average being small and painless while metastasizing through circulatory and lymphatic system.' Then she talks about the uncertainties of a 'viral delivery system,' whatever that is, and then she says they opted for 'recombinant fusing of viral and *E. coli* DNA to produce lethal plasmids for reabsorption by *E. coli* intestinal bacteria.' They were all upset because they didn't have any human beings to test this stuff out on, and then they got hold of some young fellow who was in a motorcycle accident—'cerebral cortext partially sheared away and level EEG brought to Bay State'—"

"Bay State Medical Center?" Leffingwell asked. "That's only an hour from here. Stackpole and I could go down with a camera and do the exposé—"

"She goes on to say how they 'outfoxed transplant team hoping for kidneys and heart, then subject brought to our floor and maintained mechanically for plasmic introduction and tumor maturation. After six months, Walinski and surgical team perform orchiectomy. Testes forwarded to me for gross analysis and histological profile.' "

"What happened to the man?" Father Tim asked.

"He was already clinically dead," Buridan said. "I

doesn't matter. Now here's the *really* provocative part. 'Excised teratoma nineteen millimeters long and one-point-five grams enclosed in unusual sac apparently connected to arterial system. Inside sac surprised at chance formation of tumor into differentiated head, eyes, leg and arm buds, finger ridges of perfect five-week embryo. Then noticed movement of bluish mass in chest cavity. A heart, actually beating.' "

"Stop!" said Father Tim.

"No," Leffingwell said. "This is a dynamite story!"

"Well," Buridan said, "she goes on with the details of keeping it alive in some kind of artificial womb. Let's see. . . ."

Father Tim closed his eyes, listening to Buridan read. He could imagine them, faceless under surgical caps and masks, working feverishly to save this monstrosity that nature, perverted by man, had somehow endowed with independent life. He listened to the litany, the undiminishing rapidity of growth, the child's removal from the artificial womb and his APGAR score of ten, then the factions and tensions within the team as some came to think of it as a human child to be nurtured and others regarded it as a useless by-product.

And then something went horribly wrong. One by one the members of the team fell ill. *Orchiectomy of left testicle with peritoneal bilateral lymphadenectomy, but retroperitoneal node dissection indicates extensive lymph node and abdominal involvement.* Sometimes they lived, at least for a while. More often they died, the men with teratomas, the women with dermoid cysts. Some thought the plasmids were somehow released and contaminated the staff; others thought the child itself somehow oncogenic. *Ames mutagenicity series run on epidermal scrapings and biopsy specimens from child using cultures of Salmonella typhimurium; results positive, bacteria mutating at high rates within forty-eight hours. Walinski orders termination.*

"They *killed* the child?" Father Tim asked, looking up.

"No, no. The woman who wrote this kidnapped him to save him, even though she was scheduled for surgery herself. She'd become infected, too."

"Then what happened?" Leffingwell asked. "What's the rest?"

"You know the rest, between the two of you. Here, Mr. Leffingwell—the picture you were showing me just before the accident on the mountain. I forgot to give it back in the confusion."

Leffingwell took the picture. "I *knew* it! The Mother Superior across the street!"

Startled, Father Tim leaned over to see. It had been cut out of an old Academy yearbook. It was Mother Margaret as a young nun.

"Yes," he said. "I'm afraid I *do* know the rest. The woman brought the child here, then?"

"I don't follow," Leffingwell said. *"Is* she his mother or not?"

"Of course she's not," Father Tim said. "Macduff, Elephant Man—I tried to ignore the coincidence of the name. He was only a child five years ago when his uncle came for him. But now I see—the man wasn't his uncle, he was sent by the surgical team in that document to recover the . . . the thing that had been kidnapped from them."

"Elephant Man's the *child* she's talking about?" Leffingwell marveled. "And . . . and I suppose this so-called uncle wore sunglasses." He paused. "And if all this is true, then that means they're after him because . . . well, he could be a one-man plague."

"Possibly," Buridan said, "but it's clear they were never sure. They could have poisoned themselves with their own research. But you're missing the point. Say there *is* a God, and posit he chooses not to violate the physical laws of his creation. Then how is something like the Virgin Birth possible? This tells us—"

"John," said Father Tim, "I don't think—"

"But dermoid cysts can develop in the womb with skin, teeth, hair, partially formed mandibles, even working adrenal glands—all from an unfertilized egg," Buridan went on. "What if just once, against all the probabilities, somehow the same thing happened naturally and the agency that controls the proper proportioning of cell types—"

"Stop!" Father Tim shouted.

"But if it could happen in a clinically dead man, then why not in a virgin's womb? And if the first was somehow divine, then couldn't this second one be—"

"Blasphemy, John."

"What are you going to do, call in a troop of Dominicans? Technically it's *still* a virgin birth. You remind me of Ivan's dream in the *Brothers Karamazov* where the

Grand Inquisitor tells Christ that Mother Church couldn't withstand the disruptions of his second coming."

Father Tim looked at Buridan's mad torturer's grin and saw no point in answering.

"But he's not human. So if he's not divine, then what is he? Just a man-made viral mutation, a mind without a soul?"

"Life is life, I think," Father Tim said, "but I'm no theologian. I'm not qualified to answer. I've got to go home. I've got to think."

Father Tim made his escape without apologies or formalities, but it took several minutes of walking in the cold December night, mindlessly feeling the hard pavement shivering up through his thin soles to his shins and knees, before his head began to clear.

How long ago those pleasant evenings in John's living room seemed, while his mother bustled in and out serving cookies or cake or pie and brewing coffee for them, proudly listening to her son explain philosophy to a priest. John had always been fondest of medieval theology, and his rambling discussions always brought back Father Tim's seminary days. He'd liked the subject well enough in seminary—indeed, the puzzles had always delighted him because, he told himself, he wasn't a deep thinker and those kinds of puzzles always had answers.

And what would the medieval Schoolmen have made out of what he'd learned tonight? Would they have said Macduff was just another manifestation of the pox, the goiter and the tumor that were visited on mankind to disrupt Creation by the same cunning intelligence that had tempted Eve and would, at last, raise up the—

Yes, he thought, remembering his incoherent sermon of that afternoon. Raise up the monster Leviathan and the Antichrist of disease, death and heresy before Christ's Second Coming.

When Father Tim reached St. Anthony's, he went directly to the church instead of his rooms. It was too early for Saturday midnight mass, and he could have a few minutes to himself there for meditation and prayer.

He let himself in by the side door, genuflected and went to the altar rail to kneel.

Head down and hands clasped, he thought of his boyhood at St. Ambrose's, the priest's back hiding the altar's mystery from the congregation, before Father Tim had learned that even God's stewards were cursed with human frailties. *Kyrie eleison, Kyrie eleison. Christe eleison. Kyrie eleison.* The mystical power, authority, comfort of the old mass's long-dead languages.

Domine, non sum dignus ut intres sub tectum meum; sed tantum dic verbo, et sanabitur anima mea. Lord, I am not worthy that Thou shouldst come under my roof; say but the word and my soul shall be healed. *Domine, non sum dignus ut intres sub tectum meum; sed tantum dic verbo, et sanabitur anima mea.*

Still kneeling, Father Tim looked up at the church's nave. St. Anthony's had served the Italian ghetto, and its Mediterranean flamboyance troubled Father Tim's Irish soul; his heritage was the flat gray line of the North Atlantic, the wild moors and quartz cliffs of Achill in County Mayo where the eternal wind let nothing grow. Here above the altar soared a sturdy wooden canopy which supported a nativity of life-sized oak figures with faces painted unnatural pinks, dressed in real cloth costumes now faded from their former sumptuous vibrance. A worklight glowed somewhere behind the figures frozen in adoration of the skillful yet still inadequate imitation of the Word Incarnate.

No prayer, he thought. No answer. The room was overpoweringly still; the very emptiness hummed. He'd long ago conceded he'd never see visions. Icons and statues would never weep before him, and in his presence cripples would still clutch their crutches. His cross had always been the cross of mundanity, to keep the faith though the heavens never opened and to pray in the absence of a swelling heavenly chorus.

But what was he to make of what he'd learned tonight? Could so horrible and incomprehensible a thing really, as Buridan had claimed, be some kind of sign or—?

There was a distant pattering, and Father Tim felt a fine rain of dirt and dust from above settling on his shoulders. He looked up, blinking rapidly to keep the motes out of his eyes.

"Hiya, Father."

A small figure moved amongst the silhouetted oaken worshippers at the crèche, and for one insane moment Father Tim imagined the statue Child itself had stepped forward. But now the figure resolved itself into someone standing at the edge of the canopy with a pushbroom in

ts hand, looking down. Their little handyman, Justus
O'Toole.

"What are you doing here at this hour?" Father Tim
asked.

"Well, Saint Joe's got the rot, see?" said Justus. "There's
this leak in the roof and the rain's been coming right down
the back of Saint Joe's neck. This afternoon I stripped him
down on account of Christmas coming and cut out the
worst part and put on some creosote till I can get up on
the roof next spring, so I was just touching him up with
some nice healthy pink and sweeping up the shavings. But
who's gonna notice, right? Saint Joseph's a real fifth wheel
—it's all Mary and Jesus at Christmas."

"Well, I guess your surgery was a success," Father Tim
said, studying Saint Joseph's renovated likeness. "It looks
perfect."

"Congratulations on your twenty-fifth, Tim," Justus said,
a smile cracking its way across his old face. "It's coming
up, right?"

"I . . . I guess it must be. I'd forgotten."

"Yeah, I just happened to think of it, on account of
remembering your mother's been gone since right after
the war and all. You gonna have them cards printed up,
you know, remembrances?"

"For the anniversary of my ordination? I guess so."

"Well, don't forget to give me one. I got quite a pile
of them, a collection, like. Got one from Father Costello's
fortieth, just before he croaked."

"You'll get one," said Father Tim, rising. "I think I'll
be turning in now."

As he walked back down the aisle, he heard the scraping sounds of St. Joseph being turned. Frank Sinatra's
miracle in *Bells of St. Mary's*, he thought.

Later, lying in bed, he tried to reconcile the images of
the child he'd known at Immaculate Conception and the
strange, veiled creature he had walked the mountain with.
It was the perfect innocence they shared—and why not?
However much his affliction had swollen him into a parody
of adulthood, he was still a child in years. But it was more
than innocence of evil; it was innocence of all things
human. And perhaps that was the worst sin committed by
those faceless doctors.

It was well past three o'clock when Father Tim finally
dropped off to sleep. As always, his dreams were filled

with the dead gray face of the girl, blue lips set in a small knifelike line, the mirror-knife glittering beside her.

This way, he tried to explain to her, *you're condemning not only your own immortal soul, but the child's.* It was essential that the fetus be brought to term, born, baptized. In desperation he turned toward the child, glistening with the wound's fresh blood, sin-dark, rising from between the dead girl's sprawled legs. *Death came owing to guilt,* he quoted the bloody thing, *death was handed on to all mankind. You understand, don't you? Baptism——*

But does it have a soul? Buridan leered through the window.

Every child has a soul, he answered. *Even the unborn.* Even if telling her the right thing had somehow come out wrong, it could still be set straight if only the baby could be saved from the legacy of Adam.

But is the soul of a creature not created through the bodily union of two humans still heir to the sin of Adam? Buridan wanted to know, face now distorted inside the tubercle of the single light bulb hanging from the ceiling. How had he gotten inside it? *Considering the purposes it was created for, considering the conditions of its conception, perhaps its legacy is even more terrible.*

Which child? Father Tim screamed. *You're talking about the wrong one!* But already he saw quite clearly that the eyes staring from the bloody mask of the face were blank and tearless. It was Macduff, rising now to float halfway between the girl and the light bulb above.

But if it's not human, Buridan went on, voice muffled to a dull rumble by the light bulb's glass, *wouldn't baptising it be an act of blasphemy, like marrying two dogs or ordaining a pig?*

No! he answered. *No priest can make those decisions.*

*Ego sum conceptio immaculata et simul——*Macduff began

No! Father Tim shouted, hands over his ears. *I won't hear it!*

The next morning Father Tim would awaken in a darkness humid with radiator steam and his own body heat, his sweat-soaked and nightmare-twisted bedclothes coiled serpent-like about him.

Chapter 21

The Voice Out of
the Whirlwind

For a long time there was only silence in the parlor as Mother Margaret stared at her unexpected guest.

"I'm afraid you have me at a disadvantage," she said at last.

"Didn't Durwood Leffingwell tell you to expect me?" said the figure.

"Oh," she said, "of course. Why didn't you say so? So you're—but he didn't tell me *whom* to expect."

He sat with one leg drawn up like a cripple. Well, she was used to that sort of thing. "Yes," she said, lowering herself into a chair opposite, "I believe Father Tim mentioned you. It's certainly a . . . pleasure to meet you after hearing so much about you. Well, well, well. So you're the Elephant Man. Well, well."

"Just like it was," he breathed, the hat and veil turning slowly like part of an animated window display. "Nothing changed."

"Pardon?" Even when she concentrated, she could make out the slushy indistinctness of his speech only if it followed naturally from what she said or from the situation itself, like asking for a seat.

"Nothing," he enunciated very carefully. "Actually, I

225

said they *used* to call me Elephant Man. I know my real name now."

"And what's that?" she asked.

"Macduff."

The jolt of the word left her mind perfectly blank for a full second. "What did you say?"

"Macduff, Reverend Mother."

The same shudder of revulsion she'd felt on the bus shot through her, the horror of the tissue history Sykes had given her, where the half-truths told before had interlaced with what was written to form the warp and woof of a monstrous tapestry. She struggled to control herself.

"I'm glad to know you're all right," she said. "I always wondered if your uncle—"

"We drove for two days," he said. "I'm not exactly sure, because they kept me drugged. It's the only part I can't quite remember, and maybe I never will." His voice quavered and he paused. "It's very important, you see, to know who and what you are. I had to wait until I was sure, but that's why I finally decided I had to come back here to see you. I had to measure what I remembered against what I found here."

"And how do we measure up?" she asked. Despite herself she felt the same fear and hatred she'd had the night Sykes had first brought him to her. Unnatural, motherless child, sterile spawn of an eggless seed. She thought of Sykes's comments on his victims—the others in the project. She pitied them, however much they might have brought it on themselves. And poor Kevin—had Macduff's mere presence caused that, too? From anemia to leukemia, and Dr. Herzberg was so puzzled. And Sykes herself.

He was like an incubus, she thought, leaving disease festering in the wombs of the women he touched as though he had lain with them secretly in the night. More than once since she'd read Sykes's account she'd trembled for herself.

"I told you," he said. "It's just the way I remembered."

"How did you get back here?" she asked.

"I just remember something about a river and thinking about your story of how Moses was fished out of a stream."

Not Moses, she thought. Leviathan, Destroyer, Wrath of the Lamb.

"The first thing I really remember is being alone in the woods. A man named Harry found me. He took me back to his camper, found me some clothes. Later he started getting me jobs in carnivals."

"Is he dead, too?" she asked despite herself.

"Because of me?" he said. "They were never sure about that. It was one of the reasons they wanted me back, to find out."

She held herself in, waiting for him to finish, her hands on her lap below the level of the desk so he wouldn't see how they trembled.

He watched her for a long time. "You think I'm monstrous," he said at last. "I'm sorry. Somehow when I came here I was thinking you'd still see me as I was. I forgot you'd see me as I am now. You wish I were dead."

"No, I don't," she said, shocked.

"Yes, you do, and I don't blame you. I wish it myself. But it won't be long, I don't think. As I ripen, I rot, Reverend Mother. Haven't you wondered at how fast I grew? Already I'm middle-aged; at this rate I might live something like twenty years. That's not much longer than the life of a dog. I'm afraid, Reverend Mother."

Like a strong wind suddenly dropping to scuff a placid lake into ripples, something twisted and pulled back Mother Margaret's accustomed patterns of thought, and she felt directly the alien, gnawing emptiness that was his life, the absolute absence of everything she knew. It was a desolation too profound for sorrow.

"Forgive me, Macduff," she said.

"Please, Reverend Mother, I didn't come here to torment you. I came because I had to, to be sure. And to thank you."

"Thank me? For what?"

"For treating me like the others," he said. "I came here a laboratory animal, and you took me in. You taught me forgiveness, gentleness, even love. You were the thing they wouldn't give me, or couldn't. You were my mother. And this was the only place where I ever felt at home—where I didn't feel separated, cut off, *stared at*."

"Those are poor gifts," she said. "I wish I'd done something more. I wish at least I hadn't let that man take you so easily. Forgiveness, gentleness—they have no place in what's been done to you. If I were you, I couldn't keep from hating. Not God, perhaps, but the men and women who—"

"I can't hate," he said. "I am who I am, Reverend

Mother. There's no one I can hate for that." He paused again, thinking. "Do you know, Mother Margaret, when I finally began remembering things, one of the first things that came back was the time Walther and Kevin and I plugged up that old doorbell hole. Are the bees still there?"

"Still there," she said. "Sometimes it seems like their coming was the start of everything's going wrong. Now the whole building's just rotting away around them. I suppose you know about the Bishop wanting to close us down. I think this springtime when the bees wake up, they'll find they have the place to themselves."

"I hope not," he said. "Well, Durwood is probably back at the car waiting for me. I'd better go."

"Will you come back and see me?" she asked. "Today was such a strange day, I . . . I just haven't been able to talk to you the way I would have wanted to."

"No."

"But why not? You said this was your home, and it *is*. It always will be." She wanted to say more, but she could not, any more than she had been able to challenge the man she'd known wasn't his uncle or to condemn the bees that threatened her boys. She was Mother Superior, and to be mother to all things meant ultimately not committing herself wholly to any one thing, however much it needed her.

"You asked me before if they ever found out whether I was some kind of carrier. I don't know, and before I expose anyone else, I've got to find out."

She followed him to the door. She wanted to clasp him to her, but the heavy veil hung between them and the broad beekeeper's hat seemed to warn her away. Instead, she put both hands on his shoulders. "If there's anything I can do . . ."

"There is one last question," Macduff said. "I wanted to find the woman who brought me here, Sykes. She might be able to tell me more . . . about what I am, and whether I should go somewhere far away from people. She's sort of the last link with my beginning."

"I'm sorry," Mother Margaret said. "She died about a month ago."

The beekeeper's hat tipped to indicate the slightest nod. "Goodbye, then, Reverend Mother."

"Goodbye," she said, grabbing his left hand suddenly

and pressing her lips to the backs of his fingers. "God bless you."

When he was gone, she walked slowly to her room. For some reason came to her the lines of Hopkins' poem on the three nuns drowned at sea.

He was to cure the extremity where he had cast her. . . .
O Christ, Christ come quickly.

In the hallway outside, Macduff paused, remembering his first terrible night in the little room up those very stairs and at the end of the hall.

He had lain in the narrow bed, the good taste of the cheese puffs from downstairs still lingering in his mouth, but with his teeth bared in fear, because she'd turned out the light when she'd left him, and he'd never seen real darkness before.

In his laboratory home he'd seen the blackness pooled under tables and chairs; and when the flickering green-white fluorescents overhead had gone off, he'd seen the darkness rush out and fill the corners down from the ceiling and up from the floor. But always there had been the glowing yellow night lights along the wall, and the burning red of the indicator lamps over the wall switches. Never before had he seen the darkness devour a whole room.

He'd waited for the dark to try to eat him, too, but when nothing happened, he reached down and patted and found his body was still there. Then he'd let the muscles of his face relax until the lips had slipped over the teeth and covered them. So, he'd thought, he would be all right. He wet his finger in his mouth and dabbed each eyeball to stop the burning itches.

As his eyes grew accustomed to the darkness, he'd become aware of a square patch glowing blue in the wall by his feet. Cautiously, baring his teeth, he pulled his legs under himself and rose to his knees and crawled to the end of the bed to look.

It seemed to be an elongated television screen criss-crossed by lines out of which a ghostly face stared back. He raised one hand and snarled, and soundlessly the screen face showed him a raised hand. He wiggled his fingers; so did it. So, he thought, some kind of mirror.

But as he gazed at himself, he became aware of some-

thing inside his face, behind his face, the stark black forms
of trees and the deep blue of a sky prickling with the lights
of stars. A window, he thought, like the ones in the car
earlier that night. He'd never seen windows before then;
the only place he'd known had been the cavernous room
where the faceless people in green gowns and masks had
walked soundlessly on rubber soles. He pushed at one of
the panes to see if it would swing open like the one in the
car, wanting to feel again the wind hard against his face
and tugging at his hair behind. But it wouldn't move.

He turned and saw the bar of light between the floor
and the bottom of the door, and he thought of the taste of
the cheese puffs and he remembered how the woman with
wet eyes had kept telling him in the car that Rachel or
someone would take care of him. He got up and opened
the door and let himself out; he would find the cheese
puffs and he would find Rachel.

He walked everywhere that night, trying door after door
only to discover behind each the same darkness that filled
his own room. Finally, at the end of the hall he found the
stairs and scuttled down them and along the hallway to
the room where they'd brought him before.

The light was still on, but the room was empty. In one
corner he found the crumpled cellophane the puffs always
came in, but no puffs. Then he went to the shelves and
took something out and opened it and found not food but
writing, so he turned it around the right way and read aloud.

> *I have desired to go*
> *Where springs not fail*
> *To fields where flies no sharp and sided hail*
> *And few lilies blow.*

And then Mother Margaret had come huge and black
into the room and he had seen himself small, diminished,
distorted in the almond mirrors of her eyes while she had
demanded to know what he was doing.

Now, standing in that same hall, peering into the dim-
ness through his veil, Macduff could feel the muscles of
his face tugging vainly at a smile. His eyes traveled along
the wall to the stairs. That first night Mother Margaret
had scooped him up, making his stomach suddenly light
and sick, and carried him down this hall and back up

those stairs. And she had sat with him in the darkness until he had fallen asleep.

He wanted to go back up those stairs now, but he hung back at the first step, his useless right hand on the newel post, his mind traveling on, up the stairs and down the hall to his last moments there.

He had been sitting on the bed, his feet swinging free of the floor, and Mother Margaret had been standing uneasily in the doorway.

"Your uncle's waiting for you downstairs," she had said awkwardly. "He's going to take you to your real mother and father."

"You're my mother," he said.

"No, that's only a title. I'm mother to all the boys here, but I can't be like a real mother to any one of them without cheating the others."

"I don't have any other mother or father."

"Of course you do. You've just forgotten them, that's all. Why else would your uncle go to all the trouble of looking for you? You'll see—you'll be much happier when you're with them again. I know you will."

"Yes," he said, knowing he hadn't forgotten them. You couldn't forget something that never was.

She came into the room and gave him a quick kiss with cold lips and then hurried away. When she was gone, he had taken the book he'd stolen from the library downstairs out from under the pillow and torn out the picture, his dry eyes burning with sorrow. And then, picture hidden in his pocket, he had come back down the stairs.

There had been a man waiting at the bottom of the stairs, right where Macduff was standing now. He couldn't remember the face, nor could he remember much about the walk outside to the gray car. His mind refused; the memories diffused into a featureless whiteness. He concentrated as hard as he could, until at last something emerged, an image, like the playground's oak in the white morning fog, disembodied, disconnected, floating.

It was his own face. He was standing before a great mirror somewhere, and he knew it was like the mirror in the room he remembered from his beginnings, but he knew it was not the same mirror. It was so hard to remember. They kept giving him pills and shots and he fought them because he wanted to keep his memories. His memories were all he had.

But he did know that this mirror, like the first one, was also a window. Beyond his reflection cowered the doctors and scientists in a darkened room, watching him unseen. He knew because once someone had turned on the observation room's lights by mistake, and he'd seen them dim behind the mirror, frozen and then gesturing frantically like comic actors in a huge television screen, until someone had found the switch and the window had become a mirror again.

Now he looked closely at the mirror, not to see through it but to study his own reflection.

His forehead was swollen. And his nose looked wrong, a little too big. And the corners of his mouth were turned down and the upper lip raised. He felt inside his mouth with his tongue, as he had that morning and the night before. The swellings on his upper gum were still there.

Something was happening to his face. He turned to see if the mirror would give him even a glimpse of the back of his head, but he could see nothing in the matted hair that would account for the lumpish swellings his fingers had found.

Was it something they'd done to him, or had it happened on its own, a doom woven into his genes at his conception that had at last manifested itself?

He tried to smile. If only he could smile, he thought, or frown. But his forehead was already too swollen, and he couldn't make the corners of his mouth move, stretched taut by the swellings that already pressed his upper lip outward.

He wanted to hide. He wanted to draw a curtain over the mirror that was a window, and then crouch in some darkened corner of the room. But they would never let him. They were always watching him in his nakedness, even when they put aside their needles and microscopes. Those were the doctors. And then there were the others who prowled outside the building in city shirts and trousers and sunglasses carrying walkie-talkies. They watched him warily, kept their distance as though they were afraid of him. But they never stopped watching.

The only relief came with the walks outside. The south side of his room had a door that opened onto a fenced compound, and every day they let him walk there alone. It reminded him of the playground, except he could no longer picture the playground very well. There was even a river not too far away, and he would press himself against the chain-link fence and peer at it beyond the high grass.

They wouldn't tell him the name of the river or anything else about where he was, but sometimes from his compound he saw men in helmets and green uniforms moving through the grass far away, beyond the men in shirtsleeves and sunglasses, and he knew it never snowed where he was.

There had been a hole in the fence back home beyond the oak tree, he thought. If he could find a hole in this fence, he could escape. Bees or men, he would elude them, running free through the tall grass to the river. He remembered someone's story about a baby found in a river among the rushes, but he couldn't remember the baby's name. Anyway, he didn't want to be found. He wanted to let himself slip beneath the water and disappear. He wanted to die.

He looked at his face in the mirror again. They were watching him, he knew, because they wanted to see if he deteriorated. They were watching to see him die in parts, and the swelling was probably the beginning.

Beside him his foot felt the metal leg of one of the stools the doctors liked to sit on when they examined him. It moved on rollers, and it was heavy.

Without even pausing to consider, he reached down, heaved it above his head with both hands and hurled it at the mirror.

He watched the stool plunge through his own reflection, watched the mirror image of his face and the room shatter away from him in a million glittering slivers.

There was only one of them hidden there, covering his face with his arm as the glass and light cascaded over him. Macduff had clambered up and over the toothlike shards of the glass still in the frame before the man could recover; he found the door, yanked it open, stumbled out into the hall. To his left he saw a door with a window of safety glass, and through it the open grass fields.

He ran toward it, hit the release bar and found himself outside. Without a pause he plunged into the grass and headed for the river, catching a glimpse of one of the walkie-talkie men far off to his right.

The grass whipped his face and arms, the ground was rough and sharp with clumps of last season's dead growth. Behind him there was a distant buzzing that seemed to rise up and then begin to follow him, growing louder.

Admirable creatures, he thought, remembering vaguel
from a book he'd found somewhere. All identical, excep
for the drones and queen. Parthenogenic, in a way, becaus
during the mating flight the drone's genitals were extrude
into the queen and snapped off; he would fall to th
ground, dead, while the queen would return with th
injected semen. The eggs she fertilized became the female,
the workers and future queens; the eggs she laid and lef
unfertilized became the males. The most highly evolve
communal system on earth. They made perfectly duplicat
hexagonal cells for everything from larvae to honey, an
they would sting to death any intruder into the hive, eve
other bees, if they came from a different nest.

He was running downward now, and the river's broa
surface shimmered before him. The buzzing had becom
a thundering and then a rapid but distinct *whap-whap* a
the helicopter swooped overhead, banked and dipped bac
toward him.

He paused for an instant at the water's edge, caugl
a glimpse of his face and body fragmented in the broke
reflections of the rippling water and then waded in. Afte
a few steps he began to paddle forward, the helicopte
trembling almost directly above him, the motor noise dea
ening, and then he stopped moving his arms and leg
took a last breath and let the water close over him and th
current drag him wherever it chose. He remembered th
deepening darkness and nothing more.

He had gone as far back as he could hope to g
Somehow he had gotten to the other shore and elude
them until Harry had found him; the details didn't matte
because now all the important pieces had fallen into plac

He didn't like what he had found, but at least he unde
stood it. No more doubleness or multiple possibilities. N
more reruns. He'd found the rhythms and patterns of h
own life and past. No need any longer to be shackled t
the television whose soap operas were a mirror life fe
those with no other, and whose ancient movies and repeate
series were the archives and racial memory of the nation
obsolete leisures and outmoded dreams. No need any long
for a surrogate for his own alien history.

"Fuck you," snarled a voice from upstairs.

Macduff stiffened. A tall, thin figure stood at the hea
of the stairs. It wasn't addressing him or even looking

im; it seemed to be talking to someone farther down the
all that Macduff couldn't see.

"Just fuck you, that's all. If you don't want to let me
ee your *Penthouse,* then that's just fine with me, you
ot that? I don't *give* two shits. I was just trying to be
iendly, that's all."

There was no mistaking him. He was taller and his voice
ad grown deeper, but the red hair and the anger were still
e same.

Yes, Macduff thought, opening the front door. Walther,
o, was as much an outsider as he was, as much the ex-
mmunicate barred from the buzzing communion of iden-
cal souls that television enshrined.

He closed the door behind himself and limped down the
ont steps into the darkness to find Leffingwell.

Chapter 22

Bum's Rush to Judgment

Leffingwell sank deeper and deeper into Burida[
couch, cursing himself for not being quick-witted enou[
to leave under the aegis of Father Tim's departure.

"And the wonderful thing," Buridan was saying, as [
had been for the past twenty minutes, "is it's an absolut[
closed system—none of your modern loose ends. It [
a grandeur and simplicity we can't begin to comprehe[
in an age that fragments even the atom. Today's science[
still only *scientia*, the Schoolmen's 'worldly knowledg[
The higher wisdom was called *sapientia*. That's somethi[
you don't hear about any more."

"Uh, right," Leffingwell agreed, trying to recapture [
last gaggle of words he'd allowed to fly past uncomp[
hended. When he saw Buridan turn his back to rumma[
through his bookcase again, Leffingwell grabbed the m[
ment to rise decisively. "I think we've covered this befo[
and Macduff's probably waiting for me at the car by n[
But maybe you could write all this down in a kind [
position paper and send it along to me. Maybe I could w[
parts of it into the weather."

Buridan followed him, chattering amiably all the wh[
and waved a ferocious goodbye from the front door. "[
you planning to tell Macduff the truth about himself?"[
called.

Leffingwell paused at the foot of the porch steps. "I don't know. I hadn't thought about it."

"You *do* think I'm right, don't you?"

"About what?"

"The Virgin Birth, of course."

Leffingwell turned and plunged into the darkness. "Sure," he said, flipping his collar up around his ears against the cold and walking with a snow-shoer's exaggerated steps to keep his balance in the Mr. Laffy horse pants. "Absolutely."

If Buridan said anything more, it was lost to Leffingwell amongst the dry and hollow cracking of his vinyl hooves across the frozen turf of Holy Assumption's football field.

What, he thought, what in the world had he been keeping in his house since September? If only he'd listened to Claudine. He missed her, he realized. It wasn't just the inconveniences of Dawn's two-room apartment or her cramped Honda just when he was getting used to the Mercedes. Maybe what he'd told Stackpole was true—he was addicted to the level of hostility.

No, Dawn was just as hostile in her combination of consumerism and sex, but younger and more sullen. He really did miss Claudine.

And Stackpole, for that matter. They still saw each other during working hours, but the home-grown joints were gone, and so were the jokes between them, and for Leffingwell jokes were acts of love because they made light of a world of abominations and chaos. That, ultimately, had lain behind his jokes with Claudine, as well, no matter how bitter or sarcastic they might have seemed on the surface.

If there was a hell, Leffingwell thought, it would be just like earth—except nobody ever laughed. Vaguely he remembered Buridan's comment on the mountain about sinners being blind to the silliness of human folly.

The mountain. That brought him back to Stackpole and Macduff. So he'd traded his wife and his best friend for a live-in plague. What were the chances, he wondered. If Macduff were some kind of carrier of those plasmids neatly packaged in everyday bacteria. . . . He imagined himself alternately castrated or terminally ill, and Claudine swelling with the seeds of her own death. And every bit of it was his own goddamned fault.

He found the parking lot deserted except for Dawn's empty Honda and, at the far end, a nun pacing back and forth in some kind of meditation.

Idly, Leffingwell watched her. She was surprisingly tall
he noticed, maybe six foot five. Even odder, she was carry
ing a paper bag about the size generally favored by wine
for concealing their pints of muscatel, and every now and
then she raised it and seemed to speak into it.

And then the nun turned, and beneath the shadow of
her wimple Leffingwell saw a pair of sunglasses glint in the
streetlight.

Nervously he edged around to put the Honda between
himself and the ersatz nun's boustrophedon. At that, the
nun stopped pacing and moved to the side of the parking
lot nearest the street, as though to cut him off. After what
had happened at the biodegradables', Leffingwell had no
wish to wait and find out if she had reinforcements. If he
were smart, he thought, he'd take off right now.

And leave Macduff behind to fall into their clutches?

Why not?

"Leff?"

Macduff's voice startled him. "Over here," Leffingwell
called. As he spoke, the nun retreated into the darkness
and a moment later Macduff's squat figure limped from the
gloom.

"Sorry if I kept you waiting," Macduff said. "I had a lot
of things I wanted to go over with Reverend Mother. Un
finished business, in a way." He suddenly noticed Leffing
well's agitation. "Is anything wrong, Leff? Are you mad?"

"Mad?" Leffingwell said, keeping his distance. "No, no,
I just think we'd better get back to Dawn before it's too
late."

Leffingwell kept glancing in the rear-view mirror as they
drove. The phoney nun could have been a spotter for a
carful of them tucked away on some side street, and they'd
be madder than hornets after the escape from Encino
barn.

Leffingwell had stowed a six-pack in the back seat
against any thirsts produced by the taping, and after an
other glance at the mirror, he reached in back and twisted
a can from its polyethylene strap. With the can between
his thighs, he pulled the pop-top ring, took a swallow, and
then with a shudder realized that Macduff might want a
sip. What would he do then? Refuse to take it back, or be
polite and risk catching whatever-it-was? He stole another
glance at the strange silhouette beside him.

How much, he wondered, did Macduff know about his

self? How much should Leffingwell tell him of what he'd discovered through Buridan? He opened his mouth to say something, but his throat tightened. Was it guilt he felt? Remorse? Something else he couldn't define?

All right, he wouldn't say anything tonight. No point in making him feel worse about himself than he already did, at least until he'd figured out what he was going to do. And maybe he'd been a little silly about the beer. If he was going to catch anything from Macduff, he'd caught it already. Sharing a beer with him at this point couldn't make anything worse, he supposed. Silently, he held the beer out to Macduff.

Macduff accepted it and drew it up inside his veil to drink. Leffingwell was just about to reach out to take the can after Macduff was finished when he looked up for a perfunctory check of the rear-view mirror.

Far behind, twin pale white discs had suddenly appeared. The headlights of another car, gaining on them.

"Oh, my God," he sighed. "I think they've sent the Marines. Hold on while I give the Bat-Honda a Bat-goose!"

For the first time that Leffingwell could remember, he heard Macduff laugh at his joke. High-pitched, edged with fear, but still an honest-to-God laugh.

They were still well ahead of the other car when they screeched to a stop in the parking lot behind Dawn's apartment. Leffingwell wasn't sure what protection Dawn's place offered, but he knew he'd rather fight it out there than on some back road in a Honda—it was more dignified, maybe, and a little less cramped. With the remaining cans of beer dangling by their plastic neck-straps from one hand, Leffingwell helped Macduff out of the car and into the building.

When Dawn opened the door to their frantic knocking, her face was white and her mouth drawn. "Hello, Woody," she said, and cleared her throat. For an instant she seemed to raise her eyebrows and roll her eyes as though trying to signal them in some way, but Leffingwell ignored it as some kind of nervous tic and strode into the room quickly, pushing her aside. Then he stopped. Something cylindrical and metallic with a hole at the end was pressing the soft flesh just beneath his rib cage.

"I don't suppose that's just an old piece of pipe you've got there, whoever you are," Leffingwell said. The next moment the room came alive with dark figures rising from behind the sofa and piling in through the bedroom door.

"You're under arrest, Mr. Laffy. You have the right to have an attorney present during questioning. You have the right to remain silent. If you waive that right, anything you say can and will be used against you. And I'll take them beers as evidence."

Leffingwell pulled up his balloon-pants with dignity and turned to see what was connected to the gun barrel. Instead of the expressionless face behind the green bulges of sunglasses, he found a round, pink, rather stupid face, no different from the average carwash attendant's.

"I'm Sheriff Lurdan, pervert," said the face, "and you're under arrest. Apprehend the freak, the rest of you."

"John Doe, known as the Elephant Man," said another voice, "A k a Guppy-Man and Dog-Faced Boy, you have the right—"

"Some of you go search the car for evidence," Lurdan was saying.

Leffingwell felt his arms grabbed on either side, and the next moment he was being pushed toward the door. "DAWN!" he shouted as he was propelled into the hall. "Call Greenbaum! Sue the bastards!"

The next thing Leffingwell knew, he was hustled outside, across the sidewalk, and into Sheriff Lurdan's Plymouth. He sat stunned, staring at the wire grating between the front and back seats. Then he looked out the side window. Across the street a trimless gray sedan was just pulling to a stop— the car that had chased them. The driver did a double take and removed his sunglasses to reveal two eyes as wide with surprise as Leffingwell's own.

The other door swung open and Macduff was sent sprawling in. "Don't try that again!" Lurdan barked, leaning in after Macduff and cracking Leffingwell on top of the head with his gun barrel.

Right you are, sir, Leffingwell thought, drifting off into unconsciousness. Whatever it was, never never never never again. . . .

His sleep was troubled by vague dreams. A gas station attendant pulling off his belt, another yanking at the beer can's pull-tab that still dangled from Leffingwell's finger.

"What about this ring here?" said the faraway voice.

"Personal effects," said another, depositing it in a manila envelope with Leffingwell's belt and billfold. He extended a large purple tongue and licked the flap, and then he faded away.

Leffingwell awoke, a lump just behind his ear throbbing, to find himself in a fold-down bunk. "Where am I?" he mumbled.

"Bumberry Center, the county seat," answered a familiar voice. "The sheriff's office in the District Court Building."

Leffingwell opened his eyes to see sunlight streaming through a small barred window onto a toilet without a seat. A man at least seven feet tall, a kind of animated foothill, was slumped on the opposite bunk in laced hunting boots, a red-checked woolen shirt buttoned to the neck and a tie that said "Expo '67." A French Canadian arrested in his Sunday best, he thought.

"Over here, Leff."

Leffingwell had to turn his head slowly in order to keep the pain at a manageable level. He found Macduff by the cell door, shrouded under a makeshift blanket hood. His hat and veil had been confiscated. Through the bars he could make out a crowd of teen-agers staring at Macduff from the juvenile cell.

"Is this the drunk tank?" Leffingwell asked, trying to sit up. The pain surged to a point above his ear and exploded. "Has Dawn sent Greenbaum yet?"

"Here we go," said a voice. "Breakfast and the papers." A deputy pushing a tray-covered cart appeared. He pressed a slack face against the lower bars as he pushed first one tray and then another in through the six-inch space between the floor and the bottom of the door. "Don't usually give hotel service, Mr. Laffy, but the sheriff figured you show business types always want to see your notices first thing." He shoved a newspaper in after the trays.

"That's *Leffingwell*. If you guys are going to arrest the wrong guy, at least you could get the name right. And where's Macduff's hat?"

"No hats in the cells," the deputy said.

"Why not?" Leffingwell said.

"Rules," said the deputy, clattering back down the hall with his empty cart.

Leffingwell sighed and picked up the paper. It was a local giveaway, the *Shopper's Yodel*. There was nothing about him or Macduff on the front page, but three pages in, under the IGA ad for tender chicken thighs at 69¢/lb., he found "LOCAL GIRL VICTIMIZED BY CELEBRITIES." In smaller type appeared "Hoofer Fingers Kiddy-Show Horse and Elephant Man."

"Miss Fern Adams," he read, "aspiring local girl and danseuse, last night, to her sorrow, met face to face the dark side of man's deepseated animal lust as the rapee of alleged area television personality and neighbor Durwood Leffingwell and his so-called Elephant Man."

He looked up, stunned. "Macduff, we're being accused of . . . God, it says we gang-raped *Fern Adams!*"

"I know," Macduff said.

"Listen to this," Leffingwell said, reading aloud. " 'The thirteen-year-old Miss Adams, student for numerous years at "Miss Nicky" Nackalis' "Top Hat Tap 'n' Toe Studio" appearing with the Nick-Nackettes in such as Kiwanis Entertainment Night, old people's homes for the aged, the Senior Class Revue "Gobs in Gotham" and fourth runner-up in the Rotarians' "Olde Tyme Talente Showe," reported that the Elephant Man and Mr. Leffingwell, known to local viewers of Channel 29 as "The Weather Man," last night made advances on her behind her home shortly before the "10:00 O'Clock News" on which he was not on due to being the weekend, which is near Quidnunck, New Hampshire, and forced her to commit acts.' "

Leffingwell looked up at the hooded face. "Well, *that's* a relief. I was worried for a second, but that time means we've got air-tight alibis—I was with Buridan and you were talking to that nun. I'll tell Greenbaum to—say, where *is* he? You don't think Dawn forgot to call him, do you?"

"You know her better than I do," Macduff said.

"Yeah," Leffingwell said. "That's what worries me." The other day he found Dawn reading "It Pays to Increase Your Word Power" in *Readers Digest,* and he suspected she was outgrowing them. He went back to the newspaper article. " 'Being that Miss Adams is a minor, the victim's mother called the authorities, Sheriff Lurdan, which swiftly arrested the perpetrators and apprehended them to Bumberry Center Jail where they were held without bail with the assistance of Corporal Tillson of the State Police and Sheriff's Deputies Harrow and Bolt. Miss Adams is the daughter of Mrs. Rose Adams of Quidnunck, and the former John Adams, who is available as a secretary part-time while she pursues her Dance Career.' "

Leffingwell carefully refolded the paper. "I guess this is

all because I kicked her butt when she was in that chicken suit."

"This seems a lot worse than what you did to her," Elephant Man said.

"Well, that's inflation for you," Leffingwell muttered.

"I guess she just wants someone to blame," Macduff said. "She wants everything that's wrong with her life to be *somebody's* fault. I feel sorry for her."

"Don't waste your time," Leffingwell said. "It's just fate, that's all. It's my rotten luck."

"No," Elephant Man said. "It's my past. I used to be so worried about finding it, and now it seems the whole time it's been looking for me instead."

"Oh?" Leffingwell said, wondering how much of what he knew, Macduff knew as well. "You referring to that gray sedan that was following us last night?"

At that moment, the door swung open with a clang. Greenbaum stood there, a briefcase dangling from one arm and an index finger in his left nostril.

"Thank God you got here," Leffingwell said. "Dawn got through to you after all."

"What the hell is *that?*" Greenbaum shuddered, peering into Macduff's blanket hood.

"Allow me to introduce the key figure of Elephant Man Enterprises, Inc.," Leffingwell said. "This is Macduff."

Greenbaum switched hands and fingers. "I'm supposed to defend *him*? No way—no one's going to drop charges against anything *that* ugly. Some kind of accident?"

"Never mind," Leffingwell said. "Now the first thing you've got to do is tell that cretin with the badge to give Macduff back his hat and veil."

"We'll see," Greenbaum said. "Now assuming you still could afford me, I went over to the Prosecutor's house this morning. I don't do criminal law," he added, wrinkling his face as though something smelled, "and he was P.O.'d at not getting to *Dick Tracy* first thing, but he was willing to listen."

"And he realized the whole thing's a huge mistake?" Leffingwell asked.

"Right. He'll accept a lesser offense."

Leffingwell was shocked. "Plea bargain? But we're not guilty in the first place."

"Look, the charges are aggravated kidnapping, aggravated assault, illegal restraint, forcible rape, statutory rape, lewd and lascivious carriage, maintaining an elephant inside town limits without a license *and* sodomy and other crimes against nature."

"So we're supposed to settle for contributing to the delinquency of a minor and despoiling virgin woodland?"

"Something like that. It works out to only ten years with a recommended three and a half. You'd be up for parole in an easy fourteen months."

"Fourteen months! shrieked Leffingwell. "That's over a year in jail for *nothing!"*

"Be reasonable. If you waste the judge's time with a trial, he's apt to get pissed off and hit you with the maximums for everything."

"What would that mean?" Leffingwell asked.

"For kidnapping, assault, restraint, two rapes, a carriage, an elephant and a sodomy? You'll be up for parole in early A.D. 2051."

Leffingwell paused. "You talk like somebody's going to believe these charges."

"Right," said Greenbaum. "The preliminary hearing's being handled by Judge Abraham Steele." He checked Leffingwell's bunk for vermin, wiped his finger on the coverless pillow and sat down. "He's what they used to call a hanging judge in the old days. Don't know him myself, but the only case of his I could get a line on this morning was ten years for a third offense driving without a license."

"I have a vision," Leffingwell said. "It's the *Bumberry Shopper's Yodel.* The headline is 'HORSE'S ASS GETS HOT-SEAT.' "

"Of course Steele's had more decisions reversed than any district court judge in the state," Greenbaum continued.

"That sounds promising."

"But he's just been appointed to Superior Court starting next month as part of the Governor's election promise to get tough with the courts—so in all probability he'll be reviewing his own decision and presiding over your trial in Superior Court."

Leffingwell slumped against the bars.

"Well," Greenbaum said, "'what we need is a good, sound courtroom strategy by Tuesday."

"Tuesday? I'm on the air tomorrow night!"

"Sorry," said Greenbaum. "Judge Steele's taking tomorrow off to get his hearing aid fixed—keeps picking up

CB from truckers. So, how many friends can you get to swear this Fern Adams is the town pump?"

"You mean *lie?*" asked Macduff.

"What else?"

"I spent the whole evening with a philosophy teacher and a priest, and Macduff was with a nun," Leffingwell said, lowering his head into his hands. Things just got crazier and crazier. A virgin birth and an imaginary rape all in the same evening. He looked up. "Why should we lie when we're *that* innocent?"

"Damn it," said Greenbaum, disappointment and despair ringing in his voice. "You don't expect me to believe *that.*" He rose and went to the window as though to peer dramatically through the bars into the mysterious complexities of the lawyer-client relationship. Leffingwell came up behind him and found he was looking at the loading platform at the rear of S. S. Kresge's.

"A client's got to level with his attorney," Greenbaum said. "Now tell me the truth—why did you do it? Because you couldn't get along with your wife? Remember, I know all about *Dawn.* Or was it because *Dawn* started getting headaches and you and your friend were striking out at the Holiday Inn Singles Night?"

"We didn't do it," Leffingwell said. "The whole thing's a rotten frame. The kid hates me, that's all. Or . . . hey! Maybe it was her *mother* put her up to this! She knew Macduff here had some money. Not long ago she was talking to me about suing people. I wonder if *this* was what she had in mind."

"If she just wants the money, why not give her some?" Macduff asked.

"Never," Leffingwell said.

"Wait—you're saying the charges were fabricated for revenge and profit?" Greenbaum said.

"Something like that."

Greenbaum shook his head. "Too simple—no one'll ever buy it. What if you both plead joint insanity?"

"We're not the ones who're crazy," Leffingwell said, thinking of Buridan.

"Doesn't matter—insanity's a top-flight strategy. We'll say you were driven by deprivation to self-abuse, which in turn brought on dementia—"

"BULLSHIT!"

"Look, take it from me, no judge in the world wants to

hear you're innocent. He wants at least to hear you admit you're nuts. After all," Greenbaum added more kindly, putting a hand on Leffingwell's shoulder, "which of us in this crazy, mixed-up world is *really* innocent?"

"We are," Leffingwell said. "Will you at least get that dippy sheriff to send someone to talk to Buridan? He can *prove* my alibi. And get him to give back Macduff's hat while you're at it."

"What's this?" Sheriff Lurdan was lounging in the doorway, chewing on a toothpick. Must have seen *Heat of the Night* once too often, Leffingwell thought. "What alibi, Laffy?"

"His name's John Buridan, if you can get *that* straight, and I was with him all evening."

"Okay, smart-ass," said Lurdan. "I'll call your bluff. I'll send one of the boys over first thing tomorrow—don't hardly have nobody on weekends, you know."

"Yeah, you call my bluff. And then, cow-flop, we're going to sue those jodhpurs off you, because this guy Buridan is unimpeachable, alibi-wise. I mean, he's a sound, stable, *respected* member of the community, and if *that* isn't enough, he teaches *citizenship* at a *Catholic* school." A huge smile broke out across Leffingwell's face, and he put his arm around Macduff's shoulder. All this had somehow made him feel even more warmly toward him. "Macduff, we're going to be out of here in two shakes of a lamb's tail."

Chapter 23

Ockham's Razor

Buridan was still too agitated to make any sense of the strange officer's questions, so he played with the sash of his bathrobe for a while, then looked around his new white room. How clean, he thought.

No, he didn't remember. What he did remember was coming into his old living room—was it this morning?—books for class and *Commonweal* under his arm, hoping the Maxim would disperse in the hot tap water, and then finding them in the window.

Not unattractive, really, as buttocks went, a bit reddish, thrust impudently over the windowsill directly above Mother's picture on the Motorola.

"Good morning, Mr. Buridan," had mouthed the vertical cleft between. They'd had a kind of crooked, sideways smile, but that was because Buridan's head was cocked to one side. He tilted his head the other way and made the buttocks mildly depressed.

It took him a moment to realize it had to be a wretched schoolboy prank. Softly he went to the front door, tore it open and peered down the porch to the window. Nothing. No movement anywhere except Justus O'Toole, who had just arrived to keep his promise to retar Buridan's roof and was unloading supplies from his pickup at the curb.

"You see anyone run past?" Buridan called. "Maybe someone with his pants down?"

"No, thanks," Justus yelled back. "Just finished breakfast. Mind if I store the tar on your porch the next day or so? Hate leaving it out overnight."

"I SAID DID A BOY RUN PAST WITHOUT PANTS?"

"Nope, nothing to worry about. Course, you better keep your open fires away from it, see?"

Buridan turned back in, but on the threshold, where the outdoor and indoor worlds butted together, the exterior wall looked baby-bottom smooth, while inside the buttocks still hung over the television.

To have a buttocks thrust through a window without a legs and torso on the other side defied every philosophical precept Buridan could think of. At once he marched in to put the hallucination to an empirical test, and brought his hand down on the buttocks with what ought to have been a resounding slap. Instead, his hand passed through, sending little shards of buttock wafting upward like translucent jello. A moment later they reassembled themselves.

"Mercy me," Buridan said.

"Not from us," the buttocks replied. "We are the Devil."

"You can't be—I'm an atheist!"

The potential for the loss of one's faith had been his mother's principal objection to a career in Philosophy. "I *want* you to be happy," she had said once. "Didn't I let Roger take those chemistry courses even though I knew he'd blow up in a lab?" In fact, Buridan had thought sullenly at the time, Roger had never blown up, not even once. "But *Philosophy*, John! They'll make you say obscene, sacrilegious, dirty things. You'll get black rings around your mouth. What will my dear cousin the Bishop say?"

"Nonetheless," the buttocks continued, rudely interrupting Buridan's thoughts, "we are here to make you a proposition."

"What kind of posture is that for making propositions?" Buridan sneered.

"Martin Luther admired it very much."

"Martin Luther was a Protestant."

"Actually," the buttocks said, "we chose it because he was German. We've found our present manifestation highly effective with them, along with librarians, model railroaders, Danish plate collectors—anal types generally."

Buridan thought perhaps he was lucky not to be a phallic personality.

"But to business," the buttocks continued. "It would be the standard contract, of course, your soul for your heart's desire."

Buridan looked around the comfortable room. There really wasn't anything he wanted, he thought. Mother was gone and he had the house to himself.

The buttocks made a raspberry sound, then drooped dejectedly over the sill. "No imagination at all," they sniffed. *"Ubi sunt* the overreaching Fausts of yesteryear? What about the fact you might lose your job? What about football?"

"You could save my job?" Buridan asked, suddenly interested. "You're not thinking of something like *Damn Yankees,* I hope. I hate football."

"Never mind. Like Him, we work in mysterious ways."

"Empty assertion," Buridan said. "You can't expect a philosophy teacher to sign his soul away on that basis."

"Very well. Proof will be provided." With that, the buttocks' twin globes had rolled in upon each other, compressing themselves, and had begun to revolve, centrifugal force bulging one toward the top and the other toward the bottom into a fleshy Yin-Yang that had whirled faster and faster, smaller and smaller, into nothingness between the window and the sill.

Buridan slammed the empty window down like a guillotine and marched off to class. Nothing unusual happened. In Civics he corrected Harbutt's "But I thought—" with a curt "At Assumption, we deal in facts. Now mark me— and this is your Memory Gem for the day, so prick up your ears—efficient local government is the noblest work of Nature." Really, he had thought, what some of them want is an old-fashioned whipping. And in European History they began his favorite lesson sequence, Philip II and the Spanish Inquisition. Buridan liked to particularize for impact.

"Imagine yourself, Walther Peters, with your feet manacled to one end of the kitchen table and your hands tied to a huge winch, being stretched taut as piano wire . . ."

As he spoke, he glanced down at his notes and found to his surprise a note addressed to him in a microscopically precise script recalling charters he'd seen in museums one summer with Mother in Europe.

Buridan:

Re larger specimens for football. As our new administration's recruiting shows results, will need bigger jerseys and smaller helmets. Requisition same at once.

Dom Diablo,
Headmaster

New administration? Dom Diablo? Headmaster? What did it all mean? Suddenly Buridan heard an insistent ringing. "All right," he said. "That's the bell. You may go."

"What bell?" someone asked.

Really, in the last year or so students had grown astonishingly stupid. The bell was loud enough to wake the dead. "*THE* BELL! Class dismissed!"

Confused, they rose and stumbled sheeplike toward the door. He waited until the room was empty, then walked briskly to Mother Margaret's office to confront her about the mysterious new headmaster, noting as his heels clicked neatly on the linoleum that all the Sisters were keeping their classes late.

He brushed past Sister Ursula's reception desk and went directly into Mother Margaret's office. She looked up, surprised. "Not again!" she said. "Don't you have a class at this hour?"

"About the new headmaster," Buridan began, turning to see Sister Ursula in the door behind him. He was struck by how visible the moustache on her upper lip was this morning, and missed what she was saying. Something about two men. Perhaps the new headmaster sent by the Chancery?

"Tell them I don't have time for questions," Mother Margaret said.

But even as Sister Ursula turned, two priests in black monastic habits with full cowls glided into the room. Both were dark eyed and swarthy, the first tall and gaunt, the second short and stocky.

"Good afternoon," the tall one said, a strong Spanish trill to his *r*'s. "Allow me to introduce myself. I am Dom Diablo, Abbot-General of the Fratres de Scelestis Agnis Perditis—a small and humble order. And this is my assistant and confessor, Dom Legarto."

The shorter one smiled toothily to Reverend Mother and turned to Dom Diablo to ask some sort of question. To Buridan, it sounded like "Rrrrk?"

"No, no," Dom Diablo smiled. "This is the very fine Reverend Mother—beyond reproach."

Dom Legarto looked disappointed.

"I have come," Dom Diablo continued, "to see to the orderly transfer of teaching assignments and other duties."

"Perhaps," Buridan ventured, realizing he had to take control of the situation in view of Mother Margaret's incapacity to deal with so sudden a change, "you will need an auto to bring your luggage—?"

"Alas," Dom Diablo said, "we have no luggage. We are sworn to poverty and travel light." He turned to Dom Legarto, who had become visibly excited. "No, no, my friend. "Auto-*mobile*. Horseless tumbrel, yes?" Then he turned back to Mother Margaret. "Always he is so full of desire to begin the good works, it is hard to believe such dedication can stuff in so small a stature, yes?"

Dom Legarto moved toward Buridan. "Rrrrk?" he asked again.

Dom Diablo placed a restraining hand on his shoulder. "Have you forgotten Ockham's Razor, little one? *Pluralites non est ponenda sine necessitate*. This gentleman is cut from the same virtuous cloth as the Reverend Mother. Senior Juan Buridan, the very fine footballs coach, I presume?"

"The same," Buridan said, surprised to hear Ockham quoted. He had only recently rediscovered Ockham in his plunge from the comfort of Augustinian universals toward the terrifying chaos of a Creation of discontinuous, unrelated items.

"Mr. Buridan," Mother Margaret interrupted firmly, "I think you're overtired—your concern over football, your mother's passing—"

"I only asked the Dom—"

"Who? Please, go home for the day and rest."

Mother Margaret had recently developed a patronizing tone with him, Buridan thought, unintentionally, perhaps, but obviously treating him as though he were like some mad and gloomy Russian, Gogol's Poprishchin or Ivan Karamazov, needing gentle treatment. He made a face and left, thinking it was she who, distracted and agitated, needed the rest and understanding. On the way out he told Sister Ursula that Reverend Mother might be close to a breakdown.

When he reached home, he found Justus O'Toole on

the porch cleaning his hands, the flesh stained dark brown, pores and wrinkles etched in black by the tar. His ladder stood against the house, and nearby a five-gallon pail of tar over a butane heater.

"This to warm the tar?" Buridan asked, to be polite. "What's it made of?"

"Car?" Justus was unwrapping his sandwich with dirty hands. "Oh, *tar*. Coal, trees, peat, old tires—whatever."

"A kind of universal residue?" Buridan asked, intrigued. He stepped carefully over the sticky blobs Justus had spilled on the porch, but inside he found he had tracked it across Mother's rug. He rubbed with his finger, but the black spots merely spread into deep brown blemishes. He went up to the bathroom for the thorazine Dr. Herzberg had given him for worry and the cleaning fluid, but at the door he stopped short.

The toilet paper had been unrolled and draped from towel rack to faucets to curtain rod, back and forth. Who? Justus O'Toole? But there was writing on it. He looked closely. A memo. He read from section to section. It was from Dom Diablo, a plan for making sure the football team obeyed training regulations. Infractions were to be reported to a new disciplinary body called the Suprema, and the accused would be bound over to the secular authorities for—

Elated, Buridan stuffed the toilet paper into his pocket and bounded down the stairs, only to find Dom Diablo himself in his living room.

"Ah, Senior Buridan," he smiled. "The first of our new football recruits has arrived, and we have appropriated your kitchen to administer the S.S.A.T. tests required for admission. He is twenty-seven years of age and plays for the Rams, but his parents, very devout, wish for him a religious postgraduate year. Still, we must have the tests, for we cannot automatically—"

"RRRRK?" Dom Legarto asked excitedly from the corner. Buridan realized he must have been there the whole time without his noticing.

"No, no, sweet Hammer and Anvil to our Faith," Dom Diablo corrected. "Auto-*matically*. Will you excuse us, Senior Buridan?" He smiled and led his associate into the kitchen. The door shut.

"Now, the first question," Dom Diablo's voice had said. "In the figure before you, the length of the rectangle *A* is

ne more than X, and its width one less. If the area of
is twice that of B, then the perimeter of A is (a) 10,
) 12, (c) 24, (d) 30 or (e) none of the above?"

A lengthy pause. "None of the above," a desperate
oice said.

"Alas," Dom Diablo said. "We are sunk deep in Error.
om Legarto . . . ?"

The door burst open and Dom Legarto hurried past. A
oment later he bustled back again, carrying the tongs
om the fireplace in the parlor. "Rrrrk," he smiled with
l the teeth in his head.

"Aaaagh," came from inside.

"All can be forgiven if you recant." Dom Diablo's voice.

"I recant."

"Excellent. Do you wish to hear the question again from
ur new perspective?"

"No, it's . . . is it . . . number 'a'?" A pause. "Oh,
od, it's not? *Tell* me, *please*."

"The rules forbid our interfering. Alas, how obstinate
ose sunk in Darkness can be. Dom Legarto, is it 'a' as
e so foolishly believes?"

A pause and a creaking sound.

"Aaaaaaaaagh!"

"You confess to relapsing into Ignorance?" Dom Diablo
ked on the other side of the door.

" 'B' then! It's got to be 'b.' "

"*Ad majorem dei gloriam,* how gratifying to see you
eturn to the bosom of Rightwiseness. Dom Legarto, help
ur friend to blacken the space of his choice on his
nswer sheet using his electrically conductive pencil. Oh?
ery well, try the *other* hand, then."

It seemed an eternity before the interrogation ended
d the kitchen door opened again. Dom Diablo emerged.

"Would you believe it?" he exulted. "A perfect score!"

Behind him came Dom Legarto with the tongs. "Rrrrk!"
e leered. Buridan glanced inside. There was no sign of
e student, but on his kitchen table were ropes and a
and winch. At last he understood. The word was "rack."

Dom Diablo saw him wince. "Do not alarm yourself,"
e smiled. "It is sanctioned in the papal bull of Innocent
V, 1252, *Ad extirpanda*. Now, as our prospective student
ill be staying to dinner, I think it would be—how do you
ay?—*nice* to have a special meal." He leaned over and
hispered instructions, which Buridan jotted down on the

nearest available surface, a doily. Then Buridan headed out the door to find Sister Refectorian about the menu change.

On his way across the empty football field, he four young Trivet, the mascot-keeper, walking his charge. " think Agnes is sick, sir," he said, patting the small, wool thing, yellow-white stained brown around the ears, no and tail. "She's acting funny."

"I'll see to it," Buridan said, taking the leash. "Where the team?"

"Team? The season's over, sir."

Buridan waved him away and headed on toward th main building. He literally had to wrestle the butcher kni from Sister Refectorian's hands, and she screamed at hi the whole time he was following the recipe. When he wa done, he put the knife in his coat pocket, washed his hand and dried them on the recipe, which got ink all over h fingers. Then, still trailing a tail of toilet-paper memo fro his pocket, he went to the faculty lounge to wait for th supper bell.

He knew perfectly well what was going on from h history test. Dom Diablo's Fratres de Scelestis Agnis Perd tis were the only order of inquisitorial friars ever suppresse for excessive cruelty in Spain, the Lost Black Lambs. An they had been sent by the buttocks to grant him his wisl a winning football team that would save his job. But why The answer was obvious—God wanted to trick him int damnation for discovering that the Virgin Birth was simple freak of nature that required no God at all.

But he was crafty, and he could still use these hell-sen shades to his advantage if he were careful. It was lik dealing with leprechauns or Greek gods—spell out wh you want and don't assume anything. Otherwise you woun up like Tithonus, whom the gods granted eternal life b not, because he'd neglected to mention it, eternal youth.

As the dinner bell tolled, Buridan went to take h accustomed place at the head table. It was very confusin because sometimes he saw Dom Diablo and Dom Legart across from him, and sometimes Mother Margaret an Sister Ursula.

"You're feeling better?" Mother Margaret asked. "I' like to know why you came back when I told you to sta home and rest, but now you're here, would you mind e plaining the requisition you left on my desk for eight gross of extra-large football jerseys?"

Buridan waved away the distracting sounds and winked broadly at Dom Diablo. From behind his face came a gasp that sounded like Sister Ursula, but at that moment in came the student waiters with their laden trays.

"And Sister Refectorian had to be taken to her room," Mother Margaret continued. "She was babbling about your having changed today's menu for the head table. Can you explain?"

"It was Dom Diablo's thoughtfulness," Buridan protested mildly, thinking that if he ducked, the sounds would fly right over him.

"Who? Never mind. Sit up, please. Sister Refectorian also claimed you threatened her with a knife. And now little Luis Trivet says our mascot is missing."

"Dom Diablo thought we needed a new image—a big, black ram," Buridan said.

"Where *is* Agnes, Mr. Buridan?"

"She has, alas, gone on a journey elsewhere," Dom Diablo said.

"I can't hear you with your face so close to the plate, Mr. Buridan," Mother Margaret pursued. "Did you say she ran away?" Mother Margaret sat back. "Well, she can't get far. She'll turn up sooner or later in this kind of neighborhood."

"Sooner," Dom Diablo had said.

The waiter had handed her the platter. She had looked as it and put it down. "Is this meat?"

"It's a special Roman Easter dish," Buridan had said. "Dom Diablo said it would be all right. *Abbaccio al forno.*"

"True, Reverend Mother," Dom Diablo said.

Mother Margaret pretended not to hear. She held a piece under her nose. "What does *forno* mean?"

" 'Baked,' I think." He turned to Dom Diablo for support. "I know it sounds like a sin, but I think *fornaro* is only 'baker' in Italian."

"I see. And—what is it . . . *abbaccio?*"

"Milk-fed yearling la—"

Mother Margaret dropped her fork and leapt up, muttering something about telephone calls—but Buridan realized right away no telephones were ringing. "Must talk with someone," she managed. "Excuse me." She made her way among the tables toward the door.

The verge of chaos, Buridan thought. Reverend Mother leaving head table before announcements. Unheard of. Students restless—without organization they're beasts.

He rose masterfully to take control, leaning across the table to ding Mother Margaret's little bell with his spoon. He would save the day by announcing the new method for handling infractions of training rules. Ding ding ding ding. But as the brutish little faces turned up toward him, he decided he needed something more dramatic. "Gentlemen, tonight we will have a rally for tomorrow's game. A demonstration of unity of spirit and team support. Please follow me in an orderly fashion to the bonfire."

Dom Legarto bounced up and down in his chair with glee.

"Yes, Little One," Dom Diablo said. "At last, the purifying fire; at last, the *auto-da-fé!*"

"Precisely!" Buridan called back to them over the students' heads, moving swiftly through the tables. "Purge past humiliations, cleanse our spirits, unify ourselves!"

At first they only stared, but then Trivet rose, white faced, and another, then a third. A cheer was what they needed to unify them, Buridan thought, walking backward toward the door.

"KILL!" he shouted, at once exhilarated by the oneness of their voices as they answered.

"KILL, KILL, KILL, KILL, KILL!"

As they crossed the street and then the field, Buridan dashed ahead to string Dom Diablo's long memo from the barrel to the steps and then slosh cleaning fluid on it.

"Stop him!" he heard someone shout—a creature of the trustees—but he was not to be stopped. A match to the memo, yellow light licking up the white pathway, down inside, then a dull, muffled "whump" from within the barrel. A column of cleansing flame had leapt up.

Someone vaulted the railing and came toward him.

"Get away," Buridan yelped. "Dangerous!"

"Grab him!" someone yelled.

"Tackle him!" called another.

The game already? Buridan saw Dom Legarto frenziedly hopping up and down as Dom Diablo watched the plays impassively. Stokes had downed the Cranmer Tech ballcarrier at the forty and the others had piled on, then red whistles, handkerchiefs, sirens marked a penalty. Then the players disentangled themselves, leaving the ball-carrier stretched on the field, ankles shackled to a fathom of iron chain ending in a sixty-pound ball.

"Illegal holding," the referee signaled. "Against the Paschal Lambs."

"Don't just stand there!" Buridan told the man who had appeared next to him. "Get a hacksaw!" But the man didn't move. Uniformed, Buridan thought. Official score-keeper?

"Let's come quietly, pops," the man said, his face melting into the buttocks perched atop his shoulders beneath the police cap. "Enough demonstrations," they said. "Take your choice. Sign or not."

"Watch it!" some hysteric shouted. "He's got a butcher knife!"

"This is the usual way, I think," Buridan said to the buttocks as he inked the knife. "Isn't it supposed to clot as a warning or something?"

A violent tremor suddenly shook the knife from his hand, turning him so that he found himself looking through the buttocks' window into the heart of the flame. There in her wingback sat Mother, running like tar.

"Oh, John," she wailed, shaking her head so violently that molten globs of face flew outward in all directions. "Why couldn't you have taken Chemistry?"

"You never understood," he spat back, feeling himself going away. "Philosophy every bit as dangerous. Crucible of gunpowder—explode in your face any minute."

But somehow he found himself already somewhere else, in a car with the lattice-screen of the confessional between front and rear seats. He clung desperately to it.

"I didn't see it at first, Father," he told the priest at the wheel. "But it just shows the justice of Ockham's Razor —'multiplicity ought not to be posited without necessity.' The Elephant Man's not discontinuous at all! Shave away the accidents of disparate appearances, merely deceptive exteriors, and you've got the common existence shared by everything from the Virgin Birth to cancer viruses. And do you know what that Essence is, Father? Tar. People think it's sticky and dirty, but absolutely everything can be reduced to it. A crucial discovery—well worth the risk of consorting with devils. But you needn't worry about that because I'm an atheist."

The uniformed priest turned around in the front seat and Dom Diablo's face smiled at Buridan through the screen. "Don't be apologetic," he soothed, the fire bathing his face in red. "*We* have no admissions requirements. Welcome."

"Mercy me," Buridan murmured, letting the buttocks-scorekeeper press him back against the seat so he could see the red flame dance as tiny stars on the chrome of the auto fixtures. "Mercy me."

The still-warm ground made a slight sucking noise as Mother Margaret walked to the ruins of what had been Immaculate Conception's door. Black and glistening with hose water, the wooden posts and lintel stood like an empty picture frame, within which swirled the smoke and steam of the still smoldering fire. The air reeked of wet, charred wood.

The sparks. That was what they had said. Like fireflies they had ridden the night wind from Buridan's house and lighted on the wooden shingles of Conception. It was hard for her to believe, but firemen spoke of fires with a churchman's authority on religion and morals. One didn't argue.

And poor John Buridan. Faced with her own loss, it was tempting to ignore his suffering or even to blame him, but she knew better. If only she had recognized the seriousness of his symptoms, but she had been so preoccupied with her own worries. And her fears.

She looked down. On the wet stone steps a bee lay curled. A bee in December? The fire, of course—its false spring warmth had wakened them from winter sleep and they had begun to crawl from their nest only to tumble into the flames or perish in the cold hovering at the fringes of the fire. They too had been betrayed.

It would not do to blame God. What seemed like cruel chance to man was really divine providence, God's plan which worked eternally toward universal good even though the mortals it touched might see in it only personal calamity. Still, the bee brought back to her the thing that had preoccupied her every moment until the fire itself—Macduff.

Was there anything in the overwhelming calamity of that poor creature to argue for the workings of a greater good? It wrenched her faith to think that mere men could so pervert the very atoms of God's perfect Creation. Where were the bolts of lightning from the sky that should have struck such monsters dead? Not only had they been spared, they had prospered, come to her door yesterday, and she could not help but wonder if they had not somehow had a hand in what had happened here last night. And what part had she played? Might she have prevented that spurious uncle in sunglasses from taking the child five years ago? Had they done something to him after they got him back that had turned him into the creature he was now?

Unnatural, motherless creation of disease. She could not suppress that shudder of revulsion whenever she thought of him, and yet she knew what she felt was a mother's guilt. All her other charges had been saved from the fire, and they would find lives just as good in the Order's other homes, but she could think only of the one lamb lost. If she had gone to the authorities . . . ? No, as far as she could tell, these people *were* the authorities.

"Mother Margaret?"

She turned to see Father Fagan making his way through the blackened debris toward her, his breath smoking in the December cold.

"I came as soon as I heard," he said. "They tell me everyone's all right."

She nodded, trying to swallow the burning lump in her throat.

He was silent for a moment. "They asked me to tell you that they're holding the last bus for you, but if you'd like to stay here awhile, I've got the parish station wagon . . ."

"No," she said. "I'll go with my children."

"I understand."

"All the records were lost, you know," she said. "I wonder if that was the reason—wiping out all evidence of him."

"Pardon?"

She smiled. "Never mind—I'm giving in to my worst thoughts. You know the poor soul they call Elephant Man?"

Father Tim looked worried. "Yes?"

"I know this will sound impossible, but—"

"He's Macduff? I know." Father Tim paused. "John Buridan found out . . . somehow. It seemed to disturb him very deeply—the philosophical implications, I mean. It's even possible that what happened last night . . ."

"He knew? Then I understand even better why he finally lost control." Mother Margaret stared at the wisps of smoke leaching from the fallen timbers. "I want to ask you a favor, Tim. It seems almost as though I had been put here to look after Macduff. And I failed—failed then, and failed now because I've got to go where I'm called. It's unfair to pass my burden on, but—"

"Don't worry, Margaret. I'll look after him."

She was afraid even to allow the truth to take shape in her mind. She wanted more than anything to cast off her vows, to go to Macduff and help him, protect him in any way she could. *Not, I'll not, carrion comfort, Despair, not feast on thee. . . .*

"Years ago I took a vow of obedience, and that's still my first duty. But I know God wants me here, too. As soon as I can, I'll be back."

"Of course you will. And don't you worry in the meantime," Father Tim smiled.

"I just can't help thinking that I've already failed. That somehow his fate is beyond anything mere mortals can stop. But that would be like saying that God allowed Macduff to be created and then cared nothing about what happened to him."

"We'll still do our best."

The deep honk of a bus drifted up from the street.

"Yes," she said. "We'll do our best. God bless you, Tim."

"And God bless you, Margaret, old friend."

Chapter 24

Well, Maybe Three Shakes of a Lamb's Tail

"He *what?*" Leffingwell yelped.

It was Tuesday morning, and he and Macduff were waiting to be taken upstairs for their preliminary hearing.

"I *said,*" Greenbaum explained patiently, "that your alibi set fire to his house and the whole school burned down. Said he did it because the Spanish Inquisition had taken over the football team so he wouldn't have to sell his soul to the Devil's rear end. Lurdan's deputy found him at the state mental hospital."

"Was he able to make a deposition, at least?" Leffingwell asked.

"Oh, great. A deposition from an off-the-wall fruitcake who keeps talking about Frankenstein and the Virgin Birth in Latin—he's one great alibi. Very convincing."

The guard, slumped in his chair like a used teabag, raised one heavy eyelid. "You clowns want to keep it down?"

"All right," Leffingwell went on in a lower voice. "What about Macduff's alibi, the nun?"

"After the fire, the nuns and kids were bussed all over the place—wherever somebody had room. Nobody seems to know exactly where this Mother Margaret of yours wound up."

The words were like a bolt of electricity. Macduff stiffened and looked away, dry eyes burning. He tried to imagine the old building as a smoldering ruin, saw the dark shape of Mother Margaret move forlornly through the devastation.

She had been the nearest thing to a mother he'd ever known, the immutable reality he had sensed existed even before he had rediscovered her on the television screen that day. How he had struggled to retrace his footsteps back to his beginnings and her.

And now she was gone. Like Sykes, like everything else he'd ever touched. His life was one long disappearing act. It was as though some force were methodically obliterating every trace of his past, slowly working its way forward in time. Soon, he felt, he too would suddenly wink out. Only the triumphant men in sunglasses would be left, and it seemed there was nothing he could do. He did not fear for himself; it would be a relief, after all this, to have his monstrousness wisp into the nothingness he had imagined on the other side of that hospital door so long ago. A relief for himself, a blessing for everyone connected with him. But he feared for Leffingwell.

Silently he wet his finger and dabbed at his eyes.

"*Which* places?" Leffingwell was saying.

"How should I know?" said Greenbaum. "Have I got Paul Drake and Della Street doing legwork for me? My secretary won't even sharpen my pencils. I'll find her, I'll find her—as soon as I've got a minute. In the meantime, what about reconsidering insanity pleas?"

On the far side of the room a belch rolled down from the heights of the French Canadian in the Expo '67 tie and rattled the windows. As far as Leffingwell knew, he hadn't moved since Sunday morning.

"My alibi's in the cuckoo bin, I'm being held on the hallucinations of a thirteen-year-old fatty, and you want *me* to plead insanity?"

"Okay, make it a moral issue if you want to," Greenbaum said, picking his nose indifferently. "I'll see you in the Big House."

"That's how much you know," Leffingwell said. "You couldn't even get Macduff his hat."

"They don't allow hats in court," Greenbaum said.

A second deputy appeared at the door. "Five of ten. Let's move it, Laffy."

"Leffingwell," Leffingwell hissed. Why was it everyone connected with the law from Greenbaum to Lurdan kept getting his name wrong?

"Whatever. You, too, Gruesome. And Frenchie over there—you're first this morning."

Greenbaum, Leffingwell and Macduff followed the Man-Mountain and the second deputy down the hall, up a flight of stairs and through a doorway at the side of the courtroom. They found a small audience of social security pensioners, drop-ins from the unemployment compensation line upstairs and a compact cluster of prepubescent girls led by a spidery older woman—Miss Nicky and the Nick-Nackettes or a civics class come to see the judicial branch in action. And two men at the back in light suits and sunglasses.

As their little procession came forward, gasps rippled through the crowd and head after head turned to stare at Elephant Man's trembling excrescences.

With surprise, Leffingwell found Capella and Stackpole in the first row on the defense side. Capella raised a Sicilian fist to show he too desired to obscenity the obscene mother of the law, and Stackpole flashed the kind of smile he hadn't given Leffingwell for a month. Had they really skipped work just for him? But Dawn was nowhere to be seen, nor, for that matter, was there any sign of Fern or Mrs. Adams.

As Leffingwell slumped down between Greenbaum and Macduff, Stackpole leaned forward.

"I know a brother's got a Schmeisser burp gun stashed away," he whispered encouragingly. "I can be back here with it by lunch. Five hundred ten rounds a minute. Think about it."

At least an hour passed before the bailiff announced Judge Abraham Steele and the court rose to watch him hobble in. He was deep into his seventies, but still thick and bullish under his robes, like a retired Mafia mechanic. A kind of hit-man for the far right.

First on the docket was the Man-Mountain, who turned out to be one Pierre Labouchere up for manslaughter. He was serving as his own attorney.

"And would you tell us again, Mr. Labouchere," said

the nervous young Prosecutor, several fat files tucked under
one arm spewing papers out of their back sides at regular
intervals, "how it was you happened to shoot Mr. Immelman?"

"Ah," said Labouchere. "I am hunting, you know, and
I see something, and I say to myself, 'Hey, you one lucky
sonofabitch, Pierre! Look there—a fine gophair!' So then
I shoot him, boom!"

"You're saying you thought Mr. Immelman was a woodchuck?" said the Prosecutor.

"Oui."

"But Mr. Immelman was driving a Chevrolet Impala,"
persisted the Prosecutor. "How many woodchucks have
you seen driving Chevrolets, Mr. Labouchere?"

"I dunno," Pierre said thoughtfully. "One, maybe."

Leffingwell sensed a stirring and turned. Mrs. Adams
was plowing hugely down the aisle in a new pair of rhine-
stone-studded glasses, her overcoat open to reveal an
equally new dress the shocking pink of Leffingwell's low-
pressure stick-on circles for the weather map. Behind, in
matching dress and glasses, slumped Fern herself. Leffingwell watched them move with the ponderous dignity of
growing storm cells and settle on the Prosecutor's side like
guests of the groom at a wedding. A moment later, Dawn
slipped in.

"Thank God," he whispered. "I was beginning to wonder if you'd come."

"Of course I came," she answered. "I was subpoenaed."
Leffingwell noticed she had shed her woolen shirt and
fatigues for a prim gray suit.

"By the prosecution? You mean you didn't come to give
me moral support or something?"

"Why did you do it?" she asked sternly.

"What? *Fern?*"

"I just met her in the corridor," Dawn said, fingering a
bulky manila envelope in her lap. "She's a very, very sincere person. She, uh, gave me some stuff to help Lance and
Oberon cover your story."

"Let's see it," Leffingwell said. There was something
terribly wrong about this. Sincerity wasn't one of the qualities Dawn specialized in. He took the envelope.

Inside were four 8 x 10 glossies of Fern in tap shoes and
a distressed leotard looking like an ambulatory potato, and
a two-page, typed press release:

Miss Fern Adams, aspiring local girl and danseuse, last night, to her sorrow, met face to face the dark side of man's deepseated animal lust as the rapee of alleged area television personality and neighbor Durwood Leffingwell of the highly regarded and often viewed Channel 29, and his so-called—

Leffingwell looked up. The same mangled prose retailred for Channel 29. Across the room, the pair in pink ully blinked their lizard eyes, witless but huge and danerous. His chicken nightmares come true. So that was ow the incident had gotten such amazing coverage—the ern Adams Wire Service and Public Relations Corp., with nishing touches by her *Tattler*-reading mother. He rearned the pile to Dawn.

"You know where this kid is coming from, don't you?" e asked. "She's either out to get our money or she's so razy she thinks the publicity's going to put her in show iz."

"I'd like to believe you, Woody," Dawn said. "But really, ho'd be gullible enough to think anyone could get anyhere by smearing a local UHF hack?"

"UHF hack?" bleated Leffingwell, but at that moment a uccession of "ooh's" of recognition from the spectators lerted him to the progress of Lance and Oberon Ricketts own the aisle. They squeezed in beside Capella.

"Hi," Leffingwell said. "Hope you're not sweating toight's weather. We'll be done here in plenty of time."

"The new Weather Girl will handle it," said Oberon.

"Weather Girl?"

"Since last night's show," Oberon smiled.

Leffingwell's eyes moved slowly from Oberon to Dawn, ho was staring at the floor. So *that* was why she'd believed ern. At some point Dawn had decided Elephant Man nterprises, Inc., was no longer a growth industry and had quidated her interests in the firm. Like Fern, Dawn was oing into television. He turned back to the Ricketts.

"How come you're here?"

"Witnesses," whispered Oberon.

Leffingwell pondered. "For the Prosecution?"

"What else?" Oberon beamed. "And afterwards we can o a live remote of you and your friend in manacles going prison. Didn't Capella and Stackpole tell you? The van's arked right outside, all ready to go."

Leffingwell glanced back at his two former friends. Skipped work for his sake indeed, he thought, angry with himself for not suspecting the worst. He should have known he and Macduff were nothing but ratings fodder. He turned back to his one remaining friend with a cold, numbing hopelessness creeping over him. "We're fucked, Macduff," he said. "Just because one kind of rape gets all the publicity doesn't mean there aren't other kinds."

Macduff said nothing, and Leffingwell suddenly realized the words "Leffingwell" and "Elephant Man" had just been spoken aloud. He looked up to find Pierre Laboucher gone, and the Prosecutor, armed with a new set of folders, was specifying the charges against them.

When he was done, the judge leaned forward to Green baum. "Counsel, how do your culprits plead?"

Greenbaum flashed them a last, desperate look, but Leffingwell was adamant. "Not guilty, Your Honor," Green baum sighed.

"Let the record show the defendants refused to plead guilty," said Judge Steele. "But let me assure you, gentlemen, this isn't going to be any bed of peaches."

Leffingwell's faith in the power of innocence began to dribble away like antifreeze from the old Rambler's radiator. So this was a hanging judge.

The first witness was the arresting officer, Sheriff Lurdan. He recounted Mrs. Adams' telephone call, the arrest at Dawn's love nest, and identified each of the six confiscated beer cans, now curiously empty, by their individual tags. "They was tanked up something fierce," he added.

The Prosecutor heaved a duffel bag from the floor onto his table with a resounding clunk and pulled out several lengths of rope and twenty feet of heavy-duty chain. Leffingwell recognized them as the emergency tie-ropes and tow chain the ever-efficient Dawn kept in the back of the Honda.

"Yep," said the sheriff. "Found 'em in his trunk. Guess they carry them with 'em *wherever they go*," he added darkly.

Leffingwell looked questioningly at Greenbaum, but neither could fathom it. Then Greenbaum rose for his cross-examination: had Fern been taken to a hospital for semen test? She hadn't. Greenbaum dismissed him.

"Doesn't that mean they've got no case?" Leffingwell

whispered hopefully. "Doesn't there have to be a witness or something?"

"Not under the new get-tough-on-rape statute," Greenbaum answered. "One sworn statement or two significant rumors."

Leffingwell slumped back, despair congealing into icy terror. He knew how the Rambler had felt, smashed and abandoned at the foot of that hill. Damn it, how could Macduff just sit there without so much as blinking? Didn't he understand?

"Call Mr. Tanker Hackett to the stand," said the Prosecutor.

Hackett limped down the aisle in a leg cast, Henry Adams Elementary School Athletic Squad sweat shirt, baseball cap and whistle. "Got to be back by third-period medicine ball," he said before taking the oath.

Dutifully he testified that Leffingwell had been drummed out of the Tooth Brigade Monday morning to prevent further contact with innocent children. "I'm just a simple soldier in the war against decay, sir, but—well, gee whiz, every dogface knows there's times a man's got to do what a man's got to do."

"Are you saying you *regretted* firing Mr. Leffingwell?"

"No, sir, not at all. I was *glad* to do it. Anyway, the Weather Girl's taking his place in the horse."

Greenbaum cross-examined. "Whatever WHCK's present PR worries, Mr. Hackett, wasn't Mr. Leffingwell perfect for his part? Isn't it a fact he never harmed a child on the show?"

"Well," said Hackett, "I saw him kick a chicken once."

"A *chicken?*" asked Greenbaum.

"Maybe she was a rooster," said Hackett. "I forget."

"What's that got to do with—"

"There was a *kid inside* the chicken," said Hackett. "A little girl."

The spectators gasped. The Prosecutor smiled and called Oberon Ricketts to the stand.

"If they find out *Fern* was that chicken," Leffingwell whispered, "we've really had it." He cast a sidelong glance at Macduff's great, misshapen head, tipped slightly forward as though in meditation. Why didn't he *do* something? How could he just *sit* there?

Oberon Ricketts was in the process of testifying that Leffingwell had been the kiddy commentator at the Butler

Barnum Labor Day Parade while under the influence of a powerful narcotic. "I found it personally *humiliating,*" she said.

"No further questions," said the Prosecutor.

"There were no children physically present at this incident, were there?" asked Greenbaum.

"No, just thousands of them watching."

"I see," Greenbaum said, his index finger trembling dangerously close to his nostril. "Now, in his capacity as a weatherman——"

"Objection, Your Honor," said the Prosecutor. "This wasn't covered in direct examination and it's outside the area of the witness's competence."

"Objection sustained," said the Judge. "Please refrain from this line of questioning, Counsel."

"Witness may step down," said Greenbaum with a flourish and returned triumphantly to his seat.

"What the fuck did *that* prove?" said Leffingwell.

"Nothing," said Greenbaum, still smiling at the judge and Prosecutor. "But you've got to *look* like you just scored a point. That's how the law works."

"You are Mr. John Miasma?" the Prosecutor was saying.

"*Professor Jack* Miasma," he answered, turning his eyes into slits by pushing back his hair with the bases of his palms.

"Would you tell the court what you do, Professor Jack?"

"I am a highly regarded cinematographer, widely read younger poet, dedicated teacher, and Director of the Creative Writing-slash-Cinema Program at Cambria College."

"Thank you, Professor Jack."

"I'm also the entire staff as well."

"Thank you."

"Not to mention *Unlisted Numbers,* a collection of my poetry which has been considered by several *major* publishers."

"*Thank* you."

"I just thought the court would want to know my stature so they could evaluate my testimony. Whenever I write a student recommendation, I always include a page about myself."

"Professor Jack," said the Prosecutor, "would you mind telling us what your connection with Mr. Leffingwell and the Elephant Man is?"

"*Are,*" corrected Jack.

"Excuse me," said the Prosecutor. "Connection are."

"I swear I only knew his wife as a student in my classes. There was nothing between us."

"No," said the Prosecutor. "I meant the Encino incident."

In measured tones, Jack Miasma recounted how Durwood Leffingwell had, in his presence, aided and abetted the Elephant Man in ravishing America's widely regarded concrete poetess for a porn film. She had not been seen since.

"Now," said the Prosecutor, "we've already heard how Mr. Leffingwell earlier assaulted an unidentified child disguised as a chicken. Did you yourself ever witness any act of violence committed by Mr. Leffingwell?"

"I certainly did," said Jack. "The accused attacked me with a *loaded* camera. Knocked me *senseless.*"

"Do something," said Leffingwell.

"No questions, Your Honor," said Greenbaum.

"Did you just say ten-four, Counsel?" asked the Judge, giving the side of his head a smart rap with the base of his palm.

The Prosecution called Mrs. Rose Adams to the stand. Leffingwell guessed the tenor of her testimony even before she spoke. One November night, she told the court, she, anxious and worried mother, had discovered Durwood Leffingwell accosting her daughter in the parking lot beside his gleaming new Mercedes.

So it was just as he'd feared that night, Leffingwell thought. Whether or not Fern had known it herself, she'd been sent out to get him into a compromising situation by her *Tattler*-inspired mother.

"Now, Mrs. Adams," said the Prosecutor, "during the period before Leffingwell deserted his own wife and went to live in sin with a *mere girl,* did you ever have cause to suspect either him or the Elephant Man?"

"Well, Fern and I was both scared to death of the elephant one. My Fern knew right off it was some kind of sex maniac. He actually lured her into the house the first day he was there."

"I see. And did you ever witness any of the violent outbursts already documented as a dominant aspect of Mr. Leffingwell's character?"

"Well," said Mrs. Adams, "last September he come over

to my house to use the phone—never bothered to have one of his own put in, see—and he stomped my little Fernie's kitty dead as a pancake."

Ugly rumblings from the spectators. "Beast!" someone shouted.

"Course, I could forget the whole thing," Mrs. Adams went on, "so long as he wanted to make amends in cash or certified check. After all, there's so much chlorine and radiation in the water, it's no wonder he's crazy."

"I read that too!" shouted a voice from the back.

"What a Christian woman," said another. "God bless you."

"No questions," said Greenbaum, licking his fingernail.

"If you don't come up with something fast," Leffingwell said, grabbing Greenbaum's arm, "I'm going to staple your nostrils together."

"If you'd learned how to control that nasty temper of yours," Greenbaum said, "you wouldn't be in this mess now."

A profound silence spread across the courtroom. Leffingwell looked up to see pink-frocked Fern bearing down on the witness stand, fat arms flopping at the elbows, feet slapping with hip-jarring force, thighs whooshing, a Tyrannosaurus on the scent of small early mammals. At the witness's chair she stopped straining and let gravity seat her. Then, guided by the Prosecutor, she began in a squeaky nasal to recount how Leffingwell had enticed her from her home into the darkness and the waiting arms of the hideous Elephant Man.

"And then they . . . then they forced me to commit those . . . acts," Fern said softly, almost sobbing.

"*Tell* us, child," panted the Hanging Judge. "However painful, we want *every* detail. In your own words."

"Well, after the elephant one had affixed the leather cuffs to my slender ankles and wrists and had fastened the chains and ropes to four iron ringbolts I had not previously noted on our apartment siding, Mr. Leffingwell began to disrobe me."

"Excuse me, Miss Adams," said the Prosecutor, straining to lift Dawn's Honda tow chain from his table. "Is *this* the chain they used?"

Fern's eyes bulged at the massive links. "Yes," she said uncertainly. "For sure."

Leffingwell slumped lower. Now he understood the significance of State's Exhibit A.

"First he rolled my sweater up until it had bunched beneath the pendulous undersides of my breasts. Then the Elephant Man yanked the coil of sweater upward——"

"Her mother's taught her the whole thing," Leffingwell said. "It's straight out of *National Tattler* or *Rec-Room Torquemada* or something. *Do* something, Greenbaum!"

"——and my milky-white, full and magnificently rounded boobies, suddenly freed, quivered naked in the moonlight like two twin hillocks of——"

"OBJECTION!" shouted Greenbaum, rising.

Leffingwell squirmed with delight. They'd get her for memorizing books not for sale to minors.

"There was *no moon* that night!" said Greenbaum.

"Overruled," came the Judge's strangled voice. "Go on, child, for God's sake."

Greenbaum collapsed into his chair. "It worked for Abe Lincoln," he shrugged.

"Thank you, Your Honor," said Fern primly. "Then, leaving my face half-smothered by the sweater bunched around my shoulders, one of them——"

Leffingwell drifted off at her description of someone's "lust-inflated member, its awesome blood-engorged dome pulsating like a Nazi helmet," and tried to assess his options.

First, there was Stackpole and his Schmeisser burp gun. Second, he could try slipping into the comfortable rear end of the Mr. Laffy suit they'd confiscated downstairs and amble out under the deputies' noses. Neither one struck him as likely.

"I've *got* it!" Greenbaum said, some of his old fire returning. "How about the *Wronged Woman Syndrome?* Your wife finds out about Dawn and wants revenge. So she impersonates you——"

"In a rape?" said Leffingwell.

"Sure—you know, like those *Mission Impossible* reruns," Greenbaum said. "I find Claudine's disguise, then I ask Fern if she recognizes the latex mask of your face and the latex——"

"*Flare*," the Prosecutor was repeating for emphasis. "*Burning*. And may I remind the court, in light of what we've just heard, that Sheriff Lurdan at no time testified to finding an *unused* flare in the defendants' trunk." He looked witheringly at Macduff and Leffingwell.

"Well, how about it?" Greenbaum asked.

The mention of Claudine had sent a pang of regret through Leffingwell. "Leave her out of this," he said.

"—reminded me," Fern was saying, "of what that nasty Ron Becker did to poor Peg on *Young and the Restless*. He raped her *and* her sister, you know."

"Ron Becker is *innocent!*" Macduff shouted, so clearly that everyone understood him. Leffingwell sank lower in his chair.

"Hah!" sniffed Fern. "They showed the *repeat* of the mysterious intruder with those pantyhose over his head to disguise himself."

"That was just Peg *remembering* what happened," said Macduff.

"No, that was Peg's memory the *first* time," said Fern vehemently. "But the *second* time they faded away to show it was *Ron Becker* remembering it. And how could it be *his* flashback unless he's the raper?"

"Counsel!" shouted Judge Steele. "Restrain your client or I'll have him bound and gagged and tied to a chair in the hall! And which of you keeps calling herself Beaver-Two and asking for Ten-Wheel Charlie?"

"She's *right*," Macduff breathed, sagging back to his seat. "I must have missed that episode when I stopped watching TV."

"Will you shut up about that stupid soap opera?" Leffingwell snapped. It was suddenly quite clear to him that if it hadn't been for Macduff and his money, none of this would have happened. And Greenbaum was obviously right —standing trial with anyone as ugly as Elephant Man guaranteed their conviction.

Judge Steele was pounding ferociously at the side of his head. At last the disc of his hearing aid clattered onto the bench before him. *"There,"* he said. "Much better. Did you wish to cross-examine, Counsel?"

"Yes, Your Honor," said Greenbaum. "I'll do my best," he said to Leffingwell, "but frankly, you two are cooked."

"Maybe I could reconsider that suggestion of yours," Leffingwell ventured. "Insanity?"

"Great," said Greenbaum. "We'll lay the groundwork and get right on it after lunch." He approached Fern with renewed confidence as she tugged her tortured hemline oward her knees. "Would you please tell us, Miss Adams, hen you first had some hint of their deranged intentions?"

"Oh, I always knew Mr. Leffingwell lusted me," said ern, smoothing her pink dress on her enormous thighs.

"And how did you know that?"

"I could see it in his eyes. Two limpid pools aflame, um, flame . . ." She closed her eyes to concentrate. "Oh! flame with animal passion."

"When was that?" asked Greenbaum.

Fern leaned forward confidentially. "The *very first time* e ever saw me. They cut away from the five-day forecast oard, and there he was—"

Greenbaum whipped around, confused but suspecting he ad somehow stumbled onto something. "There he was *hat*, Miss Adams?"

"Looking right at me, his both eyes two limpid pools a—"

"On the *television screen?*" he asked, barely hoping.

"Of course. That's where he first started sending me ose secret messages."

"Wait a bit, Miss Adams," said Greenbaum, his eyes traying his jubilance. "Let's clarify this for the court. ou say he looked through the TV camera in the studio here he was doing the weather and he could see you in ur *living room?*"

"Oh, no."

Greenbaum was deflated. "No?"

"No, I keep the TV in my *bedroom*."

"I see," said Greenbaum steadily.

"It's *my* TV, not Ma's. Daddy left it to me."

"Of course," said Greenbaum.

"So I guess it's partly my fault, in a way. I should *never* put the TV in my bedroom. It gave *all* of them the ong idea."

"What do you mean '*all* of them,' Miss Adams?" Judge eele interrupted. He turned toward the Prosecutor. "Is e some kind of tart?" he asked in a lower voice.

"I always clicked them off in time," Fern said, looking at the judge. "But certain individuals got huffy. Some of m even called me names to ruin my career."

"Who?" asked the Judge. "Tell me, my dear."

"Well, Walter Cronkite, for one," she said with a toss of r head. "I was watching *CBS Evening News* with a TV ner in bed cause Ma and I weren't speaking. I admit I should have known better, but I didn't *mean* to lead him on. The minute he got funny with me, I clicked him off. So the very next day at the end of the news he says, 'And that's the way it is, Wednesday, April twenty-fourth. By the way, I'll be on vacation sailing for the next few days, and Fern Adams is a musk ox.' I remember the date because I was too humiliated even to go to dance class that week."

The Judge shook his head. Then he scowled at the Prosecutor and motioned him to the bench.

"This is it!" Greenbaum exulted, bending close to his clients. "He's going to dismiss the charges!"

The judge leaned forward to the Prosecutor, round-shouldered with shame and disappointment. "Your office hasn't done its job, has it, Mr. Webster?"

"No, Your Honor. We should've checked her out more thoroughly."

The courtroom was hushed.

"So I'll have to do it for you," said the Judge.

The Prosecutor nodded, waiting for the roof to fall in.

"I'll see that the subpoena is made out," the Judge continued, taking out a handkerchief.

"Excuse me?" said the Prosecutor, confused.

"The subpoena. For this Crockett." He blew his nose. "Cronkite?"

"Thank you," said the judge, putting the hankie away.

"Why, Your Honor?"

"Why? He's clearly involved. You heard the child's testimony. There's some kind of conspiracy here."

"Conspiracy, Your Honor?"

"Among these TV personalities," said the Judge. "You know, the Northeast Liberal Media Axis."

"Chet Huntley said I was a sea cow when I was little," volunteered Fern.

"Thank you," said the Judge to Fern. "And for this Chet Hunter, too, Mr. Webster."

Webster slumped against the bench, burying his face in his arms. "I can't," came his reply.

"And why not?" asked the Judge. "Speak up, man."

"Huntley's dead, Your Honor."

"All right, all right," said the Judge, angrily shoving papers away from himself. "Sometimes a felon slips through the eye of justice. But this Crockett isn't going to get away."

The Prosecutor stood transfixed before the bar of justice; Fern sat unperturbed in her chair.

"Mr. Greenbaum," said the Judge, "have you anything further to ask the witness?"

Greenbaum snapped back to reality and swallowed. "No, Your Honor. I move the charges be dismissed on the grounds of the complainant's demonstrable insanity."

"Motion denied," said the Judge. "Really, you're not going to get anywhere chasing will-o-the-wisps like that."

Greenbaum looked desperately to Webster, but the Prosecutor seemed to be studying the ceiling intently, as though to discover why it hadn't fallen.

"In that case, Your Honor, I *do* have further questions, but, ah . . ." Greenbaum was out of syndromes and needed time. "In view of the hour, may I suggest we recess for lunch first?"

Leffingwell admired Greenbaum's tenacity, but he was now convinced there was nothing anyone could do. He glanced at the awful, immobile face of Macduff. Now he understood something of what Macduff had endured. The hopelessness of being a victim.

"Court will stand adjourned until two o'clock," the Hanging Judge said.

"Oh, thank you," gushed Fern. "Now I won't miss to-day's episode of *Young and the Restless*. My Auntie Em lives right down the street, and she said we could come over and watch it if we got recessed in time. Snapper and his wife *might* get back together, you know, and that Ron Becker——" She stopped herself, confused and excited.

"Don't mention it, child," said the judge, rising.

Steele was barely out of the room before Greenbaum was shaking the Prosecutor by the shoulders. "Webster, why didn't you ask him to dismiss the charges? The kid's psycho!"

"Sure she is, but so's Steele," said Webster. "*You* ask him. He's liable to charge me with receiving stolen goods or taking his time."

Leffingwell watched Fern lumber by, eyes down and arms flapping. The only way to Steele was through Fern's testimony, but Fern was so crazy she was going to visit a relative in the middle of a rape trial so she wouldn't miss her favorite soap opera. Well, after all, that was the essence of her madness. Plumbed to her shallow adolescent depths, she was simply a tiny soul possessed by Demon

Television. But how did you go about exorcising the greatest triumph of modern technology?

Between Fern's TV and the nightmare *National Tattler* world her mother inhabited, Leffingwell and Macduff were about to become the first recorded victims of the mass media. An insane joke, like Buridan's notion of sin as a string of follies whose humor only the blessed could see. Or was the joke that his punishment for this imaginary crime was justified by all the unadmitted sins of his past?

He let out a long, involuntary laugh.

Chapter 25

The Exorcism of Fern Adams

"What's the matter, Leff?" Macduff asked. The fleshy protuberances along his neck quivered with worry, though his face showed no emotion except in the bright eyes.

"Something just struck me funny, that's all," Leffingwell said, catching his breath. Macduff's concern made Leffingwell feel terrible. He was always so quick to be angry with him, to ignore the good, compassionate soul within. Maybe it was just too easy to see the elephant and forget the man inside.

"Well, Durwood, you've really done it *this* time," said a voice behind them.

Leffingwell turned to find Claudine at the railing. "Oh, hi," he said. "Nice of you to make it to the hanging." He felt a surge as he looked at her. He *had* missed her, damn it.

"I came because I was worried," she said, looking down.

"Of course," he said. "I didn't mean it. It was just another one of my stupid jokes."

"But don't get the wrong idea," she said. "I just came as a friend, you know? I wanted to see if there was anything I could do to help." She cast a quick glance at Macduff. "Both of you, I mean."

277

"You ask her if she's got that latex disguise?" Green-baum called.

Claudine gave him a quizzical look and went on. "Actually, I'd have come to see you during visiting hours yesterday, but it was my first day on the job."

"A job?" said Leffingwell. "That's great, Claudine. I really mean it."

Macduff nodded.

"Nothing much," she said. "I'm a clerk at this little insurance office, but they said they'd let me try sales after I knew the business."

"Well, I'm really glad for you," Leffingwell said. "I hope everything works out the way you want it. By the way, your friend Jack was here this morning trying to help us, too."

"Jack Miasma?" she said. "I haven't seen him since . . . you know, that night."

"Oh?" said Leffingwell.

Claudine glanced at Macduff again. "I'm sorry about that night, Macduff. I can't tell you how sorry. I just wish it had never happened."

"It's all right." Macduff said. "It doesn't matter."

"But *is* there something I can do?" she asked. "I just heard the last little bit, but it all sounded so crazy. She thinks the TV talks to her?"

"Yeah," Leffingwell said, glancing idly around the room. Oberon and Dawn had wandered off after Fern, but Capella, Lance and Stackpole were still there, looking awkward and ashamed at attending a friend's persecution for the sole purpose of doing a live remote. "Now if we could just get the TV to tell her to shut up. . . . Hey! What if it did? Greenbaum, forget the latex mask—how about a real *Mission Impossible* gambit?"

"Remember," Greenbaum said, biting something off the end of his nail, "I'm an officer of the court."

"Claudine?" said Leffingwell.

"Of course," she said. "Anything."

Capella and Stackpole, catching the excitement in Leffingwell's voice, had already begun to lean over the railing, and even Lance side-stepped along the aisle to join the little group. Hurriedly, Leffingwell explained.

"That's the dumbest thing I've ever heard," Lance said. "There's not enough time."

"We've got till *Young and the Restless* goes off at twelve-thirty," said Leffingwell. "She said her Auntie Em's just down the street. If you move the van into the alley behind the lockup window, the cables might just reach."

"Nobody's going to let you fool around their house," Capella said. "This Mrs. Adams may be some kind of empty closet, but there's no reason to think Auntie Em is, too."

"That's where Lance comes in," Leffingwell said. "He flatters the housecoats off them by asking for an interview, keeps them distracted. Think you can pretend to be a reporter?"

Lance looked offended.

"If the kid believes the TV talks," Stackpole said, "her aunt's bound to believe Lance is a real newsman."

A moment later the deputy had come to return the prisoners to the lockup.

The lockup seemed infinitely larger this time: the Man-Mountain's woodchuck defense had failed to move Judge Steele, and Pierre Labouchere had been packed off to County Jail to await trial.

"Hey, hey, hey!" chorused the juveniles from across the hall. "You going to trial or you plead guilty?"

"The hearing's recessed," said Leffingwell.

"Recess?" said one. "I remember that. Used to have it right after metal shop."

Inside the lockup, Leffingwell went directly to the window to watch for Stackpole. Elephant Man, who hadn't spoken since Leffingwell outlined his plan, followed close behind.

"You can't do this, Leff," he said. "It's too cruel."

"It's survival. Her or me. Remember, she's out to get you, too."

"It's not us she hates," Macduff said. "It's the world. Or TV—they're the same thing to her, and you're the link between what she sees out her window and what she sees on her television screen. You make it that much more real, and she can't understand why you can be part of the glamorous side of the world and she can't."

"I already admitted it was all my fault for booting her in the ass—I should have kicked her in the head where it would've done some good. Don't tell me now it's my fault for being a weatherman, too."

"I didn't say it was anybody's fault," Macduff shrugged. "But it's true TV people never worry much about respon-

sibility. Maybe TV can't show the truth, but at least it could
be careful about which lies—"

"Responsibility? Who's got the time? Television's all
rush rush rush. I don't even get the time to think about an
hour from now, let alone—"

"I imagine that's what Sykes and the others would have
said. But in a very real way, Fern's only a creation of
WHCK."

"So I'm Frankenstein and she's my monster? Don't hand
me that." From the corner of his eye, Leffingwell saw the
white van pulling into the alley. "If television made her,
then let it unmake her. It's only fair." He reached through
the bars and opened the window. "Hot in here," he announced loudly for the benefit of the deputy outside the
door.

It was almost twelve-ten and cold enough to liquefy
hydrogen by the time the second deputy opened the door.
"The perpetrators' lawyer's here with the wife," he told the
first. "Lurdan said it was okay—hardship case."

In came Greenbaum with the furtive eyes of a child
molester, and after him Claudine, her face buried in her
collar and scarf, the front of her coat horribly distended.

The first deputy nodded understandingly. "Something in
the oven, little lady?" She nodded demurely. "What a life
that kid's going to have. If I was you, I'd tell him his
father died like a hero in Nam or something. Let him grow
up without being ashamed."

Leffingwell saw something silver-gray snaking through
the open window and between the bars—Stackpole was
feeding the first of the cables up into the lockup. He
grabbed it and pulled it behind him. "Look, can we get a
little privacy? We want to see what we can salvage out of
the wreckage of our lives."

The deputies hesitated.

"I mean, what do you think I'm going to do?" Leffingwell asked, wire piling up behind him. "Squeeze through
the bars and make a mad dash through the Kresge's check-
out?"

The two deputies let themselves out and retired a respect-
ful distance down the hall. In a flash Claudine opened
her coat and gave birth to a minicam and remote back-
pack. Leffingwell hooked up the cables and helped Claudine slip the rig on while Greenbaum fitted himself with
the earphones and throat-mike.

"Stackpole explain what you need to know about working this stuff?" he asked. They nodded. "Okay, come on, Macduff."

Macduff shook his huge head. "I won't have any part in it."

"Okay, I'll do it myself," Leffingwell snapped. "Greenbaum, you're floor director. You ready?"

"Check," Greenbaum said, listening to his earphone. "Capella says Lance's interviewing the mother and aunt on the porch, and Stackpole says he ought to do more of his interviews like this, without the camera plugged in. Capella says he's up in a tree and he's got a good view of Fern, too. She's in the living room, glued to the set."

Leffingwell took his position in front of the blank lockup wall while Claudine focused.

"Move to your left," she said. "I can see 'Fuck Judge Steele' on the wall over your shoulder."

Leffingwell moved.

"Forget it," she said. "Now I'm getting 'Burn, Bumberry, Burn' over your other shoulder."

"Who could forget the sixties," Leffingwell said.

"Okay," Greenbaum said, "Capella says it looks like Lance can't think of anything else to ask the aunt and mother, so Stackpole's going to start transmitting right away."

Leffingwell smiled into the camera, praying that everything was working and his smile was flying from Claudine's camera through Stackpole's van console and along the video cable stretched along the sidewalk to Capella's alligator clips on Aunt Em's antenna and thrusting itself into the backside of Fern's set to flood all nineteen inches of her screen.

"Hello, Fern," Leffingwell said with an unctuous sincerity and measured cadence somewhere between Eric Sevareid and a funeral director. "I'm sorry to interrupt *Young and the Restless,* but I have something very important I've got to tell you, and Snatcher—"

"*Snapper!*" whispered Macduff disgustedly.

"And *Snapper* said it would be okay. Is my brightness all right? Would you like to change my contrast?"

"She just got up and adjusted something," Greenbaum mouthed.

"Thank you," Leffingwell said. "That feels much better, Fern. Did you want to get a snack or use the toilet before

I start? I'm not like those *other* rude shows—I'll wait for you."

Greenbaum shook his head.

"No? Okay, now I want us to think very hard about something. About the story you've been telling in court. I think we both know none of that ever happened."

"She's nodding her head," Greenbaum mouthed.

"Good, I'm glad we agree," Leffingwell smiled. "Now, I think it's too late to admit the whole thing was a lie, because the police would probably put you in jail for a zillion years if you did. But you wouldn't want the Judge to be confused the way Elephant Man was confused about Ron Becker, would you?"

Elephant Man turned to stare out the window.

"So the only thing to do when Mr. Greenbaum asks you in court this afternoon is to say we're not the ones who did it. And you want to be extra convincing, because there could be a talent scout out there in the courtroom who's looking for someone very sincere to replace Marie Osmond. Well, I don't want you to miss any more of *Young and the Restless,* so now I'm returning you to your regularly scheduled program."

Greenbaum nodded when Stackpole confirmed that all the connections had been broken and Fern was back with her soap opera.

"None of this helped her at all," Macduff said. "She's still completely deluded."

"I serve a higher truth," Leffingwell said. "And I'd rather go free with a guilty conscience than serve ten to twenty with a clear one. Moral victories suck."

In the meantime, Claudine had reassembled her pregnancy under her coat, and she and Greenbaum departed. For Leffingwell it now became a matter of waiting through the recess to find if his plan worked. When they had been returned to the courtroom and Judge Steele summoned, Fern mounted the witness stand glassy eyed.

"Now, Fern," said Greenbaum, "I want you to tell me if either of the men who committed those indescribable acts you described this morning is present in this courtroom."

She nodded yes.

Leffingwell's heart sank. What had gone wrong?

"Would you point him out to us?" Greenbaum quavered, obviously worried.

Slowly Fern's eyes scanned the courtroom, studying each face—the Prosecutor, her own mother, Lance, Oberon, Capella, Stackpole, Claudine, Dawn, Greenbaum—pausing at Leffingwell and Macduff. Then her eyes swept on and stopped at last. She raised her arm and pointed. A gasp went up.

"Let the record show the witness identified Judge Abraham Steele," Greenbaum intoned calmly.

It was Macduff who smoothed things over by getting Greenbaum to persuade Judge Steele to release Fern in her mother's custody. "After all," Greenbaum argued, expanding on Macduff's whispered suggestion, "we can only pity this poor child, possessed by a dark and alien force of more than mortal powers—from which none of us is safe."

Judge Steele agreed on condition Miss Adams seek psychiatric help. "And an experienced exorcist." Then he dismissed the charges and departed as quickly as his dignity and infirmities permitted.

"Squee-awk," the tiny voice of his hearing aid called after him from the bench. "Say again, Beaver-Two. Missed that last bit trying to make the Hookset hill. Over."

Leffingwell turned to thank his friends just in time to see Dawn hurrying down the aisle. Obviously she was hoping to claim her new berth as Weather Girl before Leffingwell could get back to the studio with his exoneration.

"Let her go, Leff," said Macduff quietly.

"Let her go? I'm going to tell the nearest deputy she photographed our trial with a camera hidden in her bra. Knowing this place, by the time they've found a matron to do a body search, I'll be back at the weather map finishing up the day's highs and lows."

"That's worse than what she tried to do to you," Macduff said. "It would be another deliberate lie."

"I told you before, we live in inflationary times," Leffingwell said. "What are you, my goddamned conscience?" He caught himself before he got angry; he wasn't used to Macduff's moral superiority any more than he was used to his naked head, but he realized Macduff was right, as always. And it was as it should be: Macduff was still in essence a child, and only a child understood such things well. "Sorry," he said.

"It's all right, Leff," Macduff said. "We're all tired."

"Speaking of inflation," Greenbaum interrupted, "what about my fee?"

"Send me a bill," Leffingwell said, glumly watching Dawn get away. "But you'd better get that tool Lurdan to bring up Macduff's hat."

"Actually, Durwood," Claudine said, "there's something I didn't tell you before because I didn't want to worry you. You might have a little trouble paying Greenbaum's bill."

Leffingwell looked at her blankly.

"The IRS was over yesterday. When Dawn drew up the articles of incorporation, apparently she forgot to make you a nonprofit organization."

"That figures," Leffingwell said. "She's never heard of a nonprofit anything. How much?"

"Well, since Dawn wrote herself a check for the entire balance as back salary, you should have enough to cover back taxes for this quarter if you sell the Mercedes."

"Easy come," said Leffingwell.

"By the way," Claudine said, digging into the bag that hung from her shoulder, "I imagine you'll want these, now." She handed him the three cans of film, the sum total of what had been done of *Elephant Man Story*.

Leffingwell took them. "Does that mean I could drop over tonight?"

She shook her head. "I meant there was no money to argue over in the divorce. Goodbye, Durwood. And you, too, Macduff. Goodbye and good luck." She turned suddenly, head down, and hurried away.

"Hey, the two of you," said Lance. "We're setting up on the steps outside. We figure at least we can get a live remote of the winners going free."

Leffingwell felt the weight of the cans of film in his arms. "No," he said. "No more TV, no more pictures. I promised Macduff. Matter of fact," he said, turning to Macduff, "why don't you take these?"

"I don't want them," Macduff said.

"They're yours. Destroy them, whatever you want. They're just not mine to keep."

At that moment, Greenbaum returned. "Here," he said. "I got the hat."

Proudly, Macduff reached out and took the bundle Greenbaum offered, flapping it loose and swishing it onto his head with a single grand motion. "Thank you," he said from behind the veil.

They were making their way toward the back door to avoid the TV camera on the front steps when Stackpole stopped them, his hand extended in congratulations.

"I couldn't have done it without you," Leffingwell said.

"It's all right, my man. I owed you one for even coming along with those vultures to immortalize your trip to the slammer."

"Yeah, well, that's television."

"And I guess that's the problem," Stackpole said. "Ever since I saw Dawn on the monitor doing the weather, I've been thinking I've had about enough of this. Figure I could make it tree farming, or something."

"Hey, come on, I couldn't stand working there without you. Speaking of which, any chance I can hitch a ride with you back to the studio?"

Stackpole shook his head. "Came down in the van. It's already crowded with me and Capella and Lance—Oberon won't let him in the Sunbeam with her."

"Let me give you a ride," called a voice. It was Father Tim, squeezing his way through the crowd toward them. "I'm parked right out back. And congratulations to both of you."

"It's good to see you, Father," Macduff said.

"And you," said Father Tim.

Leffingwell wrinkled his nose but said nothing. If he got a ride out of the priest and saved his job, it would be more than he'd gotten out of all the years he'd gone to confession.

Chapter 26

Winking Out

Macduff limped slowly after the others into the gathering night of the rear parking lot. A light snow was just beginning, and the black asphalt glistened in the street lamps with flakes melting at the pavement's touch. Between the dark shapes of the buildings beyond, Macduff could see the sparkle of Christmas lights on Commercial Street and the shabby tinsel boas and plastic stars strung from street lamp to street lamp. The indistinct rumbling of a worn record drifted toward him from a loudspeaker under the lights.

God rest ye, merry gentlemen, sang the chorus.

Rest, he thought. Not catnaps through the long night with his head cradled on his knees while the television kept the vigil, but real rest. That was what he wanted. Yearned for.

Oh, tidings of comfort and joy, comfort and joy,
Oh, tidings of comfort and joy.

Small comfort for Mother Margaret, or the Sisters and boys this night, split up and sprinkled from orphanage to orphanage. She was strong; she would manage. And yet Immaculate Conception had meant so much to her. And she had done so much good there.

Winking out, he thought. Maybe there was a kind of

justice to it that went beyond the wishes of the men in sunglasses. He was an aberration, a mistake, something nature should never have been forced to endure. The sooner he was gone, the sooner universal balance would be restored. Comfort and joy—he had never had either, and now, he realized, he no longer wished for them. His was a destiny apart.

> *I have desired to go*
> > *Where springs not fail,*
> *To fields where flies no sharp and sided hail*
> > *And few lilies blow.*
>
> *And I have asked to be*
> > *Where no storms come,*
> *Where the green swell is in the havens dumb,*
> > *And out of the swing of the sea.*

He heard a faint humming sound and looked up. His neck prickled with fear. A gray sedan, lights out but motor idling, hovered in the shadows by the courthouse, almost breathing. His eyes swept the parking lot. Two others on the far side.

He quickened his pace to catch up with Father Tim and Leffingwell.

"The trouble is," Leffingwell was saying in a low voice, "we don't know whether he's actually a . . . carrier. A danger to other people. So I was thinking, maybe we could go away somewhere, and I'd be like those canaries they take down into the mines to warn them of gas pockets."

"But you'd be putting yourself in danger, wouldn't you?"

"No, there are things doctors can do. The options aren't really, um, attractive, but if you kept getting checkups and all . . . I mean, everyone who's come near him ought to be monitored, and we'd probably know in a year or so."

"Is it because you feel responsible for him?"

Leffingwell paused. "No, it's because, well, he's my friend. I'd want to be with him to keep him company."

"You're a fine person, Durwood Leffingwell."

"Not really. I've just got a lot to make up for."

Macduff stopped, his eyes burning with gratitude. He couldn't let Leff make a sacrifice like that because he himself didn't want to go on. Couldn't. He glanced toward the sedan. If he simply went to them now, it would be over so fast Leff and Father Tim might not even notice. It was too late to spare Mother Margaret; his selfish desire to know had brought down destruction on her. But he might still keep these two friends from getting further involved.

"Don't you whine at me!" bellowed the unmistakable voice of Mrs. Adams from the darkness. "You ruined everything! How am I supposed to pay for this car now? Or these damn dresses? You get in, you hear? And when we get home I'm taking that damn TV down to the living room where it belongs, will or no will."

They might be endangered, too. Resolutely Macduff walked directly toward the sedan.

"Next time I exercise visiting rights to the Afghan," Leffingwell was saying darkly, "I'm going to show that one the *real* dark side of man's animal passions. I'll . . . I'll— I don't know. Expose myself or something." He turned to glance back at Macduff and saw him walking in the other direction. Then he noticed the first of the gray sedans. "MACDUFF!" he shrieked. "COME BACK!"

But it was too late. Suddenly men in light suits exploded from the car, peering through the bulbous insect-eyes of their sunglasses, converging into a pulsing knot around Macduff, swarming over him, while two more cars lurched up to disgorge their occupants. There was the muffled report of a pistol.

Leffingwell ran toward them.

He plunged into the swarm, fists flailing, and went down, pummeled, nose bleeding, sliding on the pavement. He found his face opposite Macduff's on the ground.

The hideous head lay naked, wisps of hair wet with blood and melted snow. A fine net of rivulets of blood had formed around the base of the pinkish stub that passed for a tusk, more blood was pooling in the creases and hollows between the gums and perpetually opened lips. Then the deep-set eyes fluttered open, and in them Leffingwell saw his own anxious face reflected.

"I tried to get you to go on to the car," Macduff whispered.

"It's all right, deputy," Leffingwell heard one of them shout outside their tight circle. "Official business. Keep everyone away, especially that TV crew out front."

"You're going to be all right, Macduff," Leffingwell said. "They can't do this. We'll get you to a doctor."

The eyes stared at him, betraying neither confidence or fear.

"Probably won't need a doctor," said a voice. "Always healed right up, from what I hear."

"All right," said Leffingwell, his voice trembling with rage, "just who the fuck *are* you guys?"

"Hustle those two fatties over there out of the lot," said the first voice. "And make sure you tell them to keep this to themselves. Be *persuasive*."

Leffingwell felt one of the figures slip away. Then the circle above him opened and Father Tim stumbled in. He knelt on the other side of Macduff. "Macduff," he said. "Did they hurt you?"

"No," Macduff said, barely audible. "It's all right, Leff, really. This is the right way, after all."

"What about these two? With Buridan and the nun taken care of, they're the only civilians left who know. Do we neutralize them or—?"

"I *hate* that word," said the first. "What are we, thugs? Give both of them the shot and see if that doesn't clear their minds a little."

"This can't be real," said Leffingwell. "I get it—you're the bad guys and this is *Man from Uncle*, right? This is the part where you spill your guts about your diabolical plot while you're gloating over us."

"Leff," said Macduff weakly, "*they are* the Men from Uncle. I tried to warn you. Now get away. I'll be all right."

"But why did they just lurk around all this time?" he asked, getting to his knees. "Was it you guys weren't sure? Yeah—you didn't know if Elephant Man was the right one—till he went to Immaculate Conception. That's why you started to move in that night, except the sheriff's deputies got in the way and took us off to a public jail. Local lawmen unwittingly thwart federal plot—how's that for tomorrow's headline?"

"Stick motor-mouth first," said the leader.

It happened so fast Leffingwell had no time to react. Suddenly his arm was being twisted behind him, and he caught a brief glint of streetlight off the metal casing of a hypodermic needle, and then there was a sharp sting in

the back of his neck. The man let go of his arm. For a bri[ef]
instant he knelt there, swaying, his eyes trying to pierce t[he]
gray gathering into black that crowded everything from h[is]
vision. At last he thought he could make out Macduff. H[e]
reached out to him vaguely as though to protect him wi[th]
his palsied hands. "Sorry, old friend," he mumbled. "I . [.]
never did manage to take you to the opera." Then [he]
crumpled to the pavement.

While Leffingwell had been talking, Father Tim ha[d]
leaned over Macduff. Still through his mind raced t[he]
doubts and uncertainties that had tormented him sin[ce]
Saturday night. The soul, he thought. Would there be [a]
soul or not? But that wasn't a question for mortals; it wa[s]
a question for God.

He was so preoccupied he barely felt the sting of t[he]
needle in his neck. All at once some mad portion of h[is]
mind in sympathy with Buridan broke loose, told him [he]
was a lost and giftless king before the Word, told him [to]
curse these simple killers for seeking to out-Herod Hero[d]
who had but slain innocent babes.

No oil or salt or chrism, but with a hand wet with melt[ed]
snow he made the sign of the cross on Macduff's heart a[nd]
forehead, and with his thumb he signed the forehea[d,]
mouth, ears, nose, hands, eyes.

He sagged down, vision blurring, retreating into t[he]
safety of the Latin of his boyhood's worship, paraphrasi[ng]
not from the Passion of Christ, but deliberately, fearfull[y,]
hopefully, from the simple commemoration of the depart[ed]
faithful, the generations of Mother Church's common m[en]
and women: *Ipsis, Domine, locum refrigerii, lucis et pac[is,]
ut indulgeas, deprecamur.* To these, O Lord, we beseec[h]
Thee, grant a place of comfort, light and peace.

He wanted to keep on praying lest in the Edens of the[ir]
bodies grow monsters of corruption sown by this innocen[t]
creature of chaos, boy and man, child and father of deat[h.]

He struggled to see, reached out to touch with his thum[b]
and his own body's salt the tongue lolling slack at the corn[er]
of the gaping mouth. He wanted to explain about being a[l-]
lowed at last to exercise the priestly function once deni[ed]
him by the mother of an unborn child. And Thou sha[lt]
sprinkle me with hyssop, O Lord, and I shall be cleanse[d.]
Thou shalt wash me, and I shall be whiter than snow.

"Thank you," he gasped, half to Macduff and half to God. Then he crumpled beside him, guilt expiated, nightmare over, child able to sleep at last. And it seemed to him in that last moment of consciousness that when he had touched the tongue, he had seen a smile flicker at the corners of Macduff's mouth.

Chapter 27

Storm's End

Snow was general all over New England. It was falling on the squat pink cinder block studio of Channel 29, on the slush-streaked streets of Butler and the empty windows of Immaculate Conception, falling softly upon the Cambria College campus and, farther northward, softly falling on the Bumberry Center Courthouse and on the silent slopes of Mount Shadrach and into the dark currents of the Merrimack River. It was falling, too, upon Durwood Leffingwell.

He stood alone in the cold and dark, his head buzzing and, it seemed, monstrously swollen. He blinked to free the snowflakes trapped like netted fish amongst his eyelashes. Somewhere deep within him was a half-formed sense of loss, a sense he ought to weep, as Saul once wept for David, and David for Jonathan. If only he could remember.

The door and lighted window were familiar. He stumbled across the lawn, clumps of grass and rain-rills frozen into a moonscape lava flow in the Sea of Tranquillity.

He paused in midstride, arrested by the matching door and window one apartment over. "Cockadoodle-doo," he mumbled, fumbling with his pants, trying to collect his thoughts. There was something he wanted to do, but even before he could call it to mind, he shook his head and staggered across to the first door and pounded on it with his fist.

Claudine opened the door, her face a black, empty space outlined by the light behind that caught the graceful curve of her neck and made the tips and edges of the random hair-swirls glow.

"Durwood?"

He grunted, shivering.

"What are you doing here?"

"Don't remember."

She peered into the darkness for a car but could see nothing. "How did you get here?"

He said nothing, looking inside toward the warm light.

"Where's Macduff?" she asked.

"Who?"

"Macduff. Elephant Man."

Elephant Man, he thought. He should know that one, but he didn't. There was something tucked under his arm, and he brought it forward to clutch against his chest. It was the empty top of a film can, wrapped in an elephantine pair of costume pants with vinyl hooves.

"God, Durwood, you're a mess. All right, you can come in for a minute, but zip up your fly. I think you came over with the wrong idea."

The hot room vibrated with the sound of a man's voice.

—*other local news, the Channel 29 News Team just missed filming a hit-and-run accident behind the District Courthouse in Bumberry Center, New Hampshire*—

Leffingwell knelt on the rug and looked under the sofa, ignoring a low growl from behind him. The snowflakes in his hair were beginning to melt and trickle down onto his scalp and forehead.

"Be still, Krishna," Claudine said. "Durwood, I just got a call for you from someone named Tim Fagan, but when I asked him what he wanted, he didn't seem to know. I think he was drunk. What *are* you doing?"

"I'm *looking* for something. . . ."

—*unidentified victims apparently left the scene unaided, according to Deputy*—

"Aha! See?" he said. "Hairbrush. Full of Afghan hair."

"Durwood, you came all the way over here for *that?* I could have sent it to you."

"And my . . . tennis racket," he said, reaching under and pulling it out, trailing a dragnet of dust and hair. He started to get up, but somehow he was suddenly too exhausted. He collapsed onto the couch. "Have to play a few sets soon," he said. "Out of shape. Lose the balls, or they somewhere around?"

"Have you been drinking with that Fagan person?" Claudine asked.

—we'll be bringing you tonight's weather with our Weather Girl. But first, this important message.

Leffingwell glanced over at the television screen. Thousands of people in eighteenth-century costumes were streaming by what looked like the statue of Nike and the Butler Public Library. Then came a close shot of one of them, a female figure carrying the French tricolor in her right hand and a rifle with fixed bayonet in her left.

Liberté! she shouted, clambering over a barricade. The camera zoomed in for a tighter shot of the head and shoulders. The face was somehow familiar.

Égalité! she called.

Oh, my God—

Chevrolet!

It was Crazy Stan Melchizedek, Crazy Stan with a flag and rifle, Crazy Stan wrapped in a bedsheet with one nippleless breast of a flesh-colored padded bra peeking over the Roman fold of his garment. Evolution had struck again.

It is a fah, fah bettah sale I offah dan I have evah offahed befoah—

"Durwood!" Claudine said. "I just realized! Why aren't you at the station? Who's doing the weather?"

A moment later Dawn appeared, face contorted in a vacant, professional smile, in front of Leffingwell's snowflake-bedecked map over which a cigar-chomping crow, trembling violently, peered.

—expecting fifteen to twenty-four inches of that old white stuff, she was saying.

At that moment the switcher in the booth cut from the first camera to the second, and onto the screen flashed a long shot of the entire studio. Wires, trash, old cans littered the floor, and in the center of the chaos Dawn could be seen still talking to the dead camera. She was standing on top of two telephone directories piled on an ancient Coca-Cola case. Off to one side, beaming hugely, a pudgy little man watched her.

"Who is he?" Claudine asked.

"That," Leffingwell said, not quite sure how he knew, "is Uncle Mr. Trammel, Vice President for Programming."

"Why are they showing that shot? It's awful."

"That's Stackpole's work up on the bridge," Leffingwell said. "I think he's just decided to make this his last night at WHCK."

Suddenly the little man glanced at the monitor, saw himself, looked back horrified toward the camera and scampered off.

"You know," Claudine said thoughtfully, "he reminds me of that drawing of the little round man who was really the Wizard of Oz." Without thinking, Leffingwell closed his burning eyes and inclined his head toward her until it rested on her shoulder.

"Durwood—" she began, and then stopped herself. "Oh, all right," she said, pulling him down and gathering his head and shoulders against her breast. "Poor drunk Durwood," she said. "I guess we deserve each other. We're unique, baby. The world's worst-matched couple."

"Turn off the television," he murmured, desperate for peace.

"I can't get up," she whispered.

"Doesn't matter then," he said, barely awake as Claudine began to rock him gently. He lay with his limp hands over the tennis racket and the hairbrush and the costume pants and the empty film tin, eyes closed against the darkness of those breasts into which his face was pressed, swaying, swaying, trying to remember.

Explicit liber viri elephantini.

"Why didn't you tell me?"

The man standing before Kerry looked intense and extremely sexy as he glared at her.

"Hello, Alexi," she said hoarsely, past a lump that she couldn't attribute to morning sickness.

"It's been three months! Dammit, Kerry, you should have phoned me immediately."

"And what could you have done? I'm having this baby whether you like it or not."

"You think I don't want you to have my baby? Don't be absurd. I would never—"

"I don't know that. We didn't have much time to discuss the subject."

"We managed to talk about almost everything else."

"Including your upcoming nuptials to the contessa."

Alexi's expression grew fierce. "First of all, I'm not marrying Contessa Di Giovanni."

"But—"

"Second, you and I are getting married. Our child will be the *legitimate* heir to the throne of Belegovia."

Dear Reader,

It's that time of the year again. Pink candy hearts and red roses abound as we celebrate that most amorous of holidays, St. Valentine's Day. Revel in this month's offerings as we continue to celebrate Harlequin American Romance's yearlong 20th Anniversary.

Last month we launched our six-book MILLIONAIRE, MONTANA continuity series with the first delightful story about a small Montana town whose residents win a forty-million-dollar lottery jackpot. Now we bring you the second title in the series, *Big-Bucks Bachelor*, by Leah Vale, in which a handsome veterinarian gets more than he bargained for when he asks his plain-Jane partner to become his fake fiancée.

Also in February, Bonnie Gardner brings you *The Sergeant's Secret Son*. In this emotional story, passions flare all over again between former lovers as they work to rebuild their tornado-ravaged hometown, but the heroine is hiding a small secret—their child! Next, Victoria Chancellor delivers a great read with *The Prince's Texas Bride*, the second book in her duo A ROYAL TWIST, where a bachelor prince's night of passion with a beautiful waitress results in a royal heir on the way and a marriage proposal. And a trip to Las Vegas leads to a pretend engagement in Leandra Logan's *Wedding Roulette*.

Enjoy this month's offerings, and be sure to return each and every month to Harlequin American Romance!

Melissa Jeglinski
Associate Senior Editor
Harlequin American Romance

THE PRINCE'S
TEXAS BRIDE
Victoria Chancellor

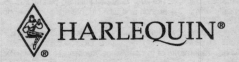

TORONTO • NEW YORK • LONDON
AMSTERDAM • PARIS • SYDNEY • HAMBURG
STOCKHOLM • ATHENS • TOKYO • MILAN • MADRID
PRAGUE • WARSAW • BUDAPEST • AUCKLAND

To our Thursday Lunch Group, for your continued
encouragement. Thank you Judy Christenberry,
Jane Graves (w/a Jane Sullivan),
Barbara Harrison (w/a Leann Harris),
Tammy Hilz, Karen Leabo (w/a Kara Lennox)
and Rebecca Russell.

ISBN 0-373-16959-0

THE PRINCE'S TEXAS BRIDE

Copyright © 2003 by Victoria Chancellor Huffstutler.

Visit us at www.eHarlequin.com

Printed in U.S.A.

ABOUT THE AUTHOR

After twenty-eight years in Texas, Victoria Chancellor has almost qualified for "naturalized Texan" status. She lives in a suburb of Dallas with her husband of thirty-one years, next door to her daughter, who is an English teacher. When not writing, she tends her "zoo" of four cats, a ferret, five tortoises, a wide assortment of wild birds, three visiting chickens and several families of raccoons and opossums. For more information on past and future releases, please visit her Web site at www.victoriachancellor.com.

Books by Victoria Chancellor

HARLEQUIN AMERICAN ROMANCE

844—THE BACHELOR PROJECT
884—THE BEST BLIND DATE IN TEXAS
955—THE PRINCE'S COWBOY DOUBLE*
959—THE PRINCE'S TEXAS BRIDE*

*A Royal Twist

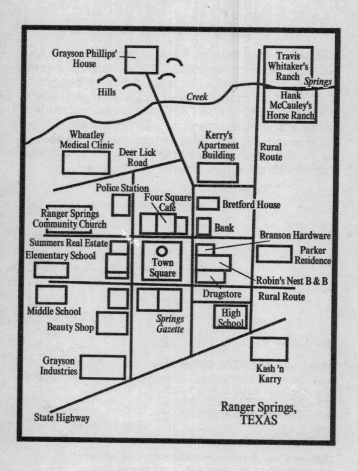

Grayson Phillips' House

Hills

Creek

Travis Whitaker's Ranch

Springs

Hank McCauley's Horse Ranch

Wheatley Medical Clinic

Deer Lick Road

Kerry's Apartment Building

Rural Route

Police Station

Four Square Café

Bretford House

Ranger Springs Community Church

Bank

Branson Hardware

Summers Real Estate

Parker Residence

Elementary School

Town Square

Robin's Nest B & B

Drugstore

Rural Route

Middle School

Springs Gazette

High School

Beauty Shop

Grayson Industries

Kash 'n Karry

State Highway

Ranger Springs, TEXAS

Prologue

Kerry Lynn Jacks pulled her blue chenille robe tight around her, fought back another urge to run into the bathroom and headed instead for the insistent pounding on her door. This had better be important. Mornings were *not* her best time of day. Hadn't been ever since that little test strip had turned blue—and she'd started turning green.

She wove her way around her coffee table and chair. The tile in the entryway to her apartment was cool on her bare feet even though August in Texas was anything but temperate. "This had better not be someone selling magazine subscriptions," she murmured to herself as she stood on tiptoe and peered through the peephole.

Her heart began to pound and she sucked in a much-needed breath. Either her friend Hank McCauley had started wearing designer clothing or there was a prince on her doorstep. Either way, she had to let him in.

She turned the deadbolt and doorknob, then took a shaky step back as the door swung open.

The man standing before her looked intense and

extremely sexy as he glared at her from beneath furrowed brows.

Definitely the prince.

"Hello, Alexi," she said hoarsely past the lump in her throat that she couldn't attribute to morning sickness.

"Why didn't you tell me?"

She couldn't pretend not to know what he was talking about. "I was going to." She shrugged, then crossed her arms over her chest. "I just hadn't decided how or when. You're not exactly the easiest person in the world to get in touch with."

"It's been three months!"

"Well, yes, but it's only been about a month and a half since I was sure."

He ran a hand through his hair, looking suddenly weary. "Can we go inside and talk about this?"

"Of course." She stepped back and gestured toward her living room. "Make yourself comfortable."

She followed him, adjusting her robe, smoothing her blond hair into some semblance of order. The very feminine part of her wished she looked better—more pulled together, with a bit of makeup to hide behind. But Alexi would probably see through whatever cosmetics she might apply, so why bother? And since she'd already decided to tell him the truth, what did she have to hide...except her pride?

"If you want some coffee, you'll have to make it. My stomach... Well, let's just say I've given up on my morning jolt of caffeine for a while." She sank into the chair across from the couch and curled her feet beneath her.

"I didn't travel thousands of miles for coffee, even though I'm sure yours is excellent."

"I've had a lot of experience making coffee," she commented casually, reminding Prince Alexi Ladislas of Belegovia that she had been a lowly truck stop waitress when they'd met. Reminding him that they lived in separate worlds and always would.

"Dammit, Kerry, you should have phoned me immediately."

"And what could you have done if you'd known a month or two ago? I'm having this baby whether you know about it or not."

"Then you admit it? This is my child?"

"This is *my* child," she stated, placing her hand over her slightly rounded stomach. "Maybe conception was an accident, but I want this baby. I don't need permission from you or anyone else to deliver my son or daughter."

"You think I don't want you to have the baby? Don't be absurd. I would never—"

"I thought I did at one time, but now I realize I don't know you well enough to know how you would react. We didn't have much time to discuss the subject in the short time we spent together."

He leaned forward and placed his forearms on his knees. "We managed to talk about almost everything else."

Kerry bowed her head and took a deep breath. She would not cry in front of him, even though her nerves were as jumbled as her thoughts. Even though her stomach clenched with tension and she had the urge to run out of the room.

"I suppose you found out from Gwendolyn." The

idea that her friend had called him and revealed a confidence sickened her. Kerry thought she was a good judge of people, and Gwendolyn had seemed like such a loyal friend. But she'd been Alexi's childhood buddy and then a trusted employee for years. Maybe that went beyond a three-month friendship based mostly on a set of bizarre circumstances that few people would believe...and even fewer knew to be true.

"She didn't call me to reveal your secret, if that's what you're thinking," Alexi said. "I was actually on the phone to her when you came to the ranch."

Kerry frowned, remembering yesterday's conversation clearly. "She told me she had to put a call on hold."

"Gwendolyn has many good qualities and abilities, but anything above the technology of a manual pencil sharpener is beyond her. She obviously thought she'd put me on hold, but she didn't because I heard every word. I immediately flew to Texas and went to your mother's house so we could resolve the problem, and she informed me where your apartment was located."

"My baby is not a problem!"

"I didn't mean it that way," he said quickly. "I meant that I wanted to talk to you about the situation. At least your mother was glad to see me."

"I'll bet. She had your autograph framed, you know." Charlene Jacks had probably loved playing matchmaker. It's a wonder she hadn't phoned to tell Kerry that a prince was on his way to her apartment. Of course, her mother didn't yet know *why* Prince Alexi might be in such a snit. And if he'd asked her to remain silent so he could surprise Kerry with his mere presence, she would have complied in a heartbeat.

"Why did you tell Gwendolyn instead of calling me?"

"I was so upset. I didn't know who else to talk to. I didn't even tell my mother, for Pete's sake!"

Kerry took another deep breath, wishing she had some soda crackers and ginger ale to calm her queasiness. She wouldn't go into the kitchen to get them when she and Alexi were in the middle of this conversation. Even though she didn't want to discuss her baby at this moment, she knew she'd have to face him sooner or later.

"I just needed advice," she admitted in a small voice. She looked into his eyes and saw a fading of anger. A smidgen of sympathy. "I needed to determine what I should do that would be the most fair to everyone. You, me and the baby."

"And she told you about Belegovia's laws of succession."

"Yes." She'd been surprised when Gwendolyn had volunteered the information, but then Kerry had realized that she had to consider all these factors to decide what was best for her baby.

"So you know that whether you have a boy or a girl, this child could succeed me as king or queen."

"Yes," Kerry said, lifting her chin, "but only if you declare it as your heir. Otherwise, any children you and—" she choked out the words "—the contessa have after your marriage will be your legitimate heirs. This baby would still be the half sibling of the royal heirs, but wouldn't be in line for the throne."

Alexi leaned forward, his expression once again

fierce. "First of all, I'm not marrying Contessa di Giovanni."

"But my mother told me that there was a big party this weekend where your engagement was going to be announced." Charlene Jacks was an avid royal watcher and had kept Kerry informed of every event involving Belegovia—until she'd realized her daughter was hopelessly in love with the prince.

Alexi held up his hand, obviously impatient. "Second, there won't be any half siblings."

She knew that as the crown prince he'd be expected to have at least two children to ensure the succession. His father, King Wilheim, had given him a deadline of age thirty to find a bride. Which had led him to run away while on a trip to Texas in May.

He'd run away with *her*.

Kerry's stomach clenched as she asked, "Why?"

He covered her hands with his, making her look into his sky-blue eyes. Her heart pounded at the warmth and strength of his grasp, the scent of his cologne. She hadn't seen him for three months, but it seemed like only three days.

When he spoke, his voice was softer, more intimate. "Because you and I are getting married as soon as I can arrange for the ceremony at the cathedral in Belegovia. Our child will be the undisputed *legitimate* heir to the throne."

Kerry took one look at his intense expression and knew it was too late for soda crackers and ginger ale. She leapt from the chair and fled to the bathroom, remembering in vivid detail just exactly how she'd gotten herself pregnant by the prince.

Chapter One

"Hank McCauley, you devil!" the young woman squealed, throwing her arms around Alexi's neck. "Did you remember to bring me a present?"

Alexi, stunned by the feel of her firm breasts pressed against his chest, her soft-as-silk blond hair brushing against his neck and her light floral fragrance filling his senses, could only wrap his arms around her petite, curvy body and hold on tight.

Sooner or later he was going to tell her he wasn't Hank McCauley...whoever that might be.

Before he could gather his wits, she pulled back, grinned and placed a smacking kiss on his lips.

Her lips were as soft as her breasts were firm. She tasted of cinnamon and mint, and he immediately wanted her.

When she pulled back, her smile faded. Her arms slipped away from around his neck and he allowed his hands to slide down her arms until they were both standing in the truck stop, breathless and confused.

Her light brown brows drew closer together over a cute little nose sprinkled with freckles.

"You're not Hank."

"No, I'm not."

She tilted her head. "But you look just like him." She stared, leaning forward to examine him as though he were an interesting new species of insect. "You don't have the little scar above your lip."

"No, I don't." He folded his arms across his chest, expecting some accusation or scorn. "I didn't mean to deceive you. You took me by surprise."

"Are you British?"

"I was born and raised there, but I live in Belegovia now."

"Belegovia. Where have I heard that name?"

"Perhaps on the news?" he offered.

Comprehension dawned swift and sure. "You're the prince." She grinned and shook her head. "You don't look very much like the grainy photo I saw in the newspaper this morning." She placed a uniform down on a stool—she'd obviously just changed clothes also—and reached for a section of the paper resting beside the cash register. It was crumpled from many people sharing the newsprint. "See. You look a lot more…stern in the paper."

"Thank you, I suppose," he replied, more and more fascinated by this young woman who seemed completely unimpressed by his position. He was about to ask for an introduction when Lady Gwendolyn Reed walked up, frowning. She'd probably witnessed the whole incident from her position by the double glass doors. Gwendolyn didn't miss much.

"No, I mean you look better," the petite blonde

continued, sparing a quick look at Gwendolyn. "Like Hank McCauley. He used to be my boyfriend…well, for a little while. Not that we were ever serious. We're just friends now. I thought maybe he'd come to visit me here at the truck stop."

"And bring you a present," Alexi finished.

The cute blonde grinned. "I like surprises."

Alexi felt his answering smile all the way down his body. "So do I." *Especially when they come in such attractive packages,* he thought.

"Your Highness, we really should be leaving," Gwendolyn said. She looked businesslike and slightly severe in her purplish woolen suit, black pumps and combination purse and briefcase. Her dark hair was pulled back in a simple clip. She appeared the exact opposite of the slightly disheveled truck stop waitress whose blond hair curled in an attractive style around her head.

"I'd introduce you," he said to his public-relations director, "but I have yet to learn the name of our new friend."

"Oh, I'm sorry." The young woman in question tossed the paper back onto the counter and thrust out her hand. "Kerry Lynn Jacks, from Ranger Springs."

Alexi turned it over so he held her fingers and kissed the back of her hand. "Pleased to meet you, Kerry Lynn Jacks. I am Prince Alexi Ladislas of Belegovia. May I present Lady Gwendolyn Reed, the formidable woman who is urging me ever closer to San Antonio and another round of boring public appearances?"

Kerry laughed. "Sounds like a difficult job."

"You have no idea," Gwendolyn said, her nostrils

flaring as her eyebrows rose. *Don't give me any trouble,* she seemed to be saying. *Please, just get back in the Land Rover and we'll forget all about this little encounter.*

Fat chance, he'd learned to say when he'd lived in the States several years ago. Sometimes he simply couldn't resist tweaking Gwendolyn's nose—figuratively, of course, as he'd done when they were much younger. She preferred a much more restrictive view of his public life than he favored. He enjoyed much of the baby-kissing and hand-shaking, but Gwendolyn scheduled a plethora of those appearances. He would rather focus on promoting tourism and stimulating economic development in his country, which he'd just done in Dallas. As far as he was concerned, he'd accomplished his mission to Texas. Gwendolyn, on the other hand, still believed he had several days of public appearances to endure before finding out if he'd be meeting the president on his Texas ranch late Saturday.

''Well, I'd better let you go. I'm sorry about assaulting you. I'm sure that doesn't happen often.'' She frowned. ''Not that women wouldn't want to throw themselves at you. I just meant that I'm sure you're not usually confused with someone else.''

Alexi smiled. ''I can honestly say that has never happened before.'' And he couldn't have imagined a more pleasurable case of mistaken identity, either.

''Nice to meet you, Lady Gwendolyn,'' Kerry replied with a smile. ''I hope y'all have a nice time in Texas.''

She turned away with one more friendly smile over her shoulder. Alexi stood rooted to the spot, still tast-

ing her lips and feeling her petite, curvy body pressed
to his.

"We really should be going," Gwendolyn reminded him. "Between the incident in the Land
Rover and this distraction, we're nearly an hour behind schedule."

The "incident" involved a soft drink Alexi had
purchased on their last stop. He loved American soft
drinks. They tasted different in the States than in Europe. This particular bottle, however, had either been
shaken on purpose or dropped by clumsy hands, because the minute he'd twisted open the lid, cold,
sticky liquid had spewed from the bottle, soaking his
shirt and the seat of the Land Rover, and saturated
his hair and face.

He'd needed a change of clothing and the truck
stop seemed a perfect place to wash his face, neck
and hands. To his surprise, the large facility contained
showers for both men and women, clothing, a variety
of recordings and books, and every type of food imag-
inable. The combination showers and rest rooms separated the retail part of the truck stop from the restaurant, which occupied about one third of the
building.

He'd chosen jeans, a Western-cut shirt in bright
stripes and a tooled leather belt that he knew would
remind him of Texas long after he returned to Belegovia. With his new wardrobe and impatient looks
from Gwendolyn, he'd slipped into the men's showers.

When he'd emerged clean and in his new clothes,
Kerry Lynn Jacks had launched herself into his arms.

Alexi narrowed his eyes and watched her hug two

waitresses and wipe a tear from her eye. "She's certainly an interesting young woman."

"One we don't have time to linger over."

"You are no fun," he told Gwendolyn, who was single-minded in her duties. Mainly she scheduled, then escorted him from event to event, competently and without any surprises. And she never scheduled any temptations.

With one last look at Kerry, who had picked up a canvas tote bag and was waving goodbye to her friends, he turned away also. "Okay. Let's get on the road."

"You don't need to sound so disappointed," Gwendolyn chided. "This trip was your idea."

"The *meetings* in Dallas were my idea. The photo ops were for you and my father."

"Whatever."

They emerged into the bright morning sunlight. The newly cleaned Land Rover with their Texas driver, Pete Boedecker, and Alexi's man, Milos Anatole, stood ready at the door.

"We're off to San Antonio, Mr. Boedecker," Gwendolyn announced. She stood beside the vehicle door, waiting for Alexi to enter first, as was his right. He still had a hard time remembering to observe the formality when he was in the States. He'd lived in Boston for five years, never once failing to act courteously to women—most of whom knew him only as Alex.

Just when he was getting ready to enter the vehicle, a loud compact car, partly blue and partly rusted, pulled up beside them. Milos immediately stepped in front of him, but as soon as Alexi saw who was driving the disreputable automobile, he smiled.

"It's okay, Milos. I don't think the young woman is going to abduct me."

"Prince Alexi," Kerry called out breathlessly, "I almost forgot to ask you for a big favor."

"What is that, Miss Jacks?"

"My mother is a huge fan of all the European royalty," she explained as she stepped out and walked around her sorry excuse for a car. "If she found out I'd met you and didn't get her an autograph, she'd tan my bottom."

The image of Kerry Lynn Jacks's firm, round bottom popped into his mind and wouldn't leave. Not that he wanted to "tan" her, but he would like a peek at what was hidden by her jeans.

"What would you like me to autograph?" he asked, straight-faced.

She handed him an envelope from the truck stop and a pen that had been chewed on the plastic end. "Would you make it out to Charlene Jacks, please?" Kerry asked, peering at the paper he held as though she didn't trust him to give a proper autograph.

He smiled. "Of course. Are you going home now?" he asked, to make conversation while he worded an appropriate message.

"No, I'm on my way to Galveston."

"Galveston!" He looked up, remembering the island from his check of the map before his trip to Texas. "Surely not in—"

"Now, don't say anything rude about Delores," Kerry admonished with a grin. "She may be old, but she's been real good to me for the past eight years. We've been through a lot together.''

''Really?'' Alexi wondered if any of those memories involved the back seat of the aging vehicle, but a quick glance inside confirmed his suspicions. The back seat was too small for any decent-size man.

''I don't want to demean Delores, but perhaps you should reconsider driving all that way. Surely you're not going alone?''

''I am. My mother is working and my sisters are busy. I have to be back on Saturday for my college graduation ceremony, but I'm going to see my aunt and uncle. I'm getting my aunt's mother's car. It's in real good shape—only twenty-one thousand miles and not a dent or a scratch.''

''I see.'' College graduation? How old was Kerry? She'd appeared several years older than an undergraduate. ''What type of degree?''

''My bachelor's in business. It's taken me ten years, but I'm finally finished.''

Alexi breathed a sigh of relief. At least he hadn't been lusting after a twenty-one-year-old. Kerry was at least twenty-seven or twenty-eight—just a few years younger than his age of thirty.

''Your Highness,'' Gwendolyn said, warning him she was serious by the use of his title, ''we really *must* be going.''

''Lady Gwendolyn, I've just learned this young lady is driving all the way to Galveston by herself in this rather questionable automobile. Surely I can't let that pass.''

''Surely you *must*, Your Highness,'' she insisted.

Alexi laughed. ''How far is this trip of yours?''

"In hours, I'd say around six or so."

"Six hours in Delores," he said, turning to Gwendolyn. "That seems rather unfortunate, don't you think?"

Gwendolyn tugged on his sleeve. When he leaned down, she whispered fiercely in his ear. "So buy her a bloody ticket on an airplane and let's be on our way!"

Alexi laughed. "You can't solve everything with money, Gwennie."

"Alexi Ladislas," she whispered, reverting to the tone of voice she'd used when she was peeved with him, "forget any idea that might be forming in your head."

"I can't imagine what you're talking about."

"I can see you're busy," Kerry said with a sigh. "Thanks for the autograph. My mother will be so proud."

"Just a moment, Kerry," Alexi said.

"Alexi, no!"

He smiled down at Gwendolyn. "This is fate, don't you think? If that soft drink hadn't exploded. If we hadn't stopped in this particular place."

"Fate is sticking to your schedule. Who knows what momentous events await you in San Antonio?"

"I've never been to Galveston."

"You've never been to San Antonio, either!"

"Yes, but Galveston has a beach." He turned to Kerry. "It does have a beach, doesn't it?"

"Yes," she answered, obviously confused. "Galveston is actually an island."

"Ah, you see, an island. You do remember how I love the islands. Besides, all my important meetings

are complete. Relax for a few days, Gwennie. You
need a holiday as much as I do.''

"Alexi, don't!"

"I must, dear Gwendolyn.'' He turned to Kerry.
"As a gentleman, I cannot allow you to make the
treacherous trip alone. It would be my honor to accompany you to Galveston in your faithful steed, Delores.''

KERRY COULDN'T BELIEVE she was driving State
Road 46 toward Interstate 10 with a genuine prince.
He was sitting on the passenger side, his backside
resting on her Wal-Mart imitation leopard-print car
seat cover, looking as though he were having the time
of his life. The wind blew his brown hair across his
forehead and plastered the Western shirt he'd bought
in the truck stop to his chest. His really nice, impres-
sively muscular chest.

She was usually a good judge of character, but
Prince Alexi had poleaxed her from the moment she'd
kissed him, so she might not be thinking straight.

She almost moaned aloud. Jeez, she'd kissed a
prince! She still couldn't believe she'd done that. The
only explanation she could come up with was that
today was her last day as a waitress. She'd said goodbye to her fellow waitresses and regular customers,
all emotional about this change in her life, including
her college graduation on Saturday. Then a prince
walked into her life. And not just any prince, but one
who was so good-looking he made her eyeballs hurt.

She wanted to watch him instead of the road, inhale
his scent instead of the dusty highway breeze, and
most of all, she wanted to kiss him again. Which was

crazy. She had to keep reminding herself that he was a prince.

Why was he sitting in her aging Toyota? If he'd wanted to see Galveston, why hadn't he hopped on a jet or into his fancy Land Rover? Why would he care if she drove there in Delores when he didn't even know her?

"What kind of music do you like?" he asked, reaching for her radio.

"Almost everything but rap," she replied. "It might be hard to pick up a station between towns, but I have a CD player. CDs are in the back seat, in that black zippered case."

"You have a CD player?"

She glanced over at her passenger. "What, you don't think Delores deserves a nice stereo?"

"I'm just surprised, that's all."

"The new CD player and stereo radio was a gift from my mother two years ago. I spend—spent a lot of time commuting from home to school to work."

"Where is Ranger Springs?" he asked as he reached for her CDs.

"West of the truck stop, about twenty-five minutes." She grinned. "In Texas, we often give distances in the minutes it takes to drive rather than the actual miles."

"I only visited Dallas. I have some business contacts there."

"I thought you were in the business of being a prince."

"I have some other interests."

"Really?" She glanced over and saw him flipping through her CDs. Garth Brooks, vintage Bee Gees, the music from *Phantom of the Opera* and a half-dozen other groups.

He sighed as if he didn't want to talk about himself. "Some investments of my own."

"Ah. So you're not just another pretty face with a crown." Maybe if she joked about his good looks, she wouldn't keep thinking about how interested she was in him as a man.

He laughed. "Thank you for the compliment, I think. I suppose that is the view of royalty, especially in Texas, where everyone values their independence."

Kerry nodded in agreement. "We're big on independence, but fascinated by everything bigger than life. Rich folks. Movie stars. Royalty. My mother is one of the biggest fans of the British royals, but she doesn't discriminate. When I give her your autograph, she's going to be doing the happy-happy dance all around the living room." Kerry chuckled as she imagined her mom squealing in delight. "As a matter of fact, I may have to keep that car seat cover just because you sat on it."

"Maybe you should bring me home and really make her day." He slipped one of her favorite Dixie Chicks CDs into the stereo.

Kerry shook her head. "I'm not sure her heart could stand it." Maybe *her* heart couldn't stand it, either.

"Is she ill?" he asked, concern evident in his voice.

Kerry chuckled again. "No, she's as healthy as a horse. And she's not that old, either. She just turned fifty. I was exaggerating."

"That's another trademark of Texans, isn't it?"

"Only when we're talking to Yankees."

He laughed and turned up the volume on the CD player. "I'm having a good time, Kerry Lynn Jacks."

"I'm glad...."

"Call me Alexi."

"That seems kind of wrong. I mean, just because you and I are on a road trip, you're still a prince."

"Can you put that aside for a couple of days?"

"I don't know," she answered truthfully. "I can try."

"Please, try," he asked, placing a hand on her shoulder.

She tried not to react, even though her skin felt suddenly overheated...and not from the warm May temperature. "Okay." She passed a pickup truck heavily laden with bales of hay as she thought about forgetting that the man beside her was a prince. The name Alexi sounded so foreign. Maybe if she had a nickname for him, she wouldn't think of him as the prince. And what about when they stopped, or got to her aunt and uncle's house? She couldn't call him by his real name without alerting everyone that the prince was slumming around Texas with a truck stop waitress he'd just met.

"What's your middle name?" she asked as the Dixie Chicks sang about women striking out on their own. What appropriate music. Kerry was just getting ready to start her new life. A professional life in which she would never have to wear a uniform again. And she'd have an apartment all her own. She could stay out late without anyone worrying. She could sleep late on Saturday morning and only wash dishes when she felt like it.

"Which one?" Alexi asked, breaking into her fantasy. "I have several."

She made a face in his general direction. "Just tell me, okay? I need to call you something besides Alexi, or Your Highness, or whatever else is appropriate, because people are going to be a bit suspicious. They'll either think I'm crazy as a loon for calling Hank a prince, or that you're crazy for running off with me."

"My full name is Alexi Karl Gregor MacCulloh Ladislas."

"Wow."

"My sentiments exactly. While attending college in Boston, I rarely used anything but my first name, usually shortened to Alex. And I found the computer forms weren't understanding about more than one middle initial."

"All your names sound real European except MacCulloh. Where did that come from?"

"My mother is English. Her grandfather was from Scotland and honored him by giving me his surname."

"That's nice, and it's also perfect. Can I call you Mack? Anyone who hears us talking will think that you're Hank McCauley."

"Ah, yes. The man who looks like me. Tell me, now that we've spent some time together, do you still think we resemble each other that closely?"

She glanced over at him again. "Yes, you do, although your expressions are different. Hank's more...well, I guess you could say he's spontaneous.

He's also a big tease, and he's a Texan through and through.'' He also didn't make her heart race with just a smile.

Alexi was silent for a moment. Kerry glanced quickly at him and noticed he was frowning. Finally, he asked, ''What does he do for a living?''

''He trains cutting horses now, but he used to be a champion bronc rider. He's retired.''

''Retired…at what age?''

''I guess he's thirty-one now. Around your age, I suppose.''

''You cut me to the quick,'' he replied with mock indignation. ''I'm a relatively young thirty.''

Kerry chuckled. ''Sorry. I wouldn't want to add a whole year.''

''I was dreading my thirtieth birthday enough. I can't imagine the next one.''

''I thought women worried more than men about aging.''

''Oh, I'm not worried about getting older. It's just that my father, King Wilheim, has decided that thirty is a magical number. It's the age at which I should settle down and choose a bride.''

''Choose a bride? That sounds so…archaic.''

He shrugged, then rested his arm on the open window and stared at the passing flat plains dotted with patches of wildflowers and barbed-wire fences. ''What can I say? I'm a prince. You can't get much more archaic than that.''

As she neared the intersection of Interstate 10, Kerry wondered if that was what this whole ''road trip'' incident was all about for Prince Alexi. Running away from his life. Running away from the responsibility of finding a bride.

She wondered if the men in her life would always lack reliability and maturity. Her father had loved gambling and excitement more than his family. Hank was a nice guy, but he flirted and teased his way through life. And now she was on a road trip with a prince—a prince, for goodness' sake!—who'd left his entourage with the drop of a hat. What did that say about him? That he didn't care? Or that he couldn't be trusted? Or maybe both.

He certainly didn't seem excited about marrying one of the ''beautiful people'' among the elite in Europe. He'd marry someone tall, slim and elegant and within a few years they'd produce the next generation of tall, elegant royalty. She'd never seen a photo of royalty in which the women were petite, freckled and ''wholesome''—a description she'd heard from family and friends one too many times.

The difference between Prince Alexi and her long-gone father, Kerry mused, was that dear ol' Dad had run away *after* he'd fathered three daughters. He'd left four people confused and angry, while Alexi had infuriated his public-relations director...and maybe disappointed his king. He certainly wasn't married yet, so maybe he'd settle down someday soon.

She risked a glance at him, wondering why he didn't remind her more of Hank since they looked so much alike. Alexi's striking profile was highlighted by morning sunlight streaming in through the windshield. His handsome features and confidence probably came from generations of blue blood. She imagined that he was used to getting whatever he wanted, even if his whim was a trip to Galveston in an un-air-conditioned car named Delores.

Perhaps he was a little like her dad, she thought as she headed east on Interstate 10, but not much. Not too much, anyway...

Chapter Two

Alexi settled back against the fake leopard fur seat and let the warmth of the Texas day seep into his bones. He'd taken several short vacations in the past year or so, but they'd involved rushed trips to the Mediterranean or skiing in the Alps, hiding from the paparazzi, trying to have a personal life in impersonal fancy suites and ski lodges. Nothing at all like a long drive across the Texas prairie in an aging Toyota.

Nothing at all like a trip with Kerry Lynn Jacks.

"You have a real 'cat ate the canary' smile on your face," she said, her voice drifting through the drowsy noontime like feathers through mist.

"Hmm. Well, I do feel rather contented at the moment."

She chuckled. "You're an easy man to please... Mack."

"I know a score of people who would disagree with you. Starting with my public-relations director, who is probably still fuming."

"That was kind of mean of you—leaving her standing there in the parking lot, stamping her foot."

Alexi smiled. "Yes, that was rather bad of me. I'll

make it up to her, though. Besides, I told her I didn't want to make the appearances in San Antonio. She was filling in some time until we discovered if the president was going to come to his ranch for the weekend.''

The car swerved as Kerry gasped. Alexi opened one eye and looked around.

''*The* president! You mean you were supposed to meet with *the president* and you ran off to Galveston with me instead?''

''The meeting wasn't assured. We had no idea if he'd be traveling to Texas. You know how things come up.''

''Oh, of course,'' she said in a highly stressed voice. When he glanced at her, she made a sweeping gesture with her hands. ''I know exactly how things can just *come up* with you heads of state.''

''Really, Kerry, I doubt that the meeting would have occurred. Congress and world events can be very unpredictable. Besides, originally I had wanted to take a few days of holiday, but Lady Gwendolyn insisted we keep to a tight schedule.''

She shook her head. ''I can't believe I'm in my car, having a conversation with a prince who was going to spend the weekend with the president.''

''No, you're driving to Galveston with your good friend Mack.''

''Hey, I'm the one having the fantasy, okay?''

''Are you so sure?'' he asked. Kerry might not look like the models and aspiring actresses who attended the events he usually frequented. She was cute rather than beautiful, petite rather than statuesque and honest rather than calculating. He found her honesty and nat-

ural charm extremely desirable. "I can't imagine anyone I'd rather spend time with, and that includes your
current leader."

She opened her mouth, but no words came forth.
For once, he'd managed to silence her somewhat
saucy remarks.

Closing his eyes, he settled back against the seat
once more. The sound of the tires rolling down the
highway lulled him into sleep, and he dozed, a vision
of Kerry's amazed expression bringing a smile to his
lips.

"WHERE ARE WE?" Alexi—or Mack—slowly opened
his eyes. Lord, he looked good when he woke up.
Really, really sexy. How was she going to keep her
hands off him for three days?

"We're in Sealy, about an hour outside of Houston." She drove past the Wal-Mart and several fast-
food places until she spotted a service station with a
food mart. "Are you hungry? We can get a snack,
although I'd like to wait to eat supper with my aunt
and uncle tonight, if possible."

She pulled off the interstate onto the service road.

"Very good. I could use a cold drink." He raised
his lean, muscular torso off Delores's seat and
stretched, as much as possible, inside the tight con-
fines of the car. "I hadn't realized I was so sleepy,"
he said as she pulled to a stop at the gas pumps.

Kerry tore her eyes away from his tempting body
and reached for the door handle. "You can get a soft
drink or some water if you'd like. I won't be long."

"I'll help you," he said, opening his own door.

"No, that's okay." She needed a few minutes apart

from him. For the past several hours, she'd had time to think about this trip. About him. About what she was doing driving a real, live prince around Texas.

Maybe this adventure was a big mistake.

"It's been several years, but I think I can remember how to fuel up your vehicle."

"You don't have to—"

"Kerry, if I truly were Hank, wouldn't you let me help?"

"Well…"

Right there beside the gas pumps, Delores's poor old engine popping and wheezing beside them, he used one finger to tip up her chin. "I'm Mack, your friend, remember? Treat me just like you would Hank."

"I'm having a hard time with that," she whispered.

"Kerry Lynn Jacks, you are thinking too much," he answered with a smile.

His smile slowly faded. Her lips slowly parted. He leaned closer, closer… Just when she thought he might kiss her, her car let out a particularly loud ping. Blinking, Kerry stepped back.

"Seriously," she said. "I'll pump the gas. If you'd like to do something nice, you can buy me a soft drink. Anything cold with caffeine."

"Very well," he said with a sigh.

"Oh, and *Mack,*" she said, emphasizing the nickname, "whatever you do, don't use the word *schedule.*" His pronunciation of "shed-yule" would give him away immediately.

He chuckled, waving off her concern, and she went back to filling up Delores's tank, probably for the last time.

After they'd both used the facilities, they piled back into the car. In the few minutes they'd been apart, Kerry had gotten herself under control again. Okay, so she was chauffeuring a prince around Texas. And pretending he was someone else. She could do this.

But he had to help.

"Look, if you're going to be 'Mack' instead of Prince Alexi," she said as she started Delores's reluctant engine, "you need to talk like you're from Texas instead of London."

"We can work on that on the way to Galveston."

"Okay. So tell me about your family—your real one, that is, not something you'd make up to fit your Texas persona—but use your best Texas accent."

"Hmm, very well," he began.

"Wait just a minute. Don't say 'very well.' Texans just don't talk that way. You can say 'okay' instead."

"Okay," he responded with a tight smile. "I'm the oldest son of King Wilheim of Belegovia. I have a brother who lives in our country and a sister who is attending university—"

"Nope, she's 'goin' to college,'" Kerry interrupted.

"Okay, she's goin' to college at my alma mater, Harvard."

"Pretty classy," Kerry said with a grin. "You're getting better, by the way. Just relax. Go ahead."

"Let's see... Oh, yes. My mother lives in England."

"Are your parents divorced?"

"No, but they haven't lived together since shortly

after our country became a separate entity after liberation from the Soviet Union.''

"Okay, tell that to me again in Texas-style English.''

Alexi laughed. "Sorry. Belegovia is an old monarchy that was swallowed up by the Soviet Union after World War II. My grandfather fled the country with his family and sought asylum in England.''

"So the queen took you in.''

"Actually, I—''

"No 'actually,' either. Just go ahead and tell me.''

"Very...er, sorry,'' he responded with a grin. "My father was a very young man when they settled in England. I wasn't born yet.''

"Oh, so that's why your mother is from England.''

"Right. And she prefers to live there. You see, she never expected my father to become king. After all, he didn't have a country when they married, and there wasn't any clue that we'd ever get it back.''

"So she didn't want to be a queen.''

"She didn't want to give up her life, her home, her friends,'' Alexi said, his expression showing he'd resigned himself to his parents' situation long ago. "My father taught history. She was much happier being married to a professor than a king.''

"I suppose I can understand her point. I mean, there's got to be a lot of hassles when you're a monarch. Lack of privacy, lots of expectations.''

"And don't forget all those public appearances,'' he said with a grin.

Kerry gave him what she hoped was a chastising frown.

"To give her credit, she tried to fit in for a short

while, but the country was still chaotic when we returned to Belegovia. The parliament and some of the courts were in operation, but the palace had yet to be restored and the role of the king was still tenuous.''

"Texas talk, remember?'' she prodded.

"Oh, of course.'' He frowned for a moment, then brightened. "The place was a damned mess,'' he finally said with a grin and a drawl.

Kerry laughed. "By George, I think he's got it,'' she said in her best Henry Higgins imitation.

She sipped her soft drink as they drew closer to Houston. She hoped they missed most of the rush hour traffic, which could be brutal, from what she'd heard from her aunt and uncle. They avoided ''the city,'' which meant anywhere in or near Houston, whenever possible, preferring the slower pace of life on the island.

"Tell me about yourself, Kerry Lynn Jacks,'' Alexi said, breaking into her thoughts as she passed a semi.

"I have a mother and two sisters. No father, at least not for years. He left when I was thirteen.''

"That must have been difficult for your mother.''

"Yes, it was. She's a waitress at the Four Square Café in Ranger Springs, which doesn't pay really great. I've been helping out as much as I could, mainly because tips at the truck stop are a lot better than at the local diner.''

"I see. What about your sisters? How old are they?''

"Carole is just a year and a half younger than me—nearly twenty-seven. Cheryl is twenty-six. Both of them live in Ranger Springs.''

"Do they resemble you?''

"Your Texas accent is slipping," she said, mostly to collect her thoughts. "And yes, sort of."

"Then they must be very beautiful."

"Oh, puleeze," she said, already feeling her cheeks heating. "You don't have to say things like that just because I'm giving you a ride across the state."

"That's not why I said it."

"Look, I'm slightly cute, okay? But beautiful people are tall and thin and dress in incredibly fantastic clothes. They live in New York and California and exotic places, not Ranger Springs, Texas."

"You've been reading too many fashion and celebrity magazines."

"No, I've just learned to be a realist. I'm not unhappy with who I am. I'm content to be short and cute." She took a big breath, then smiled at him. "Besides, I'm also smart and stubborn. That makes up for a lot of slinky clothes and exotic locales."

"So what is a smart, cute woman like yourself doing after graduation on Saturday?"

She brightened at his question. "I have a great job at Grayson Industries as a financial analyst. Gray Phillips moved his company to town two years ago and married our doctor, Amy Wheatley. Business is booming, so he's expanding his financial staff. I'll be looking at things like cash flow, financing and inventory management."

"Sounds interesting."

"Are you just saying that?"

"No. Why do you think I went to Harvard? They don't offer degrees in 'princely deportment,'" he teased. "I got my MBA to help manage my own investments and help my father. Besides, there was a good chance I'd need to get a job, since the title 'prince' doesn't translate into a living in the real world. There was no guarantee that Belegovia could successfully return to a parliamentary-style government with a titular monarchy.''

''Really? I guess I hadn't thought about it.'' She'd assumed that he'd always been assured of his position in the world. But now that she knew more of his background, she understood that being a prince wasn't something he'd grown up with, not like the British royal family. From the day they were born, they knew what their role was going to be. Alexi had grown up as the son of a history professor who happened to have royal blood.

And now that he'd turned thirty, his father demanded he get married. A princess bride. If she'd read about it in one of her mother's royalty magazines, Kerry knew she'd think the situation romantic. After all, hadn't she watched the last big royal wedding with tears in her eyes over the fairy-tale quality—the ivory satin gown with the long, long train, the tiara, the beautiful flowers?

Now that she knew the situation from Alexi's point of view, she understood the pressure he felt. This trip was obviously a rebellion against his father's mandate. She'd taken only one course in psychology, but she understood such motivation.

''If you get tired of driving, please let me know. I'll be glad to take over,'' he said, breaking into her thoughts.

''We're almost to Houston. The traffic is pretty bad and it's almost rush hour. I wouldn't wish that on my worst enemy.''

"Actually...sorry." He slipped into his version of a Texas accent. "I meant, I was a darned good driver when I lived in Boston."

"Do you even *have* a driver's license?"

"Of course," he said with mock indignation. "Duly issued by the Belegovian Department of Transportation. I even took the written test. And I drove a Formula One racer in a charity event in Monte Carlo last year."

Kerry laughed as she shook her head. "Just hang on, Mario Andretti. I'm taking you into the final lap. We'll be in Galveston in less than two hours."

ALEXI ENJOYED viewing the sprawling metropolitan area of Houston. He could barely see the downtown area from the eastbound interstate highway, just south of Houston. Various groupings of high-rise buildings gave the impression of several different "downtown" districts as Kerry deftly dodged traffic.

She would have been a big hit in the charity race in Monaco, he thought with a smile. He could just see her layered blond hair peeking out from a helmet, her petite, curvy body encased in the one-piece, form-fitting, emblem-emblazoned driver's suit.

His smile faded as his body responded to the image. Shifting in Delores's fake-fur seat, he glanced at Kerry. She was absorbed in the heavy traffic, so he looked his fill. She was right; she was cute. Her skin was lightly freckled, her hair naturally streaked by the sun. But her animated features and endearingly honest personality made her beautiful in his eyes.

When he'd impulsively decided to accompany her on this trip, he'd wanted to explore the instant attrac-

tion he'd felt for this Texas sprite. Now that he knew
more about her, he liked her even more. He wasn't
sure how many days he could spend with her—surely
they'd return for her graduation on Saturday—but he
would savor each moment.

He really hoped the president was too busy to go
to his ranch this weekend. After all, they had nothing
of substance to discuss; Belegovia's contract with the
United States for the removal of old Soviet Union
missile silos was secure. The U.S. had granted much-
needed foreign aid for Belegovia's cooperation in
making sure the region was safe from nuclear accidents.

Besides, Alexi knew he'd much rather spend time
with Kerry than the leader of the free world.

They exited the loop and headed south for Galveston, passing one of Houston's airports, Kerry informed him. Soon the buildings and the traffic
cleared. The flat plains of south Texas met the water
in marshes on either side of the highway.

"How much farther?" he finally asked.

Kerry smiled at him. "You sound like a little boy."

"Those are fightin' words," he said, mocking a
Texas accent.

Kerry laughed. "Actually, you sounded a lot like
Hank then. Keep it up and Aunt Marcy and Uncle
Bob will never know you have blue blood in your
veins."

"So my goal is to be a little over the top?"

"That's Hank. And to answer your original question, about half an hour."

Alexi settled back in the seat and watched the salt
marshes whiz by. Hank. He kept coming up in con-

versation. Had Kerry been in love with the cowboy? Was she over their romance? The questions bothered him more than he wanted to admit. But that was probably because he was so curious about all aspects of Kerry Lynn Jacks. Wondering about her previous relationships was normal…right?

So what if he couldn't recall ever thinking about the previous lovers of any of the women he'd dated. Kerry was different in so many ways, but they both knew their time together was limited. Perhaps that made the experience so much more intense. They had a lot to learn in three short days.

He'd love to learn how she would look, flushed with desire, her blue-gray eyes smoky and mysterious. She was so expressive, so spontaneous. Kerry would be a wonderful lover, he was certain. But she was also a delightful person, and until they arrived at their destination and he knew what sleeping arrangements were offered, he was content to watch her drive and listen to her speak of her friends, family and home state.

"I should warn you that Aunt Marcy is in a wheelchair. She gets around so well that sometimes I forget, but I didn't want you to be too surprised when we get to their house."

"That's fine. Was she in an accident?"

"No, she was one of the last cases of polio before the vaccine was developed in the 1950s."

"Bloody horrible disease," he muttered, then held up his hand. "And no comments about saying it in Texas English."

"I wasn't going to," she said softly. She drove for a few more minutes, then gestured to the left. "I know you went off without much from your luggage. If you need to get anything, there's a mall up there. Galveston clothing shopping is pretty limited unless you want souvenir T-shirts and tropical shorts.''

''That's very thoughtful. I should pick up a few things. If you wouldn't mind...''

''Not at all.''

They shopped at several stores for khaki slacks, another pair of jeans and a package of underwear. He let Kerry pick out several shirts since he wasn't sure what Hank would wear. They both laughed over the wide variety of swim trunks, which he'd need for the beach. She playfully suggested bright green baggy tropicals with huge pink and purple flowers. He preferred solid blue with a discreet red stripe up the side. They compromised on a moderate red and white pattern.

At the cosmetics counter, he picked up a bottle of his usual cologne, some lotion and sunscreen, since they were going to the beach. Kerry appeared a bit surprised, but he couldn't see ignoring personal grooming just because he was on a road trip.

Within an hour they were back on the road, his new duffel bag stowed in the back seat. He looked forward to meeting Kerry's aunt and uncle and spending time in a typical American family home. He hoped his presence didn't disrupt their sleeping arrangements. If so he could always get a hotel room, which he assumed were plentiful in this island city.

Or he could offer to bunk with Kerry, he thought with a grin. He'd be willing to sacrifice sleep for the opportunity to hold her in his arms and get to know her much, much better.

Just then they approached a high bridge.

"This is the only bridge on and off the island," she explained. "When a hurricane warning is issued, Aunt Mary and Uncle Bob told me traffic is a nightmare."

They passed over a bay with boat docks lining the shores. A little farther ahead, he saw waterside homes to the right, and a strange pyramid structure. "What's that?"

"Moody Gardens. The Moodys are a wealthy Texas family who give a lot to different charities and universities. I've never been to Moody Gardens, but Aunt Marcy loves to go. They have a tropical habitat with butterflies."

Soon the highway turned into a city street with a wide, tree-lined median as they went past small businesses and modest, sometimes shabby houses. So far, except for the scruffy palm trees and blooming shrubs, the city didn't look like a semitropical island, but he hadn't seen the beach yet.

"The old part of Galveston is up ahead," Kerry said, pointing to the left. "Tomorrow we can tour some of the homes if you'd like. Or we can go to the Strand, this Victorian section near the pier, with shops and restaurants."

"Anything is fine with me. Whatever you'd like to do, I know I'll enjoy it." He was especially looking forward to seeing Kerry in her swimsuit. He didn't suppose he'd be lucky enough to discover she wore a bikini. "When will we go to the beach?"

"Almost anytime. As a matter of fact, we can take a walk along there tonight. My aunt and uncle live only two blocks off the seawall."

"Fabulous," he said with a grin when Kerry turned off the main thoroughfare onto a numbered side street. He couldn't wait for a romantic moonlit walk along the beach with his Texas tour guide.

KERRY PULLED DELORES to a stop in the driveway behind her aunt and uncle's van. She had to stop herself from running for the door and giving them both a big hug. She hadn't seen Aunt Marcy and Uncle Bob for almost a year. She'd taken more class hours this last year, but continued to work a full shift at the truck stop. Between family, school and work, she hadn't taken a vacation. And her aunt and uncle didn't enjoy traveling much. Most houses didn't accommodate Aunt Marcy's wheelchair, so visiting was difficult.

Uncle Bob opened the door, grinning as he spread his arms wide. Kerry smiled and ran up the ramp to the front porch.

"It's so good to see you," she said against his pipe-tobacco-scented shirt.

"We're so proud of you, Kerry girl," he murmured as he gave her a bear hug. "It's good to see you, too."

She looked back at the car. Alexi was standing by Delores's bumper holding his duffel and her suitcase. She gestured him forward.

"Uncle Bob, I want you to meet my friend, Mack."

"Mack? Why, isn't that Hank McCauley? Your mother sent us a picture of the two of you at a rodeo a couple of years ago. I thought you called him Hank."

"Oh," she said, waving her hand dismissively, "Mack is my special nickname for him.

"Mack, this is my uncle, Robert Jacks, but you can call him Bob."

"Pleased to meet you," Alexi said, holding out his hand and grinning. He sounded enough like Hank to fool someone who had never actually met the cowboy.

As the men shook hands, Kerry slipped behind them to find Aunt Marcy, just inside the living room. She leaned down and gave her aunt a big hug.

"I'm so glad to see you."

"I'm so glad you brought a friend with you. I was worried about you driving across the state all by yourself in that old car."

"Delores did just fine, thank you very much," Kerry said, smiling at her aunt. "She might be a little old and have a lot of miles on her, but she's never let me down yet."

"I'm sure your new car will be just as good."

"Oh, I'm sure it will, too. I'm just going to miss my old clunker. You'll try to find her a good home, won't you?"

Aunt Marcy nodded her head. "Of course we will, but you should have never named that car."

Grinning, Kerry turned to see "Mack" and Uncle Bob enter the room. "Kerry brought a friend—Hank McCauley."

"Wonderful," Aunt Marcy said, reaching out her hand. "We have plenty of room and an extra sofa bed, Mr. McCauley."

"Please, call me Mack," Alexi said, giving his words a slight twang even as he bestowed his most charming smile on her aunt. ''And as long as you're sure I won't be in the way, I'd love to stay in your home. If not, I can get a hotel room.''

''Nonsense,'' Aunt Marcy said, turning her wheelchair around and heading for the hallway.

Kerry breathed a sigh of relief since the introductions were out of the way and no one was suspicious of her prince. They moved into the kitchen. Aunt Marcy was in the process of preparing dinner. Kerry hadn't eaten since an early light lunch just before she met Alexi at the truck stop.

Aunt Marcy scooped fried okra out of the skillet and onto a paper towel-lined platter. The unique smell filled the yellow-and-white kitchen, which had been modified for a wheelchair. Most of the countertops and appliances were low, so they could be reached from the sitting position. As the vegetable cooled and drained, Aunt Marcy transferred ground beef patties to the sizzling skillet.

''Need help?'' Kerry asked.

''No, I've got everything pretty well prepared. We weren't sure when you'd get here, and I didn't want dinner to get cold.''

Kerry smiled as Alexi eyed the fried okra. ''Try it,'' she urged. Of course, Hank had eaten this type of food all his life. He selected a single piece and, after testing the heat in the palm of his hand, he placed the okra discreetly into his mouth.

He even chewed neatly. Politely. She'd never seen him eat a meal, but she was certain he had perfect manners. She couldn't imagine Prince Alexi doing anything badly.

''I'll get some clean sheets for the Hide-A-Bed sofa

in the den,'' Uncle Bob informed Alexi as he also popped a piece of fried okra into his mouth. ''I put both your bags in Kerry's room, temporarily.''

''That means you can get your bag anytime you'd like, as long as it's not in the middle of the night,'' Kerry explained.

''Sure,'' Alexi agreed casually.

Uncle Bob folded his arms across his chest and faced them both. ''Not that I don't trust you two kids, but we have a rule in the house—no wedding ring, no hanky-panky.''

''I respect your principles,'' Alexi said.

''Uncle Bob! We're just friends.''

''Enough said,'' he muttered. ''I just wanted to make myself clear. Kerry, you never have brought a *male* friend to visit us before.''

''Well, Mack rather...insisted. He was worried about me driving down here in Delores.''

''I respect you, son,'' Uncle Bob said with a laugh.

''I'm glad I'm not the only one who was worried,'' Aunt Marcy added.

Kerry threw up her hands. ''Gesh, I'm twenty-eight years old and I've been driving for twelve years. You'd think I could find my way from Ranger Springs to Galveston on my own.''

''We just worry about you, dear. You're so independent,'' Aunt Marcy said, patting Kerry's hand. Her aunt turned to Alexi. ''Kerry helps her family so much, and not just moneywise. She pitches in until we wonder how she gets her schoolwork done. But she must, because she's graduating cum laude even though she works full-time.''

''Okay, now I'm embarrassed,'' Kerry said, feeling

her cheeks heat up. "I'm taking A—Mack away before you reveal any more family secrets." She grabbed his hand and dragged him toward the small bedroom she'd stayed in many times when she'd visited. Once inside, she drew open the curtains, but couldn't see anything outside due to the early evening shadows. A mirror image of her and Alexi, standing close together, stared back.

"My aunt and uncle are just curious. Plus, they want to impress you with how wonderful I am," she added flippantly to lighten the mood. "They always say I'm their favorite niece, but I suspect they say the same thing to my two sisters."

Alexi laughed. "I don't need them to expound on your virtues. I'd already figured that out on my own."

She grabbed her suitcase and slipped it onto the bed. "I'm disappointed. I wanted to be a woman of mystery."

"Oh, I'm sure there are many layers I have yet to uncover," he responded in a sultry tone that made her breath hitch and her palms grow damp. He leaned against the door frame and crossed his arms over his chest, confident, powerful and just a little mysterious himself.

She wished he didn't make those suggestive comments in such a sexy voice. Her mind filled with all types of "uncovering" possibilities.

"I'm going to unpack real quick, then help Aunt Marcy get supper ready. If you'd like to wash up, or look around, go ahead."

He didn't immediately take the hint, watching her intensely from the doorway. She wasn't locked in a room with him; she could push by him if she wanted and be in the hallway of the relatively small house. Or she could just shout her aunt or uncle's name and they'd be here in an instant. But she didn't feel threatened...at least not in an uncomfortable sense. A kind of a welcome, yet edgy sense of awareness flowed between them.

This felt different from their time together in the car, probably because they hadn't been staring at each other. This felt...dangerously thrilling.

Could Prince Alexi be her reward for ten long years of hard work?

Chapter Three

After a dinner of surprisingly tasty hamburger steak with grilled onions, mashed potatoes and fried okra, Alexi welcomed a walk along the beach. He and Kerry took a towel to sit upon and a flashlight to see their way to what she called "the seawall."

"Your aunt and uncle are charming," he said as they neared the busy thoroughfare that ran along the coastline. Several other couples, some young people and a few families were also out on foot tonight. When there was a lull in the automobile traffic, he could hear the waves breaking against the shore. The smell of saltwater coated the warm, humid air.

"They are wonderful people. It was their idea for the family to take up a collection and buy Marcy's mother's car. She went into an assisted-living facility in Alvin, which is just south of Houston. Since Aunt Marcy is in a wheelchair and needs a specially equipped van, they didn't need an extra car."

"I'm sure everyone will feel more confident now that you have a much newer car," he commented, remembering their earlier conversation.

"Yes, but the funny thing is now that I've graduated, I'll only be driving about four miles round trip."

"That's all the distance from your mother's house to this Grayson Industries?" he asked as they crossed the street.

"Actually, I'm getting my own apartment. I'm moving in next week." She turned to look at him, her face alight with joy. "You have no idea how much I'm looking forward to having my own place for the first time in my life. No sharing a bathroom. No being quiet because everyone else is sleeping. No one to steal my food from the refrigerator."

Alexi laughed. "I know what you mean. My first flat in London was absolute heaven. I did all the typical bachelor things. My flat was messy, smelly and tastelessly decorated."

Kerry laughed. He felt his own smile fading as he remembered other things about living on his own. Girlfriends, some attracted to his title, some hoping for an introduction to one of the British princes, some just looking for a good time. Easy sex, although not nearly as much as some might have assumed. He didn't want to think that Kerry would have the equivalent experience. Boyfriends. Easy sex of any sort.

"What's wrong? Don't you like the beach?"

He turned his attention back to the present and Kerry. Forcing a smile, he took her hand. "I adore the beach."

"You're slipping into your British accent again."

"I know, but let me be myself for a while. I've been very good at playing Hank McCauley, if I do say so myself." He pulled her aside as three people on in-line skates whizzed past. Kerry's leg brushed his as their hips bumped briefly before she stepped away.

"Yes, you have." She swung their linked hands while strolling along the sidewalk, apparently not as affected as he by their contact. "This seawall was built after a huge hurricane in 1900. The whole island was raised to keep it from ever being submerged again, and this seawall was built of concrete and rock to keep the water from washing away the shoreline."

"Very impressive—both the history and your knowledge of the area."

"My aunt and uncle are great history buffs. They have a book on Galveston you might find interesting, just in case you have trouble sleeping."

"Good to know," he said as they started down the steps that took them to the beach. He had an idea he *would* have trouble sleeping with Kerry so near, yet so far away. Ever since seeing the cozy bedroom she'd be occupying, he'd envisioned her stretched out on that small bed, an alluring smile lighting up her cute, freckled face.

The smell of the ocean was stronger here, the sand deep as they stepped off the wooden steps onto the beach. The sound of the waves was even and reassuring as he again took Kerry's hand. Lamps from the seawall illuminated the area enough that they could see where they were walking. Other couples strolled closer to the water, where the sand was firm and wet. White foam on the waves gleamed silver in the artificial light.

"I suppose it's not as wonderful as those Mediterranean beaches you're used to."

Alexi chuckled. "Actually, European beaches are

almost all rocks. We have very little sand, especially something this fine and pale.''

"Really?''

"For truly wonderful beaches, we go to the Caribbean or Central or South America.''

"I'd love to travel someday,'' she said wistfully. "I get two weeks of vacation a year, but I have to wait six months to take part of that. After five years, I get three weeks.''

"Sometimes shorter holidays can be very relaxing.''

"Yes. We have Memorial Day, the Fourth of July and then Labor Day coming up. Maybe I can plan a long weekend someplace fun. Corpus Christi or Las Vegas or New Orleans.''

He didn't correct the impression she'd gotten from his use of "holiday." In England, the word was used instead of the American "vacation." But whatever Kerry called time off from work, he wondered if she would venture somewhere alone. Or would she have a boyfriend to accompany her on one of these upcoming weekends?

Perhaps he could fly over and take a holiday with her.

Perhaps their brief relationship didn't have to end with him going back to Belegovia on Sunday. Unless, of course, he immediately became involved with someone else at the insistence of his father. Unless he became engaged to one of the European elite who had been selected for him.

"I love it here,'' Kerry breathed, barely above a whisper. He had to lean close to catch her words over the rhythmic pounding of the surf. "The sound of the waves is so peaceful. Sometimes I just sit on the rocks,'' she said, pointing to a man-made rocky pier that jutted into the surf, ''and watch for hours.''

''I feel that way when I'm on a boat,'' Alexi admitted. ''Especially a sailboat. There's nothing like the rocking motion of the water, the slap of the waves against the hull, to lull your brain into semiconscious bliss.''

''Exactly,'' Kerry said softly, turning toward him. ''I knew you'd understand.''

She wants you to kiss her. The knowledge was so certain that for a moment, Alexi thought someone had spoken the words into his brain. But he was only reacting to Kerry. Her wide eyes and parted lips beckoned him.

Semiconscious bliss. That's what he felt when he pulled her close, their bodies touching everywhere. His brain shut down, giving over to sensations. Her rapid breathing. Her small, shapely breasts brushing his rib cage. Her thighs nestling against his.

He looked into her luminous eyes until he lowered his head. She tasted like the orange sherbet he'd eaten for dessert—sweet and tangy, just like Kerry. Then he lost himself when she parted her lips and her tongue touched his. His hands tightened against her back, pulling her closer. She met his passion with equal enthusiasm, kissing him thoroughly until neither could breathe.

They broke together and sucked in air, still clinging tightly. Her breath tickled hot against his chest as his hands moved restlessly over her back. He longed to reach lower, cup her bottom in his hands and pull her higher, until she wrapped her legs around his waist, but he didn't dare. Not in public. Not yet.

But the urge was there, stronger than ever. They had two days, possibly three, before they each began new lives. Could that be enough for either of them?

As KERRY FIDGETED restlessly in the guest bedroom, she couldn't stop thinking about that kiss. Wow. Alexi might look like Hank, but the two men were worlds apart. She'd never reacted to her former boyfriend like she did to this prince. The chemistry was just so…intense. Different. She didn't know why, but Alexi brought out a side of her she'd only slightly explored. Sure, she and Hank had kissed a couple of times, but there hadn't been any sparks.

Now she felt like a Fourth of July firecracker waiting for the match to strike.

Rolling onto her back, she stared at the ceiling. When she was a child, she used to imagine she could see the shapes of animals in the plaster of this bedroom. Directly above the bed was a lion's head. Near the window was a flying bird. And beside the closet door was a lamb. She'd indulged her fantasies by making up stories of why they were here, what they were doing. Especially at night. The animals romped around a lot at night.

Now she had more grown-up fantasies. Of romping on the beach with Alexi. Of falling to the cool sand with him. Of making love to him as the waves surged around them. Her girlhood fantasies were as tame as that lamb, but she was really a lion as an adult. Especially when she imagined raking her fingernails down his back as she pulled him closer, closer…

Sighing, she flopped onto her stomach and hugged a pillow. She'd thought earlier that Alexi might be her reward for years of hard work. For studying during her work breaks, for staying home when her friends were going away for the weekend, for helping her mother and sisters instead of partying.

She'd been a good girl—with just a couple of unremarkable lapses—and now she wanted it all. Her freedom, her career and her prince.

Except he wasn't *her* prince. He was going to marry someone from European royalty or at least blue blood. Someone his father would approve as the future queen of their beloved country.

But while he was in Texas, he was hers. She didn't have to use her imagination very much to indulge that fantasy.

ON THURSDAY they ate a hearty breakfast of pancakes and sausage with Aunt Marcy and Uncle Bob, then headed out for a tour of the island around ten o'clock. Kerry thought Alexi might enjoy the Victorian sights, since he'd grown up in such historical settings. England was steeped in tradition, and Belegovia probably had one of those old, drafty castles. A few of the houses in the historical district were made of stone and looked like castles.

"Where should we go first?" Kerry asked, driving her new car. Actually, the Saturn was three years old, but it still smelled new. Aunt Marcy's mother had never so much as nibbled a French fry inside this sedan.

"Have you gone on any of the tours or visited any

of these sights? I'd like for you to see something new.''

Oh, I like what I'm seeing right now, she wanted to say, but kept quiet as she negotiated the narrow streets of the residential section. ''Let's go to the Bishop's Palace.'' The huge mansion looked like a castle. ''I've never toured that house and it's supposed to be spectacular.''

Galveston wasn't that large, and within a few minutes they arrived at the huge red stone mansion. A new tour wasn't starting for ten minutes, but after Alexi offered a substantial contribution to the historical society that operated Bishop's Palace, a private tour was offered.

He looked perfectly comfortable in his ''Hank clothes,'' walking beside the middle-aged tour guide, making the woman blush and stammer with his compliments and charm. Kerry watched it and smiled, thinking she'd created a monster by encouraging him to use a Texas accent and swagger like a cowboy. While Alexi appeared every inch a prince, Alexi as Hank could charm the spines off a cactus.

After the tour they drove to the Strand, which had a unique Victorian waterfront charm. There was one really nice hotel with a restaurant, but Alexi opted for soft drinks, burgers and fries they could eat outside, to take advantage of the warm weather. Since the tourist season hadn't started yet, they had the small patio to themselves.

The Strand was only a block from the piers. The smell of saltwater mingled with city odors such as exhaust and food, but the mix wasn't unpleasant.

''This trip was just what I needed,'' he announced

as he polished off his burger—very neatly, Kerry noticed as she struggled with her second paper napkin. He'd lapsed into his "prince" mode, but she didn't remind him since they were alone.

"What were you expecting when you hopped into my car?" she asked. After spending all day with him yesterday, kissed him on the beach, then spent most of the night fantasizing about him, she felt comfortable asking the question. Although she never forgot he was a prince, he seemed much more of an ordinary person.

An ordinary person with excellent manners and lots of money, charm, good looks, etc.

"The wonderful thing about my impulsive action is that I didn't have any expectations. Oh, I wanted very much to get to know you. And, I must admit, I wanted to tweak Gwendolyn's nose just a bit to make up for her scheduling of the public appearances in San Antonio. But as for what we'd see and do, I had no idea." He spread his arms and smiled. "I was perfectly willing to leave myself in your hands."

Kerry smiled. "I could have been a crazy woman. Or someone who'd go to the tabloids with the story. Or any number of other unpleasant possibilities."

He shook his head. "I knew you weren't. I'm an excellent judge of character and I trust my instincts."

"So you're not...disappointed?"

"Not at all! Why would you think such a thing?"

"I don't know. I thought maybe you were expecting a woman who was a little more...demonstrative."

He appeared confused, so she forged ahead. "You know, affectionate."

"I find you very affectionate. You are especially

loving with your aunt and uncle, which is a charming quality.''

''No, I meant with you. Someone who would jump in the sack with you because you're a prince.''

He appeared genuinely surprised. ''Don't be silly. That wasn't what I expected at all.'' His expression softened, and he leaned closer. ''Although if you get the urge, by all means, I'll cooperate fully.''

Kerry laughed, knowing he was joking...sort of. ''I'm not a prude, but I don't... I mean, I'm not into one-night stands.''

''I never thought you were, Kerry Lynn Jacks,'' he said, covering her hand with his. ''You are delightfully honest and refreshing. I'm having a wonderful time, although I do rather miss the king-size beds in those nice hotels.''

''I'm sorry about that. If you'd rather, I can tell Aunt Marcy and Uncle Bob that you have an old rodeo injury and need a firmer mattress. They'd understand if you want to go to a hotel.''

''No, I wouldn't think of it. The couch bed is fine for tonight.''

''What else would you like to do while you're in Texas? I have one more free day and a fairly new car to chauffeur you around.''

''Tell me, if I weren't along, what would you want to do?'' he asked, squeezing her hand slightly.

''Me? Well, I'm not sure. Probably just hang out at the beach, then head back home.''

''But if you could do anything, what would you like?''

She had to think about it for a minute. Sipping her soft drink, she stared out at the brick street lined with

Victorian buildings. She'd always been drawn to old architecture, and one thing she'd wanted to do was stay in one of those beautiful, gingerbread houses built around or before the turn of the century.

"I suppose if this were my vacation and I had the time and money, I'd like to go to a bed-and-breakfast. One of those really nice ones with two or three stories and wide porches and lots of bric-a-brac, as my mother would say. With big trees and lacy curtains. There are a lot of them in East Texas."

"Then that's what we shall do," he announced.

"Oh, but—"

"No, I insist. My treat. We'll find a lovely bed-and-breakfast wherever you'd prefer. It will be my graduation present to you."

"That sounds...wonderful." But would they be staying in separate rooms, or would he want to find a place with a king-size bed that two could share?

LATER THAT NIGHT, after sightseeing, a dip in the Gulf—when Alexi learned that Kerry wore a modest one-piece instead of a bikini—and dinner at the family's favorite restaurant, Gaido's, they settled into the living room to watch the evening news. Kerry had stated earlier that she needed to check on the weather since they'd be driving tomorrow.

The idea to go to a bed-and-breakfast had been an impromptu one, but something Alexi felt was a great opportunity. While he enjoyed getting to know Kerry's family, he longed for more time alone with her, where he could be himself. Where they could talk without fear of anyone discovering his deception. Where he could fantasize about coming back to

Texas, or having her fly to Europe, so they could continue their relationship. He didn't know where this attraction was going, but he wanted to find out.

He hoped they had enough time before he had to choose a bride. Once he was engaged, he wouldn't dishonor his future wife or Kerry by having an affair.

"Would anyone like popcorn?" Bob asked.

Everyone groaned. "I couldn't eat another bite," Alexi stated, making sure he rubbed his stomach and put a little extra twang on the word *bite*.

Kerry grinned at him. "Me, either."

Alexi felt perfectly relaxed in his role as "Mack," although he still had to be careful when he spoke. Kerry usually found a way to remind him gently when he began to speak, which helped tremendously. Sometimes he forgot to be so "over the top" as Hank McCauley, but no one seemed to notice. As he'd heard somewhere, people saw what they expected to see; a man dressed in boots, jeans and a Western shirt was a cowboy.

Not that he was a real cowboy, but he did feel differently than he had yesterday morning, before running away with Kerry. Perhaps the relaxed pace of life in Texas, perhaps the intimate homey atmosphere of the Jackses' home. For whatever reason, he felt more attuned with his "softer side." He'd never really known what that silly phrase meant until now. The tender feelings he rarely had time to acknowledge seemed to swell with each hour spent around Kerry and her relatives.

"Look, there's a story about the prince who's visiting Texas!" Marcy exclaimed. "I'll bet Charlene is just about to wet…er, I mean she'd be jumping for joy to have some real, live royalty so near.''

Alexi tried to hide his amazement as he saw ''himself'' admire some animals at a zoo, then hold a baby and grin at the doctors at a hospital. Whoever was wearing his clothes was doing a damn fine job. Even the hair looked perfect.

''Prince Alexi of Belegovia made two appearances in San Antonio today,'' the reporter stated, ''charming the local residents. His spokesperson stated that the prince is suffering from laryngitis, but wouldn't think of missing his public appearances.'' A shot of Lady Gwendolyn at what appeared to be a press conference at the hospital, with ''the prince'' leaning close and whispering in her ear, gave a clue as to how she was pulling off this deception.

''Why, that prince looks just like you, Mack!'' Bob stated.

''He sure does!'' Marcy added.

''I've heard that everyone has a double,'' Kerry said.

''Yes, but—'' Marcy began.

''What an interesting story,'' Kerry commented tightly, jumping up from the sofa. ''Mack, would you like to take another walk along the beach?''

''Excellent idea,'' he said, forgetting to use his Texas accent. Three pairs of eyes stared at him.

''Was my imitation of the foreign prince that bad?'' Alexi asked with a grin.

Only someone who knew him relatively well would realize that smile was bogus. And so was his claim that he'd been imitating the prince. He'd forgotten to use his Texas accent, but to give him credit, he'd covered his blunder really well.

Uncle Bob laughed and Aunt Marcy smiled. "I don't know if you sound like him or not. He has laryngitis, remember?"

"Right," Alexi drawled. "Well, Kerry darlin', are you ready for our walk on the beach?"

"I sure am." She'd better get him out of the house before he drawled himself into another problem. She was also really interested to hear how and why his public-relations director had talked Hank into cooperating. Hank wasn't easy to talk into things he didn't want to do.

Kerry picked up her key from the side table, and Alexi took her hand as they walked out the front door.

"We'll leave the light on for you two kids," Uncle Bob called out.

As soon as they were out of earshot, Kerry turned to Alexi. "How did she talk Hank into impersonating you? That's just not like him."

"Lady Gwendolyn can be very persuasive. I must admit, I never thought she'd use your friend in my place. I assumed she'd simply cancel the events. As I said before, they were hardly major appearances. We were simply killing time until we heard whether we'd be going to Crawford or back to Belegovia."

"Do you think she offered him money?"

Alexi shrugged. "Perhaps. You seem inordinately interested in your former boyfriend's motives."

"I am not! I'm just surprised. I mean, here I am with you in Galveston, and the newscasters say you're in San Antonio. And darn it, Hank really looks like you!"

"Yes, he did. Compliments of Milos Anatole, my valet, and Lady Gwendolyn, no doubt. They can work wonders with anyone."

"Hey, Hank is pretty cultured. He's just not good with languages. No matter how much anyone worked with him, he couldn't fake a British accent."

"Few people could. Even professional actors use voice coaches, and they often work together for months." He shrugged. "I can probably fake a Texas accent because I did live in the States for five years, plus I'm multilingual due to my upbringing."

"What languages do you speak?"

"English, of course, French and Belegovian. I can speak Russian, but not fluently."

"Why so many?"

"Belegovia is an old country with our own language, but due to the Soviet occupation, the language is dying. It was forbidden for nearly forty years—two generations. Most of the people now speak Russian, with some who also speak English and French. My father is taking the country into a multilingual society similar to Switzerland, which has three official languages."

"Wow. I had no idea just deciding what to speak would be so difficult."

"If you were to come to Belegovia," he said casually, "you wouldn't have trouble talking to most people. The people have embraced English since they appreciate the fact my grandfather and his family were given refuge there. We are also developing a tourist industry geared to English speakers."

He grinned. "Besides, they'd love your Texas accent. They'd ask you all kinds of questions about your culture, mostly based on old television shows. The fact that you live in a rural area would intrigue them.''

''Great,'' she said with a chuckle. ''It's good to know that Europeans think we're all from the 1950's Westerns or the 1980's *Dallas* series.''

''J.R. and Sue Ellen Ewing on a cattle drive,'' Alexi quipped. ''It boggles the mind.''

Kerry laughed and leaned toward him on the uneven sidewalk. He put his arm around her, supposedly to steady her, but left it there as they strolled down Seawall Boulevard.

''Maybe you'd better call Gwendolyn and let her know where you are,'' she said. ''She seemed really annoyed with you, and besides, we need to know what the plan is. I mean, how long can Hank go on being you? What if the president calls? He can't meet the president, pretending to be you.''

''No, he can't,'' Alexi said with a sigh. ''I suppose I will have to call sooner or later, but I'm not looking forward to hearing her lecture.''

''You sound like a very naughty little boy.''

''Really? Would you like to spank me?'' he teased.

Kerry punched his arm. ''Stop it. I'm trying to be serious.''

They walked down the wooden steps to the beach. The sound of the surf was stronger tonight. A storm was probably churning up the Gulf of Mexico.

''I don't want to be serious,'' Alexi said as he took her hand. ''I want to be carefree, and that's exactly how you make me feel.''

Kerry felt herself frown, but she hoped the darkness hid her expression. Her father had been carefree. He hadn't wanted to be serious about his family, his responsibilities. And one day he'd simply loaded up his truck and driven off, leaving them wondering where he was, what he was doing and whether he'd ever come back.

Alexi had driven off from Lady Gwendolyn and his responsibilities. He hadn't even called to tell her that he was fine! The poor woman was probably pulling her hair out right now, afraid that Hank would mess up and everyone would know that he wasn't the prince.

Kerry had been nervous that her aunt and uncle would find out that Alexi wasn't really her former boyfriend, but the repercussions were hardly serious. They'd never call a cheesy tabloid to tell them about the runaway prince. But if Hank were discovered, everyone would look bad.

Kerry suspected that the king would be especially angry.

How could Alexi do this to them? "I know you want to be carefree, but you do have responsibilities. Don't you think you should at least call and tell the poor woman that you haven't been abducted by aliens or murdered by a Texas chainsaw waitress?"

"My dear Kerry," he said, pulling her into his arms, "I live for my responsibilities on a daily basis. I'm even going to marry one of the women my father has approved, just to provide my country with an heir and a spare. Please, don't lecture me on duty. Please, don't deny me this one short trip before I go back to my life."

She hadn't thought of his life that way. Perhaps he wasn't running away, just temporarily retreating. "Is it really so awful?" she whispered against his chest, unable to stay upset with him when she could feel his heat and hear his heart beat beneath her ear.

"It's wonderful, actually. I love the fact that we are doing something constructive for a nation that has been suppressed for so long. But that doesn't mean I can't be a simple, ordinary man every so often. That I can't explore my attraction to a very lovely Texas lady."

"We only have a day and a half," she said.

"Then we must make the most of every moment," he said softly before his lips took hers in a passionate kiss. She wound her arms around his neck, pressing as close as possible as she responded. Like the night before, she lost herself in the heat of his body, the thrust of his tongue against hers, the feel of his arousal. She pressed closer still, restless and yearning, wishing they were someplace else besides the nearly deserted public beach. Wishing they were going back to a secluded room, not to her aunt and uncle's home and separate beds.

There was no way she could smuggle Alexi into her room without them finding out. No way she could keep that bed from squeaking or herself from crying out if they made love tonight.

He placed hot kisses from her jaw to her neck, to the sensitive place just above her collarbone that made her moan. "We have to stop," she whispered into the night, more to herself than to him.

"I know." His words tickled her damp skin, making her shiver. "But I'm not good at impulse control where you're concerned."

"I thought I was pretty disciplined...until I met you."

"Ah, then let's be crazy together, Kerry Lynn Jacks."

Just then a group of teens on the sidewalk above whistled and yelled, some of their remarks making her blush.

Alexi stiffened, then put himself between her and the hecklers. When he was about to respond to them, she placed a finger over his lips.

"They're just letting off steam. Don't bother to yell back."

"They were insulting to you."

She smiled up at him. He appeared very fierce, very old-world protective, in the low light of the lamps far above. "Thank you for being noble, but let's just forget about it. After all, we needed an interruption."

He breathed deeply, then turned his attention back to her. "Very well. I suppose you're right. I was becoming a bit too...amorous."

Kerry laughed, then took his hand in hers. "If that's the Belegovian equivalent of 'hot and bothered,' then I was, too."

Chapter Four

The next day they awoke early, even before Uncle Bob and Aunt Marcy. Kerry made coffee while Alexi showered. When she went into the hall bathroom after he finished, the space still smelled of him. She remembered the subtle scent of his cologne mixed with soap and the smell of his new shirt from last night, when she'd clung to him on the beach.

Today they were leaving the safety of her family, the restrictions of "no hanky-panky," as Uncle Bob said. Today they were going out into the world as two adults who wanted each other.

Was she strong enough to act on her desires, or would she run back to Ranger Springs, to the safety of her family and new job, and never know what she'd missed in loving a prince?

Making love to a prince, she corrected herself. She wasn't in love, but she was definitely in lust. And she liked him. A lot.

By the time she'd showered and dried her hair, Aunt Marcy was buttering toast while Uncle Bob scrambled eggs. The scent of sausage filled the air in the cozy yellow kitchen.

"You didn't have to do that for us. We could have gone out for doughnuts or bagels."

"That's not a good start to the day," her aunt said. "Besides, we want to send you two off with full bellies."

"I'd better not eat too many more of your meals," Alexi drawled, "or I won't be able to button my jeans."

Everyone laughed, and Kerry settled into a chair to sip her second cup of coffee. "This has been a great visit," she said to her aunt and uncle. "Thank you so much for everything. This trip was exactly what I needed."

Alexi reached over and took her hand. "Me, too."

After breakfast, while he had a second cup of coffee, Kerry excused herself. Using the phone in her aunt and uncle's bedroom, she called her mother at work.

"Four Square Café. This is Charlene."

"Hi, Mom."

"Kerry! How are you? Are you having a good time?"

"I'm having a great time. No problems at all."

"How's the new car?"

"It's wonderful. It still smells new."

"And Marcy and Bob?"

"Just fine. They've been cooking for us."

"Us?"

"Well, I didn't exactly come alone."

Her mother was silent for a moment. Kerry envisioned her, a worried frown on her face. "Who's with you?"

"This is going to sound really weird, so just let me

tell you, okay? When I was getting ready to leave the truck stop, a man came in who looked just like Hank. As a matter of fact, I thought he was Hank, so I kind of hugged and kissed him."

"If it wasn't Hank, who was it? The only other person I've seen who looks like him is the…prince. Oh, Kerry, tell me you met Prince Alexi of Belegovia! He was on his way to San Antonio, wasn't he? And he stopped at the truck stop at that exact moment when you were there."

"Er, that's right, Mom."

"Oh, Kerry, you kissed a prince!"

And that's not the only time, she wanted to say. But you just didn't say things like that to your mother. "He's really nice, Mom."

"I saw him on television last night. He's so handsome and cultured."

"Well, Mom, that wasn't exactly the prince."

"What do you mean?"

"You have to absolutely promise me that you'll never say a thing to anyone about this, okay? I mean, this is really important. And you know how fast gossip spreads if you said anything."

"Kerry, you're scaring me! Of course I won't say anything if you ask me not to, but what could be—"

"I'm with the prince right now, Mom. In Galveston."

"What!"

"He wanted to get away, and I told him about driving to Galveston, and then he just wanted to come along, so I said yes."

"Kerry! You mean he's there right now? At Marcy and Bob's house?"

"That's right, but they think he's Hank. We're getting ready to leave, but we've been staying here at the house."

"Prince Alexi slept there? Where?"

"On the sofa bed. Where else? He insisted I take the guest bedroom, since that's where I always sleep."

"What a gentleman," her mother said dreamily.

"Yes, he's a great guy. Like I said, we're having a wonderful time."

"I just can't believe this."

"You know what's really funny, Mom? Before I knew he was coming with me, I got his autograph for you. I told him how much you'd cherish it."

"Oh, thank you, sweetie. That's so thoughtful."

"So, the deal is, Mom, that Hank is impersonating the prince while the prince is on this trip with me. And I'm not sure when or where we're going to exchange princes, but I'll be back for my graduation on Saturday. Just don't say anything to anyone, okay? If the tabloids or the royal family or even the U.S. government found out about this, there could be all kinds of problems."

"I understand, but this is so unbelievable. I mean, things like this just don't happen to people like us."

"I admit, it's kind of weird."

"Where are you going, Kerry?"

"We're heading out for East Texas. I told Alexi I'd always wanted to stay in a bed-and-breakfast, so he's giving me that for my graduation present."

"That's nice of... Wait a minute! He's paying for a room? For each of you, or one room?"

"Mom! He's a gentleman."

"Still, Kerry, he's a man. You know that talk we had a few years back?"

Kerry laughed. "Yes, Mom, I remember, and it was more like ten or eleven years ago. Don't worry, I'm a big girl now."

"That's why I'm worried!"

"I'll call you before Saturday to see where we're going to meet at the ceremony. And don't plan anything special for Saturday after the ceremony, since we're having the party Sunday afternoon."

"Be careful, Kerry."

"I will, Mom. Don't worry. Everyone thinks Alexi is Hank, and we're having fun just being regular people."

"I love you, sweetie."

"I love you, too, Mom. See you Saturday."

Half an hour later they were packed and ready to hit the road. A growing sense of anticipation filled Kerry as they stowed their bags in the trunk of the Saturn. She felt kind of tingly. Kind of restless.

"Have you decided which city in East Texas will have the kind of bed-and-breakfast you're looking for?" Alexi asked as they waved goodbye. Uncle Bob stood behind Aunt Marcy's wheelchair. Both of them smiled and waved.

"I thought we'd head northeast and see what we could find. Kind of 'I'll know it when I see it.'"

"Sounds good," he said, settling back against the seat. "Remember that I'll be glad to drive if you get tired."

"Let's get through Houston first, then we'll see."

One thing was certain; she had to quit thinking about tonight and keep her mind on the moment. Otherwise she'd pull over, drag her prince into the back seat and see if her new car could accommodate two amorous adults.

ALEXI ENJOYED the scenery of East Texas, but watching Kerry was an even better treat. She took delight in pointing out landmarks, such as a huge statue of Sam Houston, Texas's first governor, and a large outlet mall north of the city. Before they traveled too far from civilization, Alexi used his cell phone to call his valet, Milos Anatole, for an update. He smiled as Milos recounted Gwendolyn's deception. She'd made everyone, including the Texas governor, believe Hank was a prince.

After consulting her map, they exited the interstate and drove through piney woods. Instead of perfectly flat plains, some hills emerged, lending the landscape a more familiar quality. Much of Belegovia consisted of gently rolling hills covered in evergreen trees. The areas that had been cleared hundreds of years ago grew fertile fields of grain and vegetables, while mountains separated the western portion from Switzerland.

He'd grown up in England, but he loved the home of his ancestors. The concept of a benevolent monarchy filled him with both awe and pride. His father, one of the many history professors in various universities around England, was now the head of a country. Alexi believed he would have succeeded in business if he and his father hadn't been called home to fulfill their destinies.

So when Kerry had at first been impressed that he was a prince, he could understand. For most of his life, he'd been in awe of the British royal family, with whom he'd socialized on rare occasions. The deposed monarchy of Belegovia had some social status, but were hardly important political icons. Very few people imagined that they'd actually get the country back someday.

If he'd known he was going to be a "real prince" someday, he might have been more impressive to teenage girls when he was still in public school, he thought with a smile.

"Penny for your thoughts," Kerry said, breaking into his fond memories.

"I was just thinking about how strange life can be at times. When I was a teenager, I wasn't really a prince. Now that I'm a prince, I'm running around like a teenager."

"In Texas, a lot of high school and college kids go to Galveston for spring break. I suppose this trip is an abbreviated spring break for you."

"That's a good way to look at it, although I must admit my feelings for you are much more...ambitious than the ones I had when I was eighteen."

"Oh, really? I'm not sure how to take that remark."

"You should be flattered. I had a pretty good imagination when I was a teenager."

She looked at him from the corner of her eyes. "I have a feeling you still do."

WHEN KERRY STOPPED to fill up the gas tank at a small town on State Highway 21, she didn't notice at first that the proprietor was such a rodeo fan. Then she noticed, with growing alarm, the posters of upcoming events on the windows and the advertising of rodeo-related products. By the time she'd started pumping gas, Alexi was already on his way inside to buy some bottled water. She quickly switched on the device that kept the gas flowing and followed him inside. She barely made it in before she heard someone loudly announce, ''Hank McCauley, as I live and breathe!''

Great. Now they had to deal with a loyal fan.

Alexi appeared startled for a moment, but then turned and gave the man a big smile. ''How in the heck are you?''

''Fine, just fine! Why, I never thought I'd see you inside my little ol' gas station.''

''It's good to be here,'' he drawled.

At least he didn't say ''partner,'' Kerry thought.

''What brings you to my neck of the woods?'' the man asked.

''Just a little road trip,'' Alexi answered. He finally noticed Kerry standing near the counter and gave her a big, fake smile. ''Isn't that right, darlin'?''

''That's right.'' She walked up to him and put her arm around his waist. ''We'd better get on the road if we're going to make it on time.''

''Sure,'' he said, but she knew he was trying to remember if they had an actual deadline.

''Let me get you to sign your poster,'' the man said, whipping out a fine-tip felt marker. ''I'd sure be grateful. I always watched you on TNN. When that piebald bronc tossed you at nationals two years ago, my darn heart just about stopped.''

''That was a nasty one,'' Alexi commented.

Kerry wondered if she'd even told Alexi what

event Hank had competed in, but she couldn't remember. At least he was playing along so far, although she doubted he knew a piebald from a line-back dun. Or saddle bronc riding from bareback.

Alexi took the marker and asked the man, "What's your name?"

"Ben Fix," he answered, extending his hand. "And I sure am glad to meet you."

With a choppy flourish, he wrote a quick message and signed Hank's name to the man's poster.

"Thanks a lot, Mr. McCauley."

"Call me Hank," Alexi announced with a big grin.

"We'd better be going," Kerry advised as "Hank" placed the bottles of water on the countertop and reached for his wallet.

"No, this one is on me. My pleasure."

"Thank you very kindly," Alexi said with another grin. The two men shook hands, and then she and "Hank" headed for the car.

"That was scary," she said as she removed the nozzle from the gas tank and replaced the cap.

"That was rather fun."

"You wouldn't say that if he'd figured out you were an impostor."

"Give me some credit. I would have bluffed my way out of it."

He was probably right, she thought as they got back into the car. But she didn't like taking chances with their time together. Every minute seemed more precious as the sun moved from high overhead toward the west. Toward Ranger Springs, and home, and real life.

WHEN KERRY HAD started out that morning, she wasn't sure where they'd end up. But when she saw the slate blue and pale lemon bed-and-breakfast with all types of roses growing behind the white picket fence, she knew she'd found the right place. She only hoped they had a room available. Not only was she tired of driving, but she was anxious to explore her relationship with Alexi. To see if she'd had a change of heart since last night, when she'd decided they should pursue their mutual attraction.

"This place looks very English," he remarked as she pulled to a stop at the curb. "All those roses make me nostalgic for my mother's cottage in Sussex."

"Really? I love the way it looks, but it's very different from anything in Ranger Springs. There are some houses in Fredricksburg that are this Victorian style, but I don't think I've ever seen so many roses."

"They are lovely."

She unfastened her seat belt and turned to Alexi. "It's time to be 'Mack' again. You'll have to lose all those 'lovely' British comments and get real down-home and country."

"That's fine with me, darlin'," he drawled. "So, what's our story?"

"Story?"

"Sure. We may need to tell the proprietors why we're traveling around, who we are and so forth. Some innkeepers can be real chatty." He leaned closer. "They may assume we're married."

"Don't be ridicu— Married?"

Alexi shrugged. "We're young and obviously attracted to each other. It's a reasonable assumption."

"I'm not going to tell them we're married!"

"Then we'll need to be vague about our relationship."

"No problem!" She didn't know what their relationship was, so being vague wouldn't be a stretch for her.

"Don't you think asking for two rooms will be a dead giveaway?"

Alexi smiled seductively. "Do we want two rooms?"

Kerry sucked in her breath, her mind spinning. She'd thought she was ready for this decision, but she wasn't. Saying she wanted them in one room—in one bed—would be a commitment of sorts that was difficult to admit.

She'd never been promiscuous. She'd been raised to believe that sex meant something; it wasn't just an aerobic activity or a physical release. Besides, she'd been too busy in the past several years to pursue a serious relationship. Her two previous intimate relationships hadn't prepared her to deal with the feelings she'd developed for Alexi in such a short time.

"Kerry?"

"If I told you I wanted two rooms, I'd be lying. But if I said I was 100 percent certain about sharing a...room, that wouldn't be true, either."

"Then why don't we see what they have available. Perhaps adjoining rooms? Or a suite with two sleeping areas?"

"I suppose that would work."

"Come on," he said, opening his car door. "Let's see what's inside this charming cottage."

Cottage? The house looked more like a mansion to her, but then, she supposed since Alexi lived in a real palace, anything would appear small. She wondered what he'd think of her family home, a small three-bedroom brick-and-frame house that constantly needed repairs her mother could barely afford.

Of course, Alexi Ladislas would never see her family home. They had less than a day left together. Tomorrow afternoon she'd attend her graduation ceremony and he'd go back to being a prince.

Her good friend "Mack" would be gone forever. The thought saddened her, but also pushed her out of the car. If they had only hours left, they'd better make the best of them.

Inside the B and B, they were met by a middle-aged man who looked as though he'd spent most of his life in a uniform. His graying hair was cut military-short, and his posture made him look impressive in khakis and a teal polo shirt.

"Good afternoon," he said pleasantly. "Welcome to Piney Glen House."

"We were wondering if you have any rooms available for tonight," Kerry asked.

"I have four available. Saturday is our busiest day, but Friday is slower."

"Great," Alexi drawled as he draped an arm around her shoulders. "Which is your best room?"

"That would be the Randall Suite. Would you like to take a look?"

"Sure," Kerry said.

"Follow me," the military man said as they started up the stairs. "By the way, my name is James Brody. My wife, Ellen, works part-time at the hospital in Crockett, but she'll be home later this afternoon."

Kerry smiled in awe at the carved mahogany banister, elaborate floral wallpaper and old framed portraits on the stairwell. "Your house is beautiful."

"Thank you. When I retired from the navy, I promised my wife we'd live as far inland as she wanted. Running this B and B has been great for both of us." He walked around a beautifully furnished sitting area at the top of the stairs. "Here's the suite. I think you'll enjoy it."

Kerry looked at Alexi, who smiled as he waited for her to enter first. She barely contained a sigh of appreciation when she viewed the suite.

A queen-size four-poster bed dominated the room. A wedding ring quilt in rose, green and cream covered the mattress, while a lace bedskirt brushed the wide plank floor. The curtains matched the lace ruffle, while the valances coordinated with the wallpaper. Below, beadboard wainscoting wrapped the room in warm wood, all the way up to the carved fireplace and mantel. Marble surrounded the opening, which was filled with a beautiful spring bouquet. Everywhere she looked, she noticed interesting, decorative accessories.

"This room is named after Colonel Randall, a Spanish-American War veteran who settled around here with his large family. All these photos are of his children and grandchildren," Mr. Brody said as he pointed out a few of the portaits and framed medals.

A large chaise lounge angled out from the corner, where the gardens were visible beyond the second-floor balcony. This was the most peaceful room she'd ever seen, and the most romantic setting she could have imagined.

"It's beautiful," she breathed.

"You have other rooms?" Alexi asked.

"Yes, but this one is the largest, plus it has a big whirlpool tub in the bathroom, through those French doors."

"Do we need to look at another room, Kerry?"

She felt her eyes widen at his question. She knew what he was asking; did she want to share this room, this bed, even the whirlpool tub? Her gaze went to the chaise lounge. If things didn't work out, she could sleep there.

Looking at Alexi, so comfortable in his jeans and blue plaid shirt, so confident of his place in the world, she thought things were going to work out just fine.

"This room will be fine," she answered softly.

"We'll take this suite," Alexi said with a grin.

James Brody nodded, folding his hands behind his back. "Have you two been married long?"

Her gaze flew to Alexi, whose expression seemed to say "I told you so." She turned back to Mr. Brody. "Oh, we're not—"

"We're engaged," Alexi said, stopping her confession with a shocker of his own. "I sure hope that you don't mind we're not married yet," he drawled, giving the military man a big grin.

"No, no, that's fine. I just thought, looking at the two of you, that you were already a couple."

"That's a nice thing to say, Mr. Brody," Kerry said.

"Why don't you relax, darlin'? I'll run out to the car and get our bags."

Kerry didn't have to be asked twice. With a sigh she collapsed onto the chaise lounge. Well, she'd made a decision...of sorts. She was going to share this room with her prince. One night, she reminded herself. Then back to the real world. Back to the life she'd worked so hard to achieve. A well-paying job, her own apartment and the opportunity to have a professional career.

But that was all next week. Tonight was her treat. A graduation present from Alexi.

Did he realize *he* might be her real treat?

Before her daydreams got out of hand, he arrived back in the room with their bags. "This really is a lovely place, and it seems we have the whole house to ourselves. No one is booked until tomorrow."

"Great." She could make all the noise she wanted to when she... Stop it right there, she reminded herself. She hadn't decided 100 percent that she and Alexi would be sharing that four-poster bed.

"Mr. Brody said that there's a good restaurant within walking distance. I don't know about you, but I could use a nice stroll. I rather miss the beach."

"I do, too. I always like to leave before I get tired of it. That way, it's always so nice to return for a visit."

Alexi sat on the end of the chaise, placing his arm along her extended legs. "You have such a refreshing way of looking at life. Most of the people I know schedule holidays at the beach because they always go there, or their friends will be there, or some other reason. I doubt many of them think about leaving before they grow tired of the experience."

"When you don't have a lot of money, I think you look at things differently. In our family, my mother tried to make things fun. She convinced us that watching videos and dressing up as our favorite Disney characters was more fun than visiting the theme parks because of the crowds. And every Friday we had competitions to see which one of us could make the most delicious and innovative meal out of macaroni and cheese.''

''Your mother sounds like a wonderful woman.''

''She is, and she's really excited to get your autograph for her collection.''

''Perhaps I can meet her when we return tomorrow.''

''I—I'm not sure. I have to call before the ceremony to see where we're going to meet.''

''And I'll have to check with Gwendolyn to see how we're going to exchange identities.''

''Of course.'' Kerry drew her feet up to her chest. ''Let's just see how it goes tomorrow.'' Suddenly she felt her real life intruding into her trip. Into her fantasy.

Alexi seemed to sense her mood. ''Then no more talk of what will happen tomorrow. That's a long way off. We need to explore the rest of the house, then take a walk to the restaurant.''

''Sounds good.''

Alexi stood and reached down. Kerry took his hand and swung to her feet. He looked at her intently.

''You're not upset that I made up the story about us being engaged, are you?''

''No, of course not. It was just a little fib. I'm sure it made Mr. Brody feel better to think we're an engaged couple. If he knew we'd only known each other three days, he might be a little less enthusiastic about us staying here.''

"Three days," he echoed, shaking his head. "It seems longer."

Kerry nodded, suddenly remembering how she'd met Alexi, kissing him when she thought he was Hank, agreeing to let him run off with her to Galveston. What must he think of her? That she did this kind of thing regularly? That a one-night stand was no big deal to her?

These feelings he evoked in her...they were a very big deal.

Forcing a smile, she tugged him toward the door. "Let's look around. I've never been in a bed-and-breakfast before."

"I'm sure every one is different," he said as they walked into the hallway. He stopped her before they entered the room across from theirs. "Are you sure you're fine? You seem a bit...quiet."

"And here I was trying my best to be entertaining."

"Now, Kerry, that's not what I meant."

She shook her head. "I'm fine. Maybe I'm a little overwhelmed by all this," she said, arching her hand around them. "Maybe I'm remembering who you are and who I am and why we shouldn't be here, but we are."

"Maybe you should stop thinking about those things. The truth is, we're here. I, for one, am glad I'm here and not someplace else."

"I'm glad I'm here with you," she whispered.

"Then let's have a smashing good evening."

Chapter Five

They went to dinner at a small Italian restaurant. When they arrived, the waiter was lighting votive candles, and the low lighting emphasized the faux finished plaster walls decorated with silk grape vines and clusters. There were only six tables inside and two on the small front patio, but luckily they were too early for the dinner "crowd," if such a thing existed in this town. Still, it was Friday night, and lots of people went to dinner to celebrate the start of the weekend.

She was celebrating too, Kerry thought as Alexi ordered a bottle of Ruffino Chianti Classico Reserva and a tray of antipasto. The smell of warm, yeasty, crusty bread filled the air, making her stomach rumble in anticipation.

When they each had a glass of wine, she raised hers in a toast. "Here's to the start of my new life."

"I do believe I can drink to that," he said before taking a sip. "But I was going to make my own toast."

"Oh, to what?"

"To whoever shook up the soft drink that exploded

in the Land Rover, forcing me inside the truck stop, where I was kissed by an angel.''

Kerry laughed. "Hardly an angel. More like a confused, slightly dippy waitress slash college student.''

"Ah, no. College graduate. One who is starting her new life. May I say that I am ever so grateful to be included in this special occasion?"

Kerry felt her eyes tear up. Princes could be so charming. "Yes, you may." She reached across the table and held his hand. "I'm really, really glad you came with me.''

"I am, too," he said softly.

The waiter returned, taking their order and asking how they liked the wine and the untouched antipasto. They nodded, said everything was fine, but continued to look at each other. Alexi's eyes reflected the flickering votive candle and seemed to burn away the mirage of "good girl" she'd tried so hard to maintain.

She was in so much trouble. She didn't want to be a good girl any longer. Just gazing at him across the table made her knees so weak she wondered if she'd be able to walk back to the B and B. She felt all hot and squirmy, too, and she didn't know what to do about that, either. She wished they'd already eaten dinner. She wished they were already inside the Randall Suite, with its queen-size bed and cute little steps leading up to the high mattress.

She was having some decidedly wicked fantasies about that high, soft mattress. She just knew she'd feel like a fairy-tale princess once she was lying on top...naked. With Alexi looking at her as he was now, all hot and naughty.

Sucking in a deep breath, she leaned back as the

waiter delivered their salads. She had to behave herself a little longer. Just through dinner and more polite conversation.

The task proved more difficult than she'd imagined. Although she'd been starving as they sat down, now she could barely eat. She couldn't recall if the lasagna was good or not. She only knew that if she didn't get Alexi back to the suite pretty soon and claim her reward, she was going to do something really crazy. Like kiss him in public. Like drag him into the bushes of that overgrown house they'd passed and have her wicked way with him.

"Ready?" he asked minutes later after declining dessert and paying the check.

"Absolutely," she said, pushing her chair back and rising so fast, several other diners—when had they arrived?—looked at her funny.

"In a hurry?" he asked as they walked through the front door into the pleasant warmth of the early evening.

She forced herself to walk slowly beside him down the shaded street toward the B and B. "I suppose I'd be terribly unsophisticated if I told you I wanted to get you alone."

"That depends," he said huskily, "on why."

"Because I keep thinking about that big, high bed. And how really, really good you look in candlelight. And how sexy your manners are, and—hey!"

Alexi grabbed her hand and practically dragged her down the street. Kerry laughed as she struggled to keep up.

Suddenly, her prince was in a hurry. She hoped he'd slow down later. One of his sexiest characteristics was the slow, deliberate way he did things. She wondered if he was as deliberate and thorough in bed as he was at the table.

She figured she was about to find out.

ALEXI WASN'T SURE what had changed Kerry's mind. She'd only had one glass of wine, so she wasn't intoxicated. She'd seemed hungry, but shortly after they'd sat down, she'd started looking at him as though he were a large bowl of fettucine Alfredo. Not that he minded, of course. She just hadn't given any indication that she wanted him as much as he wanted her...until tonight.

He couldn't wait to get back to their suite. His desire for Kerry had grown steadily as they'd driven across the state and taken a holiday in Galveston. Her admission that she'd always wanted to stay in a bed-and-breakfast had added fuel to his slow burning fire. Now he was even more thankful they were the only people staying there tonight. He didn't think he could tolerate hours of chitchat with others in the parlor before making their excuses and dragging her upstairs at a decent hour.

But when he pushed opened the door and prepared to rush up the steps—because he didn't imagine Kerry would enjoy the spectacle of him carrying her to their room—they were met with a smiling James Brody and his wife.

"How was dinner?"

"Wonderful," he said quickly.

"Great," Kerry said at the same time, sounding breathless. He'd probably rushed her a bit much, but she'd seemed equally anxious to get to privacy.

"I'd like for you to meet my wife, Ellen."

They all shook hands and exchanged greetings, but Alexi couldn't remember being more eager to get away from civilities, even during long receiving lines at formal state events. Of course, he didn't have Kerry waiting for him at the end of the evening in Belegovia.

"We thought you might like a little after-dinner wine or dessert," Mrs. Brody offered. "We have a delicious muscat from one of our Texas vineyards." The hopeful, inviting look on the woman's face dashed cold water on his plans to whisk Kerry upstairs and into that big bed.

"That's very nice of you," Kerry said.

"Of course we'll join you," he finished.

"Excellent!" Mr. Brody boomed, reaching for a silver tray of crystal dessert wineglasses. "Come on into the parlor. I'll show you the restoration we've done on the fireplace."

Alexi forced a smile. He hoped the restoration wasn't too extensive. He had a four-poster bed and a whirlpool tub calling his name.

KERRY FORCED a yawn and smiled at the Brodys. "This has been great, but I'm getting sleepy, honey," she said to Alexi.

She had to restrain him from jumping off the couch. "Yes, we got up real early in Galveston this morning," he said convincingly. "And we've got a busy day tomorrow. Another day on the road."

"That's right. We'd better turn in."

"We've enjoyed visiting with you," Ellen Brody

said, "but I understand. What time would you like breakfast?"

Never, Kerry felt like saying. If morning never came, she'd have more time with Alexi. They could stay in that big bed forever.

"How about eight o'clock, darlin'? Will that give us time to make the drive back to Ranger Springs?" He leaned a little closer. "With you being so tired and all, I didn't want you to have to wake up too early."

Kerry knew from the sexy quality of his voice that he had plans other than sleeping late for the morning. "Eight o'clock is fine with me."

"We'll see you in the morning, then," Mr. Brody said. "Have a good night."

Oh, yes. She certainly hoped they did. She and Alexi rose from the sofa and, hand in hand, almost skipped up the wide staircase. As soon as they were inside their suite, the door securely shut, they burst into laughter.

"I hope they don't decide we need more towels," Kerry said, clinging to Alexi's arms.

"Or want to tuck us in," he added.

Still chuckling, they stared at each other in the low light of a Tiffany-style lamp. Laughter faded as the quiet intimacy of the setting surrounded them. "Now what?" she whispered.

"This," he said softly, his mouth descending.

With a sigh, Kerry rose up to meet him, her lips parted, meeting his kiss halfway. She wrapped her arms around his neck and held on tight, ready for him to take her to new heights, ready to experience something of which their previous kisses had only hinted.

She lost herself to the sensation of melding her body with his, pressing tighter, closer. His hands roamed her back, then lower, pressing her against his desire as he cupped her bottom. Kerry moaned into his mouth, then broke away, shaking and gasping for breath.

"Too much?" he asked, sounding almost as shaky as she felt.

"No...no," she whispered, burrowing against his chest, reaching up to nuzzle his neck. His skin tasted more delicious than anything she'd eaten at dinner, and the scent of his arousal, mixed with the expensive cologne he wore, drove her wild.

Alexi lifted her, his hands holding the back of her thighs as he encouraged her to wrap her legs around him. Kerry looped her arms around his neck and held on tight as he moved toward the bed, each step causing a delicious friction that spread through her body.

She fell back onto the high mattress, her legs still locked around his hips. "I don't want to let you go," she said.

"Then don't," he said, his eyes hooded and almost glowing with the hot, blue fire she'd seen in intense flames. His hands smoothed up her legs, over her hips, up to her ribs...and stopped. "Although at some point, I'd love to remove these clothes."

"Come here," she ordered softly, and he leaned forward. She went to work on the buttons of his shirt, pulling it from the waistband of his slacks. "I've wanted to do this since I saw you on the beach."

"And I've wanted to do this since you grabbed me and kissed me at the truck stop," he replied, sliding his hands to the hem of her cropped T-shirt, then higher, bringing the fabric with him, skimming over her breasts. She'd barely gotten his shirt unbuttoned before he peeled her T-shirt over her head, dislodging her hands.

"Much better," he said, gazing at her barely covered breasts. His appreciative look warmed her from chest to tummy.

"Mmm," she said, reaching up again to grasp his shoulders, raising herself off the bed to feel the warmth of his flesh beneath her fingers. He leaned down and kissed her deeply, pressing her into the thick quilted comforter. She felt consumed by him, inundated with his smell and touch, the wet suction of his kiss, the hard press of his arousal.

But she wanted more. When he moved to her neck, she whispered, "We are still wearing too many clothes."

"You're right," he murmured against her collarbone. "Come here."

Within seconds they scooted off the bed and managed to finish undressing. He retrieved his wallet and tossed it on the table beside the bed, giving her a glimpse of several square packets. *Thank heavens.* At least one of them was thinking. She hadn't given a moment's attention to the subject of birth control.

Kerry couldn't stop touching Alexi, reveling in his warm, lightly tanned skin, the soft hair covering his chest and the strength she sensed he controlled just as carefully as his public image.

Then he pulled her tight against him again, kissing her, driving her wild. Once more he backed her toward the bed, but this time he reached behind and swept away the quilt. Her bottom touched the cool sheets, and then he lifted her. With a sigh and a smile, she fell back on the mattress.

"Climb up those steps and come to me," she said, trying to be as bold as possible, hoping she didn't disappoint him. She knew she wasn't a seductress, like he was probably used to, but he made her feel so sexy, she didn't have to pretend.

He smiled seductively and prowled up the steps, kneeling on the mattress and crawling toward her like a sleek, dangerous predator. A beast who preyed on unsuspecting—but willing—truck stop waitresses.

"I feel like I've waited years for this moment," he whispered against her neck, one hand covering her breast. His fingers worked magic on her already-tight nipples, making her move restlessly. She wanted him close, tight against her, merging hot inside her.

She caressed him wherever she could reach, but he didn't let her touch the part of him that throbbed hot and heavy against her thigh. "Too much," he explained. "Later."

The idea that this wouldn't be the only time they made love filled her with warmth. Then he kissed her again and she stopped thinking, stopped planning. She gave herself over to the feel of his large, hot body. The sound of a packet tearing, then the feel of him at her most vulnerable place, filled her with yearning. She moved against him, urging him closer, pulling him deep. And when they joined, she gasped at the rightness of the emotions that surged through her.

She closed her eyes and gave herself over to the feelings building, building, until she cried out. Alexi buried his face in her neck and joined her in a wild climax that went on and on until everything—the Victorian suite, his royalty, her humble background and their differing future—was eclipsed by a passion more profound than she'd ever imagined.

ALEXI AWOKE to the sound of rain on the tall windows. The Tiffany lamp was still burning, casting muted shadows in rosy shades across the high walls and ceiling. Beside him, Kerry snuggled closer, her hand fisting on his chest. She was holding on, he thought with a smile, even in her sleep.

But she couldn't hold him much longer. He wasn't sure what time it was, but probably the night had already slipped into a new day: Saturday. The day she needed to return for her graduation. The day he needed to find Gwendolyn so he and Hank McCauley could exchange identities.

He didn't want to return. At least not yet. Not when he'd just discovered Kerry, when he'd barely explored the passion they shared.

Although he'd taken a while to grow into his title, he loved the difference he was making in Belegovia. He wanted to be a prince. But at this moment, he thought he might be able to give up something—some part of his heritage or his title—for more days with Kerry Lynn Jacks.

He placed her hand on the bunched-up quilt, then slipped out of bed. He carefully laid their clothes on the chaise so they'd be relatively unwrinkled in the morning. Besides, he didn't fancy tripping over his shoes or getting tangled in Kerry's T-shirt in the middle of the night or the half-light of dawn. Then he turned off the lamp and made his way carefully back to bed.

She snuggled against him, moaning a sexy little sigh before her hand settled once more on his chest. He smiled into the darkness, feeling her softness and warmth so close, so real. He'd never enjoyed sleeping with a woman, always feeling a bit awkward, even if the sex had been good and he liked her as a person. But he didn't feel that way with Kerry. He wanted to wake up beside her. He didn't dread the morning-after conversation that inevitably followed a night of passion.

She stirred, slipping one smooth leg between his. Her hand drifted lower and her breath tickled his pectorals as she stirred slightly. He wanted to wake her, to show her how much her nearness affected him, but she needed her rest. She had a big day tomorrow, with the graduation ceremony and probably some sort of celebration with her family.

An event he would not be attending.

He tried not to feel depressed over the idea of Kerry off with another group of people, sharing good memories, laughing over her accomplishment. He bloody well wanted to be there, his arm around her shoulders, making new memories they could both share...at least for a while. Until he was required to do his duty and choose a bride.

He settled Kerry deeper into his arms and rested his chin on her tousled hair. This holiday had been both wonderful and terrible. He'd had a wonderful time, but that had only accentuated how his life was about to change. This time next year, he would not have been able to run off with a truck stop waitress who kissed him because, in her spontaneity and in-herent charm, she thought he was someone else.

Lost in his thoughts, he didn't at first realize that her hand was again headed south. Then she touched him. Stroked him. He responded so quickly that he felt a bit light-headed.

"Now is it okay?" she asked in a sleepy, throaty voice.

"Now is fine," he managed to whisper before losing his mind to her inquisitive fingers.

When he could wait no longer, he prepared himself, then pulled her astride him. "Ride me, cowgirl," he muttered as she eased over him, down, moaning in that sexy, throaty way that drove him crazy. Slowly, he filled her, and then she began to move. Rocking, gaining momentum, clenching tightly until she cried out.

He let himself go, losing a little more of himself to Kerry Lynn Jacks. Getting a little closer to heaven... and to hell.

KERRY AWOKE to the muted sounds of voices from below and immediately smelled sausage and coffee. She stretched, unsure of the time, but knowing the place. The suite at the B and B. The queen-size four-poster bed with Prince Alexi Ladislas.

She'd just spent the night making incredible love to her very own prince.

Well, not her very own. In a matter of months, he'd belong to someone else. Someone else would sleep beside him at night and wake him up to make love again...and again.

The thought was too depressing, too distressing, to consider. He was still sleeping, so she slipped out of bed and padded barefoot across the cool, wide plank floor to the bathroom.

She noticed that all their clothing from last night was neatly placed on the chaise lounge. Alexi, she hoped. She certainly didn't want to believe that someone else had come in to tidy up while they'd been sleeping. She'd never stayed in a bed-and-breakfast before, but she was pretty sure that wasn't part of the service.

She gazed longingly at the tub. Big enough for two, it just screamed "intimate encounter," with its gleaming brass fixtures, fluffy white towels and multiple candles just waiting to be lit.

After taking care of nature and brushing her teeth, she exited the bathroom, only to come up against a warm, wide chest and a pair of sexy bedroom eyes.

"Good morning," he drawled, even though he didn't need to pretend he was a cowboy.

She smiled in return, hugging her arms around him. He was so solid, so real.

"It's only six-thirty," he muttered against her hair, "and we never did get to try out that big bathtub."

"No, we didn't."

He walked her backward through the door she'd just exited. "I'm just dying to wash your back."

"Hmm," she murmured, her hand straying over his chest, then lower, to discover how much he wanted her…again. "I'm just dying to wash your front."

He laughed as he reached for the faucets.

She'd never taken a bath with a guy before, so she wasn't sure of the protocol. She and Alexi were both already naked, so the awkward removal of clothes wasn't an issue. But as he looked up at her from his position near the faucets, adjusting the water, she thought playful might be just the right approach. She smiled, gave him an ''I sure do like what I see'' once-over, and then trailed her fingers in the big tub. Just as he reached for her, she cupped a handful of water and threw it at him. His eyes went wide, he shook like a ferocious beast and then he reached for her.

Kerry giggled as she pretended to struggle, but he didn't seem concerned. He growled as he picked her up in his arms. ''You're asking for trouble now,'' he said as he held her over the tub.

''Don't you dare drop me!''

He moved as if he would let her go, making her squeal and throw her arms around him. His morning beard was rough against her cheek, but she didn't mind. Her fingers caressed the back of his neck, then she couldn't resist brushing away the clinging drops of water from his hair and around his face. Her mood turned from playful to passionate as his eyes turned from cunning to hooded.

''There's just one thing we need,'' he said, striding toward the bedroom with her still in his arms.

''What?''

''Our little friend,'' he said, nodding toward the nightstand. Only one lonely packet remained.

She picked it up. ''Good thing we have only a short time before we're due downstairs for breakfast,'' she joked.

''Good for whom?'' he asked with a sexy smile as his hands curled over her thigh. He walked back into the bathroom as though she weighed next to nothing.

Not for me, she wanted to say. She wanted more

time. More hours until they had to leave this suite, more hours until he had to leave Texas.

He lowered her into the tub, then reached down to turn off the water and turn on the jets. The surface erupted into bubbles and waves as she sank into the water. "This feels wonderful."

He stepped into the tub, seemingly unconcerned that he was fully aroused. Of course, he had been for some time now, she remembered, thinking back to when she'd caressed him minutes ago.

"If you think that's wonderful," he said, slipping behind her and resting against the slanted end of the tub, "wait until you feel this."

He settled her back against his chest, his arousal pressed between her legs. With his hands he caressed her breasts as she leaned back against his shoulder, moaning into his neck. Oh, he was talented. In so many ways. In so many…areas, she thought as she moved restlessly against him. The water churned around them as he brought her closer, closer to where she wanted to go. Where she'd gone so many times last night.

But with him inside her, she wanted to stay, tossing her head from side to side as his fingers parted her, rubbed her, entered her.

"Let it go," he whispered, his breath hot in her ear.

"Come with me," she urged.

"Next time." He stroked harder, faster, so deliberately she could no longer think. She came apart in his arms, in the big bathtub she'd longed to share with him.

And then, while she was still limp and sated, Alexi

donned their last protection, flipped her around so she straddled him and showed her exactly what wonderful sensations whirlpool jets and a thoroughly aroused prince could produce.

THEY WERE nearly late getting down to breakfast, but the Brodys didn't seem to mind. They also apparently didn't know—or care—that their guests had just participated in the greatest sex ever experienced in this or any other house in Texas. Or maybe North America.

They chatted about the spring weather and the upcoming summer and the joys of growing roses, and Alexi listened and seemed to be paying attention, until she discovered his hand creeping up her thigh beneath the table. Breakfast was delicious, but she didn't eat all of her French toast or sausage-potato casserole. A certain prince had her tied up in emotional knots that she didn't know how to unravel.

Before long they went back upstairs to pack. She didn't want to leave this room or the man who'd made her feel like a princess, if only for one night. But reality awaited, halfway across the state, and they needed to get on the road.

"Ready?" he asked as she zipped up her bag.

"No," she answered honestly, with a sad smile she couldn't hide, "but that doesn't really matter, does it?"

"You could skip the graduation ceremony. I could put off meeting up with Gwendolyn for one more day."

She shook her head. "No, as tempting as that sounds, I need to get back to my life. This has been wonderful, but it's not real. Having one more day would only make it more difficult.''

''Kerry, I—''

''It's okay. We both knew this, right? I mean, all along we said we had to get back. So let's just enjoy what's left of the day and have a pleasant trip back to Ranger Springs.''

''*Pleasant* doesn't begin to describe how I feel about being with you.''

''Me, too,'' she whispered, fighting her emotions. ''Now, let's hit the road before I really do abduct you. I have a feeling that Lady Gwendolyn would come looking for us eventually, and I'd hate to make a scene.''

He pulled her into his arms and held her tight. ''Last night was magical.''

''Yes, it was, but now it's morning,'' she whispered against his chest. ''It's time to go back to being a prince.''

''Are you my Cinderella?''

''Hey,'' she said, pulling away and forcing a smile. ''If the glass shoe fits...''

Chapter Six

Despite fairly heavy traffic, they made good time on Highway 21, the most direct route from their location in East Texas to San Marcos. She called her mother when they stopped for drinks, telling her that they should meet at the ceremony. She planned to drop Alexi off at the Four Square Café, where Lady Gwendolyn could recover the royal runaway. They wouldn't have much time, so there would be no lengthy goodbyes. Just a polite public parting of two people who had shared a few days of vacation.

It's been great. Have a good life. If you're ever in the area, stop by and say hello. She would never see him again, and that was something she'd learn to accept. Eventually.

Alexi was quiet. Too quiet. She felt him watching her sometimes when she was busy driving. Like when they went through Bryan and College Station, where Texas A & M was located. And lots of other small towns, with only one traffic light and the inevitable eighteen-wheelers and overburdened pickup trucks. She felt his gaze on her, but she didn't ask him why.

Maybe she didn't want to know. Because no matter

what the answer, he was leaving today. Or tomorrow at the latest. No matter what.

All she had to do was protect her heart for a few more hours. Then she'd have a lifetime to recover from these four days with her prince.

By the time they got to the outskirts of town, Kerry was running late. She didn't have time to change clothes, but luckily she'd be wearing her cap and gown, and everyone wore cool clothes beneath the graduation garb. Her stomach felt a little queasy and her hands began to sweat on the wheel.

''Nervous?'' Alexi asked as she jerked the steering wheel too hard to avoid a paper bag blown by the wind.

''Yes, because I'm running late and I don't know how long it will take Lady Gwendolyn to come for you and I don't think I'm good at saying goodbye.''

He placed his hand on her shoulder. ''Relax, sweetheart. I know today has been difficult, but we're almost there.''

She held back a sob as she turned onto the square. ''I know.''

In the center park of the square, right in front of the café, two men, one wearing an army-style camouflage vest and the other in an old-fashioned polyester suit, with large cameras stood talking to one of the waitresses. She was fairly new to town, wore too much blue eyeshadow and rarely volunteered to help Kerry's mother fold napkins. Kerry didn't like her much, but she seemed to be telling the men something very interesting.

''Those men aren't from around here.''

Alexi looked at them, squinting against the early-afternoon sunlight, and then swore. Before she could ask him what was going on, he ducked down in the seat. "Keep driving," he said. "Those two are paparazzi. I can think of only one reason they'd be in your town."

Paparazzi, here in Ranger Springs? "How did they find out you were going to be here?"

"Who knows? They're as devious as hell. Just get away from here before they see me. They might even know who you are, although they probably don't know this car."

"Good grief," she muttered. "I can't just drive off! What will I do with you during my graduation ceremony?"

"If those vultures find out we've been off together, the story will be in all the papers tomorrow. Plus, they won't leave you alone. They'll be dogging your footsteps, howling for a story. Believe me, they can be most persistent."

"Alexi, I can't just drive away!"

"Then hide me someplace. I'm not willing to explain my presence in this town to those two, nor do I believe they'll think I'm your former boyfriend, Hank."

Kerry's mind raced on an adrenaline high. Hide him? But where, without bringing someone else into their confidence? She knew several people well enough to ask, but that wouldn't be fair to them. If these paparazzi were as persistent as Alexi claimed, then she'd be putting someone else in the crosshairs of their long-range camera lens.

She drove by the side of the square where the café

was located, noticing a car parked out back, right beneath the stairs.

The stairs. To the vacant apartment upstairs. It hadn't been used since the former manager moved out two years ago. It was probably dusty and barely furnished, but no one would look for a prince there.

"I know the perfect place," she said, turning down the alley between the café and the furniture store. From back here, the paparazzi couldn't see them. At this time of the day, there weren't many people around the square. The café closed at two o'clock and wouldn't open again until Monday morning.

"There's an apartment upstairs," Kerry explained, pulling in next to the other car, right beside the brick wall. "If we can just get you upstairs, you'll be safe. You can call Lady Gwendolyn and tell her where you are."

"You're going to leave me here?"

"I don't have a choice. Look, I have to hurry. I can't be late. And trust me, you'll be safe. No one ever goes upstairs."

"Very well. Should we make a run for it?"

"I think we should just walk upstairs as if we know what we're doing. Hopefully, the key to the restaurant will open the door at the top of the stairs, too."

"You have a key?"

She shrugged. "Sometimes I help my mother out in the morning."

Alexi nodded. "All right, then. Let's go."

"Just swagger a little. Everyone will think you're Hank."

"Drawl, grin, swagger," he complained. "What else must I do to become this real cowboy?"

"Well, you could ride a bucking bronc down Main Street, but I don't think we have time for that. Grab your bag and come on."

ALEXI ROAMED the deserted apartment, trailing his finger along the dust-coated surface of the end table, looking out the hazy window to the town square below. An ornate gazebo dominated the parklike setting, which also contained shrubs and flowers of various kinds along concrete walkways.

The paparazzi were still there, although they'd retreated to a van parked alongside the curb, directly across from the café. Cigarette smoke curled from the open windows as they sat inside, no doubt arguing about their next move. They didn't seem to be in any hurry to leave.

He didn't know how long Kerry would be gone, but he assumed at least several hours. He should call Gwendolyn and tell her where he was, but he resisted going back to "work," as he considered these rather meaningless events she sometimes scheduled for him. He hadn't seen a television since watching the news at the Jackses, so he didn't know if Hank McCauley had made any other appearances as prince, but they had listened to the radio in Kerry's car. If something scandalous had occurred, surely it would have been reported.

He did have one inside source, however. Someone he'd checked with twice before in case of an emergency. He should call again, just to see what the plans were.

Slipping his cell phone out of his bag, he turned on the power. Within a moment the display informed him that he had twenty-seven messages. Alexi sighed, somewhat chastised that he'd gone off on this jaunt, but not regretting a minute. He'd needed this respite from public duties and his personal mission to bring tourism and industry into his largely agricultural country.

He needed to know Kerry, to see the world through her eyes and experience the joy of living from her perspective. She was everything fresh and wonderful, wise and yet innocent in many ways. He wanted to know her much better, but he knew there could be no future for them. As much as he'd thought about coming back to Texas for a holiday, or having her fly over to Belegovia for a visit, he knew that would never work.

He'd be exposing her to his world, with all its problems.

Such as the paparazzi that hovered around celebrities like vultures over roadkill. They would be brutal to her, calling her names, questioning her family, making her life hell until she retreated in disgust. He didn't want their relationship to end that way. He'd far rather make a clean break, and in telling her goodbye, attempt to express how much she'd meant to him. How he would never forget her.

He couldn't simply leave without seeing her again. He knew she half expected him to be gone when she returned. But he'd also seen the hope in her eyes before she'd shut the door and run down the steps. She wanted the chance to say goodbye without the press or family or other engagements threatening them. She wanted a kiss that would make them both remember this time fondly, an embrace that would imprint the other permanently on the soul. And he would give that to her, for all the joy and pleasure she'd given him.

Skimming through his speed-dial keys, he located the number of the phone Milos had been given when they arrived in the States. His valet picked up on the third ring.

"Alexi here. Can you give me an update on the situation?"

"Yes, Your Highness. Lady Gwendolyn decided she should travel to Ranger Springs to look for you, while I stayed behind in Austin pretending to be you. To date, I have talked to your father, the king, on two occasions and to various hotel persons who wished to clean the room and bring me chicken soup for my laryngitis."

Alexi chuckled. "Are you still in Austin?"

"No, Your Highness. Mr. Boedecker and I are in a rather nondescript motel in San Marcos, ready to move at a moment's notice. Lady Gwendolyn and Mr. McCauley have gone to the university to find you and Ms. Jacks."

"I see. Well, I'm in Ranger Springs. I'll call Lady Gwendolyn later and tell her where to find me."

"Very well, Your Highness." Milos paused, then continued. "I do hope to see you soon. Your father has become rather insistent. Something about sending the royal physician to Texas if you aren't recovered soon."

Alexi silently cursed. His father was meddling more and more in his life.

"Thank you for taking care of his calls, Milos. I'll

be in touch soon, as soon as I know whether Ms. Jacks is returning here.''

"Mrs. Jacks may be involved in that decision."

"Kerry's mother?"

"Yes. She mentioned something about the ceremony when she talked to Mr. McCauley."

"Bloody hell. How many people know about this switch?"

"Only myself, Lady Gwendolyn, Mr. Boedecker and Mrs. Jacks, I believe, Your Highness. I trust all of them will be discreet."

Alexi had known Kerry had called her mother, but he hadn't realized everyone involved was talking to each other. This complicated matters. The situation also made him feel as though they were ganging up on him.

"What other plans do you have? If they were to find me, what is Lady Gwendolyn scheduling?"

"Departure to Belegovia, I believe, Your Highness. She did not mention any other plans."

"Very good. Let me consider this for a while."

"If I may ask, sir, are you well?"

"I'm perfectly fine. Never better. When it is time to exchange identities with Mr. McCauley, be certain that can be accomplished quickly."

"Very well, Your Highness. I will await your further instructions."

"As they say here in Texas, Milos, just lay low."

"Yes, Your Highness. May I suggest you do the same?"

Alexi chuckled and ended the call. Oh, he'd like to lay low. With Kerry. Back in that four-poster bed where they'd spent the night loving each other. But they couldn't go back...in more ways than one. Each of them had to go forward, separately.

But they could have a little more time together. When she returned. And perhaps, just for a few moments, they could recapture some of the magic of last night.

He stood in the center of the apartment and looked around. There wasn't much to work with, but he could make their setting a bit more pleasant. He had nothing better to do, and although he hadn't cleaned in years, he used to do a decent job of it in Boston. All he needed were the right supplies. He was fairly certain the restaurant, if not this apartment, would have everything he needed.

WHEN KERRY WALKED into the apartment, the sun was setting. And although she couldn't see clearly, she knew things had changed dramatically. She distinctly remembered the sparse furnishings covered in a layer of dust. The air had even smelled stale, but now curtains fluttered in the mild breeze and brought in the fragrance of blooms from the square outside. Mixed in was the smell of lemon furniture polish.

"Did you invite Martha Stewart over while I was gone?" she asked Alexi, who was relaxing on the couch with the Saturday edition of the *Springs Gazette.*

He looked up and smiled. "Yes, she and her crew of hundreds descended upon this humble abode and transformed it into a stylish and tasteful example of rural décor."

Kerry laughed, dropping her purse and sitting on

the other end of the couch. "Will I expect to see this in a future edition of her magazine?"

"Yes, I believe it will be titled, 'Prince's Private Love Nest.'"

Kerry reached out her hand, then found herself enfolded in Alexi's warm, welcoming embrace. "Is that what it is?"

"That would be my fondest wish."

She sank down on the couch, stretching out along his body. "I missed you."

"I wish I could have been there."

"I'm sure you would have been bored silly."

"I doubt that," he said generously. "How did the ceremony go? I imagine your family was very proud."

"Very," she answered, tracing the vee of skin his unbuttoned shirt revealed. "Mom cried and my sisters seemed genuinely happy. Even my niece, Jennifer, came to see me, and she made me the cutest graduation card."

"I almost expected you to walk through the door in your cap and gown."

"And nothing else?" Kerry teased.

"Now, there's an idea," he said, tracing her bottom lip.

"I gave my stuff to my mother to take care of." She propped her hands on his chest and frowned. "Did you get in touch with Lady Gwendolyn?"

"Not exactly. I looked outside and saw that the paparazzi were still on your town square, so I decided against calling her yet. I did, however, let Milos Anatole, my valet, know where I was."

She brushed his hair back from his forehead. "So

you're staying with me tonight?'' she said, trying her best to keep the hopeful, wistful yearning out of her voice.

"I thought I would."

She felt her heart expand and glow with warmth and her eyes fill with unshed tears. "That's the best graduation present yet."

He touched the corner of her eye, his expression serious. "I really must leave tomorrow. I need to be in Geneva on Monday evening for an economic summit."

"I know, and I promise I'll let you go. No messy scenes, no clinging vines."

"Kerry, I—I don't know what to say."

"You don't have to say anything, Alexi. You gave me an absolutely wonderful four days. I'll treasure these memories always. But I know you have to go back to your country, marry your princess and have your heir and a spare. I know that." She sniffed a little, then forced a smile. "I don't have to love it, but I accept it."

He nodded, but he didn't try to smile. She felt very touched that he was genuinely sorry to leave her. She'd never imagined that a prince, a worldly man like Alexi, would grow attached to a small-town girl like her, but he had. She knew it as surely as she knew her name.

"I raided the storeroom of the café," he said, as if to lighten the subject, "after I fixed myself a sandwich. Let me light a few candles against the darkness. Would you like something to drink? I brought up some soft drinks. I'm afraid I couldn't find any wine."

"That's because this is a dry area."

"Dry?"

"We don't sell liquor."

"Ah. We don't actually need any wine, do we?"

"No," she whispered, touching her finger to his lips. "All I want is you."

"You have me," he said, nipping her finger lightly. "For as long as possible."

THE SETTING WASN'T nearly as romantic as the suite at the bed-and-breakfast, but Alexi knew Kerry didn't mind. He would love to see her lying naked on his huge bed at the palace. He would love to see her anywhere in the future, although he knew that wasn't an option. They had only tonight.

Once again he carried her toward the bed, kissing her, losing himself in her soft lips and firm, curvy body. The breeze ruffled her soft curls and flickered candlelight over her lightly tanned skin. He wanted to kiss every inch of her...and vowed he would before the night was up.

When he'd driven her wild with desire, she rolled him over and said, "It's my turn."

She explored him, making him crazy while he watched her small, competent hands and soft pink lips make love to him as he had to her. By the time he reached into the nightstand drawer for the protection he'd thankfully found earlier, they were both nearly incoherent with passion. He heard her cry out when he entered her, plunging deep, feeling her warmth and wetness all the way to his soul.

He would never forget her, he vowed as he moved inside her, framing her face with his hands, watching her eyes widen and her mouth gasp as she began to climax. He kissed her then, silencing the scream he knew was building, losing himself in the wonder of loving Kerry.

Minutes later, when his breathing returned to normal, when he could once more move, he took her with him as he rolled to his side. She sighed and smiled, snuggling against his chest as she'd done last night.

He wanted to say the words he'd never told another woman, but wasn't certain whether his emotions or his hormones were speaking. Besides, he couldn't make a commitment to her. While he wasn't promised to another woman, he was married, in a sense, to his country. He might resent his father's edict to choose a bride, but he would comply. He needed to marry and produce an heir to the throne. He needed to establish traditions that would be passed on to future generations, ensuring the continuation of the royal family.

Eventually, when Kerry relaxed against him in sleep, he pulled away. He needed to make a quick trip to the small bathroom and hoped the rusty pipes worked just a while longer. Then he would return to Kerry, curl up beside her and watch her sleep.

But when he got up from the bed, he knew something wasn't right. Memories of their lovemaking came roaring back, and suddenly he realized why their joining had felt so good. Why he'd felt even closer to Kerry than the first time they'd made love.

The condom he'd found in the nightstand drawer had obviously been there for years, because it had broken. Shredded, as a matter of fact. He had actually felt her wetness and her warmth far more intimately than ever before.

"Bloody hell," he whispered. He only hoped he hadn't also destroyed Kerry's future as an independent, carefree career woman.

KERRY WASN'T SURE how she made it through Sunday. She'd called Hank early Sunday morning, discovering Lady Gwendolyn in his bedroom. Probably in his bed. They'd met on Travis Whitaker's property, far away from prying eyes. Hank was angry, thinking Alexi had taken advantage of her, but Lady Gwendolyn managed to calm him down. Alexi tried his best to be charming, but Hank wasn't buying his apologies to Lady Gwendolyn for causing this problem.

Kerry had thrown in her two cents' worth, too, giving Hank a piece of her mind when she remembered how bad this could look for everyone involved, especially her mother and sisters, if the tabloid reporters twisted the truth. Suddenly the simple escape both she and Alexi had needed seemed vastly more complicated, with far-reaching implications for people they hadn't considered before.

After a drive to San Marcos, where they'd met up with Alexi's driver and valet, she and Hank had spent time at the Dairy Queen while Alexi changed back into a prince. She and Hank had talked, which cooled things down a bit. She knew he was crazy about the English lady, and he suspected she was half in love with Alexi, but they both knew they couldn't do anything about it. After the press conference Lady Gwendolyn had arranged on the town square in Ranger

Springs, she and Alexi would be off for the royal jet, back to their real lives in Belegovia.

They arrived in downtown Rangers Springs in the Land Rover, all four of them silent and tense. The town was decked out in Fourth of July splendor, even though it wasn't Memorial Day yet. Kerry looked out at the faces of her friends and neighbors and wanted to crawl into one of Alexi's suitcases and stay there forever.

The press conference was horrible, with all the lies and deception. Every time she looked at Alexi, all polished and proper, she wanted to cry. *This is who he really is,* she tried to tell herself as he explained how he and Hank had been mistaken for each other. Cameras flashed and video rolled as everyone, from news media to ranchers and schoolkids, documented the foreign prince in their midst.

She barely got through the event, standing stiff beside Hank, before the short reception at the café began. She didn't make it through that event, not without escaping to the ladies' room for a big cry. She prayed for numbness, but instead felt raw and exposed, like a jagged wound.

How was she going to watch Alexi walk away—or drive away, in this case—without breaking down in front of everyone? She couldn't do it. She couldn't even hide her emotions when Lady Gwendolyn came into the bathroom.

"Does he know?" Gwendolyn asked.

Kerry shook her head. "We had a good time but it's over." They were from different worlds...worlds that just didn't collide except for chance encounters along interstate highways.

"Perhaps it's not that simple."

"I'm a former truck stop waitress from Ranger Springs, Texas. He's the crown prince of an old, respected European country. What could be more simple than that?"

Gwendolyn was silent for a few moments, then said, "I'm rather fond of your Hank McCauley."

Kerry admitted she suspected as much, just as she assured Gwendolyn that she and Hank were more like cousins. They talked about Hank briefly, then Gwendolyn said, "We must go back outside and face everyone."

Kerry had never imagined that she had much in common with a classy English lady like Gwendolyn, but she did. Gwendolyn was in love with Hank. Kerry was in love with Alexi. And neither relationship had any hope of continuing.

Kerry and Gwendolyn embraced, sisters of a sort, in love with the wrong men, and then they repaired their makeup and went back out to the "party" so no one would suspect. No one would ever know Hank had been a prince, and a prince had been a cowboy, if only for a few days.

Later, Gwendolyn had pulled Kerry aside. "Alexi will be upstairs in a moment. You'll have just five minutes. I'm sorry, but we need to leave."

"I understand," she said, but she didn't. Not really.

She had only five minutes to say goodbye. Five minutes to last a lifetime. She'd known for four days this moment was coming, but she wasn't ready. She'd never be ready, because she never wanted to let him go. She wanted him to stay with her, to be a part of her new life. She wanted to kidnap him and take him away from all his responsibilities, especially the need to marry a suitable bride.

Every time she thought of him with another woman, she felt overwhelmed with jealousy. She had no right, she told herself. So she tried not to think of him courting someone else. Standing beside the faceless woman and announcing their engagement.

She pushed it out of her mind as she climbed the stairs to see him one last time.

"Alexi?" she called out as she neared the top of the interior stairs. The apartment looked exactly the same as it had this morning when they'd left here to meet Gwendolyn and Hank, but it felt different. Lonely, as though its life had ended when they'd closed the windows and locked up, their hearts heavy.

"Over here," he said, moving away from the window that overlooked the town square. "I was just watching the media circus. Most of them are leaving now. The story is over."

Yes, it's over, she wanted to say, but her throat was frozen. He looked so wonderful, so…princely. No one who'd known him from their road trip would believe this was the same man. Only she knew…and she'd never forget.

"Kerry? Are you okay?"

"I'll be fine." She wasn't now, but she'd get over him. Somehow. "I'm going to make myself very busy. I'm moving into my new apartment, then starting my job a week from tomorrow."

"You'll be fine," he said, but he didn't sound convinced.

"How about you? Other than the economic summit, what will you do?"

He sighed, took a step toward her, and stopped. Leaning against the sofa, he said, "My father has chosen someone for me to meet."

"Someone…like a woman?"

"Yes," he said, sighing again. "Contessa Fabiana Luisa di Giovanni was at the governor's dinner in Austin that Hank attended. He said she was very lovely."

"Sorry," Kerry said, holding up a hand, "I don't want to hear about another woman."

"I'm sorry. I didn't mean it like that. I just…I'm not sure about giving in to my father's edict. Why rush into anything?"

"Don't ask me that, Alexi! You need to marry someday. You need an heir. I accept it, but I don't have to like it. I don't have to think about you with another woman."

"It won't be that way. Not like it was between us."

She put her hands over her ears. "Don't!"

He pulled her into his arms. "Kerry, I'm sorry. I just wanted to have a good time. I didn't expect—"

"For me to start falling in love with you?" She couldn't believe she'd just said that, but her emotions were too raw to guard her heart right now. And since she'd never see him again, she could say what she wanted. In a few minutes, he'd be gone.

"I didn't expect for either of us to…care for each other as much as we do."

"It's not your fault you're very lovable," she said with a sad chuckle. "I mean, a real live Prince Charming who cleans apartments? You're perfect."

"Hardly. I was very inconsiderate. First to Gwendolyn, for running away from the engagements she'd planned, then to you, because despite the honesty we both professed, I think we were wrong.''

"Alexi, please. There isn't a future for us, so this discussion is useless. I can accept that you have to leave. Maybe not today, or even next week, but I'll be fine. I survived when my father packed up and left, so I have a bit of experience.''

"I'm not like your father, although God knows I've disappointed enough people in my life.''

"No, you're not like him,'' she whispered. But there was a part of him that was similar to her dad. Both meant well. Both vowed they'd never "do that again.'' Whether Alexi could keep his promise had yet to be seen, but she hoped he'd learned his lesson. She seriously doubted that he had completely changed his attitude.

He'd still hate to make public appearances booked for him; he might still run away. And he might break another heart without meaning to, just because, like she'd said, he was charming and wonderful. What woman could resist falling in love with him?

He leaned back and tipped her chin up. "Promise me you'll call if you…if there are any repercussions from last night.''

"What?''

"The condom,'' he reminded her.

"Oh.'' The broken condom. She'd nearly forgotten in the chaotic day that had followed. "I'm sure I'll be fine.''

He threaded his fingers through her hair, his blue eyes suspiciously bright. "You take care of yourself, Kerry Lynn Jacks,'' he said softly. "I'll miss you.''

Was this how her mother felt when her father

walked out? Kerry remembered all the tears her mother had cried, and to what end? Tears didn't change anything, but the pain was so sharp, she wasn't sure she could hold back. She'd read about the feeling of a broken heart; the description wasn't too far wrong. Still, if she hadn't experienced such joy, she wouldn't be feeling this pain.

She swallowed the lump in her throat. "I'll miss you forever, Alexi Ladislas. I hope you find someone who'll take care of you."

His hands tightened and he pulled her close. Choking back a sob, Kerry kissed him with all the love in her heart. She poured everything into that kiss, knowing it had to last them both a lifetime. Because she believed him; he would miss her. Maybe not forever, but for a while.

"Alexi, we must leave now." Lady Gwendolyn's voice, rising up the stairs, startled them both. Pulling away, Alexi gazed into Kerry's eyes one last time. She felt his hands tighten, then fall away from her shoulders.

"Goodbye, Mack," Kerry whispered.

"Goodbye, Kerry." And then he turned and strode across the room, taking the steps with a determined tread.

She couldn't watch him leave. Couldn't take one last glance at his back while he rushed back to his life in Belegovia.

She sank onto the couch and hugged her arms around herself to hold in his scent, the feel of him pressed close.

Someday, he might tell people the story of his trip to Texas when he ran off with the truck stop waitress.

They'd all laugh, and he might get a look of longing in his eyes. And then he'd blink, and smile, and the memory would be gone.

"Goodbye, Alexi," she whispered in the stillness of the deserted apartment before she let the tears fall.

Chapter Seven

Three months later

Alexi had never envisioned this particular scene when he and Kerry had parted three months ago. He'd done his best to be strong, but he'd nearly lost his composure and asked her to go with him. Just get on the jet and leave. But he hadn't. Asking wouldn't have been right, but leaving hadn't felt right, either. As a matter of fact, nothing had felt right since he'd left Texas.

He paced the living room of Kerry's apartment and waited for her to return. Pregnant women were often sick in the mornings, he told himself. There was nothing to be worried about. But still, he resisted the urge to fling open the closed door and hold her hand. Or her head. Or whatever part of her needed a little support.

He couldn't actually say he felt guilty about getting her pregnant. After all, the broken condom had been an accident. Although Kerry hadn't thought she was fertile then, apparently she had been. That wasn't anybody's fault. The baby she now carried was conceived accidently, but that didn't mean he or she was unwanted.

On the contrary, Alexi was elated. He'd fought against calling Kerry for three months. He'd rebelled against marrying the contessa, but in the end, he didn't have a good excuse to avoid the nuptials his father so dearly wanted.

Now he had an excuse. A very good excuse. One that would be obvious in a few short months.

His father was going to be furious, but his anger would fade as quickly as he realized he'd soon be holding his grandson or granddaughter. That the succession of Belegovia would be assured. Alexi was sure the people of his country would love Kerry once they got to know her, and the baby would be an instant hit. Belegovians wouldn't hold it against a child because he or she had been born less than nine months after the wedding.

When the bathroom door remained shut for what seemed like forever, Alexi walked over and placed his ear against the wood. Nothing. He knocked softly. "Kerry? Are you okay?"

Finally he heard the sound of water running, then moments later the door opened. Her golden skin looked pale and somewhat blotchy, and her eyes appeared watery, but not from tears. Still, she was the most beautiful sight in the world to him.

"Are you okay?"

She nodded. "For the past two months, my mornings have been pretty rocky. After about nine o'clock, I'm fine."

"Have you been able to work?"

She nodded again. "I love my job. My manager at Grayson Industries has been very understanding."

"They know you're pregnant?"

"Not for sure, but I think they suspect that's the problem. I haven't felt up to telling anyone." She rubbed her forehead. "Of course, everyone will assume the baby is Hank's, since you were so convincing at that press conference in May."

"We'll tell them the truth immediately, of course. There is no need for anyone to assume you are romantically involved with Hank McCauley."

"Especially since he and Gwendolyn are getting married soon." She started walking toward the couch, and Alexi put his hand under her elbow for support. Instead of flashing him a smile, she glared at him. "And *we* aren't telling anyone anything. At least not yet."

"Kerry, don't be stubborn. We need to arrange the wedding as quickly as possible. I'll contact the archbishop today and of course, I'll rely on my sister to take care of the details. She's very good at that sort of thing, and she knows the best caterers, designers and decorators."

"Let me get this straight," she said as she turned and leaned against the arm of the couch, facing him. "You've already decided where the wedding will be. Once your sister and a horde of other people get busy on the details, everything will be taken care of."

"That seems the most expeditious plan," he said, warned by her folded arms and serious expression that she wasn't happy with his plan. "Unless you'd like to be more involved. Which would be fine, of course.

As a matter of fact, I'll give you my sister's personal number and you can call her immediately.''

"There's one thing you've forgotten."

"What?"

"I never agreed to marry you. As a matter of fact,'' she said, unfolding her arms and advancing toward him, "I've—'' she poked him in the chest "—never—'' she poked him again "—been asked.''

"Oh.'' He forced a smile to cover that slight oversight as he gently captured her finger. Of course they were getting married. Perhaps he had been a bit overbearing, but time was critical. As soon as he'd overheard Kerry's conversation with Gwendolyn, he'd arranged for the jet while Milos had packed a bag. He'd been out the door in thirty minutes, landed many hours later in Austin and rented a car to drive to Ranger Springs.

"In that case, Kerry Lynn Jacks, will you do the honor of becoming my bride?''

If anything, she looked a little more blotchy, as if she was going to be ill again. Then she thrust out her chin and looked directly into his eyes. "No.''

"No?''

"See, that's exactly why I wanted to talk to Gwendolyn. Have a little time to consider the consequences. Now you burst back into my life—when I haven't heard a word from you in three months—and you demand that we're getting married just for the sake of the baby. Well, I'm not marrying anyone just for the sake of my child.''

He looked shocked. Of course, since this was Alexi, he looked darned good being shocked. Although she'd seen Hank several times in the past three months, he didn't remind her of Alexi. At least not emotionally. Only this man, who looked and acted just like his royal heritage, made her weak with yearning.

But at the moment, she had to think of him as the father of her baby, not as the man who had loved her so sweetly for just a few days, three months ago.

"*Our* child," he reminded her, "and this is not just any baby. This is the royal heir."

"No, this *could* be the royal heir. The baby could also be the mayor of Ranger Springs, or a champion cowboy, or an elementary schoolteacher. I believe a child should have options. Don't you remember talking about how you felt about duties? And you were an adult!"

"That's different, and has no bearing on the issue of our child's legitimacy or heritage."

Kerry retreated to the couch. She didn't feel well enough at the moment to argue with Alexi the man, much less the prince.

But, she told herself, he was on Texas soil now, subject to her country's laws. He couldn't force her to marry him. He couldn't take her baby away from her, as long as the baby was born right here in Ranger Springs. Right here where she was surrounded by friends and family, where she had a great job and benefits.

"Look, Alexi, I need a little time to think about this. I just found out yesterday from Gwendolyn about your country's laws and traditions. Now you burst into my apartment when I'm not feeling well and demand that we're getting married." She shook her head. "Let's get together later. I need a little time to think."

"Kerry," he said, walking toward her, "we don't have much time. Plans need to be made—"

"Only if we're getting married. Otherwise, I imagine a lawyer can draw up some documents."

"Don't say that. This...situation is between you and me. We made this baby together. We can work out the consequences."

"But we're not the only people involved, Alexi. It sounds to me as though a whole country might be affected. I know for sure that one small life," she said, rubbing her slightly rounded stomach, "is going to be changed no matter what decision we make."

He took a deep breath, closing his eyes as if he were debating her words. He had to know she was right. He shouldn't have come in here with demands, especially when he hadn't called her in three months.

"Very well. When would you like to meet?"

"Are you incognito, or did you plan to appear around town as a prince?"

"I really hadn't thought about it. I have no reason to hide my identity."

"Okay, then. Meet me at the Four Square Café at noon." She didn't want to be alone with him. The most public place in Ranger Springs was the best option. She folded her arms again and gave him a pointed look. "I believe you know where that's located."

She wasn't sure, but she thought he might have blushed. Or maybe he was just flushed with frustration. After all, it wasn't everyday that a commoner got to say no to a prince.

BY THE TIME Kerry pulled herself together, showered and dressed, she was running late for her noontime meeting with Alexi. She pulled her car into a slanted parking spot and walked quickly toward the café door, waving as she spotted Robin Parker placing a new painted chair in front of her antique store.

The bell over the door tinkled gaily as she walked into the restaurant. Every head swiveled toward her as she paused, searching for Alexi. He wasn't hard to find. A group of five or six people stood around his table, obviously vying for his attention.

Well, perhaps this hadn't been a good idea. She'd thought business would be slow, as it usually was on Saturdays. Apparently the news that a prince was in their midst had spread fast. Thelma Rogers was in the middle of the group, no doubt getting a scoop for Sunday's edition. Thankfully, the *Springs Gazette* didn't have a society column, because Kerry was sure she'd be in it tomorrow. "Local Girl Hosts Prince," or how about "Prince Revisits Local Love Nest." She shuddered as she thought of what might be printed if Thelma possessed fewer scruples.

At least she was thankful no paparazzi or journalists from out of town lurked, ready to snap pictures. Ready to report on the prince's illegitimate baby with his small-town lover. How tawdry that sounded!

She didn't want tawdry. She wanted what was best for her baby, but what solution gave them each what they wanted? She was afraid nothing satisfied everyone. She knew she wouldn't be content with a marriage that was forced, knowing her father-in-law had wanted a contessa, not a waitress-turned-financial analyst, for his son, knowing that the Belegovian people expected someone more suitable for their prince.

"Hello, Kerry," her mother called out, excitement evident in her bright eyes and clasped hands. Although she wore her waitress uniform, she looked very much like one of the group, admiring the man who'd given her an autograph just days before he'd impregnated her daughter. Not that Charlene Jacks knew that little fact. "Look who found his way here for lunch."

"What a big surprise," Jimmy Mack, the hardware store owner, boomed.

"I'll say," Pastor Carl Schleipinger added. Both men stood over Alexi as though guarding him from unwanted intruders.

"Hello, Kerry," Alexi said, his arm stretched out across the red vinyl booth. A paper place mat and a glass of iced tea showed that he'd been here for at least several minutes.

She nodded, unwilling to trust her voice. However, the group didn't seem to realize she'd come here to meet Alexi. They stood around, smiling, blocking the other side of the booth.

"If you good people wouldn't mind, I'd very much like for Kerry to join me."

"Oh," Thelma said, her gray eyebrows raised in speculation.

"Jimmy Mack, we'd best be getting on with our own lunch," Pastor Carl said, nudging the portly hardware store owner.

"What can I get you, sweetie?" Kerry's mom asked.

"Just water with lemon for now, Mom. Thanks."

As soon as they were alone, Kerry leaned forward, resting her elbows on the table. "I'm sorry. I didn't realize there would be so many people here to 'greet' you."

"That's fine. I'm just afraid we won't have much privacy to talk."

"I'll keep my voice down if you will."

"I'm not sure. Can Ms. Rogers of your local newspaper read lips?"

"I don't think so," Kerry replied, smiling despite the serious nature of their meeting.

Alexi pushed his iced tea aside and leaned forward. "Well, we can always go upstairs."

Heat rushed through Kerry at the memories. At the sound of his bedroom voice. At the intense look in his blue, blue eyes. "In your dreams," she said as flippantly as possible.

He smiled, one side of his mouth quirking up. "You would be surprised how often I've dreamed of that apartment."

"Really? Would that be before the vacation in Monaco? Before or after the ski trip to the Alps? Or would that be while you were courting Contessa di Giovanni?"

"Ouch," he said. "You've apparently been keeping up with the press reports of my life."

"Correction, my *mother* has been keeping up with you. I've been listening when I couldn't get out of the room fast enough."

"Ah, Kerry, you wound me. I have been thinking of you."

"Save it, Mack. I'm here to discuss our little 'situation,' not my feelings about your exploits."

"From what you've told me so far, I'm not sure you can put aside one for the other."

"Trust me, I'm going to try."

"I do trust you, Kerry," he said, leaning forward once more and speaking softly. "I trust you to do what's best for our child."

Before she could come up with a good comeback, her mother returned to take their order.

Alexi ordered the daily special—chicken fried steak, mashed potatoes and Texas toast—while Kerry's stomach revolted at the idea of such heavy food. She chose a club sandwich with chips and no pickle. Unlike some pregnant women, she hadn't developed a craving for pickles...especially not teamed up with ice cream.

"You mentioned that I'd never called you after I left in May, but I thought it was for the best," he said as soon as her mother left. "If I couldn't offer you a real relationship, I thought it best to cut our ties completely. I couldn't imagine talking to you occasionally, knowing how much I wanted to be with you, and not acting on my desire."

"That sounds wonderful, but I have to question whether you really did think of me after you got back to your real world. I mean, the trip to Texas was an...interlude. Maybe you felt differently when you got back home. When you started back into your real life."

"My feelings for you haven't changed," he said, then sat upright and smiled as his salad was delivered.

Kerry felt very frustrated. Alexi had made some remarkable claims about his feelings, but none of them could be substantiated. She wanted proof that he'd thought of her. Proof that the feelings they'd expressed to each other before he left were real, not just a product of the moment or an afterglow of the fantastic intimacy they'd shared.

He took a few bites, then pushed the bowl aside. "You've had two months to come to terms with your...condition. I just found out. I know you don't completely trust me at the moment, but please, give me a chance."

"But how, Alexi? How can you go back for those three months and prove that you were thinking of me? I've already turned down your rather high-handed proposal. And now that you know I won't marry you just for the baby, you say that you've wanted me all along. I'm sorry to distrust you, but that just sounds too convenient."

"Believe me, nothing about this situation is convenient, not for any of us."

She noticed her mother coming out of the kitchen, carrying a tray of food and beaming, so happy to have a real live prince here in the restaurant.

Kerry wasn't happy. She was confused and hurt. Because no matter how she looked at the situation, there was one indisputable fact. She hadn't been good enough to be Alexi's princess before she got pregnant, and no one would believe she was good enough now. She'd always be the poor, small-town girl who trapped him into marriage.

She'd always know she was second best, outclassed in the eyes of royal society by a contessa who, by Hank's account, was lovely, polished, beautiful and...tall. Just like a real princess was supposed to be. Just like Kerry would never be.

ALEXI FELT his frustration level rise as they finished lunch—not that either of them had managed to consume much for the palpable tension in the air—and made their excuses to Charlene Jacks and a plethora of others to whom he'd been reintroduced. Three months ago he'd met some of the people at the reception given in his honor at the Four Square Café, but he'd been in a turmoil then, too. What was it about Kerry that turned his usually logical brain to mush?

Unfortunately, nothing else was the slightest bit "mushy." Despite her rebuff of his proposal, despite the fact she was pregnant, he still wanted her. Rather desperately, as a matter of fact. Convincing her to marry him would give him the advantage of husbandly rights, or whatever sharing a bed was now called.

When they walked into the sunlight, the heat hit him like the smack of a large, thick piece of lumber. Whack! How did these Texans stand it? In Belegovia the temperatures were mild, around eighty degrees. When the sun set behind the mountains to the west, there was a decided chill. Nights were good for snuggling, small fires in the hearth or candlelight playing off the walls.

"Where are you staying?" Kerry asked as they strolled along the covered sidewalk.

"I came here directly from the airport. I haven't made arrangements yet. Can you suggest a place?"

"London?" she quipped.

"A bit closer, perhaps," he replied, hiding a smile. She might be pregnant and suffer from morning sickness, but she hadn't lost her sense of humor. "I'd prefer a hotel, but a motel would be fine, as long as it's clean.''

"We don't have any hotels or motels in Ranger Springs."

"You don't?"

"Alexi, have you lost your hearing in the past three months? Because you keep repeating my statements in the form of a question."

He glared at her as she stopped in front of her car. Beatrice looked fine, all shiny and well cared for. Of course, she didn't have Delores's fake fur car seat covers, nor did she have that well-driven look of a 100,000-mile car. "Do you miss Delores?" he asked.

"Not really. She was a good car, but I like this one, too. And you're changing the subject."

"My hearing is fine, thank you very much for asking. I'm just a bit incredulous about this whole trip. My mind is reeling. As I mentioned, you've had three months—"

"Two," she corrected. "I've only known for almost two months."

"Whatever," he said, waving his hand in dismissal. She wanted to defend her decision to keep the news from him, but he was still not happy about her actions. He deserved to know he'd fathered a child. He wanted to share the experience with Kerry, not be an insignificant bystander. "You're familiar with the…situation. I'm not. And until we can come to an agreement," he said, knowing he meant that until she agreed to his proposal, "we can't move forward."

"Speak for yourself. This baby is growing whether we agree on anything or not."

He felt his eyes widen, then he frowned. Was she

trying to drive him mad? If so, she was doing a good job, reminding him how ineffectual he'd been so far in making her come to her senses.

He decided not to try to reason with her anymore for the moment. He needed time, and time meant he needed a place to stay. He'd noticed that Kerry hadn't offered to share her apartment. And, although the apartment over the café held fond memories, it wasn't air-conditioned or completely furnished.

He wondered if any of the old condoms in that nightstand drawer were still there, waiting for the next unsuspecting user.

"Do you have a suggestion on where I can stay?"

Kerry sighed. "Robin Parker has opened a bed-and-breakfast over her antique store." She shielded her eyes and pointed across the square. The building looked like an old movie theater, except instead of posters, the display cases sported antique fabrics, lace and other decorative objects. He believed the style was called "shabby chic." At least, that's what his sister had told him when he'd remarked on the "old, worn-out furniture" he'd seen in a friend's house in England.

"I'm sure she has a room available. I haven't heard of any visitors to town. Most people don't take a vacation in Ranger Springs when it's this hot."

"Will you go there with me to meet Ms. Parker?"

"Sure. I like Robin. She's the wife of our chief of police, so make sure you walk the straight and narrow while you're there."

"I'll be on my best behavior," he promised, which might not mean much to Kerry. Apparently in the past three months, she'd developed a poor opinion of him.

He didn't remember any severe criticism of his actions while they were together, yet now she found him irresponsible, with the potential for frat-boy antics.

They crossed the street, then walked past the bank. He wanted to talk to Kerry, as they'd done so easily before, but there seemed to be a barrier between them. The trip they had shared had seemed ages ago—almost another lifetime. Since returning to Belegovia, he'd tried to throw himself into his duties and goals. He assumed Kerry had done the same things, since she'd been so excited about her new job. Going back to that carefree time seemed impossible, but going forward was proving difficult, as well.

He'd naively thought that he'd come to Texas, propose, sweep Kerry off her feet and whisk her back to Belegovia to begin her new life as a princess. Now he realized that his plan was far too simple; he hadn't taken Kerry's feelings for her new life into consideration, nor had he considered she'd be averse to marrying him.

The air-conditioned interior of the store rushed out to meet them when he opened the door for Kerry. He followed her into the fragrant interior. Candles and that mixture of dried things women loved to put in bowls around the house, he supposed.

"Kerry, how are you?" a cute woman with honey-blond hair and stylishly casual clothing greeted them, her hands full of silk flowers.

"Fine, Robin. My friend here needs a room," Kerry said, some of her good humor returning.

"Hello, Your Highness," she said, walking forward and dusting her hands on a denim apron. "I believe we met at the reception."

"Yes, I remember. Please, call me Alexi. It's good to see you again. I need a room for an indeterminate period of time."

Robin looked surprised, glancing between the two of them. Had she bought into the story they'd spun of Hank and Kerry taking off together three months ago, or did she know the truth? "I have two rooms. Both of them are available. Would you like to take a look?"

"Yes, thank you," Alexi said, relieved that he'd at least have a place to sleep until he could make Kerry see reason. He had no intention of allowing his child to be born out of wedlock.

"Here are the keys," Robin said, handing them to Kerry. "I can't leave the shop right now, so take your time and decide which one is more to your choosing. I think I know," she said with a wink, "but you might have another idea."

They climbed the stairs behind the counter. Alexi could tell the steps had once led to the balcony, when this had been a theater. Original lighting cast a dim glow on the vintage red walls.

Upstairs, more old-fashioned lights installed from the ceiling lighted the hallway along the balcony railing. Walls had been built where seats had once faced toward a screen below. Now the scene consisted of rows of antiques and decorative items.

"Robin has really done a lot with this old theater," Kerry commented, unlocking one of the doors.

The room was decorated in shades of rose, pink and green. Flounces, lace and frills adorned almost every fabric surface. Ornate furniture and gilded accents screamed ''feminine'' from the rafters of this old building.

''How beautiful,'' Kerry said in awe. They walked farther into the room, which had a cozy, equally feminine bathroom and Jacuzzi tub. Even the smell was...frilly.

''I wonder which one of the European paparazzi stayed in this room—the camouflage guy or the polyester cigarette smoker?''

Kerry laughed. ''Either one would have been grossly out of place. Let's take a look at the other room.''

They closed and locked the door, then entered the next room. This one was done in cowboy décor—obviously a tribute to the Old West. Rustic lumber, cow-patterned accents and bandanna material gave this space a masculine appeal. ''Now, this is more like it,'' Alexi said. ''I might feel like your friend Hank in here.''

''Robin obviously has a sense of humor,'' Kerry stated. ''As if there was any doubt which room you'd choose.''

''Perhaps she thought you were staying here with me.''

''Perhaps that's just wishful thinking on your part.''

''I'm always wishful where you're concerned,'' he said, reaching for her.

She stepped around a big denim chair, eluding his grasp. ''If I didn't know how busy you've been, I might be tempted to believe you.''

He gazed into her eyes and stalked around the chair. ''I think it should be obvious to anyone, especially an astute observer like Mrs. Parker, that I'm very tempted by you.''

Kerry breathed deeply, unsure how much longer she'd be able to resist his persistence…and his proposal.

Chapter Eight

Kerry gave a breathless, nervous chuckle. "She doesn't know anything about *us,* so I don't see how she'd come to that conclusion."

"Will she know soon?" he asked, stepping in front of Kerry so he could look into her eyes. His hands lightly rested on her shoulders to keep her from turning away again. "I want everyone to know the child you're carrying is mine, not some faceless stranger's baby. Not your Hank McCauley's."

"I'm not ready to tell everyone yet. I haven't even told my mother and sisters!"

"Then let's tell them together. Tonight, or tomorrow. Let me take the family to dinner, wherever you'd like, and we'll break the news."

"Alexi, I just don't know."

"Surely you've been thinking about telling them."

"Of course, but I haven't decided how. No matter how I visualize the scene, I can see disappointment." She caught her bottom lip between her teeth and frowned. Then, with a sigh, she continued. "My sister Carole ran off when she was just a teenager and had a baby with a would-be country-western star. That's my niece, Jennifer. We all love her, of course, but I remember how difficult the situation was for my sister, who was married for just a few months. And for my mother. She felt as though she'd failed Carole. Like if she'd been a better mother, this wouldn't have happened. That wasn't true, of course. My mom is great. But now she has another pregnant daughter, and I know that's going to hurt.''

''Then that's one more reason we should get married.''

Kerry shook her head. ''As much as I love my family, I'm not getting married to make them feel better, just like I'm not going to marry you just because you think it's the most expeditious thing to do.''

''It's the *right* thing to do.''

''Right for you, maybe,'' she said, raising her chin. ''I'm not sure it's right for me or the baby.''

Alexi sighed and dropped his hands. ''What can I do to convince you we should be together? I know I left three months ago, but you understand why. At the time, I didn't think we had a future. You were so excited about starting your new life. I felt it would be best to select someone from Europe to become the princess bride my father wanted me to select. But that doesn't mean I wouldn't have pursued you had the situation been different.''

''You mean if you'd been a regular guy.''

''Exactly.'' He was glad she was finally seeing his point of view.

''So what has changed? You're not a regular guy now. You're still a prince. I'm not a truck stop waitress any longer, but I'm still a small-town Texas girl, the daughter of a waitress and a runaway father. I'm hardly princess material.''

''I may still be a prince, but first of all, I'm a man. Soon to be a father. And I take my responsibilities seriously. One of those is to acknowledge and care for my child.''

Kerry sighed and sat down in an overstuffed chair upholstered in denim, pillowcase ticking and red gingham checks. ''I know, and I'm not trying to deny you access to your child. I even understand why you're excited about becoming a father.''

''You do?''

She nodded. Alexi walked to the chair and hunkered down so they were eye-to-eye. ''When I found out I was pregnant,'' she said, her eyes suspiciously bright, ''I was scared and thrilled and excited and just about every other emotion. I knew the timing was all wrong. I knew the situation was all wrong. But I wanted this child just the same.''

She paused, looking down at her folded hands. ''When you left, I knew I'd never see you again. And then when I realized I carried your child, it's like a part of you would be with me forever.''

Alexi enfolded her in his arms, pressing his cheek against her soft curls. ''I'm sorry I wasn't here for you then. Let me be with you the rest of the journey.''

She pulled back slightly to look into his eyes. ''Part of me wants to lean against you, hold your hand and let you support me. That's the part of me that gets morning sickness, mood swings and indigestion,'' she admitted with a smile. ''Another part of me wants to stand up tall and say this is my baby and I'll make all the decisions. Thump my chest and say I'm in charge of my body.''

"I rather like the first one better," he said, tipping up her chin.

"I know you do. But the problem is, neither one of them is practical. Neither one is right."

"Then what do we do, Kerry? Very soon you must tell your family, your boss, your friends. And you know I want to be acknowledged as the father."

She sighed again. "I suppose I want to know that you will be around for me if I need to lean on you. That this sudden desire to marry me and proclaim this child a royal heir isn't just a whim."

"What can I do to show you I'm completely serious?"

"Stay here in Ranger Springs. Show me that you can be a regular guy, not just a prince."

"You want me to pretend to be 'Mack' again?"

"No," she said softly. "I just want a chance to know the real Alexi Ladislas."

KERRY LEFT ALEXI at the Robin's Nest B and B, then returned to her apartment. She needed a nap, but her brain wouldn't shut down long enough to sleep. She lay in her double bed, staring at the ceiling and wondering if she was doing the right thing.

Tonight, she and Alexi were going to tell her family that they were expecting a baby next February.

Happy Valentine's Day, Mom. You're going to be a grandmother again.

The afternoon sun slanted through her blinds, warming the room and casting shadows on the white walls. She'd been so excited when she'd moved into her first apartment. For the first time ever, she'd been alone. No one to bother her if she wanted to sleep late, or stay up to watch old reruns of *Family Ties* or *The Cosby Show*.

She'd been so stir-crazy after one week that she'd shown up on a Saturday night at her family home, ready for a hamburger skillet dinner, refrigerator dinner rolls and brownies from a mix. She'd never tasted such good food or been so glad to be overwhelmed by the noise of three other women and one child all talking at once.

Of course, after dinner her mother had regaled her with stories of Alexi's return to Belegovia following the economic summit. Pictures of him from several Internet Web sites showed a smiling, designer-dressed prince at the opera in Vienna, the opening of a visitor's bureau in Belegovia and escorting a beautiful, tall brunette to a reception at the palace.

The contessa. The woman his father wanted him to marry. They sure hadn't wasted any time getting together. Kerry still remembered how jealous she'd been when she'd seen the couple. Her mother hadn't realized, of course, how much it hurt for her daughter to see the man she secretly loved with another woman.

So in the weeks that followed, Kerry endured news and photos from Belegovia until one day, she'd simply run from the room in tears. She'd flung herself on her old bed and held a pity party. Finally, her mother had interrupted the tears with apologies for her inconsiderate obsession with royalty, especially Alexi. She'd eventually confined her Alexi-worship to the framed autograph in the living room and, Kerry was sure, private viewings of *Royalty* magazine and her favorite online sites.

Now Kerry and Alexi were going to show up for Saturday-night dinner with the family. They were going to share news that would shake up their world. Nothing would ever be the same for the Jacks family again, no matter what decision Kerry made about her baby's father.

Rolling to her side, she looked out the open doorway of her bedroom into the living room. Her apartment wasn't luxurious, but it was hers. She'd furnished it with a new couch and chair, coffee and side tables, a breakfast set, television and entertainment center. It must appear very plain and ordinary to Alexi, but it suited her. She could relax after work, read a book and dream about the future in this space.

She was happy here. Well, mostly happy. Sometimes she was a little lonely. Sometimes she longed for Alexi's strong arms and powerful loving. And sometimes she worried about what the future held for her baby. Whether he or she would be happy in a modest home in Ranger Springs rather than a palace in Belegovia. Whether her child would drive a used car instead of being driven in a chauffeured limousine.

How did a mother know what to do? Was there a crystal ball someplace she could use? None of the alternatives were perfect, but there had to be a way to weigh her options. She didn't know what to do; she wasn't even sure how she felt about Alexi right now, except she was pretty sure she'd never fallen out of love with him, despite his high-handed reaction to the unexpected news.

But he was right about one thing—they needed to tell her family. Putting off the inevitable would only hurt everyone's feelings.

WHILE HER NIECE, Jennifer, played on the back porch with the family cat, Kerry nervously asked everyone to have a seat in the living room.

"Alexi and I have something to tell you," she said as she sank into one of the dining chairs they'd pulled into the living room for additional seating. Alexi took the chair beside her, pulling it close.

Her mother's eyes lit up like gray-green Christmas bulbs. Carole appeared calm, as usual, and Cheryl looked as if she wanted to jump off the couch. Kerry felt the silence stretch on until Alexi took her hand.

"Mom, you've known the truth all along, that I was really with Alexi when I drove down to Galveston."

"What?" Cheryl said, perched on the edge of the sofa as if she was going to use the springs inside to propel her forward. "Why didn't you tell *us?*"

"Please, don't be angry at Kerry," Alexi said. "I made her promise not to tell anyone else. I thought it best for everyone involved."

"But we're your family, Kerry," Carole said. "I don't understand."

Kerry tensed, but continued. "What's done is done, and we did what we thought was best at the time. That's not the only thing we need to tell you. You see, Alexi had to hide from the paparazzi that were hanging around town, so we went to the vacant apartment over the café."

"I'm not sure your family needs to know all the

details," Alexi advised, giving her hand a little squeeze.

"I'm not going to tell them *all* the details," she whispered, squeezing back harder.

He laced his fingers through hers and held tightly. "It sounds as though you're very close."

She tugged her hand away and continued. "So, one thing led to another, and we spent the night there."

Three gasps filled the silence of the living room.

Before her sisters could start questioning her again, Kerry surged forward with the news. "And that leads to what we have to tell you tonight." She paused and took a deep breath. "I'm, er, well, that is, *we're* going to have a baby."

Her mother emitted a strangled, gurgling sound. Everyone turned to help her, but she waved them away. "I'm going to be a grandmother again?" she asked when she caught her breath.

"That's right, Mom. I'm sorry to tell you this way, but—"

"And you're going to be a princess!"

"Well, no, not exactly. That is—"

"I have asked Kerry to do me the honor of becoming my bride. She has yet to affirm, but I am still hopeful."

"Kerry Lynn Jacks, you'd better say yes!" her mother exclaimed, jumping up so fast, Kerry eased back against her chair. "You need to get married as soon as possible. Do you have any idea how hard it will be to find a maternity wedding dress?"

"Mom, the decision's not that simple."

"Yes, it is."

"You just want a prince for a son-in-law!" she

shot back, then realized how that sounded. Okay, her mother was royalty obsessed, but she loved all three of her daughters. She'd never insist on something that wasn't in their best interests. Or what she *thought* was in their best interests.

"I'm sorry, Mom. I didn't mean it that way. I just need some time to think this through. I have a great job, and I love my apartment and—"

"And none of that is important when it comes to raising a child. Kerry Lynn, this is different than when your sister Carole ran off." Charlene turned to her middle daughter. "Pardon me for saying this, sweetie, but that was just poor, teenage judgment."

"No, you're right," Carole said, turning to her older sister. "Kerry, this is different. I did marry Jennifer's dad before I got pregnant, but there was no way that marriage would have lasted. He didn't want to be a father. I assume Prince Alexi does?"

"Absolutely. I'm very excited about the prospect."

"Right. And, Kerry, you're what, eleven years older than I was when I ran off? The situation is totally different."

"Still, there's a lot to consider beside the fact that I'm having a baby."

"That's a huge consideration," her mother advised in her practical parent voice, "and it's not going to get any smaller in the next six months."

"Thanks for reminding me that I'll be waddling around soon enough," Kerry said, throwing up her hands. "Does anyone understand why I might not want to marry a prince from a foreign country?"

Three pairs of nearly identical eyes stared back at her as if she'd just spoken in tongues.

''Kerry, they just want what's best for you and our child,'' Alexi said gently.

''So do I, but obviously no one else understands.''

''What would be so bad about marrying Alexi?'' her mother asked. ''Beside the fact he's a prince, he's a really nice man.''

''Thank you, Mrs. Jacks.''

''He's also impulsive and irresponsible...well, sometimes,'' Kerry said, rising from her chair. ''He ran off with me on the spur of the moment, and he ran back here just as fast when he eavesdropped on my conversation with Gwendolyn and found out before I was ready to tell him.''

''Thankfully, yes, I was on the phone when you burst into her house and told her the truth,'' he said, almost growling. ''Something, I might add, you should have told *me* first.''

Kerry folded her arms under her breasts and glared at him. ''And what were *you* supposed to be doing this weekend? I think I heard from someone,'' she said, glancing at her mother, ''that you were going to announce your engagement to the beautiful, cultured and *tall* Contessa di Giovanni!''

He placed his hands on his hips and glared back. ''I thought it was more important to ask the mother of my child to marry me!''

''You demanded—you didn't ask—and I still think you're too impulsive.''

''Children, quit bickering,'' her mother said. ''This is getting us nowhere.'' She gave Kerry a pointed look. ''What will it take for you to believe Alexi?''

''I already told him I needed to know he was a regular guy.''

"Excuse me," Cheryl piped in, "but he's single, gorgeous, probably rich and a *prince*. And you want him to be a regular guy? What's wrong with this picture!"

"You don't understand. I need to know he's reliable. That he won't go off and leave me on a whim if he gets tired of being a married man. Or a daddy."

Kerry's mother walked across the room and put her arms around her oldest daughter. "Oh, sweetie, Alexi isn't like your father. Don't refuse to marry him just because you're scared."

Kerry hugged her mother tight and burst into tears.

"I'M SORRY I fell apart like that," Kerry said as they drove back to Robin's Nest B and B. "I suppose my hormones are going crazy."

"I'm sure that's part of it." Alexi watched her drawn face from the dashboard lights. She looked tired and tense. He wished he hadn't put her in that situation, but her family needed to know first. Now they could tell the world. Perhaps he could get Gwendolyn to write the press release.

After a while, Kerry said, "I'm just a little sensitive about my father."

"I imagine so, since he walked out on your family. You've never seen him? Even as an adult?"

She shook her head. "He died about five years ago."

"I'm sorry."

"He was driving back to Texas from California and must have fallen asleep at the wheel. The strange thing is that we never did know if he was just passing through, on his way home, or going someplace else."

She shrugged. "There's no way to find out what was in his mind."

He reached over and covered her hand on the steering wheel. "Perhaps he was coming home."

"I'd like to think so, but I'm still angry at him." She pulled the car to a stop in back of the B and B, since the front door was locked after hours. "I don't ever want to feel that way about you, Alexi," she said softly.

"I'll never let you down. I'll be there for you and the baby."

"I want to believe you, but—"

"I know. You want proof." He leaned closer. "I'm going to show you I'm a regular guy, Kerry."

She briefly leaned against his arm, then blinked and sat up straighter. "Can you really stay here in Ranger Springs?"

"For a short time. Not forever, but you know that."

She nodded.

"Everything will be fine. You'll see."

"I hope so, Alexi. I want things to work out for the best."

And he knew what was best. Marrying her. Being a father to their baby. "We've had a busy day. Things will look better tomorrow."

She nodded. "Do you have any plans?"

"No, but I would like to see Gwendolyn. I'll call her tonight and see if she and Hank are available. Is there someplace we could go for lunch?"

"Bretford House. It's the only upscale local place."

"Good," he said, leaning closer. "I don't suppose

you'd like to come up to my room and play cowboys and Indians. Or perhaps I should say cowgirl and Native American. The vintage decorations are spurring my imagination.''

Kerry smiled for just about the first time tonight. ''No thanks.''

''May I kiss you good-night?''

''I don't think that would be a good idea.''

''Why?''

''Because,'' she said rather breathlessly, ''you might take advantage of me.''

''Only if you want me to,'' he said, just a few inches away from her lips.

''That's the problem, Alexi.'' She leaned away from him and put the car into gear. ''I'll see you tomorrow.''

Alexi shook his head and laughed. ''Until then, Princess.''

''Don't call me that!''

He grinned. ''You'd better get used to it.''

As soon as she drove away, he went up the back steps and unlocked the door to the upstairs. He had several phone calls and arrangements to make. First, he needed to reach Gwendolyn and arrange lunch tomorrow.

Settling into the denim chair, he dialed her number from memory. Hank answered on the second ring.

''Alexi here. How are things at the ranch?''

''Couldn't be better, as long as I keep Wendy out of the barn.''

Alexi laughed. Wendy was Hank's pet name for Gwendolyn, given to her as an irritant. However, over the period of time when Alexi and Kerry had been off on their road trip, Gwendolyn had apparently morphed into Wendy.

"I suppose you heard I was in town."

"Word reached me, yes. We were expecting your call."

"Kerry and I would like to invite you to lunch at Bretford House tomorrow. Are you available about noon?"

"I'm sure we can arrange that. Do you want to talk to my lady?"

Alexi smiled. Gwendolyn was indeed a British lady, the daughter of an earl, but Hank made the phrase sound endearing rather than formal. "Yes, please."

Gwendolyn came on the line after a bit of shuffling and what sounded like a lingering kiss. Alexi certainly didn't want to think about the love life of his former public-relations director and his cowboy double since *he* wasn't getting any kisses yet.

"So, you had the jet filled with petrol and came to Texas posthaste."

"I thought that was the right thing to do, yes."

"Is that what this is about? Doing the right thing?"

"You know I would never do anything I didn't really want to, even if the world considered it right."

"Yes, I know you're a notorious free spirit. But in this case, the people who are most important to you may think you're making a mistake. Not to mention the press. They will be brutal to Kerry when word gets out."

"I know, and I'm going to warn her again, but first I have to get her to agree. So far, I've only heard no and maybe."

"Then perhaps you are making progress."

"I hope so, although right now I am definitely alone at Robin's Nest B and B. Hank said you could meet us at noon at Bretford House. Does he know about the pregnancy?"

"Yes, although I'm afraid I made him extremely nervous. My wording wasn't too clear, it seems—or perhaps it lost something in translation from proper English to Texan—but in any case, he believed *I* was the one who was expecting."

Alexi laughed, imagining Hank's surprise. "Are you still planning on an autumn wedding?"

"Yes, we're waiting until the temperatures lower so we can follow in the Ranger Springs tradition and have an outdoor wedding. You'll see the place tomorrow—Bretford House. The gardens are lovely. Not proper English gardens, mind you, but very fitting for Texas. Lots of wildflowers. And my family will be flying over to see where I'll be living. I hope you can come back also."

"Just let me know when and I'll be there. Hopefully, by then Kerry and I will have already been married at the cathedral in Belegovia. So perhaps I will see you and Hank over there before we come back here for your wedding."

"I will keep my fingers crossed for you, Alexi. I know she loves you. I could tell that day we left. She was so devastated, both after your speech and when I told her she had only five minutes to say goodbye."

His heart seemed to skip a few beats. He wanted to believe Kerry loved him still, but she'd only admitted to "beginning" to fall in love with him. She'd never actually said the words he longed to hear.

Of course, neither had he. He hadn't felt free to profess his feelings when he knew he was going to marry another. And, at the time, he thought perhaps his feelings weren't real because he'd only known her for days. Now he hadn't said anything because she would naturally be suspicious. He'd tell her later, after she agreed to marry him.

"Thank you for the vote of confidence. I hope you're right."

"She needs time, Alexi, although I know you feel that is the one thing you do not have. But think about what has happened to her in the past three months—she's graduated after ten long years of part-time classes while working full-time, she's helped support her family since she was a teenager and she finally has a wonderful job and a place of her own. Now she must give up her independence for a life in the spotlight? This will be very hard for her."

"I know that," he said, although he probably hadn't spent enough time considering Kerry's feelings. All he could think about at first was the baby. His baby.

"When I decided to stay here with Hank—at your strong suggestion, I might add—I had to give up a career I loved and the friends I had made in Belegovia, plus I was separated by more miles from my family and friends in England. But Kerry will be even further estranged from everything she loves."

"I know! You don't have to make me feel even worse. If there was something I could do, something I could give up, don't you think I would? But my situation is different. I can't give up being Belegovia's crown prince. It wouldn't be fair to my father or the people.''

''I know, and that's all true, but sometimes the heart doesn't understand. All I'm asking is to be patient. You were my friend first, Alexi, but Kerry and I have grown close over the past three months. Partly, I'm sure, because I was her closest link to you.''

''Now you're really making me feel like a heel. Look, I'll be patient. I've had to adjust to a lot in the past twenty-four hours, too, not that I'm unhappy in any way with the news. Believe it or not, I've wanted to call Kerry a hundred times, at least, in the past three months. I did what I thought was best at the time, and I think Kerry understands now.''

''I'm sure she does. She's an intelligent, independent young woman.''

''Point taken—again. We'll see you tomorrow.''

He hung up the phone, glad that he'd had this conversation with Gwendolyn. She understood both Kerry and the situation, so she could be fair. And she brought up a good point; he did need to work on his patience.

''Wendy'' was obviously happy living here with Hank. Soon they would be married and, he guessed, they'd be expecting a child before long. Like him, she was thirty, and he supposed her biological clock was ticking despite her new career as a public-relations consultant in Austin and San Antonio.

Alexi just hoped that Kerry would be equally contented married to him...and living in his country.

That was one small detail he hadn't truly considered until talking to his old friend. Could Kerry actually be happy living someplace besides her beloved hometown?

Chapter Nine

Kerry knew they'd draw attention when they showed up at Bretford House, but she wasn't quite prepared to have every eye in the place turn on them. Everyone was dressed for church, some in short-sleeve shirts, some women in sandals, but some in suits and ties, the women in hose and heels. All of them looked with undisguised interest at the two look-alike men and the two very different women.

Gwendolyn and Hank greeted the others who were waiting for a table. She'd made a home for herself here, despite coming from a vastly different background. She didn't like the heat, Kerry knew, but had given up milder summers and snow-capped peaks for Hank.

Kerry wondered what she'd be willing to give up. Her career? Her hometown? Could she do what Gwendolyn had done for the love of a man? She just didn't know. But before she could even consider it, she had to be convinced he'd be there for her if she gave up almost everything for him.

"And what brings you back to Ranger Springs, Your Highness?" Mrs. Biggerstaff, the wife of the banker, asked. She gazed up at Alexi with a rather unholy gleam in her eyes, clasping her hands as if to keep them from roaming all over his body. Kerry couldn't really blame the slightly pudgy, middle-aged lady; she'd had a difficult time turning down his invitation last night.

"I came back to visit my very close friends," he said, smiling blandly.

"Will you have time for an interview?" Thelma Rogers asked. "I'd love to run an exclusive in the *Springs Gazette*. Scooping the big papers in Austin and San Antonio would do a lot for our local press."

"I always try to cooperate with the press, so please give me a call at Robin's Nest," he said, again evading a direct answer. He was very good at that—smooth evasion.

Even knowing why he needed to hedge, Kerry recognized her unease over that trait. She'd grown up around Texans who were praised for straight-talking. Her family might have been poor, but they were known for their honesty. Even Hank, who could talk rings around anyone and tease unmercifully, was so inherently honest that people did business with him on a handshake.

"I think our table is ready," Hank said, putting his arm around Gwendolyn and leading her through the small crowd. Kerry looked at Alexi, who simply raised an eyebrow. She definitely didn't want him holding her hand or anything else while they were in public, so she followed Gwendolyn. They were led through one room, which at one time was probably the parlor, into a second room that looked as though it had been a bedroom back when the building was a private residence. Purple flower-sprigged wallpaper and gleaming hardwood floors gave the room a cheerful quality. Sheer curtains were tied back on both tall windows.

"What a quaint restaurant," Alexi said, holding out Kerry's chair. "Turn of the century?"

"Probably. Ranger Springs was founded in the 1870s, but most of the houses you see were built from the mid-1890s to the mid-1900s," Kerry explained. "But I'm sure that seems really recent to both you and Gwendolyn. Everything's pretty old in Europe, isn't it?"

"Not everything, although we do have many famous old buildings and monuments," Gwendolyn said. "Why, in Alexi's country, there are both beautiful picturesque villages and magnificent buildings. You should see the palace! It's been completely restored with marble, stone and wood. Even the original murals and vaulted ceilings are intact."

"I certainly hope she will see the palace," Alexi said, leaning forward and speaking in a low voice the diners at other tables couldn't hear. "And the cathedral, also. We have a magnificent red carpet that just begs for a long white dress and a sprinkling of rose petals."

Kerry grabbed her cloth napkin and spread it in her lap, not looking at anyone else at the table. Alexi flustered her. He could make his words sound personal and intimate, even in the midst of a crowd.

"So, Hank," she said to change the subject before someone else overheard the conversation, "how's business?"

Fortunately, the waitress came with glasses of wa-

ter and menus, so she was spared from any more bla-
tant references by Alexi to his intentions. The conversation changed to Texas weather, Gwendolyn and
Hank's wedding plans, and things Alexi should see
while he was in Texas.

Before their food arrived, Pastor Carl and his wife
came by the table to say hello. As soon as they left,
when the salads arrived, two more couples arrived to
say they were so glad Prince Alexi was visiting their
town. He was offered a discount at the clothing store
and a free ham at the grocery—although they admitted he probably didn't need a ham, but could give it
away.

Hank was getting a little tired of the attention, but
Alexi was gracious. When their dinners arrived, along
with three older ladies from the community center,
Hank obviously had enough. He stood up and addressed the room.

"Friends and neighbors, we're real glad to see y'all
here today, but we'd like to eat our meal in peace.
Why don't you come by and see the prince later at
the gazebo? We'll make sure he gets there after lunch.
Thanks." He ended with a wave.

"Well-done," Alexi said, cutting into his barbe-
cued brisket as soon as Hank sat back down. "Now,
perhaps we can get back to our conversation. Kerry,
what do you have planned for us tomorrow? Perhaps
we should visit one of the locales suggested by the
nice couple with the extra hams."

"I don't know what *you're* going to do tomorrow,"
she said, picking up her own knife and fork, "but *I'm*
going to work. Maybe you can get someone else to
come out and play."

Gwendolyn chuckled and Hank laughed out loud. Alexi didn't look angry, but he wasn't happy, either. Well, that was just too bad. She wasn't going to change her life just because she had a VIP visitor. Or because she was pregnant. Or because he wanted her to get married on that red carpet sprinkled with rose petals.

Nope. Tomorrow she was going to work as usual. Alexi was on his own...until she got off at five o'clock.

ALEXI WOKE LATE in the morning after tossing and turning most of the night. He kept thinking about Kerry, so close and yet so far away. Yesterday had been a very busy day, one where he'd failed to make progress with her. After lunch they'd all gone to the gazebo in the center of town, where he'd greeted people and signed autographs until Hank had rescued him with a promise to show him the ranch. They'd all driven out to see the horses and improvements made to the facilities, but Kerry had spent most of the time indoors with Gwendolyn while he and Hank toured the barns. He'd barely had time to speak to her because she'd left to visit her mother and do a few loads of laundry.

The harder he pushed—like mentioning the cathedral's red carpet strewn with rose petals—the more she retreated. He was going to have to face the fact that winning Kerry's hand in marriage was much harder than courting any European princess. As a matter of fact, all he had to do was decide which ones he *might* want to marry and they became instantly available.

He was in Texas now, he thought as he stretched his arms over his head and looked around the room. Bright sunlight streamed in through shutters that looked like old barn doors, highlighting various cowboy paraphernalia hanging on the walls and decorating the furniture. Yes, he was definitely in Texas, and he had to approach Kerry on her terms.

Her mother was on his side, and probably her sisters, as well. Gwendolyn was remaining neutral, which was exactly in her nature, and Hank seemed to find the situation amusing—as long as no one "bothered" his friend Kerry too much. Deep inside, Hank had a gallant streak a mile wide.

But Alexi needed more support, and he needed to understand more about what would sway Kerry's decision to marry him. Her friends would be a good starting point. And what better place to start than the Four Square Café, where he could talk to both her mother and others who knew Kerry.

Of course, he'd have to be careful. He couldn't tell anyone else of the pregnancy until she was ready. Then, after they were married and she'd been accepted by his people, he was going to crow like the proudest rooster. *This is my baby,* he wanted to proclaim.

Stretching again, he rolled out of bed. He needed a good breakfast, insightful conversation and lots of luck. Later he'd work on getting more clothes, since he was going to be here a while, and he needed to establish a "home office" in this room so he could keep up with his investments and his country's business. He might also need Gwendolyn to help him draft a press release about where he'd run off to this time.

Half an hour later, freshly shaved and showered, he quickly descended the steps. Robin was at the counter, looking through a magazine and making notes on a yellow pad. "Good morning," she said, looking up with a smile. "How was your weekend?"

"Good. And yourself?"

"Busy. We're working on an addition to the house and there's always something to do."

Alexi nodded. "I'm out for several hours. The room is superb, by the way."

"I'm glad you're comfortable, but what about breakfast?"

"I believe I'll go to the café. I'd like to talk to Mrs. Jacks, so I might as well eat breakfast there."

"They fix a good one. All I have," Robin said with a smile, "are muffins, coffee and juice."

"Perhaps tomorrow. I feel as though I should talk to Kerry's mother about our...situation."

"I absolutely hate to be so nosy, but were you and Kerry really together in May when you came here?"

"Yes, we were."

With a definite sparkle in her eye, she asked, "Then was Hank McCauley impersonating you?"

"Yes," Alexi said with a conspiratorial wink, "except he couldn't get the accent right—I believe Gwendolyn said they didn't even try—so that's why he pretended to have laryngitis."

"That certainly makes sense, especially when she suddenly decided to stay in Ranger Springs, then moved in with Hank. His friend Travis Whittaker seemed to have it all figured out, but nobody would confirm the romance.''

''Hank and Gwendolyn are getting married in the fall.''

''Yes, I know. She's asked me to design some floral arches and large baskets for the wedding.''

''Wonderful. I hope we can come back for the ceremony.''

''We?''

Alexi grinned. ''Would you believe I used the royal 'we'?''

''Not really,'' she said with a mischievous smile. ''Well, have a good day, and I'll keep my fingers crossed for you.''

He pushed open the front door of the shop and was hit with a blast of hot, dry air. He nearly retreated back into the air-conditioned interior, but his mission was too important to let a little thing like unbearable heat keep him inside.

As he passed the hardware store, he noticed the proprietor placing some gardening-related items on the sidewalk in front of the large window.

''Why, good mornin', Prince Alexi! Are you havin' a good time in our little town?''

''Yes, I am, Mr....''

''Jimmy Mack Branson.''

''Ah, yes. It's nice to see you, Mr. Branson. I was just on my way to breakfast.''

''You go right ahead. I imagine you want to talk to Charlene.'' He grinned and winked. ''You'd best get in good with the mama. I heard you were courtin' our Kerry. She's a fine, fine young woman.''

''Yes, she is.'' The grapevine certainly worked

fast. Just yesterday he'd had lunch with her and their friends at Bretford House, and now word was out.

"You have a nice day, and make sure you come in if you need anything. Anything at all."

"Yes, I will. Thank you." He smiled, waved and walked on past. Perhaps he could purchase a large platter for his free ham.

Across the street, several pickups were parked in front of the café. In the center of the square, a dark-haired mother watched while her two children played around the gazebo.

He remembered the gazebo well from the rushed press conference he'd given there three months ago. He'd apparently been very persuasive in his contention that Hank had been traveling around Texas with Kerry. Now he was going to have to tell everyone that he and Kerry had, in fact, been more than mere acquaintances. They had made a baby together.

Both of them were going to have to face questions about why they'd kept the truth from the public, he realized as he crossed the street. Gwendolyn could put a good spin on the situation. He'd have to consult with her before the national press interviews, which were sure to follow.

He certainly didn't want people to think he'd been lying on a whim, or that he and Kerry had jumped into some torrid yet meaningless affair. He needed them to understand that there had been instant attraction, and that in only four short days, they'd created something very special. He also wanted everyone to know both he and Kerry were thrilled to be expecting the next royal heir.

Of course, first he needed to convince Kerry that

their child should be born after a wedding, and be raised to his or her rightful place in the Belegovian monarchy.

The bell over the door tinkled gaily as he strolled into the air-conditioned café interior. Breathing a sigh of relief, he spotted Charlene Jacks, smiled and waved. In just a second she walked to the front and picked up a menu and flatware rolled inside a paper napkin.

"Why, good morning, Prince Alexi. Will you be having breakfast with us?"

"Yes, I will. Any chance you can take a break and join me?"

"I think that can be arranged," she said, standing up straighter and smiling broadly. "I'll go get us both a cup of coffee."

After a cholesterol-laden but delicious breakfast of scrambled eggs, bacon, hash browns and biscuits, Alexi learned more about the woman who carried his child. After listening to what a great job Kerry had landed, plus her excitement over her first apartment— which made him feel like a heel because he was attempting to take her away from what she'd worked so hard to achieve—the conversation turned to Kerry's younger years.

"I just don't know what I would have done without her when her father left. She was only thirteen, but she pitched in like a trouper and baby-sat her younger sisters after school without a complaint. When she was old enough to get a job, she worked summers and weekends, even though I told her to take time off, have some fun with kids her own age."

Alexi nodded and buttered another biscuit.

"I mean, she participated in some things in school, but only after her sisters were old enough that they didn't need her. I just always wondered how different she might have been if she'd been more carefree. I felt so bad about depending on her, but she insisted. She said she *wanted* the responsibility."

"Mrs. Jacks, no one, least of all Kerry, resents you for giving her the opportunity to help her family. In fact, that's one of the things she and I have in common. We're both the oldest of three and we both have been put in situations where we had to assume leadership."

"You make it sound so...positive. It's hard for me to think I didn't let my oldest baby down."

He covered her hand with his. "You've been a great mother. Kerry told me so when we were traveling together. She's very proud of *you*."

"That's very sweet," she said, smiling and giving a little sniff. "I'm proud of all my girls."

"To tell you the truth," Alexi said, "I was a little worried you would be angry with me. I wouldn't blame you if you thought I had taken advantage of your daughter."

"Prince Alexi, you might have done a lot of things with my daughter, but never once did I think you'd taken advantage of her," she said with a chuckle. "Kerry might have lived all her life in Ranger Springs and gone to school in San Marcos, but she's no fool."

"I'm aware of that. Her strength and zest for life were the two qualities that drew me to her originally."

"And my first choice wouldn't be for the two of you to, er...team up like you have," she said, looking around to see if anyone was listening. "Any mother would like her daughter to have choices rather than feeling pressured to commit. But," she said with a shrug, "at least you want to do the right thing. And I think Kerry must have strong feelings for you, otherwise she wouldn't have...well, you know."

"Yes, I know." He knew *exactly* what she meant, and he didn't feel at all comfortable talking about *that* with Kerry's mother. "I hope I can talk her into accepting my proposal."

Charlene Jacks placed her hand over his and leaned closer. "Honey, you won't be able to talk Kerry into anything. But if you play your cards right, you might make her realize what she already wants to do— marry the father of her child."

THERE WAS A PRINCE waiting for her in the parking lot of her apartment building after work that day. He looked hot and a bit disheveled, leaning against his rental car under one of the cottonwood trees lining the complex. Of course, since this was Alexi, he looked darn good hot and disheveled.

When she retrieved her purse and stepped into the heat rising from the asphalt parking lot, he walked over.

"I believe the correct saying is 'Hi, honey, how was your day?'" Alexi said, taking her arms and smiling down at her.

"My day was fine," she said, "and don't you dare kiss me right here in front of everyone."

"I don't see a soul."

"They're lurking behind closed miniblinds, so don't think that we're alone."

"You make me—and your neighbors—sound devious."

"I just think that you're going to do whatever you can to put pressure on me."

"I'm only trying to be a nice, regular guy." He leaned closer and her heart skipped a beat. "Am I doing a good job?"

A job. She had to remember that he was very good at being deceitful. He'd fooled his father and the public for days by playing the role of both cowboy, then prince. He was approaching this…situation with his usual dedication. Of course, he could get tired of this role at any moment.

What if he did give up? How would she feel? Her stomach churned when she tried to imagine life without Alexi, now that he'd come back into her life.

"Let's get out of this heat," she said, dismissing her thoughts as quickly as possible. She didn't want to think about Alexi coming and going, showing up in Ranger Springs to disrupt everything, then retreating to his rich and famous lifestyle. Playing the role of daddy until that, too, bored him.

Stop thinking about what might happen, she told herself as they marched up the steps to the second floor.

"So if I were a regular guy, what would we do tonight?"

"Well," she said, putting her key into the lock, "we'd talk about what we did today, maybe beside the pool with a cold drink. Then we'd fix dinner or get something—maybe even at the Dairy Queen or the pizza place—and watch a movie or a television show."

"The pool and a cold one sounds good to me, and I love American pizza. Thick crust, everything but anchovies and onions."

"Did you bring swim trunks?" she asked as she placed her purse and keys on the side table, then kicked off her low-heeled shoes. Her feet were slightly swollen, maybe from the heat, maybe from the baby.

"Not with me, but I can get them from my room."

"I might have an old pair in my apartment. I remember moving some things friends had left around the house."

"I may get jealous if I discover you're in possession of men's clothing."

"Try to control your rage," Kerry answered with enough sarcasm to stop that line of thinking. *On second thought, try to control how much of your clothing you remove...or I may not be able to control myself.*

Her hormones were raging, causing more than morning sickness and tender breasts. Ever since Alexi had returned to town, she'd been craving his touch, his kisses. She didn't know if this was a natural result of the pregnancy or a response to his presence. She wanted him, but couldn't give in to the passion that would only confuse the issues. Sex was not a strong basis for a good marriage...or so she'd always been told.

Probably by someone who wasn't being pursued by a hunky prince who happened to be the father of her baby.

Her apartment seemed much smaller with Alexi inside. "Let me see if I can find the box with the extra clothes, then we can both change."

"Sounds promising."

"Don't get your hopes up. I meant you can change in the bathroom while I use the bedroom."

"Ah, I see," he said, smiling so intimately that she almost changed her mind and pulled him toward the bed.

She found a pair of Hank's old, formerly navy swim trunks in the bottom of a box of miscellaneous stuff she had yet to unpack. Handing them to Alexi, she said, "I know these will fit because they belonged to Hank. We used to take my sisters to a neighbor's pool and he'd change clothes before driving home."

Within a few minutes she'd found her one-piece and put it on. Unfortunately, her tummy had rounded a little in the past few days. She suddenly felt pregnant. Noticeably pregnant. Rubbing her hand over the very slight mound, she wondered whether she'd have a boy or a girl. A brown-haired, blue-eyed miniature of his daddy or a daughter with mischievous eyes and a slight dimple in her cheeks? In six months, she'd know. But would she ever be certain about Alexi's proposal?

When she walked into the living room, Alexi was looking through her CD collection, wearing only the swim trunks and a killer tan.

"You did a lot of sunbathing in Monaco, I see," she said, pulling a plaid shirt around her to keep him from seeing what he'd already seen several times before.

"You've been keeping up with my trips."

"My mother has. I've just heard." She shrugged. She'd looked at the photos and read the captions about Alexi and the rest of the royals, even when her heart was breaking. She'd tried to keep her mother from knowing how she was both fascinated and depressed by the coverage, but when Charlene Jacks had caught her daughter quietly sobbing, she'd put away her prized magazines. "Okay, maybe I noticed a few of the articles she has around the house."

"I went down to Monte Carlo for a charity fundraiser."

"And you went skiing in the Alps, and visited friends in London and flew to Moscow for the opening of an art gallery."

"The artist is a friend of mine. What's wrong with my trips?"

"Nothing's wrong. It's just that they are so common for you. Your lifestyle is so different that people like my mother are amazed. They live through you. Do you know what I've done in the three months since you left? Started a new job, which is nine-to-five, five days a week. I moved into this apartment, I have Saturday-evening dinner with my family, and I occasionally drive to San Marcos to see some college friends. Those trips consist of a casual meal and maybe a movie or a little shopping, if my budget allows. That's my life, while you're flying to Moscow for the opening of an art gallery. I'm pretty certain I couldn't afford the frame on one of those originals!"

"Is money really the issue, Kerry? Because if it is, when we are married, my money will be your money. You won't have to work unless you want to, and if you do, you can select a position that will give you some added perks."

"What kind of perks?" she asked suspiciously. She

hoped he wasn't talking about government kickbacks, which she'd read about in other countries.

"We have many important functions, such as charities and my ongoing efforts to promote tourism in Belegovia. With your knowledge of business and your position as princess, you could make a difference in the lives of many people."

"I'm not a princess."

"You could be. All you have to do is say yes."

She wasn't sure accepting his proposal would make her feel any more like a princess than putting on a rhinestone tiara and dressing up in a pink froufrou dress. Not that she'd ever done either one of those things. But how did one feel like a princess, other than being born to the position or knowing one day you'd marry a prince? The contessa obviously didn't have any trouble feeling like royalty, from what Kerry could tell from the photos of her with Alexi.

"Let's go sit by the pool and have a cold drink. In a half hour or so I'll call in for a pizza to the new place that delivers."

"You know I'm going to keep asking," he said, following her into the kitchen.

"About the pizza?" she asked as she opened the refrigerator and took out one of the beers she kept for friends and a lemonade for herself.

"No," he said, shaking his head. "About accepting my proposal. We were meant to be together."

"I just don't know how you came to that conclusion."

He picked up the two towels he'd brought from the bathroom as she grabbed her keys and portable phone from the table. "Because of all the people in the world, I ran into you at the truck stop, and you thought I was Hank. Of all the people in the world who could have been my double, the one man I resemble lives in your hometown.''

"Okay, I'll give you that one. The two of us running into each other was a wild coincidence.''

"Exactly right. Then, we got along splendidly on our trip, were going to part, but didn't, which resulted in the condom breaking.''

"So you think that was fortune smiling on us? I kind of think it was just an old condom.'' He followed her down the stairs and toward the pool.

"No, I believe it was fate that put you and me in that abandoned apartment over the café.''

"That was the paparazzi,'' she reminded him as she pushed open the squeaky iron gate surrounding the pool.

"Where is your sense of destiny? Your flare for romance?'' he asked with a dramatic sweep of his hand.

"I'm a financial analyst, not a poet,'' she said, holding back a smile as she selected two lounge chairs nearby.

"And then there's the timing of your big news.''

"I didn't contrive anything. You eavesdropped on my conversation with Gwendolyn.''

"Yes, but what about the timing? That was right before I was going to announce my engagement to Contessa di Giovanni. What if I had found out a day or two later?''

Kerry shrugged out of her shirt and sat on the lounge chair. "Good question. What if you had found out after the announcement? What *would* you have done then?'' she asked, squinting up at him through the late-afternoon sun. ''And while we're at it, doesn't it strike you as slightly irresponsible that you flew off at the drop of a hat and abandoned the poor contessa?''

Chapter Ten

"I did not abandon the contessa," Alexi defended himself. "I explained to her that because of my earlier trip to Texas, I was unable to commit to her at this time. I can't say that she was happy about my decision, but she understands." He took a sip of beer and hoped Kerry understood.

"How very nice for her," Kerry said, pushing her sunglasses down so they hid her eyes. "So she's probably beside the phone right now, waiting for your call."

"I believe she's probably in Paris with friends, hardly pining away for me."

Kerry looked away, apparently watching a middle-aged man swim laps in the pool. Other than him, they were blessedly alone. Finally, she asked, "Does she love you?"

Alexi took a deep breath. How could he explain the relationships of the European nobility? They formed a small, elite group of mostly interrelated people who often had careers and interests far outside their titles. But some lived for the role to which they were born. There was an unspoken bond between them, and sometimes a remarkable competition for greater titles, wealth or prestige.

"The contessa was born to nobility and has moved in the circles of her counterparts in many other countries. She knows how to interact on all social levels. She's beautiful and cultured, but she's not looking for the love of her life. She's looking for the *title* of her life."

"So she wants to marry you because she'll be a princess."

"No, she wants to marry me because someday she would be queen, and our children would become the future rulers."

"That sounds so archaic. And you make her sound so cold and calculating."

"As I've told you, this wasn't a love match. My father picked out a number of young women whom he thought I might like. He realized I wasn't going to marry a woman I couldn't stand. After all, he wants grandchildren. And he wants the royal line continued."

Kerry shook her head. "All this talk about royal heirs and princesses and queens has me overwhelmed. I can't believe you think I would fit into this 'small, elite group' of people who have these remarkable lifestyles that are written about in magazines."

"The paparazzi can be annoying, but you'll learn to live around them."

"What about all your peers? They wouldn't accept me."

He reached over and took her hand. "Kerry, my darling, you will someday be a queen. You are carrying the royal heir. Of course they will accept you.

To do otherwise would be to commit social suicide. Besides, there are many kind and relatively 'normal' royals you would truly enjoy.''

She pulled her hand from his and shook her head. ''This is too much for me to think about right now. I'm going for a swim.''

Alexi settled back on his chaise and watched her walk resolutely to the side of the pool, crouch and dive into the deep end. She was running away from his words, but she was at least thinking about marrying him. Otherwise, she wouldn't be worrying about being accepted by his peers.

He had to find a way to expose her to his life, although he didn't want to rush her. She'd had so much occur in her life in the past three months that he felt guilty pushing her. But they didn't have all the time in the world. He didn't want to walk down the aisle with her, worrying whether she was going into labor before they said their ''I do's.''

He placed his beer on the concrete and pushed up from the chaise. With a smile, he walked to the side of the pool and dove in. The cool water surged over him, enveloping him in a pleasant cocoon. He loved to swim; he'd been in competition when he was younger, before his own life had become disrupted by the restoration of Belegovia's monarchy. Kerry would adapt; she was both a fighter and a pragmatist.

With sure, strong strokes he caught up with her, allowing himself the luxury of looking his fill of her toned muscles, soft skin and alluring curves. He wanted her—in his bed and beside him on the throne when they were both older, with their children secure in their heritage. He knew he didn't always get what he wanted; he wasn't entitled to a happily-ever-after life any more than a taxi driver, a teacher or a business executive.

But he could try his best to get Kerry to be his wife. His princess. And someday, a country's queen.

ALL DURING DINNER, which consisted of pizza, bread sticks and salad, served at her small table in the equally small dining room of her apartment, Kerry thought about Alexi's description of his world. Or, more specifically, the people in his world. They were so different than the folks she knew. Thelma Rogers, owner and editor of the *Springs Gazette,* wasn't anything like the European paparazzi. The "rulers" of Ranger Springs were neighbors and even friends elected to the city council, served as police chief, or provided other city services. And the social elite weren't looking for titles and personal legacies. Well, at least most of them weren't. There were a few people who thought they were a little better than ordinary people, but not many. And besides, everyone knew who they were and worked around their foibles.

She couldn't imagine how a little nobody like her would fit into the social scene in Europe. Despite what Alexi said, she knew they'd laugh her right across the Atlantic. He just wanted her to accept his proposal, so he was telling her things would work out. Maybe he even believed it, but she couldn't. How could she, when she couldn't imagine what life might be like inside an actual palace?

Maybe she should talk to Gwendolyn. She'd lived in Alexi's world, and she was honest, if guarded, in answering questions.

"What are you doing tomorrow?" she asked Alexi after toying with her salad and breaking off pieces of bread stick.

"I thought I'd see if Gwendolyn was busy. We might have lunch. Could you join us?"

Drat. He was going to talk to their friend first. "Hmm, I don't think so. I may have a meeting."

"You're not eating your pizza. You need to make sure you're taking in enough calories."

Kerry chuckled. "That sounds a lot like you're trying to fatten me up."

"I just want you and the baby to be healthy."

"I'm really healthy, except for the morning sickness. And I get sleepy during the day. I think my symptoms are getting better, though. I'm going to ask the doctor. I have an appointment on Thursday."

"Really? I'd like to go with you."

"You would?"

"Yes. I don't feel very involved in the pregnancy at the moment, and going with you to talk to the doctor would help ground me. Besides, I have a few questions I'd like to ask."

"Alexi, I'm not sure I'm ready for that. If you go with me, then people will notice. They'll ask questions that I'm not sure I'm willing to answer."

"We have to address this issue soon. You'll be showing before long, even if you don't agree to marry me quickly. Like we talked about earlier, I want everyone to know the baby is mine, not some unnamed man's or your Hank McCauley's."

"I know." And she did understand. Back in her mother's day, women were pregnant and men weren't involved. Now a "couple" was pregnant. She'd heard men on television say "When we went into labor." She didn't know about this "we" stuff; from her perspective, she was the one with morning sickness and she was the one who'd be pushing and groaning in about six months.

"I'll think about it, okay. I'm going to a doctor in San Marcos because my regular doctor is Amy Wheatley, or Amy Phillips, I should say. She's the wife of my employer, so I didn't think that was a good idea at first."

"Why? Were you ashamed that you'd gotten pregnant?"

"No, but I wasn't ready for anyone to know, either."

Alexi reached over and covered her hand. "Kerry, I want to be involved. Let me go with you. Let me ask my questions and be assured that you and the baby are healthy."

She looked down at their hands and sighed. "I'll think about it." Her list of things to consider just kept getting longer.

As KERRY sat next to Alexi in the waiting room of her OB/GYN, she wondered how her life had gotten so out of control. First, she'd run off with him. Then she'd made love with him. Now she was actually considering his proposal—or, she should say, ultimatum—that they marry quickly.

Monday beside the pool, she'd considered their conversation more of an intellectual argument. A speculation. Somehow, in the course of defending her position, she'd actually started thinking about the logistics of marriage to a prince. The problems she would face, not the obstacles she *might* have to overcome *if* she were to accept his propoal.

And then on Tuesday she'd agreed he could go with her to the doctor's appointment, even after she'd decided that was a bad idea. It was in San Marcos, she told herself, so there wouldn't be much chance of being observed. And he could dress down, so he looked like Hank. And this was Alexi's baby.

With a sigh, she shifted on the seat. She needed to talk to Gwendolyn. She'd called her friend immediately, but they hadn't been able to get together since Wendy, as Hank called her, was going with him to pick up a horse on Tuesday. That had left both Kerry and Alexi without their mutual friend, so they'd spent the evening together, eating stir-fry from Kerry's kitchen and watching a movie she'd rented.

She glanced around the waiting room. A thirtyish woman was reading a magazine and a middle-aged woman was staring at the fish in the built-in aquarium. Kerry leaned close to Alexi and whispered, "If we were married and living in the palace, would we have been able to cook a meal and watch a movie?"

He looked at her with a gleam in his blue eyes. "Yes. My suite has a small kitchen, similar to one of your suites hotels. But if that isn't enough, it can be enlarged. And I also have a parlor, a small dining room, two bedrooms and two baths."

"Oh." So maybe there was room for her. Maybe one of the bedrooms could be converted into a nursery.

"Of course, the easiest way for you to judge whether you'd be comfortable with major renovations is to come back home with me."

"I—"

The door to the exam rooms opened. "Ms. Jacks?" the nurse called.

Kerry sprang up. "Right here." Alexi rose also, but she motioned him down. "You can't come in for the exam."

"Why not? I thought that's why I was here."

"Just…just because!"

"Would you like to wait in the doctor's office?" the nurse asked. "That way you can both talk to Dr. Norman."

"Okay, you can talk to the doctor after I'm finished with the exam," Kerry conceded. "I'm just not ready for you to go into the room with me. It's kind of embarrassing."

Alexi sighed, but followed them behind the door. The nurse showed him into the office, while leading her on to the exam room.

Kerry undressed, thinking about Alexi and how he might react to her increasingly sensitive breasts and slightly rounded tummy. Thinking about how good he'd looked Monday at the pool. She'd loved the excuse to touch him, even briefly, when they were in the water together.

She waited for the doctor for what seemed like forever, but in actuality was only ten minutes. She'd had the exam a month ago and knew she'd be having a lot more in the next months, but this time felt different. This time Alexi was in the other room, wondering what was going on, feeling left out.

He wanted to be a father. He wanted this child. She sighed, turning her head to the side and closing her eyes.

"Are you okay?" Dr. Norman asked when she finished the pelvic exam.

"I'm fine. I was just wondering if you're going to do the test for the baby's heartbeat."

"Yes, in just a minute."

"Would you call in Alexi? He's in your office. He wanted to be involved, but I told him I didn't want him in for the exam."

The doctor pressed the intercom and advised her nurse. Dr. Norman prepared the equipment, and within a few minutes Alexi was in the room.

"Is everything all right?" he asked, his forehead puckered with worry.

"I'm fine," Kerry said. "I thought you might want to hear the baby's heartbeat."

"I'd love to hear the baby's heartbeat," he said, holding her hand and gazing down at her with genuine affection. And maybe something more, like gratitude that she'd included him. Whatever he was feeling, she was glad she'd called him in.

"Thanks for making me bring you with me today," she said while the doctor draped her lower belly and pulled up her gown.

Alexi was such a perfect gentleman that he didn't even look until the doctor turned on a machine and they heard a beeping. After spreading a cold gel, she passed a hand-held device, which looked like a large computer mouse, low over Kerry's tummy, just above the drape, and a strange noise filled the room. Then the rapid, suction-gurgling sound of the heartbeat pulsed loud and clear.

"That's your baby's heartbeat," Dr. Norman said. "Everything sounds fine."

"Great," Kerry said, although she hadn't been worried. She didn't suppose Alexi's child would have the audacity to have an irregular heartbeat. Of course, if he or she were anything like the daddy, the baby might give them a reason to worry just for the heck of it.

"Amazing," Alexi whispered. He cleared his throat, then asked, "Are you sure there's just one heartbeat? Because that sounded a bit confusing to me."

Dr. Norman laughed. "Yes, there's just one baby, unless they are coordinating their rhythms."

"When could we know the sex of the baby?"

"Depending on the test, almost anytime now."

"Do you want to know?" Kerry asked.

"I don't know. Do you?" Alexi answered.

"I don't think so. Does it matter?"

Alexi thought about it for a moment, then said, "No, I don't think so."

Dr. Norman smiled. "Why don't we have the daddy wait in my office while you get dressed?"

As soon as Alexi left the room, the doctor turned to Kerry. "Is that the prince who was here about three months ago?" For a forty-something woman who had family pictures on her desk and credenza, she sounded a bit awestruck. Kerry had noticed he had that effect on women.

"Yes, he is. I guess you can put two and two together and know that he didn't spend all his time giving speeches and shaking hands."

Dr. Norman smiled. "I suppose not." She folded her arms across her chest. "Well, congratulations.

I've never had a prince as an expectant father before.''

Kerry smiled weakly. ''Believe me, he can be very stubborn, extremely persistent and quite frustrating. But I think he's worth it.''

ALEXI HAD SO MUCH to consider on the drive back to Ranger Springs. His mind overflowed with the image of Kerry lying on the table, her rounded abdomen exposed but all other parts strategically draped. The sound of their baby's heartbeat pounded in his memory; he couldn't believe that something still so tiny could produce such amazing noise.

And then Kerry and the doctor had joined him in the office, explaining the changes Kerry's body was going through. He knew little about pregnant women. If he hadn't exposed himself—and Kerry—to speculation, he would have checked a book out of the library since Ranger Springs had no bookstores. Thanks to Dr. Norman, he now possessed several pamphlets to guide him through the pregnancy, plus he had a new appreciation of the wonder of carrying a baby.

''I can't wait for the sonogram next month,'' he said as he turned onto the road that led to Kerry's apartment.

She smiled back shyly and he felt the intimacy of the exam room flooding back. She'd included him on this trip to the physician; did that mean she was softening toward him in other ways?

''Tell me more about your country,'' she said, startling him out of his speculation.

''What do you want to know?''

"Well, let's say that I were a tourist who was going to visit. What would I see when I got off the plane?"

His heart raced as he slowed for a stop sign. Could she be thinking about visiting Belegovia? Could she be thinking of moving there?

"The airport was built for military aircraft on a former Soviet air base, but was renovated recently. We tried to incorporate many of the innovations going on in U.S. airports, like shopping and dining options, so people might visit there even without traveling by plane. Recently we added additional security, so the airport is safe by any standard."

"What about when I leave the airport?"

"You'll see rolling hills and small farms, then apartments and homes closer together mixed with industrial shops and small businesses. The airport is about twenty kilometers out of the capital, so the drive is a nice one.

"Inside the city, there is still much to be done. Many of the buildings remain vacant and in need of repair, but I have hopes that some of the warehouses will eventually be converted into lofts such as in the trendy areas of your big cities. We are trying to attract people back to the country who might have fled, like my father, when the Soviets took over."

"I see. You have a lot of plans, don't you?"

"Yes, I do. I never really understood how much needed to be done until I set foot on Belegovia soil. Somehow, my 'job' as prince didn't seem real until I was there."

"I know exactly what you mean," Kerry said, staring down at her clasped hands. "I've been wondering what role your family might play, what they do for the country.''

As Alexi pulled to a stop, he took in her white knuckles, furrowed brow and pinched lips. His heart raced again. ''Do you mean what I think you mean? That you want to go to Belegovia? That you want to see for yourself?''

''I don't see how I can make a decision about moving there unless I see it for myself.''

''Kerry,'' he said softly, unhooking his seat belt and moving closer. He slid his hand along her jaw and turned her face to look at him. ''You're serious, aren't you? You're thinking of marrying me and moving to my country.''

She closed her blue-gray eyes briefly, then looked at him. ''I realized today that the life we've created together will bind us in many ways. I can't keep our baby from knowing his or her heritage, both in Texas and Belegovia. And I can't deny that I've never stopped wanting you.''

''I never stopped wanting you, either, even when I knew that I couldn't offer you what my heart said you needed.''

''I didn't want to be a princess.''

''But that is exactly what I must offer. Can you be happy as my queen?''

''I honestly don't know, Alexi. But I need to go to your world. You've come to mine. You've proved you can be a regular guy, just as I asked. Now I have to see if I can be something besides a small-town girl.''

Chapter Eleven

The plane landed gently, but even so, Charlene Jacks held on to Kerry's hand so tightly, she thought a few fingers might be broken.

"It's okay, Mom. We're on the ground now."

"Oh, thank goodness. I didn't mind the flying, but those takeoffs and landings are nerve-racking."

Alexi leaned forward and patted her mother's hand. "You did splendidly, Mrs. Jacks. Before long, you'll be a seasoned world traveler."

"Yes, you did marvelously well," Gwendolyn added, sitting next to Alexi in the plush leather seats. "Soon you'll be flying back and forth between Belegovia and Texas with ease."

Kerry had asked Gwendolyn to accompany them so she'd have someone familiar at the palace besides her mother, who thought marrying Alexi was a "done deal." Gwendolyn could also help her with the transition of living inside the palace, since she'd gone though a similar scenario when she moved from England to Belegovia several years ago. Of course, Gwendolyn was a member of the British aristocracy, the daughter of an earl, and not a small-town Texas woman who'd taken ten years to finish college because she worked as a truck stop waitress.

"I'm not sure I want to fly around that much," Charlene Jacks, who had never been farther than New Orleans, said.

"We'll see," Kerry said, not wanting to encourage anyone to believe she was going to live in Belegovia with Alexi. Maybe things would work out. She might not like his country; his family or his people might not like her. But she had to try, for herself and the sake of their baby.

"It will take a few minutes to power down and get the steps in place. Our captain will let us know when we can depart. Until then, you might want to get your personal belongings together. I have a feeling there will be a crowd at the airport to welcome us home."

Home. Alexi's home, not hers. Or at least Belegovia had been his home for almost half his life. He'd lived an eclectic lifestyle, from England to the United States and now Belegovia, apparently fitting in just fine no matter where he settled. She only hoped that she'd fit in half as well. If she decided to stay...

She'd never expected to leave Ranger Springs. All of her family lived there. Many of her friends were in the area, from San Marcos to Wimberley to Austin. She'd always wanted to travel, but never expected to settle someplace else. Never thought she'd have to learn a foreign language or pretend to be someone she wasn't.

At least her boss, Grayson Phillips, had been understanding. He'd granted a two-week leave of absence so she could make this trip...and possibly make a decision that would affect her life forever.

With a sigh, she gathered her magazine and paperback, put everything back in her tote bag and dug in her makeup case for lipstick and powder. She wanted to look her best for Alexi's countrymen. She wasn't even sure if there was a local television station in Belegovia, but if there was, she didn't want his people to see a Texas bumpkin stumble off the royal jet.

"Will there be press outside?" she asked.

"Perhaps," Gwendolyn answered. "If there are, just look ahead and keep walking. Don't stop, don't respond to their questions."

Kerry put a hand over her stomach and exhaled.

"You'll be fine, sweetie," her mother said.

Kerry smiled. Now that they'd landed, Charlene Jacks had regained control. She was going to reassure her daughter no matter what the situation.

Suddenly the door of the plane opened and a burst of warm, fragrant air rushed into the cabin...along with a flock of imaginary butterflies that seemed to settle in Kerry's stomach. She'd gotten over morning sickness, but she'd never faced this kind of situation.

"Hold my hand," Alexi said calmly, "and smile if you can. No one knows why you are here. No one knows about the baby. Just be calm and you'll get through this fine. Before long we'll be inside the limousine and you'll get to look at the sights on the way to the palace."

"Royal jets, crowds of admirers, limousines and palaces. I think I'm going to hyperventilate."

"No, you're not. You're going to hold your head up and act like you belong here," Gwendolyn advised.

Alexi framed her face with his strong, warm hands.

"Let me give you something else to take your mind off all these superficial trappings," he said softly before he kissed her.

His mouth devoured hers, gently and sweetly, making her forget everything but his minty taste and firm lips. She kissed him back, dropping her tote bag and wrapping her arms around his waist.

Far too briefly he ended the kiss, breathing heavily. He smiled and her heart skipped a beat. "Ready?"

She nodded, not trusting her voice.

"I'm ready," her mother said, gathering her purse close to her body as though a horde of Belegovian purse snatchers waited outside the jet. "I'm ready to meet the king. Just imagine—a real, live king!"

Kerry smiled at Alexi, and together they escorted royal watcher Charlene Jacks off the jet and into the bright sunlight, clicking cameras and cheering crowd.

ALEXI RELAXED into the plush rear seat of the limousine, enjoying the feel of Kerry beside him, leaning forward to look out at the passing scenery. Her mother perched on the lengthwise seat like a four-year-old at a county fair. Gwendolyn sat opposite Mrs. Jacks, already on her cell phone to the palace. Old habits died hard; she was probably making sure that Kerry's welcome was complete. He couldn't keep a slight smile off his face, and he didn't even try.

For the first time in longer than he could remember, he felt as though his life was coming together. He felt at peace with his role as prince. His father's edict to marry no longer hung over his head like a heavy shroud, and the future looked bright with Kerry beside him.

One thing he was certain about: he wouldn't be bored. She brought a vitality to life with her honesty and passion. Her approach to living was so different than what he was accustomed to, at least for most of his adult life. She made him remember his youth, with all the hopes and dreams that made the future exciting.

For the first time, he felt completely comfortable in his role as crown prince. With Kerry by his side and their children someday surrounding them, they would have a good life and help the country of his ancestors achieve its rightful status in the world.

"You seem happy," she commented.

"I am, now that you're here."

"That sounds like a line," she teased.

The smile faded as he reached for her hand. "It's not. I've never been more serious," he said softly. "It's like everything clicked into place when we landed. You were here beside me and I knew things were working out. We're going to have a baby we will both love, and even your mother is getting the vacation of her dreams, including getting a 'real live king' as an in-law."

"Only if I decide to marry you."

He grinned at that piece of foolishness. "Of course you will. You'll love my country and the people will love you."

She took a deep breath and gazed out the window. "I hope you're right."

He placed his arm around her shoulders and hugged her close. "I know I am. This is going to be wonderful."

KERRY SMILED at Alexi's confident comment, but she didn't feel nearly as assured as he did. Of course, she didn't know his father, his country or his friends. Maybe they would accept her, despite her small-town, working-class Texas background. Maybe they'd find her "quaint" rather than assuming she was a gold-digging waitress who'd gotten pregnant to catch a prince.

Oh, Lord, she hoped so. She really didn't want to read any negative press accounts of her arrival in Belegovia, although she was sure someone would make tacky comments and engage in rampant speculation. Her imagination made her stomach clench more than the motion of the jet or the limo. She'd just gotten over her morning sickness, but the feeling was coming back big-time with every mile—or kilometer—closer to the palace.

"Oh, Kerry, look," her mother said, breaking into her queasy musings. "The buildings are so old and pretty, just like a postcard. And the trees! There are so many, and they're so tall and green."

"Many different types of evergreens grow in Belegovia," Alexi informed them, "plus several of the deciduous trees you're used to. In the fall, the foliage is quite beautiful, much like Boston's."

"Just think, Kerry. You'll get to see real changes in the seasons. I'll bet you even have snow in the winter."

Alexi smiled. "Yes, we do."

"There are some things more important than the climate and scenery."

"I know that, sweetie, but isn't it a nice bonus that you'll have a beautiful country?"

"If I stay here," she reminded her mother.

"Of course you'll stay. You and Alexi are crazy about each other, and you have the baby to consider."

Kerry was about to say something to set her mother straight—if she could just think of the right words—when the limo turned off the more modern highway onto an older, narrower road.

They drove between brick-stuccoed and stone houses and shops, past awnings that covered fresh fruits and vegetables on narrow shelves, and beneath a mossy stone arch that looked as though it had been created in the Stone Age. Iron-railed balconies graced some of the buildings, while other buildings sported signs in both English and Belegovian, naming pubs and shops.

The limo took up most of the narrow street, forcing pedestrians and people on bicycles and motorbikes to either side of the road. They stared with interest, not resentment, into the dark-tinted windows.

At least they weren't rioting in the streets, Kerry thought. Of course, they hadn't found out yet that their prince had brought a Texas truck stop waitress to their history-rich country to be a princess. Perhaps if Gwendolyn issued a very tactful press release, she could put a good spin on the situation.

"Oh, Kerry, isn't it beautiful? Just like one of those travel specials on cable TV."

"It's very quaint and interesting," Kerry answered, one part of her wanting to stay safely inside the limo forever, another part wanting to open the door and say hello to the regular people—folks she had more in common with than the ones waiting for her at the palace.

As if he were reading her mind, Alexi said, "We'll be at the palace in just a few minutes. Koslow's Arch marks the entrance to the old city. It was built around 1650, and survived two world wars and numerous uprisings."

"That's amazing. There are a few missions in Texas going back that far, but they're mostly rubble," Kerry said.

Then the limo turned again, crossing a stone bridge over a narrow stream. Or maybe it was a moat. The palace loomed large and tall, constructed of blocks of stone covered with ivy and anchored in flowering bushes and trees pruned into decorative shapes. Leaded windows gleamed in the sunlight and reflected the puffy white clouds floating high overhead.

"Merciful heavens," her mother whispered. "Will you look at that? Why, it's prettier than Buckingham Palace."

"We did quite a bit of restoration on the palace. The Soviets had used it for their government center, so it was fairly well maintained. However, they'd installed lower acoustic ceilings and new walls, so we had to take it back to nineteenth-century splendor."

Kerry felt her breathing quicken and instinctively placed a hand on her stomach. Breathe deeply, she told herself, afraid that she'd hyperventilate and faint in front of Alexi's father.

"This gives a whole new meaning to 'meeting the family,'" she said in a shaky voice.

"Everything will be fine," Alexi told her as the limo pulled to a stop inside the courtyard. "I have a very good feeling about this."

She wished she did. At the moment, she alternated

between numb and terrified—and she hadn't even gotten out of the limo yet.

Maybe she should just stay here.

"Is that the king?" her mother asked, squinting against the sunlight and probably wishing she'd worn her glasses. Kerry noticed a snowy-haired man in a well-cut but severe black suit standing beside the huge carved door.

Alexi chuckled. "No, that's the butler, Radko."

Kerry groaned. Would she ever feel comfortable around butlers who looked like kings, living in palaces and being driven in limos?

"I HAD NO IDEA your story was so romantic," Ariel Ladislas sighed, one hand propping up her chin. At twenty-five, she was the youngest and obviously the most idealistic sibling. She was also charming and beautiful…and tall, although Kerry didn't feel jealous of Alexi's sister as she usually did with women who could pass for models. Ariel was just too friendly and nice.

Alexi had told them how Kerry had mistaken him for Hank, then they'd gone on the road trip and visited her relatives. He'd skipped over the parts where they'd stayed together at the B and B and made love in the apartment above the Four Square Café, but he had told them she was pregnant. Of course, being Alexi, he'd said it much more politely, emphasizing that they'd have a niece or nephew next February.

And, of course, his brother and sister assumed Kerry was going to marry Alexi. The king hadn't looked convinced. Or maybe he was just being hopeful that his future daughter-in-law wouldn't be from Ranger Springs, Texas.

"You did the right thing," Andrew, Alexi's twenty-eight-year-old brother, stated. He was more serious than Ariel, a little bit less handsome than Alexi—in Kerry's opinion—but equally welcoming to both her and her mother.

"You know me, brother," Alexi said with a smile. "Marrying Kerry is what I want, and it's a bonus that it's the right thing to do."

"Obligation is important," King Wilheim stated. He was an older version of Alexi, tall, darker-haired, and very stately. Very British, even though he was the Belegovian king. Apparently, living in England from his teenage years to middle age had an enormous impact on his personality, because he was the prototypical upper-class Brit: cool, reserved and highly educated.

He wasn't exactly the warm-and-fuzzy father-in-law Kerry had envisioned when she'd thought about getting married to some then nameless, faceless man. She'd always thought she'd marry a Texan and she'd have lots in common with her husband's father.

What did she have in common with King Wilheim? She couldn't even think of a topic of conversation that didn't sound lame!

"Family is important, too," her mother said, breaking the silence after the king's statement. "You have a lovely family, King Wilheim."

"It would be more complete were my wife here to welcome you," he said with barely disguised bitterness. "A wife carries the burden of most social obligations."

"Invite her to visit," Alexi advised. "She'd come if you asked."

"She knows where we are," the king said. And that seemed to put an end to that topic of conversation. And clearly stated his views on the importance of a suitable wife.

"Anyway," Ariel said, jumping up to refill everyone's wine glass but Kerry's. She was drinking bottled water at the advice of Gwendolyn. "I think Gwendolyn will be able to make everyone understand what a love match this is. The fact that there's going to soon be a royal heir will be icing on the cake."

"My thoughts exactly," Alexi said.

"Any statements will need to be cleared through my personal office," King Wilheim said. He waved off more wine, then stood. "If you will excuse me, I have an early-morning meeting with the finance minister." He turned toward Kerry's mother. "It was a pleasure meeting you, Mrs. Jacks. I hope you enjoy your visit."

Then he turned to Kerry. With a perfectly emotionless expression, he said, "Good night, Ms. Jacks. Have a pleasant evening."

She imagined he was thinking his evening would be much more pleasant if she'd fly back to Texas.

After the king left, Kerry said, "I should probably be turning in also. We've had a busy day."

"And an exciting one," her mother added. "I sure never thought I'd be in the private parlor of the royal family, sipping wine after a formal dinner."

"Father likes to use the good china and crystal," Ariel said, wrinkling her nose. "He'd throw a fit if he knew I use paper plates most evenings when I'm in my apartment. I got used to them in college and can't break the habit.''

Kerry smiled. Ariel was so down-to-earth. She'd make a great sister-in-law. And Andrew was nice, too, although he wasn't as naturally friendly as his sister. But Kerry was afraid that the king would never come around. He just didn't seem to like her, or at least not as a bride for his son.

''I'll walk you to your room,'' Alexi offered. ''If you don't mind, Mrs. Jacks.''

''No, of course not. I'm sure someone can guide me in the right direction after I finish this last glass of wine.''

Kerry leaned over and kissed her mother's cheek. ''Have sweet dreams, Mama.''

''Sweetie, this whole trip has been a dream come true.''

Kerry smiled, glad that she'd given her mother this gift. Even if things didn't work out with Alexi, they would have wonderful memories of their trip to Belegovia.

''Good night, Ariel, Andrew,'' Kerry said before Alexi took her arm and steered her out the fourteen-foot-tall, carved double doors of the family parlor.

They walked down silent hallways carpeted with long runners that appeared faded with time and were probably at least a hundred years old. Gilt wall sconces cast dim, romantic lighting on the way to the guest bedrooms. Kerry was glad Alexi was walking with her, because she wasn't sure she could find her room without his help. Tomorrow she'd try to get her bearings.

"Gwendolyn is preparing a press release announcing our engagement," Alexi said.

"Your father isn't going to be happy about that."

"Don't worry about him. He doesn't take well to sudden change, but he'll come around."

Kerry wasn't sure about that, but Alexi knew his father better than she did. If she decided to marry him, which she was leaning toward at the moment, she hoped he was right.

"What do you have planned for us tomorrow?" she asked as they went down another hallway.

"I thought you might like to see more of the country than just the airport and the city. We can take my car and go for a drive. I know a wonderful little country inn where we can have dinner."

"That sounds wonderful. My mother will be excited."

Alexi stopped in the dim corridor. "Actually, I thought your mother might like to see some other sights. I've asked Ariel to take her to a few cultural events and a dressmaker so she can be fit for the dinner on Saturday night."

"Oh." So she and Alexi would be alone tomorrow. Well, that was an interesting idea.

He took her shoulders in his hands. "You know I'd like to join you inside the guest suite, but I think I'd better say good-night out here."

"That would be best," she whispered.

He stepped close and lowered his head. This time she was ready for his kiss. This time she rose on tiptoe to meet him halfway. He tasted of sweet German wine and Alexi's unique flavor of male self-confidence and bold determination. His tongue thrust and retreated and she matched him stroke for stroke until they both breathed hard and fast, and clung tightly together even after the kiss ended.

"That was some good-night kiss," she whispered against his neck.

"Just one of many we can share if you'll say yes."

Kerry rested her forehead against the hard wall of his chest. "Don't pressure me. I just got here. I'm keeping an open mind about your country."

"I know." He sighed. "I just want to marry you so much."

"And your father doesn't want us to marry, maybe almost as much."

"No, that's not true. Don't focus on the negative. He'll come around once he gets to know you better."

Kerry nodded, not knowing what else to say. If she told Alexi that she hoped his father changed his mind, then she'd be admitting that she wanted to get married. Which she wasn't ready to say out loud, especially to a man who was pressuring her to make the commitment. If she said it didn't matter, then she'd be blowing off his proposal as if she didn't care.

"What time should I be ready in the morning?"

"How about ten o'clock? I think that will give you time to have breakfast and try on some of the clothes Milos has arranged for you."

"Oh, the clothes. I'd almost forgotten."

"I think you'll be pleasantly surprised. Although Milos is my valet, he has a certain flair for fashion."

"I trust you and Milos not to make me look like a reject from the Oscar ceremony."

"I promise, you won't make anyone's worst-dressed list in the gowns he's selected."

She smiled. "Good-night, Alexi."

Chapter Twelve

"So about the king," Kerry said the next morning to Gwendolyn after Milos Anatole and Mrs. Tamburg, the dressmaker, had spread out two ball gowns and several other dresses on the bed and left to get accessories. "Alexi says he'll eventually like me, but I'm not so sure."

"The king is very traditional," Gwendolyn said carefully, as though she was weighing every word. "He was intent on Alexi marrying one of the young ladies he had chosen."

"Yes, I heard all about the contessa from Hank, Alexi and even my mother. Alexi was going to announce his engagement to her, and instead he flew to Texas."

Gwendolyn looked up from a claret-colored silk gown with subtle beading on the bodice. "What did you expect? You are carrying his child."

"I know, but it seems a little...cold. I mean, I asked Alexi about the contessa, but he said she was only after a title. That she wasn't in love with him."

"I believe that's right. She's cordial and very polite, but hardly full of passion."

"Still, she might care for Alexi."

"Kerry, I seriously doubt that she cares even a fraction as much as you do."

She was saved from any more comments when Milos and the dressmaker entered with shoes, purses, fringed and beaded shawls, and some boxes she suspected contained lingerie. She didn't even want to think about Alexi's valet picking out underwear!

"Have you thought about what issues you might want to address if you marry Alexi?" Gwendolyn asked as all the clothing and accessories were sorted on the bed.

"Issues?"

"The royals always have projects, much like first ladies in your United States. Literacy, mental illness, childhood nutrition and so forth."

"Oh." Kerry frowned. She hadn't thought about her role except to give birth to the heir and attend state functions. But she would have to have something to do. After seeing the palace, she knew she wouldn't be keeping house or shopping for groceries.

"I'll have to give it some thought, if I decide to say yes, that is."

"Of course," Gwendolyn said, shaking the folds out of an iridescent lavender dress that looked sophisticated but had a fairy-tale quality Kerry found appealing. A subtle gathering of fabric under the strapless bodice would help disguise her tummy.

"You'll have some time," Gwendolyn said. "No one will expect decisions right away."

Again, she felt the pressure building as she stared at a beautiful pair of high-heeled sandals. Everyone wanted something—a princess daughter, a princess bride, a mother, a career woman. Even the king wanted something, or namely, someone else to be his son's wife. The stress must have shown on her face, because when she looked up, Gwendolyn wore a sympathetic expression.

"Milos, would you and Mrs. Tamburg excuse us?"

Within seconds Alexi's valet and the dressmaker were closing the door behind them, leaving Kerry alone with perhaps the one woman who could understand her dilemma.

"Now, tell me exactly what's wrong. And no more bosh about feeling sorry for the poor contessa."

Kerry dropped the shoes on the bed and sank onto a silk moiré slipper chair. "I'm not sure I should marry Alexi, for several reasons, one of which is painfully obvious," she said, sweeping her arm around the room. "I don't belong here, and the king knows it."

"Don't be absurd. You belong by Alexi's side. I knew that from the moment I saw the two of you together."

"Love doesn't conquer all."

"And why not? You can learn to be a princess. After all, Hank learned to be a prince in just one day! You'll bring a breath of fresh air into this palace and the country. Plus, you'll be adding some desperately needed genes to the rather limited pool of European aristocracy."

Kerry smiled, but couldn't quite manage a laugh. "But what about Alexi? I have to tell you, friend to friend, that I have some doubts about his ability to be a good husband and father."

"Why?"

"Well, for starters, he ran off with me at the drop of a hat, leaving you to worry about his previous engagements."

"Yes, but I found Hank, so everything worked out just fine."

"That's not the point. Things could have worked out disastrously. We were all lucky that Hank wasn't caught and Alexi covered his...bases with that impromptu press conference."

"Yes, well, all that's true, but surely you're not still angry at him?"

"No, I'm not angry at all, but I think I'm seeing a pattern of behavior."

Gwendolyn pushed aside a cocktail dress and perched on the bench at the foot of the bed. "Alexi does have a history of running off, usually because he's bored. When we were in school together, he would be the model student for months on end, then get a crazy urge to drive to Scotland for the weekend, or cross the channel into France for decent croissants, or gather up several chaps for a game of soccer on the lawn of a girls' school. When he got older and had money, his adventures escalated accordingly, but there was always a reason."

"You see," Kerry said, her voice unsteady and faint, "my father got bored with his family. He used to rant and rave about being tied down, but he'd never left for long. Maybe just a day or two to go drinking, then he'd be home. But one day he just packed up and left for good. Completely sober. He said he didn't want to live in a house full of women—although it was really just my mother and three girls—and he was going off to live like a man should. We never saw him again.''

"But Alexi wouldn't leave you or your baby. He's the most considerate, nicest man I know." She gave a shrug. "And that includes Hank, and you know how much I love him."

"Alexi is very kind and considerate, except when he gets one of his urges to run off. How can I ever trust that he won't disappear someday? Or that he won't run off and find another woman, someone who is more suitable to be a princess than a small-town Texas girl like me?"

Gwendolyn reached over and took her hand. "Because he loves you. I can't imagine him ever hurting you."

"He went back to Belegovia and never called or wrote. Not once."

"He asked me how you were doing," Gwendolyn admitted. "He always wanted to know if you were okay. Did you ever ask him why he didn't call you directly?"

Kerry nodded. "He said he didn't think it was fair, since he didn't feel he could offer me anything."

"See, that's how highly he thinks of you. He didn't want to conduct a clandestine affair. He wanted it all or nothing."

"Then that proves he's marrying me because of the baby. If it weren't for this," Kerry said, rubbing her hand over her stomach, "I'd still be in Texas and Contessa di Giovanni would be engaged to Alexi."

Gwendolyn sighed. "That's all true, but what does it matter? You *are* pregnant with his child. He *has* proposed to you, not to the contessa. And although there are no assurances that he will never run off and desert you like your father did to his family, I can tell you that would be out of character for Alexi."

"He dropped the contessa at the first opportunity."

"Yes, but he never loved her. That, my dear friend, is the difference."

Kerry wiped a tear from the corner of her eye and sighed. "I want to believe you."

"Believe in Alexi," Gwendolyn advised, rising from the bench. "Now, let's get back to work so you won't be late for your auto tour he has planned."

Kerry nodded, but she still wasn't sure. Maybe the only way to know what was best was to listen with her heart, but her father's desertion still hurt, even after all these years. The memory of her mother, crying alone in her bedroom when she didn't think anyone could hear, lingered as a vivid reminder of how deeply a man could hurt the woman he loved.

If Alexi ever left her for someone else, especially someone more suited to be a princess, she would be harmed even more deeply. Because then not only would she mistrust her judgment of him as a person, but she would know, once and for all, that she wasn't cut out to be royalty. That like he'd realized three months ago, she simply wasn't good enough to be his wife.

ALEXI HAD PACKED a picnic lunch and a few other things, just in case he was lucky enough to keep Kerry away from the palace for the whole day. And the whole night. He kept thinking back to their road trip in Texas and remembering the sense of joy and wonder of their first time at that quaint bed-and-breakfast. He couldn't re-create the entire experience, but the country inn he'd selected for their dinner was charming and picturesque, with proprietors who could keep a secret.

Like the crown prince and his pregnant, almost-fiancée.

Alexi pulled his favorite automobile, a vintage Jaguar convertible, to a stop at the rear drive. Kerry stood by Gwendolyn on the stoop, looking petite and adorable in jeans and a yellow cotton sweater, with a matching sweater tied around her neck. Gwendolyn must have helped her with that look; his friend was somewhat obsessed with clothes and always dressed appropriately for the occasion.

She probably had had trouble knowing what to wear for a short road trip on the sly, a picnic lunch and a would-be seduction at a country inn.

"Good morning, ladies," he said as he cut the engine and opened his door. "How was the fitting?" ·

"Splendid," Gwendolyn said, a big smile on her face. That meant something had gone wrong. He'd have to see if Kerry would talk to him about it later.

"Are you ready?" he asked Kerry, reaching for her hand.

She nodded, linking her hand with his, walking down the three steps to the Jag. "Nice car," she said.

"Thank you. It's the perfect auto for a short road trip."

She walked around the shiny green exterior. "Well, it doesn't quite have the character of Delores, and I'm sure those leather seats aren't as cozy as the fake fur from our last road trip, but it'll do."

Alexi smiled and opened the door. At least Kerry

hadn't lost her spunk. Yesterday, she'd been subdued, somewhat in awe of the royal jet, the limo and the palace. Not to mention his siblings and overbearing father. But today she was back to normal.

He hoped she could stay that way—feisty and smart and sexy. He didn't want the role of princess to change her personality.

They headed out of town on a curving road designed just for sports cars. Trees grew right up to the low stone fences that lined many of the roads in Belegovia. Through the trunks he glimpsed white sheep and goats, then golden-brown dairy cows.

"This is beautiful," Kerry said. "It's so green and pretty."

"I'm glad you like the country. Wait until you see the mountains."

As they drove on, past farmhouses and small villages, he sensed Kerry relaxing even more. She soaked up the sun and let her head roll back against the headrest. He wanted to stop the car, lean over and kiss her neck.

Maybe later.

The elevation changed so gradually that unless you knew the hills were slightly steeper, the valleys more shallow, you wouldn't notice. He'd chosen their picnic spot carefully, both for privacy and the view.

"Oh, Alexi, look!"

The mountains rose majestically across a wide valley with a ribbon of water running down the middle. The view always took his breath away, too.

"I love coming here. I thought you might like it."

"I love it. This is the most beautiful view I've ever

seen. It's like the Hill Country in the spring, only bigger and better, and with mountains.''

Alexi smiled and pulled the Jag off the road. Without needing a four-wheel drive vehicle to access the site, the top of the tree-covered hill provided privacy and a terrific view.

Within minutes they had spread the blanket and set out the picnic lunch the chef had personally prepared. Flaky croissants, smoked chicken and marinated vegetable spears, with the chef's special-dipped tiny éclairs for dessert, made up their menu.

''I'm seeing some definite advantages of being a prince,'' Kerry said, nibbling on a carrot stick. ''And I can tell your sister didn't pack this, because there are no paper plates.''

''No, Ariel didn't help, but she would have if I'd mentioned it. As you can tell, she's the true romantic of the family.''

Kerry leaned forward and teased his lips with the carrot stick. ''I think you're pretty romantic, too.''

''Hmm. I'm glad you do. I like being romantic with you.''

''This is really nice, but you know what was the most romantic thing you did?''

''No, I don't think I do.''

''When you cleaned the apartment above the café. Now, that was romantic.''

''So the way to your heart is through a dust rag?''

''I think you've already found the way to my heart.''

His smile faded as he gazed into her eyes. ''Have I?''

She nodded, as though she didn't trust her voice.

"Then will you stay with me tonight? Let me love you as I've wanted to do ever since I left your town three months ago?"

"Won't that cause the tongues to wag at the palace?"

"No, because we'll be at the country inn I was telling you about. It's someplace quiet and secluded. I think you'll like it."

Kerry took a deep breath, all teasing forgotten as she gazed into his eyes. What did she see there? He hoped she saw the truth; he wanted her today and always.

"All right," she whispered. "After all, what road trip would be complete without a romantic rendezvous?"

"You know I want more than one night."

"I know," she said softly. "I know."

THE COUNTRY INN had a name that Kerry couldn't quite pronounce, but Alexi said it translated into "plump chicken roost," which made her laugh. She felt a bit like a plump chicken after the delicious lunch, the hearty dinner of Belegovian classics and the extra pounds she was carrying with the baby.

Not that Alexi seemed to mind, she thought as she watched him carry in what looked like a canvas gym bag. He'd apparently planned ahead. She walked toward him and put her arms around his waist.

"You must have been pretty sure of yourself, with an overnight bag in the car."

"No, just hopeful," he replied, kissing her nose. "I try to always be prepared."

The only time he hadn't been "prepared" was in the apartment over the café. Neither one of them had anticipated making love one last time, so they'd felt lucky to find several condoms in the nightstand drawer.

"You're thinking too much again," Alexi chastised.

She broke from his light embrace and walked across the room, needing some space. "Just about how fate throws us a loop every now and then. We made love thinking we were protected, but I got pregnant anyway. Was that the best or the worst thing that could have happened?"

He followed her to the window, where the sunset appeared much as it did in Texas. Strange how some things were universal.

"I don't know about you, but for me, this baby is the best. The very best, except for one thing."

"What's that?" she asked, leaning back against his chest.

"Being married to the mother," he whispered against her neck. "Marry me, Kerry. I'll do everything possible to make you happy."

She closed her eyes, knowing she had to give him an answer, but also knowing she had to try one more time to be sure.

"I know it's hard to make promises, so I won't ask that of you. Just tell me this, why do you think you won't run away and leave me—us—if you get tired or bored?"

"That's easy. Because everything I want is right here," he said, sliding his hands down her arms, then over her hips, her stomach. She moaned as he caressed her lower, the fire building as hot and fast as before. And then he smoothed one hand over her stomach, where their baby grew, and she knew she had to say yes. If she didn't, she'd always have regrets. She'd always long for this one man.

She might be her mother's daughter, she might make the same mistakes, but she had to try to make a life with this man. Her real-life prince.

"Yes," she whispered, her head falling back against his shoulder, then looked up into his intense blue eyes.

He leaned forward, angled his head and took her lips in a searing kiss while his hands played upon her body, pulling her tight against his arousal. She moaned again as he captured one sensitive breast, then the other, in his skillful fingers.

Quickly he turned her in his arms and kissed her again, pulling her high and tight against him, coaxing her legs around his waist as he carried her to the canopied bed.

"That was a 'Yes, I'll marry you' response, wasn't it?" he asked as he lay her down on the brocade spread.

"Yes, I'll marry you, and yes, I want to make love with you. Please, Alexi, I've waited so long."

He seemed to glow with satisfaction for a brief instant before lowering himself, pressing her deep into the feather mattress. Maybe it was a trick of the light, the fading sunset colors, but she wanted to think she'd truly made him happy in that instant. That she'd pleased her prince in a way no other woman ever had.

And then his hands were easing her cotton sweater higher, baring her stomach. He reached for the clasp of her bra and opened it, exposing her to his hot gaze and nimble fingers. "I want to see all of you, do everything to you, but it's been so long and I want you so much."

"That's okay. We have all night," she whispered. "And right now, I'm as ready as you are."

"I know the books say this isn't harmful to the baby, but are you sure? You're not having any problems, are you?"

"None at all. I'm as healthy as a horse."

"You are as beautiful as a butterfly in springtime. That's how I see you—brightly colored, flying free. Don't ever change, Kerry. Not for me, not for my country. You're perfect just the way you are."

She threw her arms around his neck and held him tight, tears building behind her eyes. He'd told her what she needed to hear, what she'd longed to know.

"Are you crying?" he asked, pulling away to look at her face.

"Just because I'm so happy," she sniffed.

"I want to always make you happy."

"Then love me."

"I do. I do love you."

He finished pulling her sweater off, then her bra, and went to work on her jeans after she kicked off her sandals. While he was still dressed, before she could yank off any of his clothes, he had her completely naked on this bed that appeared to be made for a king.

"You're more beautiful than before," he said softly, running his hand over her rounded abdomen.

"If you want to make me happy, Alexi, then let me watch you take off your clothes. Undress for me, then join me on this bed. I'm getting awfully lonely and restless."

He smiled and stepped back, unbuttoning his shirt with maddening slow moves, then starting work on his chinos. Next came his shoes, which he kicked across the room, making her chuckle. She almost stopped breathing when he eased his briefs down and she saw his arousal. He smiled again, shrugged out of his shirt and placed one knee on the bed.

Instead of joining her, he eased his hands beneath her and picked her up. The feel of his skin against hers made her light-headed with longing. Or maybe she'd forgotten to breathe again. Alexi did that to her.

"What?" she whispered as she nibbled on his neck and locked her legs around his waist again.

"Sheets," he said, then used one hand to pull back the covers. He kissed her hard, moving her down, against his arousal, making her squirm. Then they both descended to the cool, soft cotton, his weight pressing her into the mattress.

The feeling was heavenly. She arched against his fingers, then gasped when he filled her slowly, completely.

"I love you, Alexi," she whispered as her climax began to build, build and then exploded in all the colors of the sunset, all the brightness of the stars.

He gasped her name, then filled her with warmth, with life, holding her so tight she knew he'd never let her go.

THE PALACE HUMMED with a steady stream of workers, from florists to musicians to kitchen staff, all getting the formal dining room ready for the "big dinner," as Kerry preferred to call the celebration Alexi's family had planned. Everyone was coming, Ariel had stated with excitement, while Andrew acknowledged this would be a great opportunity for Kerry to meet the political and social leaders of the country.

She was a nervous wreck. Gwendolyn had done her best to prepare her for the dinner, but Kerry knew she was going to make some big blunder. Something that would cause the whole room to gasp, then grow silent. She could almost hear the whispers.

"She is, after all, from *Texas*."

"What did you expect?"

"I heard she waited tables for a living."

"In a truck stop, of all places!"

Every time she thought about what could go wrong, her stomach clenched with worry. She didn't have time to hyperventilate, though, because Gwendolyn kept her busy with protocol and etiquette. There were numerous fittings for the dress she was wearing tonight, plus she'd spent time with her mother during her fittings for an elegant taupe floor-length silk sheath and matching jacket.

Charlene Jacks was so excited about attending this formal event. She'd reveled in each meeting with the royal family, whether breakfast with Ariel and Alexi, tea with the king or casual contact around the palace. Kerry knew that before the big event tonight she should have told her mother that she'd accepted Alexi's proposal, but there hadn't been a good time. After they'd returned from the country inn, they had been so busy...and she hadn't felt like telling anyone, not even her mother.

When not being pinned, primped, informed or advised by Gwendolyn, Kerry discovered she actually enjoyed the palace and the people. Belegovians were cheerful and warm—unlike their British-raised king—and accepted her at the same time they were intrigued by her accent and mannerisms. Alexi was right; almost everyone spoke English. Of course, eventually she'd have to learn their language.

Their child would learn Belegovian, she thought, pressing her hand to her tummy and smiling. The baby became more real every day, especially since Alexi reveled in becoming a father. He couldn't wait to tell everyone.

"Feeling okay?" Alexi asked, entering her bedroom with a velvet box in one hand.

"Yes, just thinking," she said with a smile.

"I have something for you to wear tonight." He held out the box, then covered it with his hand. "One thing," he said before she reached for it. "It's very old, very traditional and everyone will know my intentions when you wear it tonight."

"Kind of like an engagement ring?"

"Exactly. Except, it's a necklace. It's over a hundred and fifty years old, made for one of my ancestors and worn by every Belegovian royal bride since then."

"Okay. An engagement necklace."

"Only it's not exactly…pretty. I'd hoped my father had left it in England, but he reminded me of it yesterday."

Kerry's smile faded, but then she remembered her friends talking about what odd taste men sometimes had. What women thought was stylish or attractive was often the opposite of what a man would choose. She shrugged. "I'm sure it's not that bad."

Chapter Thirteen

He opened the lid of the purple velvet box. Resting inside was a heavy gold pendant, mermaids enameled in green, purple and creamy white, with heavy pearl drops embellished in diamonds and rubies. In the center was a carved carnelian likeness of someone—probably one of Alexi's female ancestors, surrounded by small diamonds and emeralds.

"Haven't I seen this someplace before? Like maybe in a portrait or a photograph?"

"Yes, I believe more than one of my ancestors sat for their likeness wearing this pendant."

"Now I remember! The one who posed with Queen Victoria was wearing this as a brooch."

"Yes, that's right."

"So Queen Victoria was sitting next to someone wearing this exact piece of jewelry?"

"That's right."

"That is so cool!" she said. "This is a piece of history."

"It's just a piece of jewelry. Not a very pretty one, at that, but it's traditional."

She threw her arms around his neck, startling him

for a moment. Then he responded, pulling her close. "Thank you. It's wonderful. I'll be proud to wear it."

She felt him smile against her hair. "You're welcome. The good news is that I'll buy you a real engagement ring as soon as we can go shopping. Perhaps to Paris or Antwerp. You'll only need to wear the necklace on formal occasions."

"Oh, sure. Paris or Antwerp." She wondered if she'd ever get used to name-dropping cities or designers or fashion centers like she used to say, "I'm going to the outlet mall in San Marcos for some new Levi's."

"Now, there's one more thing I'd like to discuss with you."

"You sound serious."

"This affects our future." He leaned back to gaze into her eyes. "We had such a wonderful time on our short trip to the country that I wondered if you'd like to have a country home. Someplace we could go to escape the palace. Or maybe even live there and visit the palace, at least when we're first married."

"Really? We could do that?"

"Yes, we could. I thought you might be happier in a setting outside the city, since you grew up in a small town. There are several manor homes for sale. We would probably have to renovate, but that might be fun. What do you think?"

She thought he might be worrying about her living in the palace, but that would be a tacky thing to say, so she didn't. Or maybe she was just being too sensitive. After all, Alexi's idea was a good one.

"I think I'd like to have a house of our own, even if it is a part-time residence."

"Splendid. I'll get started on that right away."

KERRY WAS SO NERVOUS by the time she descended the grand staircase for the formal dinner that she felt she might become a butterfly and flit away from all the pressure. Thirty people would be eating dinner in the huge dining room, then afterward there were musicians who would entertain.

The spectacle seemed like something out of one of the historical romances she sometimes read, and she definitely felt like the not-so-innocent country miss who had been courted or seduced by the powerful lord. Only Alexi was more than one of the earls or dukes in those romances. He was a real, live prince. And this wasn't a work of fiction; this was her life. Her new life, in a palace in a foreign country.

Thankful she was wearing gloves with her lavender-purple iridescent gown, she put on her best smile as Alexi introduced her and her mother to the guests. He stood on one side of her, with her mother on his other side, next to Gwendolyn. On Kerry's right stood Ariel and Andrew, who often made amusing observations and kept Kerry from getting too serious about all the dignitaries.

All but a few spoke English, so she could at least talk to them. Although, she couldn't imagine having a lengthy conversation with anyone. After all, what did they have in common?

When she met the Belegovian finance minister, however, Alexi made a point of mentioning she was also in finance at an American company that had several government contracts. Where Alexi had learned that information, she had no idea! But the minister was very polite and spoke to her about the current world financial situation and how interest rates and the bond market impacted her employer's business, and for that she was grateful.

Just as the last few people went through the receiving line, the king departed, then returned with a striking, dark-haired woman. Kerry thought she might be the king's date, but then, he was still married to an English lady, so that seemed unlikely. Surely he wouldn't flaunt a romantic relationship in front of his family and government officials.

"Ms. Jacks, Mrs. Jacks, may I introduce Contessa Fabiana Luisa di Giovanni?"

Kerry felt the blood literally drain from her head. She must appear white as a sheet; her freckles were probably popping out all over her nose and cheeks. Beside her, she felt Alexi tense. He obviously hadn't expected to see his former almost-fiancée at tonight's gathering.

"Ms. Jacks," the contessa said in a heavy accent.

Kerry extended her hand automatically and received a very faint handshake in response. The contessa was as beautiful as Kerry had feared, with luminous dark eyes, flawless olive skin and thick, rich dark hair. And she was tall. At least five feet nine inches or so in heels.

She and Alexi would have made a striking couple. The thought popped into Kerry's head before she could stop the mental image from forming. No wonder the king wanted his son to marry this woman. She'd make a spectacular queen.

"Pleased to meet you, Contessa," Kerry managed

to say, thankful for the hours of drilling Gwendolyn had given her. "I've heard so much about you."

"Ah, I have heard so little about you. We must talk," the contessa said with a calculating smile, her eyes glued to the heavy, ornate "engagement" necklace Alexi had given Kerry earlier.

Before she could come up with a response, the king steered the contessa down the line after she'd lingered over Alexi's bow and the way he'd kissed her knuckles, just like in one of those old movies. Very gallant. What was he feeling? Was he sorry the contessa wasn't the one standing beside him?

No, she had to quit thinking that way. He'd made his feelings very clear on the subject; he didn't prefer the contessa. He wasn't in love with her, and she was only after a title.

Although how anyone could want a title more than Alexi, the man, was beyond belief. Of course the contessa wanted him. Had she ever had him? The question plagued Kerry, but fortunately, Radko, the butler, called them in for dinner.

The long dark wood table was set with beautiful china and crystal that reflected both the chandeliers overhead and the candelabra of ivory candles on the table. Flowers alternated with the gold-plated centerpieces to provide an atmosphere of opulence. Kerry found it hard to believe that just fifteen years ago, Belegovia had been a country struggling to survive the Soviet withdrawal.

Alexi and his father had done a marvelous job returning the palace and the country to its former splendor. Ariel and Andrew didn't take credit for the success since they'd been younger and in school most of the time. Still, Kerry could see the importance of the entire royal family in providing a tangible image for the country.

Dinner was a never-ending, lavish affair with multiple courses served by an army of uniformed servants. Kerry wanted to speak to them, to thank them as they removed each plate or refilled her water glass, but she didn't dare. Gwendolyn had coached her on the proper etiquette, which included not becoming too chummy with the waitstaff during a formal dinner. She'd also said that if Kerry was particularly pleased with their attention to detail, she could tell them later in the kitchens. That did seem like a sensible compromise. After all, she knew how hard it was to wait tables and could certainly identify with their jobs, even though she'd hardly equate the truck stop to a formal dinner at the palace.

Just when she thought she'd have an accident if she didn't get to the ladies' room real soon, the king announced the dinner closed with a final toast. Kerry raised her water glass while everyone else sipped wine, receiving a speculative look from the contessa. Oh, who cared! Everyone was going to know soon enough that she was pregnant.

The gentlemen pulled out the chairs for the ladies, then everyone drifted toward the music room, where a string quartet had set up their instruments earlier and played throughout dinner. Kerry understood from Gwendolyn that a local soprano and her piano accompaniment would entertain the guests. Kerry wasn't much for opera, so when her mother pulled her aside, she was glad for the distraction.

"I believe I stepped on my hem. I need to check

it,'' her mother whispered. "I hope I didn't rip the fabric!''

"I'm about to pop if I don't get to the little girls' room,'' Kerry whispered back. "What do you say we slip away from this hoopla?''

Charlene Jacks smiled. "I'm right beside you.''

The two of them made their way up the grand stairs and found Charlene's guest room without incident. Kerry made a dash for the rest room, while her mother searched in her overnight bag for the little mending kit she always carried.

"It pulled loose a bit more than I'd thought,'' she said, threading a needle, "but it's not ripped. Why don't you go back downstairs and I'll be down as soon as possible?''

"I can stay with you. We'll go down together.''

"Nonsense. You need to attend the musicale. After all, this little shindig is in *your* honor.''

"In *our* honor,'' Kerry reminded her.

"Right,'' Charlene chuckled, "like I'm the one marrying the prince. Go on. I'll be down before you know it.''

Kerry didn't see any way to stay longer, so she did as her mother had suggested. Since she didn't want to call attention to herself, however, she decided to go down the back stairs, which she believed would connect her to the hallway just to the rear of the music room. Maybe she could slip in unnoticed.

She managed to find the stairs and get her bearings, following the sound of the soprano singing in some foreign language Kerry didn't understand. She passed several closed doorways, then one partially open. Inside she heard men's voices. Alexi's voice in particular, and he didn't sound happy. Kerry stopped and pressed herself to the cool woodwork and listened.

"I CANNOT BELIEVE you invited Fabiana to the dinner," Alexi said, clenching his fists as he paced the length of the library. "You should have known that whatever relationship existed between us is over."

"She's a fine young woman. I felt very bad over the abruptly canceled event two weeks ago."

"Fine. Then send her flowers. Send her a note. But don't invite her to this dinner, which was planned to introduce Kerry and her mother to our officials and friends."

"Think about your decision. The contessa is much more suitable to be your wife than Ms. Jacks."

"Let me say this again, I am not marrying Fabiana! I have already proposed to Kerry and she has finally accepted. Everyone will soon acknowledge my decision to wed, once Gwendolyn writes a press release for Monday morning."

"I think the pendant you gave to the young woman was proof enough of your intentions."

"You were the one who reminded me of the tradition."

"I didn't realize you would be in such a rush to put it around her neck!"

"I'm in a rush to get her to the altar!"

"Only because she is carrying your child. Otherwise, we would not be in this situation."

"Yes, she is carrying my child. And unless you disown me, the child will be the future ruler of Belegovia."

"There is no reason to rush into any commitments regarding the child."

"This is my child and my decision."

"You may have more children. Take your time."

"Is that what you did, Father? Evaluate each of us to see which was the most suitable?"

"No, but the situation was different."

"Then is it because Kerry is a commoner? Do you think her child is not suitable for that reason? May I remind you that Mother is a commoner?"

"Yes, and look at how that turned out!" His father passed a hand over his face while Alexi fumed, defeated by his own argument. Was his mother's desertion at the heart of his father's resistance? And what did it matter?

"Not only is Kerry a commoner, but she worked at a truck stop restaurant in the wilds of Texas. Her mother is still a waitress. Do you honestly want the future rulers of our country to be descended from such people?"

KERRY FELT like sinking to the carpet. She stumbled several steps down the hall, but her shaking legs would hardly support her, so she leaned against the wall. When she realized how light-headed she'd become, she made herself breathe deeply. Gradually the spots she was seeing went away, her legs stopped shaking, and her stomach no longer felt as if she were on a roller coaster.

But her heart was broken, crushed and bleeding inside her chest. She had to get away. She had to get out of Alexi's life and out of his palace.

The king didn't believe she was worthy, and

chances were that others wouldn't, either. She remembered the paparazzi, so ready to dig up dirt on Alexi, Hank and even herself until Alexi had held a press conference and covered up their runaway road trip. Now he wanted to marry her, but he'd even suggested they live away from the palace. He wanted to keep her out of the spotlight so people wouldn't talk about her inadequacies, or even laugh behind her back.

He wasn't ashamed of her, but he would be. He'd be sorry he married her, and then their love would turn to something ugly and sad.

Running up the stairs as quickly as possible, she found her mother's room. Wearing a big smile and her repaired dress, her mother was ready to go back to the party.

"We have to leave, Mama. We have to leave now."

"You may not think much of their occupation, but Kerry worked damned hard to put herself through college. No one gave her a dime. And her mother supported three children after their father walked away. She didn't give up, she didn't go on welfare. Those two women are both survivors, both of them are fighters and any family would be proud to have them join their ranks."

"This family is different. We are newly established. Every decision we make has an impact on our country."

"And you don't think the people will admire Kerry? You're out of touch with reality if you believe those old British axioms about mixing classes. People now love a Cinderella story, but even if they didn't, they'll love Kerry once they get to know her.''

''You don't know that. She's only been here a few days. All I'm asking is for you to think about this decision.''

''All I've done is think about it. Mostly, thinking about how I can convince Kerry that I'm good enough for her!''

''Don't be absurd.''

''Don't be obtuse! If you don't think Kerry is good enough for a prince, then I'll—I'll denounce my role as crown prince. I'd rather be a commoner with Kerry by my side than a king married to a woman I don't love.''

His father sighed. ''If you care for her that much, what can I say?''

''You've already said enough,'' Alexi stated, turning on his heel and marching out of the library.

The soprano was still droning on in Italian—his father's idea, no doubt—when Alexi returned to the music room. Taking a seat at the back of the room, he scanned the crowd for Kerry. He couldn't see her over the taller men and women, some with high, elaborate hairdos. So he sat and waited for the concert to end.

Minutes after the soprano ended with a crystal-shattering note, he learned that Kerry had gone upstairs with her mother to repair a minor dress problem. He wanted to see her, but could hardly burst into the room and tell her what had just transpired with his father.

He mingled and chatted with the important officials until he became irritated. He wanted to talk to Kerry, take her hand in his and announce to their guests that she would soon be his princess. This evening had not gone as planned, from the arrival of the contessa, to his father's tirade, to this dress incident that was keeping him apart from the woman he loved.

Finally, as champagne and cordials were being served, he excused himself and went upstairs. Kerry and her mother had been gone long enough. People were getting restless to see the Americans again. *He* was getting restless.

He checked Kerry's suite, but she wasn't there. He then went to her mother's room, and although the maids had seen the two women earlier, they weren't there now. Frustrated, he returned to his guests and tried to put on a smile, making excuses for Kerry with the age-old excuse of a sudden headache.

Just before midnight, as most of the guests were departing, he found Gwendolyn in the entry hall, shaking hands with the minister of public affairs.

"May I speak to you, Lady Gwendolyn?" he asked politely. At the minister's smile and nod, he pulled his friend off to the side.

"I cannot find Kerry and her mother. Have you seen them after dinner?"

Gwendolyn appeared nervous. She looked around, then pulled him farther back, behind the drapes separating the foyer from the front parlor.

"She's gone." She shook her head, obviously distressed. "They are both gone."

"What?"

"Kerry said she can't marry you. That she isn't princess material and never will be, and your father won't accept her. She was very upset and said she had to get away.''

''What nonsense!''

''It's not nonsense if she believes it.''

''Why didn't you set her straight?''

''Alexi, you're not listening. Kerry wouldn't give me the details, but apparently she heard something to make her worst fears come true. She doesn't believe she can be your wife. She doesn't believe your father or your country will accept her.''

''Where is she? I'll tell her the truth. I'll——''

''Alexi! She's gone,'' Gwendolyn said, her fists holding his lapels. ''She and her mother went to the airport at least an hour ago for a flight to Paris.'' She reached inside her pocket. ''She asked me to give you this and tell you she was sorry.''

The heavy gold pendant, the traditional engagement jewelry of his ancestors, felt cold in his palm. His fingers closed over the ugly piece, remembering how excited she'd been when she'd thought about the history, the tradition. And then she'd rejected the role, running away.

How many times had he run away? Only, his episodes had been on a whim or from boredom, or to avoid some unpleasant event. Nothing like this. Nothing that hurt this much.

He stood there, feeling frozen inside. ''Why?''

''I told you. Something happened tonight. She'd been so hopeful, but then——''

''She must have heard me arguing with my father. She ran away....''

''Whatever she heard made her feel very unwelcome here. And,'' she said, smoothing her hands away from his lapels, ''something else.''

''What?''

''She thinks you are only marrying her because of the baby.''

''I told her—''

''I don't know what you said, but that's not what she heard.''

He tried to think what part of the conversation she'd overheard. Certainly not the ending, when he'd declared his feelings very clearly. So clearly that his father could not misunderstand: Accept Kerry or lose him as a son and a prince.

''I'll go after her.''

''You'd better take the royal jet. She's got a head start, and she's very determined to get out of your life.''

Alexi cursed all the way to the phone, where he ordered up the jet. Then, for the second time in a month, he stormed out of the palace to go after the woman he loved.

Chapter Fourteen

Kerry couldn't remember being so exhausted. Every muscle in her body ached. Her head pounded, her feet were swollen and her stomach felt like turning flips all the way to the bathroom.

In twenty-four hours they'd flown from Belegovia to Paris, Paris to New York, New York to Dallas and Dallas to San Antonio, paying so much money for airfare that she'd need a year to pay off her credit card bill.

She'd called Hank from the airport and asked him to come and get them. He'd been shocked, trying to talk to her about what had happened, asking why Gwendolyn hadn't come home with them. Why they hadn't taken the royal jet.

She hadn't been able to explain to Hank, even after he'd dropped her mother off at the house. All she could say was that Gwendolyn would be coming home later. The reason Kerry and her mother had come back earlier was personal. She might never be able to speak about Alexi to her friends.

Until maybe when the baby was older and wanted to know about his or her father. She'd force herself to speak of Alexi then. She'd tell their child that sometimes love isn't enough. Sometimes fairy tales don't come true.

But she wouldn't think about that, not right now. She was too tired to think, too exhausted to feel...or so she tried to convince herself as she turned the lock on her apartment door.

She dropped her overnight bag on the floor and leaned back against the door, closing her eyes to the sunlight that streamed in through her living room miniblinds. She'd thought that she'd closed them before she'd left, but maybe not. In any case, she was too tired to think right now.

All she wanted to do was sleep for a week. When she woke up, her life would be better. It had to be better.

"Hello, Kerry."

She dropped her purse and screamed.

In an instant he was there in front of her, his strong hands on her shoulders, his scent filling her with memories. Things she didn't want to remember.

"What are you doing here?" she whispered, her voice hoarse from unshed tears. "How did you get in?"

"The manager was very accommodating."

"How did you get here before me?"

"I have a royal jet, remember?"

"Oh, that's right," she said wearily, breaking away from his light grasp. "You can have anything, right?"

"Apparently I can't keep what I thought I had—namely you."

"I'm not some umbrella you misplaced at school."

"I know that," he said, walking up behind her. She

felt his warmth and smelled his cologne, that scent that smelled rich and clean and powerful, just like him.

"I couldn't stay, Alexi, not after what I heard your father say. Not after I understood..."

"What, Kerry?" He placed his hands on her shoulders and leaned close. She closed her burning eyes against the feel of him, the sensation she'd thought she'd never feel again. "What did you think you heard in the library?"

She swallowed the lump in her throat. "I heard you say that you were marrying me because I'm carrying your child. I heard your father say that I would never be suitable, not like the contessa."

"You are nothing like the contessa, and for that, I am eternally grateful."

"I'm a nobody from nowhere. That's what your father thinks. That's what everyone will think. That I trapped you into marriage by getting pregnant. That you might dress me up and put the jewelry on me, but it's as though one of the peasants wandered into the palace."

"Kerry, that's not true."

"Yes, it is. I didn't want to hear it. I didn't want to believe it."

"My father is a snob. He might be the king, but he doesn't know anything about what the Belegovian people will accept. He only knows what his friends back in England would have done."

"They would have turned their snobby noses up at me."

He leaned closer. "Did Gwendolyn turn her nose up at you? Did I?"

"That's different."

"Because we love you? Yes, that's true, but it's not the real reason. You are a special person, and I want everyone to know you. The real you."

"As opposed to the stereotype of the gold-digging waitress who trapped you into marriage? Good luck. That's what people will think. Even your own father believes I'm unsuitable. He invited a *date* for you to our engagement dinner!"

"My father is usually a good man, but sometimes he's a fool."

"Alexi, he's right. I didn't want to believe it, but it's true."

"It's not true!" he said, his hands tightening on her shoulders. "You are strong and worthy and brave, and everyone who knows you will love you, too."

"I'm not going to do that to you or your family. I'm not going to tear your family apart, or make your country ashamed of their prince's commoner wife."

"Kerry, I love you. You love me, too, don't you?"

She nodded, unable to speak.

"I don't want to marry anyone else. Yes, I came back to Texas because I heard about the baby, but you don't know how many times I wanted to return. How many times I almost finished dialing your phone number, only to remind myself that I wasn't being fair to you. Kerry, I didn't stay away because I was ashamed of you. I stayed away because I didn't think I would be fair to you, asking you to conform to my life after you had finally achieved your dream."

"What do you mean?"

"You went to school for ten years and worked hard to help your family and support yourself. You were so excited about your new job, your first apartment. I didn't think it was fair to ask you to give that up, especially for life in the palace.''

"But you were going to marry the contessa."

"Temporary insanity," he claimed, turning her around. "Yes, I gave in to my father's demands that I marry when I was thirty. I thought I was doing the right thing, for my family, myself and my country. How could I have known it was wrong? I'd never been in love before. But then I met you, and I was falling in love with you, and I thought how free and spirited you are. I didn't want to change you. I thought that if I asked you to live in my world, you'd be unhappy.''

"What changed your mind?" she whispered.

"You did. I underestimated you. I didn't realize that you could be happy someplace else. That we could compromise. That we would become even closer because of the baby."

"I won't marry you because of the baby."

"Then marry me because I love you. Marry me because you love me. I know you do. You love me enough to walk away, just because you thought you were doing what was best."

"It would be better for you to marry someone suitable. That would be best for your family and your country," she said weakly.

"But not for me." He leaned down and kissed her lightly. "I realized something on the long flight to Texas," he said with a smile that made the butterflies in her stomach flutter like crazy.

"What?"

"That I want you to be my wife more than I want you to be my princess."

"What do you mean?"

"That I would rather be your husband than my country's prince. If you don't want to be a princess, I'll learn to be a Texan."

"No, Alexi, you can't! You've done so much for your country. The people love you, and there's so much more to do. So many more plans that you have to improve their lives."

"I have a brother and a sister who can keep up the good work and the family name. Yes, I'd miss it, but I'm serious, Kerry. I'd rather have you than the throne."

She stared at him in disbelief, then threw her arms around his neck, sobbing so hard her body shook. "You can't give up your title. You are a prince, no matter what."

"I'm not giving you up, so we need to compromise again."

"How?"

"Come back to Belegovia. Let me prove that my people will accept you. My family—at least my sister and brother—already loves you. I know my mother will love you, too. We'll go see her soon in England. You'll like England, especially in the summer."

"Wait! This is too much."

"I'm sorry, but I need to tell you everything. I need you to believe that we can work out whatever doubts you have."

She put her finger on his lips. "Your father asked you if you really wanted your children to be descended from a commoner like me. Can you honestly say that it doesn't matter?''

"Kerry," he said, pulling her close, "of course it matters. It matters that you are everything I could ever want in a woman. Everything a child could ever admire in a parent. Everything a country could ever expect from a princess. You are, in short, the perfect princess bride.''

THIS RIDE from the airport to the palace was vastly different than the last one. Instead of hiding behind dark glass so no one could tell who was inside, Alexi rolled down the windows. Kerry waved to the crowds from one side, and he waved from the other.

He looked happy. Truly, deliriously happy. She still couldn't believe he'd offered to give up the throne for her. He belonged to her, but also to the people.

"That must have been some press release Gwendolyn wrote," Kerry said as they neared the palace.

"She just told the truth."

"I don't know about that, but I'm grateful."

"The reports from the social and political leaders didn't hurt. They were all singing your praises. I only wish your mother was here to see what a success you are.''

"She said she couldn't face another transatlantic flight, and I don't blame her. Besides, she wanted to tell all of her friends at the Four Square Café about her trip abroad.''

"And her princess daughter."

Kerry grinned. "She is excited about that." On the third finger of her left hand, her brand-new engagement ring sparkled in the sunlight filtering in through the canopy of trees. As Alexi had promised, they'd stopped to get her a ring, only, she'd insisted on San Antonio, not Paris or Antwerp. Her blue-collar roots screamed "Buy American" even as she was catching a jet back to Belegovia.

She settled back against the seat as they crossed the bridge to the palace. "Did I mention what the owner and my mother are planning for the apartment over the café?"

"No. Please don't tell me they're going to hang the sheets out the window. That's an old custom I would just as soon do without."

Kerry giggled. "No, but they are planning on turning it into a museum. Mama asked me what old clothes and memorabilia she could put on display, and wondered if you had some photos and maybe a suit or something to contribute."

"As one of your country's beloved cartoon characters said, good grief."

"My thoughts exactly." Kerry grinned. "I promised we'd be home for the grand opening."

Alexi moaned, but she knew he wasn't upset. Now that they'd faced losing each other for good, everything else had fallen into perspective. The idea of living in Belegovia didn't bother her because she knew she could always go back to visit Ranger Springs. And Alexi didn't feel the need to run away anymore because he had what he wanted and needed to be happy.

The limo pulled to a stop beside the front door. Radko stepped forward before the driver had a chance to open the door.

"Welcome home, Your Highness." His normally

dour expression broke into a smile. "Welcome back, Miss Jacks. May I say for all the staff that we are very glad you have returned."

Darn her hormones, but she felt teary-eyed again. "Thank you very much. I'm glad to be here." She looked around at the stone walls of the palace, the ivy climbing toward the tall trees, the bright blue sky and white puffy clouds overhead. Birds chirped and insects buzzed around the many flowers.

Belegovia wasn't all that different than Texas, she supposed.

She looked at Alexi, her real-life prince and soon-to-be husband. The father of her child, the love of her life. "I'm glad to be home."

Epilogue

"Going home for the grand opening of that silly museum was not a good idea," Alexi said as he watched Kerry struggle to get comfortable on one of the chairs in the Four Square Café. She had to sit at the table because she couldn't fit in a booth. The baby was due in two weeks and Kerry had convinced her doctor that she could travel safely in the royal jet.

No one was going to believe this baby was premature. They would just have to let people count back nine months—which would lend even more status to the apartment overhead as the "royal love nest." He still couldn't believe the tabloids had done a spread on his visit to Texas last May.

Now, the royal wedding... He *could* believe the press coverage of that event. He and Kerry had been married in the cathedral in Belegovia in September. Her side had been filled with friends and family flown over from Ranger Springs, plus many admirers and new friends in her adopted country.

Just as he'd predicted, the people had loved her as soon as they knew her. Of course, Gwendolyn had helped. He really appreciated the way she'd come through for him, despite her career in Texas and her recent marriage to Hank McCauley, which Alexi and Kerry had attended in October.

"Mama, my back is killing me," Kerry complained to Charlene Jacks. "I think I need to lie down for a while."

"Um, Kerry, are you feeling any tingles in your abdomen?" her mother asked with a frown.

"Sometimes. I guess it's those Brax-whatever contractions I read about."

"Maybe not. I think you should see Dr. Amy right away."

"Why?"

"Well, that's just how I felt before each of you was born."

Kerry leaned back in the chair and glared at her mother. "How long before each of us was born?"

Her mother looked a bit pained before she replied, "Oh, maybe a couple of hours."

The full impact hit Alexi like a fist to his solar plexus. "Are you saying that she is in *labor?*"

"Probably," Mrs. Jacks replied, pulling Kerry to her feet. "We'd best get a move on. Walking is good."

"I'm supposed to have this baby in Belegovia!"

"Well, it looks like the baby wants to be born in Texas," her mother said.

Fifteen minutes later he and Mrs. Jacks paced the waiting room of the Wheatley Medical Clinic. A small group of friends clustered nervously at the other end of the room. "I can't believe there is no hospital nearby!" He felt so powerless at the moment. There was nothing he could do to change the outcome. He should never have agreed to this trip. Kerry should be back at their country home, resting in bed with a good book and a glass of milk. Or better yet, at the palace, with his sister for company and a staff to cater to her every whim.

"Maybe there'll be time to get her to the regional hospital. Dr. Amy will see how far she's dilated."

Alexi was just about to voice more concerns when the door opened and the nurse—he believed her name was Gladys—stuck her head out. "You'd better get in here right now."

He and Mrs. Jacks collided at the door, then scrambled inside to find Kerry straining on the exam table. She looked flushed and angry.

"What's wrong?" he asked.

"Nothing's wrong. She's just having the baby. Now," Dr. Amy Wheatley added, pulling on a pair of latex gloves. "We don't have time for the usual formalities of gowns and masks, so each of you just grab one of her hands and hold on tight."

Alexi felt panic building, but he had to be strong for Kerry. He had to help her through this time.

"This is all your fault," she gritted out between panting breaths.

"I know, sweetheart. Breathe as we've learned in class."

"You're going to have the next one."

"Whatever you say, princess."

Fifteen minutes later, after much panting, yelling and swearing by his bride, a smiling Dr. Amy laid a blanket-wrapped bundle in his arms. "Prince Alexi, meet your son."

"My son," he said in awe, looking down at the

pink, wrinkled, dear face of his surprisingly robust child. He leaned over the table so Kerry and her mother could see. "Isn't he wonderful?"

Kerry reached out and touched the baby's tiny fingers and downy cheek. "He has so much hair," she whispered.

"Family tradition."

"Like his name," she said softly, her eyes shining with love. "Alexander Wilheim Charles Ladislas. That's a long name for such a little baby."

"Not so little," Dr. Amy said. "Eight pounds, two ounces and twenty-one inches long." She gave them a wink. "Good thing he was premature."

"Remember, the next one had better be a girl," Mrs. Jacks reminded them.

Alexi wondered if Kerry remembered she'd told *him* to have the next baby. Did that mean she didn't want to go through this again? Had the pain been all that horrible? Everything had happened so fast.

"Next time, Mama," she said, stroking their baby's cheek, "we'll have a girl, and just like our family tradition, her middle name will be Lynn."

Alexi breathed a sigh of relief. There would be another baby, God willing. Maybe several more, if Kerry decided she could work pregnancy into her schedule of saving the world, Belegovian-style.

"Wait until your father sees his grandson," Kerry said, looking up.

"He's going to lose that cool British composure."

"I'm looking forward to seeing that sight," Kerry said, then she frowned. "There's only one thing, Alexi."

"What's that, love?"

"Tell your father he can't invite the contessa to our son's christening. Just in case he hasn't noticed, your carefree bachelor days are over."

"Everything I want is right here. You and our son."

"And," Kerry said with a grin, "he might be a future king, but he was born in Texas."

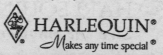

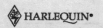

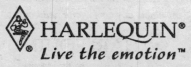

From Regency Ballrooms to Medieval Castles, fall in love with these stirring tales from Harlequin Historicals

On sale March 2003

THE SILVER LORD by Miranda Jarrett

Don't miss the first of **The Lordly Claremonts** trilogy!
Despite their being on opposite sides of the law,
a spinster with a secret smuggling habit can't resist
a handsome navy captain!

FALCON'S DESIRE by Denise Lynn

A woman bent on revenge holds captive the man
accused of killing her intended—and discovers
a love beyond her wildest dreams!

On sale April 2003

LADY ALLERTON'S WAGER by Nicola Cornick

A woman masquerading as a cyprian challenges a
dashing earl to a wager—with the stake being an island
he owns against her favors!

HIGHLAND SWORD by Ruth Langan

Be sure to read this first installment in the
Mystical Highlands series about three sisters
and the handsome Highlanders they bewitch!

Harlequin Historicals®
Historical Romantic Adventure!

HHMED29

If you enjoyed what you just read,
then we've got an offer you can't resist!

Take 2 bestselling love stories FREE!
Plus get a FREE surprise gift!

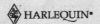
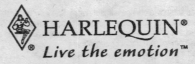